KISSING LORD LYMINGTON

"I've dreamed about kissing you here," he whispered as his tongue curled around her earlobe, licking at her before his teeth closed down in a gentle nip. He sucked the tiny fold of her skin into his mouth and teased at it with his tongue, his lips hot and demanding, commanding her response.

"Oh!" Emma gasped, shocked at the sudden heat gathering in her belly. She'd never wanted a man before, nor had she ever imagined she would.

Until now.

That it should be *him*—a gentleman, an aristocrat, a man so far out of her reach he might as well be on the moon—would lead to nothing but heartbreak, but she clung to him, grabbing handfuls of his coat in her fists, her lips opening eagerly under his.

"Is this how an innocent young lady kisses a gentleman?" he growled against her lips.

"Is this how a gentleman kisses an innocent young lady?" She nipped at his full lower lip, the only soft feature in his otherwise stony face, that pouting lip the only hint there was a passionate man underneath his cool façade.

He groaned and sank his hand into the mass of curls at the back of her neck. "Have you kissed other men like this? Brought them to their knees with that sweet mouth?"

"No. Just you, my lord." It was both the truth and a lie at once. Another man had kissed her, had done whatever he wished to her while she waited, still and cold, for it to be over.

But Samuel was the only man she'd ever kissed because she *wanted* his lips on hers....

Books by Anna Bradley

LADY ELEANOR'S SEVENTH SUITOR
LADY CHARLOTTE'S FIRST LOVE
TWELFTH NIGHT WITH THE EARL
MORE OR LESS A MARCHIONESS
MORE OR LESS A COUNTESS
MORE OR LESS A TEMPTRESS
THE WAYWARD BRIDE
TO WED A WILD SCOT
FOR THE SAKE OF A SCOTTISH RAKE
THE VIRGIN WHO RUINED LORD GRAY
THE VIRGIN WHO VINDICATED LORD DARLINGTON
THE VIRGIN WHO HUMBLED LORD HASLEMERE
THE VIRGIN WHO BEWITCHED LORD LYMINGTON

Published by Kensington Publishing Corp.

The Virgin Who Bewitched Lord Lymington

Anna Bradley

LYRICAL PRESS
Kensington Publishing Corp.
www.kensingtonbooks.com

LYRICAL PRESS BOOKS are published by

Kensington Publishing Corp.
119 West 40th Street
New York, NY 10018

All Kensington titles, imprints, and distributed lines are available at special quantity discounts for bulk purchases for sales promotion, premiums, fund-raising, educational, or institutional use.

Special book excerpts or customized printings can also be created to fit specific needs. For details, write or phone the office of the Kensington Sales Manager: Kensington Publishing Corp., 119 West 40th Street, New York, NY 10018. Attn. Sales Department. Phone: 1-800-221-2647.

Lyrical Press and Lyrical Press logo Reg. U.S. Pat. & TM Off.

First Electronic Edition: November 2021
ISBN: 978-1-5161-1040-7 (ebook)

First Print Edition: November 2021
ISBN: 978-1-5161-1044-5

Printed in the United States of America

"The world breaks every one and afterward many are strong at the broken places."
—Ernest Hemingway

Prologue

King's Place, St. James, London
November 1790

Emma Downing was the fourth.

She was fifteen years old at the time. It was too old to be of much use, in Lady Amanda Clifford's opinion, but then it was the exception that made the rule, and anomalies had always fascinated Lady Amanda.

Emma came on a wave of blood. Not all of it her own, but enough that it dropped like thick, red tears from her fingertips. The slashes on her hands would scar, of course, but Lady Amanda looked upon scars as a blessing, of a sort.

A healing, if an imperfect one.

It wasn't the scars that would haunt Emma Downing. It was the invisible wounds, the secret skin that never knit itself together again, the deep, jagged gashes on her heart that would forever alter that fragile organ's rhythm.

Even so, pity alone would not have moved Lady Amanda in the girl's favor. London was teeming with pitiable creatures, all of them victims of private misfortunes. There was nothing so extraordinary about Emma Downing's tragedy.

Aside, that is, from one small detail, the tiniest wrinkle in the page.

Against all the odds, Emma Downing had *survived*.

That made her extraordinary. No, more than that. It made her a miracle.

Fifteen years old. Too old to be of much use, but too young be a miracle.

How she'd managed to wrench the knife away from her paramour was a mystery destined to remain forever unsolved. Emma herself claimed no memory of the incident.

As for *him*, well...divine justice was an ethereal thing, and never quite worked the way one wished it would. If Lady Amanda had been given a say in the matter, he would have died at once. It was neater that way, dead men being, on the whole, unlikely to tell tales.

As it was, he mysteriously disappeared from London that night, and was never seen again. Curious, but then human justice did tend to be swift, if not quite as divine as the spiritual sort.

His blood might have proved a problem, stabbings being a gory business. Some of it had soaked into Madame Marchand's Aubusson carpet by the time Lady Amanda arrived, but great gouts of it stained the silk gown on Emma Downing's back, and the rusty smell of it permeated the bedchamber.

Lady Amanda was obliged to pay for Madame's damaged goods—the carpet, the fine silk gown, and Emma Downing herself. She handed over the notes without a murmur, well satisfied with her end of the bargain.

As for Emma Downing...

She remained mute during this transaction, her face blank, her eyes glassy. Like all of Madame Marchand's courtesans, Emma Downing was a beauty, but Lady Amanda had never put much faith in pretty faces.

The girl's eyes, though.

Such a deep blue, and so very like another pair of blue eyes, forever closed.

That another girl with eyes that shade of blue should have crossed her path...well, how could Lady Amanda interpret such an extraordinary coincidence as anything other than a command from fate?

So Emma Downing came to the Clifford School, her ghosts trailing behind her, her scars still fresh, the tender, bruised places inside her still swollen, still bleeding, the only one of Lady Amanda's girls who could recall with perfect clarity the day, the hour, the moment they'd been inflicted.

Fifteen years old, already with a world of ugliness in her head.

Memories were, alas, as often a curse as they were a blessing.

Sometimes, it was easier—so much easier—if one couldn't remember.

Chapter One

King's Place, St. James, London
April 1795

"No skirmishes this evening, if you please, Lymington."

"Skirmishes, in a brothel?" Samuel Fitzroy, the Marquess of Lymington turned a baffled look on his cousin, Lord Lovell. "Do you suppose I intend to brawl with a courtesan, Lovell?"

Lovell was far more apt to fall into a whorehouse fracas than *he* was, but Samuel clenched his teeth, lest he be tempted to share that opinion. He and Lovell could hardly manage to exchange a civil word these days as it was, without dragging the demireps into it.

"No flank maneuvers, no tactical formations, and no...what do you call them? Frontal assaults. I'm warning you now, Lymington, I won't abide any mention of frontal assaults tonight."

Ah. No objection to *actual* assaults, then, just the *mention* of them. "Strategically, there's a great deal to be said for a direct, full-force attack to an enemy's—"

"For God's sake, Lymington, I just said no frontal assaults! You're not aboard a brig in the English Channel."

"If you're referring to the *HMS Nymphe*, she's a frigate, not a—"

"The point, my dear cousin," Lovell interrupted with a long-suffering sigh, "Is that this is a drawing room, not a naval battle."

No, it wasn't a naval battle, but it was a battle nonetheless, just as everything was, in one way or another. The only difference between a drawing room and a battleship was that the ship wasn't pretending to be something else.

"And do stop glaring as if you're plotting an ambush." Lord Lovell nodded at the elegant company assembled before them. "The ravishing creatures you see before you are *ladies*, Lymington, not marauding pirates, and that forbidding frown of yours is frightening them away."

It was on the tip of Samuel's tongue to wish the ladies to the devil, but he'd rather not goad Lovell into a passionate defense of the fair sex. They didn't have all night, and Lovell's passionate defenses tended to be rambling things.

So Samuel kept his mouth closed, unclasped his hands from behind his back, and twisted his face about until he'd arranged his features into a more inviting attitude.

At least, he thought he had, until Lovell snorted. "It's not quite your usual churlish scowl, but still grim enough. Why so solemn, Lymington? You're in a bawdy house, not at a church sermon."

Samuel's gaze wandered over the drawing room, where a sea of courtesans awaited them. "Yet there do seem to be quite a lot of nuns about."

Lovell choked out a surprised laugh. "Did you just make a *joke*, Lymington? Bravo. The Sunday sermon would be much pleasanter if the congregants looked more like courtesans, wouldn't it?"

"Don't mock the pious, Lovell, or God will strike you down where you stand." God would do no such thing, of course. He seemed to have an endless amount of patience for Lovell, as well as a wicked sense of humor.

"Blast the pious. Why, just look around you, Lymington." Lovell waved a flawlessly gloved hand at the assembled company. "There's not a single plain face to be seen."

Samuel shrugged as he took in the bevy of ladies fluttering around them like a swarm of gaudy butterflies. "Choose one of them, then, and get on with it."

"Don't rush me, Lymington. Choosing a companion for the evening is a delicate business, and not one to be undertaken lightly."

If Lovell was so careful with all his decisions, Samuel would have nothing more to wish for, but as that was, again, a sentiment better left unexpressed, he said only, "Very well, then. Which lady do you fancy?"

Lovell nodded at a dark-haired creature standing beside the staircase. "That one. She has lovely dark eyes. I fancy dark eyes, as you know, Lymington."

Samuel *didn't* know. Lovell might prefer dark eyes to blue, morning chocolate to tea, John Bulls to Hessians, and Sheridan to Goldsmith, and he wouldn't know a thing about it.

Not anymore.

"Well then, why don't you go and fetch her?"

"She's an angel, isn't she?"

"A perfect seraph," Samuel replied, without enthusiasm. "Go on." He gave Lovell a nudge toward the dark-haired courtesan. "I'll wait for you here."

"Wait *here*?" Lovell gaped at him. "You mean to say you won't choose one of these delightful birds of paradise for yourself?"

Samuel let his gaze roam over the drawing room. He was a man, after all, and he couldn't deny Madame Marchand's ladies were tempting, but the few females he'd encountered since he'd returned to England had seemed faintly horrified by him.

He wasn't sleek or fashionable like Lovell. He was big and rough, his face tanned by years of exposure to sun and sea. If that weren't offensive enough to the fair sex, he also had no talent for charming pleasantries. Polite, mindless chatter bored him, and soon enough he'd start talking about skirmishes and frontal assaults, and well…there was no recovering from frontal assaults where the ladies were concerned. "No, not tonight."

"You're mad, Lymington, but I suppose there's no point in arguing with you. I can't help but observe, however, that you might not be so cross if you occasionally indulged your carnal appetites." Lovell frowned. "You do *have* carnal appetites, don't you?"

Samuel did, and rather pressing ones at that, but if he acknowledged his desires to his cousin, Lovell would set a horde of courtesans upon him, and the next thing he knew, he'd have a skirmish on his hands.

Or worse, a frontal assault.

"We're not here to indulge *my* appetites, but yours." Indulge them, and pray a tumble with a courtesan tonight would keep Lovell out of mischief for the rest of the season.

It was dangerous, bringing Lovell back to London when the fashionable crowd of debauched noblemen he'd been running with were still lurking about the city, drinking and wagering and generally making arses of themselves.

Samuel glanced across the drawing room at Lord Peabody, one of Lovell's former companions. Peabody had put away an astonishing quantity of port in the short time since Samuel had arrived, all while assessing the ladies as if they were prime horseflesh at Tattersall's. He'd just chosen a tiny girl with chestnut hair, who looked more terrified than flattered by his attentions, and was tugging her toward the stairway.

Courtesan or not, Samuel despised seeing a lady manhandled. It made him ill to think of Lovell in company with such a blackguard.

When Samuel left England eight years earlier, Lovell had been a sweet-tempered lad of fifteen. The worst that could be said of him then was that he was given to misty-eyed dreaminess. He'd fancied himself in love a half-dozen times before the age of twelve, drifting from one harmless adolescent infatuation to the next like a bee sampling every blooming flower in its path.

Samuel blamed his Aunt Adelaide for Lovell's romantic notions. She'd named the boy Lancelot, for God's sake.

Lancelot.

If ever there was a name to tempt the fates, that was it, and fate had caught up to Lovell with a vengeance. Looking at him now, Samuel couldn't find a hint of the good-natured boy Lovell had once been.

He'd been ruined, in nearly every way a man *could* be ruined.

Lovell had been seduced by the glamourous coterie of aristocratic wastrels. He'd become a London beau, flitting from one dangerous escapade to the next like a deranged insect. He brawled and wagered, trifled with demireps, engaged in endless scandalous affairs, and traded one mistress for another as often as he changed his cravat.

Predictably, Lovell's messy antics had led to an even messier duel that had landed him in bed with a dangerous fever from a pistol ball lodged in his leg.

When Samuel returned to England to bury his Uncle Lovell, he'd found his family in chaos. His uncle dead, his mother and aunt in a mutual hysterical frenzy, and his cousin bedridden from a festering wound, more dead than alive. Months had passed in terrifying limbo while Lovell fought off the fever that threatened his life—months in which Samuel had plenty of time to reflect on all the ways he'd failed his cousin.

On some level, he must have known Lord and Lady Lovell's petting would spoil Lovell beyond recovery, but even his deep affection for his cousin hadn't been enough to persuade Samuel to spend another day under the same roof as his Uncle Lovell. That it was Samuel's *own* roof, his own estate he'd left behind hadn't made the least bit of difference. It hadn't been his home since his father's death many years earlier.

It would have been a just punishment for Samuel's selfishness if Lovell had succumbed to his fever, but by some miracle, he'd survived, and now Samuel was determined to see Lovell restored to himself, and back in possession of all he'd lost. His health, his family, and the future that had nearly been ripped away from him with one pistol shot.

Starting with…well, with a courtesan, ironically enough.

But she was simply a precaution, a final wild oat to settle Lovell, who'd been cooped up inside their London townhouse in a sick bed for weeks.

"Go on, then." Samuel elbowed Lovell, and nodded at the brunette courtesan. "Your seraph is waiting for you."

"She is, isn't she? Very well, but do find something to do with yourself until I return, Lymington. I won't have you stand about glaring like a gargoyle all evening."

Lovell approached his choice, offered her a courtly bow and a charming smile, then took her hand and led her toward the staircase. Samuel watched them go, his chest pulling tight as his cousin struggled to negotiate the stairs. The surgeon insisted Lovell's limp would hardly be noticeable once it was fully healed, but there would never come a time when Samuel wouldn't notice it, no matter how indiscernible it became to everyone else.

Guilt lodged under his breastbone, sharp and heavy.

Lovell had never berated him for leaving, had never uttered a single word of blame, but the coldness between them now was as palpable as icy fingers squeezing Samuel's heart.

The duel, Lovell's injury—they should never have happened. If Samuel had been here, if he'd remained in England as his mother had begged him to do, it wouldn't have.

There'd been more than one painful scene with Lady Lymington, more than one bitter maternal tear shed in the weeks between Samuel purchasing his commission in the Royal Navy and his hasty departure, but not even Samuel's mother had been as devastated as Lovell when Samuel announced his intention to leave England.

Lord and Lady Lovell certainly hadn't shed any tears for him. His aunt and uncle had been delighted to see him go. No doubt they'd prayed he would never return. Lovell stood to inherit the Lymington title and fortune if only Samuel would have the good grace to drown, or get himself blown to bits by cannon shot.

In the end, it was his Uncle Lovell who'd had the good grace to die, and Lovell who'd nearly been blown to bits—

"Such a fierce frown, my lord. You look as if you've just shot your favorite horse."

A soft touch on the sleeve of his coat made Samuel glance down. A small hand rested there, with dainty fingers curled around his forearm. A trio of ladies—one fair, one dark, and the third red-haired—had sidled up to him, suggestive smiles on their painted lips.

"He looks bereft, doesn't he, Nellie?" The brunette gave Samuel a flirtatious wink. "Pity, but perhaps we can cheer you. Come upstairs, you poor man, and tell us all about your dead horse."

"We may even be able to coax it back to life again," the redhead put in with a smirk. "Your horse, that is."

Samuel disentangled his arm from the brunette's grasp. "There's no dead horse."

"Your favorite hunting dog, then? It must be something. We don't often see gentlemen wallowing in misery here at the Pink Pearl, do we, Clarissa?" The brunette turned to address the red-haired lady beside her.

"The married ones often look miserable when they arrive, but they're cheerful enough when they leave." The redhead fluttered a pair of pale lashes at Samuel. "I daresay you're very handsome without that scowl. Shall we go upstairs and see?"

"No, thank you. I'm not looking for female companionship this evening." Samuel had another matter to attend to, one he hadn't shared with Lovell.

"You do realize you're in a brothel, do you not?" The blonde's red lips curled in a mocking smile.

Samuel frowned. "I'm aware, madam. I'm looking for a lady—"

"Ah." The brunette clapped her hands. "Now we're getting somewhere. What sort of ladies do you prefer, my lord?"

"Not *ladies*. Just one lady, by the name of Caroline Francis. Do you know of her?"

"Must it be Caroline, or will any dark-haired lady do?" The brunette trailed her finger down his arm.

Samuel blinked down at the teasing finger. "No, it must be her."

The brunette's lips turned down. "Pity."

Rather a pity for Caroline Francis, yes. Samuel doubted she'd be pleased to see *him,* once she found out who he was, and the reason he'd come here. Ladies weren't usually eager to discuss the story of their ruination, particularly when it ended with the heroine on her back at an infamous London brothel.

Still, better to turn up at a brothel than not to turn up at all. Did Caroline Francis have any notion how fortunate she was not to have met a much grimmer fate? If not, Samuel intended to make her aware of it, and of what she owed to the two other girls who hadn't been as lucky.

"It seems Caroline's in luck tonight." The redhead touched the tip of her tongue to her bottom lip as her gaze wandered over him. "You're a big, strong one, aren't you? Such a shame, but I suppose our loss will be Caroline's gain."

"Indeed, but perhaps all hope isn't *quite* lost. I haven't seen Caroline at all this evening. Now I think on it, I believe she mentioned she had a private engagement, and would be gone all night."

All night? Damn it, what cursed luck.

The brunette gave Samuel a smoldering look from under her lashes. "If you have a penchant for dark-haired ladies, my lord, I'd be pleased to accompany—"

"That won't be necessary, madam."

Her lips turned down in a sullen pout, and she turned away from him with an offended flounce of her skirts. "As you wish."

Not having any place else to go, Samuel wandered down the nearest hallway, pausing when he reached the music room. A trill of notes spilled through the open door, and he peered inside and found one of Madame Marchand's young ladies performing on the pianoforte, accompanied by a soprano in a yellow silk gown so tight he couldn't imagine how she had the breath to sing.

At another time he might have stayed to listen, but he didn't care to fend off any more eager courtesans. He didn't fancy returning to the drawing room either, so he moved toward a door at the end of the corridor. He half-expected someone to follow him and demand to know where he was going, but it seemed Madame Marchand's guests were permitted to wander where they pleased.

The door latch gave under his hand, and he entered the dim space. It was deserted, the fire burned down to embers, but despite the chill Samuel wandered over to a large, overstuffed chair in the corner and dropped into it.

Ah, yes. This would do nicely. He might bide his time here without anyone disturbing him until Lovell was—

Click.

Samuel peered through the gloom, his eyes widening when a figure appeared on the other side of a pair of glass doors leading from a garden terrace. She was small—certainly a lady—but her face and hair were hidden by a dark, shapeless cloak with a deep hood.

He remained still, watching as the slender figure slipped inside, closed the door behind her, and glided further into the room, her movements so fluid not even the faintest shuffle of footsteps marked her progress. It was as if she were a wraith, floating inches above the ground, or some sylphlike creature too ethereal to bother with anything so mundane as footsteps.

Sylphlike, ethereal, footless wraiths?

Samuel grimaced at his fanciful thoughts. He was just about to rise from his chair and make his presence known when the wraith stopped him with a whispered word.

"Letty?"

Samuel stilled. The velvety timbre of her voice slid over his skin like the stroke of a palm, leaving shivers in its wake.

"Drat it, Letty, I haven't time for this tonight."

Good Lord, that voice. It was soft, huskier than was usual for a young lady, and so smoky at the edges it made his mouth water for whiskey. If *she'd* approached him in the drawing room, he'd have followed her anywhere.

"Letty? Are you in here?"

He froze, breath held as she peered into the gloom, but he was tucked into a corner, hidden by shadows, and her gaze skimmed right over him.

She let out a faint huff when silence was the only reply, then lowered her hood with an impatient tug. He caught a glint of moonlight on a lock of pale hair and leaned forward, eager to see if her face matched that decadent voice.

He squinted into the gloom, but most of her face was still lost in shadows.

Curious that a throaty wraith should be creeping about a darkened library in a notorious brothel, but whatever secrets this lady was hiding, they had nothing to do with him. If he could have left without attracting her attention, he would have done so, but as it was...

One by one, the muscles that had pulled taut when she emerged from the darkness loosened. Samuel let his limbs relax against the chair, and prepared to wait.

* * * *

The Pink Pearl was an explosion of light and sound, but the noise faded until there was only the faint crunch of her boots on the grass as Emma drifted through the shadows to the deserted library at the back of the townhouse.

She didn't want to think about how many people would be furious with her if they knew she'd come to the Pink Pearl tonight.

She didn't *want* to, but her brain rushed merrily along, counting them off, one by one.

Lady Clifford, Lady Crosby, Daniel Brixton, Madame Marchand...

She paused on that last name, a shudder jolting up her spine. One did one's best not to toy with Madame Marchand, in much the same way one would hesitate before threatening a venomous snake with a sharp stick.

If one couldn't finish it off with a single blow, it was best not to strike at all.

Emma slipped through the glass doors, rubbing her gloved hands together to warm them. It was spring in London, but colder than usual. The wind felt like shards of icy needles prickling her skin.

Where in the world were Helena and Caroline? She'd told Helena half-ten, and she was a few minutes late. She'd hoped they'd be waiting for her. If Emma didn't turn up at Lady Crosby's soon, Lady Crosby would alert Lady Clifford, Lady Clifford would send Daniel after her, and then there'd be the devil to pay.

But she was here now, and there was no sense in leaving until she'd gotten what she wanted. It had taken several weeks of patient prodding, but Helena had at last coaxed Caroline Francis into divulging the details of her liaison with Lord Lovell, and Emma was determined to hear the tale directly from Caroline's lips.

Except "liaison" wasn't really the right word, was it? Seduction, ruination, and abandonment made it sound ugly indeed, but Caroline's, er... association with Lord Lovell hadn't been the stuff of romantic fairy tales.

Far from it.

Emma appreciated accuracy, especially when one hoped to fit an aristocratic rake with a noose for his crimes. Not that seduction and ruination were crimes, of course. Seducing the innocent was a base, detestable thing to do, but it wasn't, alas, illegal. If it had been, nearly every aristocrat in London would have found his way to the end of a rope by now.

But Caroline Francis wasn't Lord Lovell's first, worst, or only sin.

Kidnapping and murder might prove a trifle more problematic for him, despite his noble blood, but one didn't march a man off to the gibbet without evidence. The Crown was particular that way, especially when the man in question happened to be a viscount.

As of yet, there was no proof either Amy Townshend or Kitty Yardley had met a tragic end, or even that a crime had been committed at all. Girls went missing all the time, led astray by some rogue or other, then ruined and abandoned.

But two missing servant girls, and now the third, Caroline Francis, pointing her accusing finger at Lord Lovell? That was the sort of thing that caught Lady Clifford's attention. Someone had to hold such men to account, and for better or worse, that task had fallen to Emma this time.

She wouldn't rest until Lovell's every foul transgression was laid bare.

Both Amy and Kitty had vanished from Lymington House without a trace. How Caroline Francis had escaped their same fates and instead turned up at a London brothel was a mystery. A proper villain didn't leave a witness—not without a compelling reason for doing so.

The library door squeaked open, admitting a narrow shaft of light and the faintest whiff of a scent that still made Emma's stomach tighten, even five years after she'd escaped the Pink Pearl. It was a precise balance of candle wax, snuff, rose water tempered with a sharp edge of perspiration, and underlying it all a distinctly musky smell.

No other place in London smelled like the Pink Pearl.

The door closed again, plunging the library into darkness, then there was a hurried tap of ballroom slippers rushing across the carpet.

"I'm here, Letty," Emma whispered into the darkness, trying not to flinch at the sound of Helena's disembodied footsteps. She wasn't timid, and she was accustomed to sneaking about darkened rooms, but everything about the Pink Pearl set Emma's nerves on edge.

A small, warm hand encased in a fine kid glove landed on Emma's sleeve. "I can't understand how Madame Marchand hasn't caught you and Charles out yet, given how suspicious she is."

Charles was one of Madame Marchand's kitchen boys. He had an adolescent *tendre* for Emma, and was willing to see to it the terrace door was left unlocked for her when she required it. "I imagine Madame is rather taken up with emptying the pockets of London's noblemen."

Madame Marchand was a creature of habit, and never ventured from the drawing room during the evening's festivities.

"Yes, well, there's no shortage of pockets to empty tonight."

Helena's tone was light, but Emma heard the edge in her voice, and her shoulders tensed. "Is Lord Peabody here?"

Helena threw herself into a window seat, heedless of her fine silk gown. "Here, deep in his cups, and growing more aggressive with every glass of port Madame Marchand pours into him."

"Promise me you'll stay away from him, Letty." The man had a streak of cruelty in him a mile wide.

But cruel or not, someone would have to have him. Madame Marchand wouldn't dream of turning away any gentleman. Certainly not one with pockets as deep as Lord Peabody's, not even if it meant one of her girls would end the evening with a broken finger, or bruises shaped like bootheels on her legs or back. Nothing too obvious, of course—nothing too visible. Lord Peabody knew better than to damage Madame Marchand's goods, and in return Madame pretended not to notice his violent tendencies.

Rather a tidy arrangement for all concerned, aside from the women who found themselves on the receiving end of Lord Peabody's ill temper.

There was a reason his lordship preferred the smaller, daintier ladies at the Pink Pearl.

Helena was both, but she was a temperamental handful, for all her apparent fragility. Lord Peabody generally kept away from her, unless he was in a particularly ugly mood, and fancied a fight.

"He's taken poor Lizzie upstairs already," Helena said, a hard, bleak look in her eyes. "Last time she had him he tore a clump of her hair out."

Emma's stomach lurched. "Stay away from him, Letty. Lavish your attentions on another gentleman instead. Is Lord Dimmock here tonight?"

Lord Dimmock was neither young nor handsome, but he was a courtly old gentleman, and he was *safe*. The choice between Lord Dimmock and Lord Peabody was like a choice between a plate of sweetmeats and a platter of rotted fish.

Helena sighed. "Yes, but you didn't come here tonight to discuss Lord Dimmock."

"No." Emma glanced over Helena's shoulder, her hopeful gaze on the library door. She willed it to open, and for Caroline Francis to stroll through it, but it remained firmly closed. "Since you're here alone, I take it our plans have gone awry."

Of course they had. Nothing was ever as simple as it should be.

"My dear Emma, a nobleman's lust always takes precedence over everything else. Caroline was suddenly called away to attend a private engagement this evening," Helena added, when Emma raised an eyebrow.

"An engagement?" Dash it, what blasted ill luck.

Helena hopped down from the window seat and grabbed Emma's hand. "Now, don't look like that. I'll bring her to see you tomorrow night. She can tell you her lurid tale then. It's as shocking as you could ever hope for."

"No, tomorrow won't do." By this time tomorrow evening, Emma would be at Almack's, posing as an innocent debutante on the hunt for an aristocratic husband.

Innocent. The thought brought a derisive snort to Emma's lips.

"Why not tomorrow?" Helena asked, studying Emma's face in the dim light.

"I won't be able to return to the Pink Pearl for some time, Letty." Emma tapped her lip, thinking. "Do you suppose you could get Caroline to write down an account of it?"

"I don't see why not. I can ask her, at any rate."

"Good. Give it to Charles, and I'll send Daniel to fetch it from him." Emma reached into the pocket of her cloak and pulled out a small pouch of coins, which she dropped into Helena's hand. "Here, take this, just in case."

Helena hesitated before stuffing the pouch into the hidden pockets of her silk skirts. "Why can't you come back? Where are you going?"

"I'll be in London, but I won't be able to risk a visit. If anything happens, send word to Daniel through Charles. Daniel will make certain the information gets to me."

"Yes, all right."

"If something should go awry on my end, Daniel will come for you. One last thing, Letty." Emma grasped Helena's shoulders. "Promise me you won't do anything to er...upset Madame Marchand while I'm gone."

Helena might look as fragile as a tiny filagree snuff box, but her stubbornness had earned her Madame Marchand's ire more than once. If Helena were to lose that quick temper and be sent from the house onto the London streets...

It didn't bear thinking about.

Helena tossed her head. "I don't know what you—"

"Yes, you do." Emma put on her sternest face. "You know precisely what I mean. I need you to stay safe, Letty, and Lady Clifford needs you to remain at the Pink Pearl until this business is finished. Don't do or say anything to get yourself flung out onto the street. Promise it, Letty."

Helena let out an impatient sigh. "Yes, yes, all right. I promise it. Now, off with you, before Madame Marchand catches you and flings *you* out onto the street."

Emma grinned. "She hasn't caught me yet."

"So smug, given you still have to sneak back out again."

"Oh, I think I'm safe enough. I doubt Madame Marchand even remembers she *has* a library." The woman wasn't keen on reading. She wasn't keen on anything, aside from stripping coins from the fists of London's aristocrats.

Emma pressed a hasty kiss to Helena's cheek. "Go on now, before you're missed, and remember your promise."

Helena tiptoed across the room, peeked into the hallway, then turned to blow Emma a kiss before dashing through the door. Emma waited until the sound of her footsteps faded before adjusting her hood to cover her face and slipping back out the doorway through which she'd come.

She couldn't risk returning to the Pink Pearl until she'd finished this business with Lord Lovell. It would take weeks, the rest of the season, but when it was settled, she'd return to the Pink Pearl, and this time she'd make Helena come away with her. She'd tried to do so before, dozens of times, but this time she wouldn't rest until Helena agreed.

Emma adored her friends from the Clifford School—Sophia, Cecilia, and Georgiana were as much her sisters as Helena was—but Helena had been there during the worst time of Emma's life, a time when Emma had no one else.

She wouldn't leave Helena behind again.

Until then, Helena would be all right. She *would* be. She'd promised it.

Nothing could go wrong. Not a single, blessed thing. Emma had considered her plans from every angle. She'd plotted and schemed and honed this thing down to the minutest detail, because *that* was how you caught a murderer.

She made her way through the darkened streets of London toward Lady Crosby's townhouse in Mayfair, the scuff of her half boots against the uneven ground seeming loud to her own ears, her cold hands shoved as deep into her pockets as they would go.

There would be no mistakes, and no surprises.

Emma didn't tolerate mistakes, and she'd never liked surprises.

Chapter Two

"*This* is Almack's?" Emma's gaze wandered around the ballroom, taking in the gilded columns, the silk draperies, and the row of chandeliers above their heads. "But...where's the rest of it?"

"The rest?" Lady Crosby gave her a blank look. "My dear girl, this is all of it."

This was the tribute to the nobility's vanity, the pillar of fashionable society, the altar on which England's prized aristocratic virgins were sacrificed?

Emma had seen the building from the outside many times, of course. It wasn't remarkable, but given the tremendous fuss the *ton* made about Almack's, she'd imagined the interior would be drowning in oceans of costly marble, the walls would be studded with precious gems, and golden cherubs with eyes of pearls would be tucked into every cornice.

It was just a ballroom. Elegantly done up, yes, but much like every other ballroom in London. "I, ah...I imagined it would be larger."

When she bothered to imagine it all, that is, which wasn't often.

"Oh, no, my dear." Lady Crosby gave Emma's arm a playful tap with her fan. "We must be exclusive above all else, and there's no better way to appear so than for every ball to be a crush. But don't you find it elegant?"

Emma, who knew she was *meant* to find it elegant, wasn't sure how to reply. The truth was, she didn't find it to be any more elegant than the Pink

Pearl, but one didn't compare Almack's to a brothel, no matter how similar their purposes, so she only said, "Er...the company is certainly fashionable."

Familiar, as well.

Emma's lips twisted as she took in the array of gentlemen milling about the rooms. She couldn't stir a step in any direction without stumbling over some flawlessly attired noblemen, many of whom were frequent visitors to the Pink Pearl.

To look at them now, one would never suspect them of lustful urges, or drunken brawling, or of publicly exposing parts of their anatomy best kept private. No one would think them anything other than proper, well-bred gentlemen, with their gleaming smiles and snowy white cravats.

Lord Baddeley was here, chatting with a group of young ladies on the opposite side of the ballroom. He was far from the worst of the swains, but he wasn't quite as fastidious about his personal hygiene as one might wish, and he had a quick temper. Lord Kittredge was fragrant enough, but he was the sort to find fault with everything and everyone, and his hands were always cold. Or so she'd heard from Helena, who was not as discreet as she ought to be.

And they were among the better offerings here tonight.

Emma's gaze fell on Lord Peabody in his impeccable evening dress. For all his apparent good humor, she knew his frigid blue eyes were roving over the collection of young ladies, assessing each with the same narrow calculation as he might a costly bauble at Rundell and Bridge. She pitied any lady who found herself at Lord Peabody's mercy.

If the dozens of sweet young ladies in their pale-colored silk gowns assembled here this evening knew what Emma did about London's noblemen, they'd run screaming into the night and never look back. A vague pity swelled in her breast for them. At least the courtesans at the Pink Pearl understood the fate that awaited them, but one had only to look at these poor girls to see that their every romantic illusion remained firmly intact.

How many of these hopeful young innocents would find the love they longed for in a marriage? One, perhaps two? The others would have the stars in their eyes extinguished quickly enough.

"Ah, here we are at last." Lady Crosby gave Emma's arm a discreet nudge. "Your quarry, my dear."

Emma rose to her tiptoes to peek over the shoulders around her as the gentleman she'd been waiting for made his way through the crowd to the center of the ballroom.

Her eyes widened when she caught her first glimpse of him. *"That's* Lord Lovell? But...where's the rest of him?"

Lady Crosby sighed. "Emma, dearest, I do wish you'd stop saying that."

"I beg your pardon." It wasn't quite what Emma had meant to say, but *this* man, a debaucher? A wicked rake, a despoiler of virgins, a heartless seducer?

Lancelot Banning, Lord Lovell—or, as he was called by every housemaid, matron, marriageable young lady, and courtesan in London, *Lord Lovely*— with his fine, delicate features and charmingly disheveled dark curls, was quite the prettiest gentleman Emma had ever seen.

This beautiful young man, with his soulful dark eyes and fine, elegant hands, was meant to be the scoundrel who'd seduced, ruined, and then abandoned Caroline Francis on the doorstep of the Pink Pearl? *He* was the despicable villain meant to have done away with two of his aunt's housemaids?

Of all the men crowding the ballroom this evening, he was the very last one Emma would have suspected, but *someone* had done *something* to Amy Townshend and Kitty Yardley.

Emma's throat closed, just as it did whenever she allowed herself to imagine what might have become of those two girls. Kitty Yardley had been only fifteen years of age when she went missing, the same age Emma had been when Lady Clifford took her away from the Pink Pearl—

"My goodness, look at the heads turning to follow Lord Lovell's progress. Such a fuss!" Lady Crosby gave a disdainful sniff. "One would think he was a duke."

"A prince, even." And so he was, as far as the *ton* was concerned.

If Lord Lovell had done even half of what Caroline Francis claimed he had, he deserved to be locked into a cell at Newgate, not sailing around a ballroom with dozens of admiring female gazes on him.

But Lord Lovell was a wealthy viscount, cousin to an even wealthier marquess, and even Emma couldn't deny he was as handsome as rumor claimed. Thankfully, she'd never been the sort to be felled by a fine face, but it seemed she was the only one.

The rest of the ballroom was abuzz over his presence here tonight. After all, there was only one reason a gentleman appeared at Almack's during the season. Lord Lovell was on the hunt for a wife, and half the young ladies in the ballroom this evening were imagining themselves Lady Lovell at this very moment.

Emma watched the crowd part to allow the exalted procession to pass. How lucky it was she'd had the foresight to choose a place in an unobtrusive corner of the ballroom, where she might observe the drama unfolding without attracting attention.

Still, she'd have to make her presence known soon enough, and then she'd have more attention than she'd ever wanted. Until then, she prepared to wait, and watch.

Lady Crosby tutted, shaking her head. "You'll have a number of rivals for his affections, I'm afraid."

Emma's lips curved in a grim smile. "I'll manage somehow, my lady."

Lady Crosby chortled, her powdered face falling into a dozen gleeful wrinkles. "Oh, I've no doubt of that. You look ravishing tonight, my dear. Every inch the belle, from the crown of your fair head to the tips of your slippers. One glance into your blue eyes, and poor Lord Lovell will be your willing slave."

Perhaps he would, but not for the reasons Lady Crosby supposed. It had nothing to do with Emma's face, or her gown, her blue eyes or fair hair.

If Lord Lovell's heart did end up in the palm of her hand, it would be because Emma was very, very good at pretending to be someone she wasn't. Once she discovered what sort of lady Lord Lovell wanted, it was the work of a moment only for her to become that lady.

Still, she gave Lady Crosby's hand a grateful squeeze. If she'd had a grandmother, Emma liked to think she would have been just like Lady Crosby. "Who is the lady on Lord Lovell's arm?"

Lady Crosby's mouth turned down in a frown. "That, my dear, is Adelaide Banning, the Viscountess of Lovell. She's Lord Lovell's mother, and a dreadful, cross old thing. That expression, my dear! She looks as if she's had too much of Almack's sour lemonade. Mean-spirited and overbearing, without a kind word to say for anyone other than her son, whom she dotes on."

Emma cocked her head to the side, studying Lady Lovell. The woman had a proud, unpleasant air about her, as if she thought herself very much above her company.

"Ah, now there's a bit of luck," Lady Crosby murmured as Lord Lovell and his mother paused to chat with Lord Townsley, who was standing nearby with his daughter. "Shall I introduce you to them?"

Lady Crosby came from one of England's oldest and most distinguished families, she knew everyone, and she was wealthy enough that the *ton* courted her attentions. She was one of Lady Clifford's most stalwart benefactors, and could introduce Emma to anyone here. It made her the ideal chaperone.

"There *is* something to be said for striking quickly." Emma toyed with the tassels on her fan, her gaze on Lord Lovell as she pondered her options. "But not just yet, my lady."

In Lovell's case, instinct urged her to hold off for now. Every marriage-minded mama in the ballroom was already racing toward him with their giggling daughters in tow. Emma didn't choose to be one among the crowd of his frenzied admirers.

So she bided her time, her gaze moving between Lord Lovell and the growing constellation of ladies orbiting him as if he were the sun. One could tell a great deal about a gentleman by the way he behaved when he was surrounded by beautiful debutantes, all of them right at his fingertips, ripe for the plucking.

He seemed to be making an effort to offer a polite word to each of them, and smile at their eager mamas. He bowed at the appropriate times and brushed his pretty red lips over more than one set of gloved knuckles.

He appeared, in short, to be every inch an amiable, proper gentleman.

But that was the tricky thing about appearances, wasn't it? Whichever Greek poet had said appearances were deceptive had the right of it, and never was it truer than in Lord Lovell's case. Even if he proved not to be the cold, callous murderer Caroline Francis claimed he was, he was still the sort of gentleman a lady should be wary of.

Drinking, wagering, brawling, mistresses—Lord Lovell had earned quite a reputation for himself as one of London's most appalling rakes. He was a rogue, indeed, with dozens of scandals to his name. His family was said to be at their wits' end with his antics, and eager to see him safely married off this season.

Emma smothered a snort. She wished them well with *that*. Lord Lovell's attention was already wandering, his sultry, dark eyes roving over the company as if he were searching for someone. He paused here and there when he found a particularly alluring face, but his restless gaze never lingered for long on any one lady.

Until he spied Emma, that is.

No doubt he would have spared her only the same passing glance he had the others, but Madame Marchand had taught Emma well. For better or worse—mostly *worse*, if the truth were told—she knew how to hold a man's gaze.

Emma's eyes met his for an instant only. Lord Lovell's velvety brown eyes widened, and a slow smile that likely scattered the wits of every young lady on the receiving end of it drifted over his lips.

Emma's wits remained firmly intact. She didn't simper or blush, but met his gaze directly before deliberately glancing away again, without returning his smile.

There, that would do, for a start.

Emma had no faith in beauty—her own face had brought her far more tragedy than happiness—but there was no denying it might prove useful in prying the family secrets from Lord Lovell's lips.

Such pretty lips, too. Rather too pretty for his own good.

Emma and Lady Crosby remained tucked into their corner until just after nine o'clock, two hours before the supper would be served. "I believe I fancy a dance now." Emma turned to Lady Crosby. "Not with Lord Lovell just yet, but with some other gentleman, if the thing can be managed."

"I daresay it can be. Which gentleman would you like?"

Emma gave Lady Crosby a blank look. What did it matter? One gentleman was very much like another. "Er, perhaps you'd better choose for me, my lady."

"Hmmm." Lady Crosby pursed her lips as she scanned the ballroom. "Let me see. It must be someone who displays to advantage while dancing... ah, I have just the gentleman."

Emma followed Lady Crosby's gaze to a tall, dark-haired man on the opposite side of the ballroom. "Who is he?"

"That, my dear, is Lord Dunn. Handsome, isn't he?"

"He is." In truth Emma didn't care a whit about the man's face, aside from whether or not she'd seen it at the Pink Pearl. She didn't recognize Lord Dunn, which was a promising start. "What's he like?"

Lady Crosby shrugged. "Oh, he's your typical, solid English gentleman. You know the sort—good to his sister, fond of a hearty port, never shirks his duty in the Lords. He's keen on hunting, is Lord Dunn. He's friendly with Lord Lovell, and has just purchased a hunting box near Lymington House. There's not much more to say, really. Come, my dear."

Emma allowed herself to be led across the ballroom, a demure smile on her lips. She was aware of Lord Lovell turning to follow their progress, but she kept her face averted, and avoided meeting his admiring gaze.

"Lord Dunn!" Lady Crosby waved gaily. "How do you do? Why, it's been an age, has it not?"

Lord Dunn smiled, and bowed over Lady Crosby's hand. "My dear Lady Crosby. It's a great pleasure to see you. What brings you to London?"

"I've come with my granddaughter for the season. You know how I despise society, my lord, but the young must have their chance, mustn't they? Come here, child." Lady Crosby drew Emma forward. "May I present my granddaughter, Lady Emma Crosby? Emma, dear, this is the Earl of Dunn."

"How do you do, Lady Emma?" Lord Dunn's hazel eyes swept over Emma as he bowed over her hand, his lips grazing her glove. "I do believe we've found this season's belle."

Lady Crosby cackled with delight. "For shame, my lord, flirting so infamously after only a moment's acquaintance."

Lord Dunn laughed, his gaze on Emma's face. "I beg your pardon, my lady, but I could hardly help myself."

Emma peeked up at Lord Dunn from under her lashes. He was tall and broad-shouldered, with a noble, aristocratic face, and the confident air of a man who knew his place in the world. She judged him to be in his mid-thirties, that is, young enough to catch a lady's eye, but older than most of the callow youths crowding the ballroom.

Yes, he'd do nicely. Lady Crosby couldn't have chosen better.

"How do you do, Lord Dunn?" Emma dipped into a shy curtsey, but she held his gaze for just a touch longer than a young lady should.

"A good deal better, now. Will you dance, Lady Emma?"

Emma hesitated long enough to give Lady Crosby a chance to wave a hand toward the couples assembling for a country dance. "Go on, dear, and enjoy yourself. I'll wait here and have a cozy sit down."

"I wasn't aware Lady Crosby had a granddaughter," Lord Dunn said, as he swept Emma into the dance. "Is this your first visit to London?"

"Yes, my lord. My father prefers to keep me in Somerset with him."

"Your father is a wise man, Lady Emma. If I had a daughter with such a face, I'd keep her safely hidden in the country, as well." Lord Dunn gave her a devilish grin. "How did you coax him into a season?"

"I'm staying with my grandmother while my father is engaged with business overseas. She insisted on giving me a season, and he could hardly refuse." The words flowed easily from Emma's tongue, because they were, in fact, the truth.

Or close enough to it.

The only difference between her account and the truth was that the real Lady Emma Crosby had accompanied her father overseas. With her and Lord Crosby safely out of the way, plain Emma Downing had taken Lady Emma Crosby's place. With a wave of Lady Clifford's hand, she'd been transformed into an earl's daughter.

It was merely a stroke of good luck the two of them happened to share a name. It made things much easier, yet the truth had a nasty habit of coming out, one way or another. Emma wasn't naïve enough to imagine her ruse would be an exception. Lady Emma Crosby wasn't out in society, but someone in London this season would surely have met her, and reveal Emma to be an imposter.

She could only pray the truth would stay hidden long enough for her to pry Lord Lovell's secrets from his smiling lips, because if she failed, there would be no second chance. Not for Amy and Kitty, and not for Emma. By the time the season ended, half of London would recognize her face. Once she'd lost her anonymity, she'd be of little use to Lady Clifford, or to anyone else—

"Such a pretty flush in your cheeks, Lady Emma." Lord Dunn gave her a shamelessly flirtatious smile. "Dancing flatters you."

Emma forced an answering smile to her lips. "Thank you, my lord."

He continued to chat amiably as they moved through the figures, Emma's skirts spinning around her ankles. As she had predicted, Lord Dunn kept her on the floor for a second dance, which was long enough for the company to notice her, and begin to speculate.

For her part, Emma kept her attention focused on Lord Dunn, or rather did such an excellent job of appearing to do so that no one would have suspected how aware she was of everything around her: the chatter of conversation, the curious glances as Lord Dunn twirled her around the floor, and most of all, of Lord Lovell.

His gaze wandered to her more than once. For a fleeting instant, she allowed her eyes to meet his, her lips curved in the barest hint of a smile.

With any luck, that would be the beginning of the end for Lord Lovell.

Now she'd caught his attention, there was a good chance she'd be able to hold it. Dozens of lovely young ladies graced the ballroom tonight, but Emma knew things they didn't know—things no innocent virgin *should* know.

How to entice with a glance, and lure with a smile. How to expose the barest hint of ankle with an innocent flirt of her skirts, and draw a man's attention to her lips. Emma wasn't certain whether it was amusing or tragic that her wiles should prove so useful at Almack's, but for good or ill, she could boast all the sinful, salacious tricks of a practiced courtesan.

That was how she knew not to spare Lord Lovell another glance for the rest of the dance. Even when she could feel his gaze on her, and imagined his dark eyes willing her to look his way, she never let her attention wander from Lord Dunn, who was in no hurry to relinquish her.

By the time he did return her to Lady Crosby, laughing and breathless, Lady Crosby's various acquaintances had come to bid her a good evening, and she had quite a crowd gathered around her. Among them were Lord Lovell and his mother, and several others who'd joined her while Emma was dancing with Lord Dunn.

Lady Crosby was just rising from her chair when Emma and Lord Dunn approached, her expression alight with pleasure as she held out her hand to a petite lady who'd just joined their party. "Lady Silvester? Edith, is that you?"

"My goodness, Henrietta?" Lady Silvester gushed, taking Lady Crosby's hands. "But how wonderful! I didn't realize you intended to spend the season in London."

"Why, it's been ages since I've seen you!" Lady Crosby pressed an affectionate kiss to the other lady's powdered cheek.

"You'd see a great deal more of me if you came to London oftener," Lady Silvester chastised gently. "But I won't scold, because here you are. Truly, Henrietta, I couldn't be more pleased to see you."

Lady Crosby turned her attention to a pretty, dark-haired young lady at Lady Silvester's side. "Don't ever say this beautiful creature is your granddaughter?"

"She is, indeed." Lady Silvester glowed with pride as she drew the young lady forward. "Flora, this is Lady Crosby, an old and very dear friend of mine from school."

Lady Flora curtsied. "How do you do, Lady Crosby?"

"Why, very well indeed, child. You were in pinafores the last time I saw you, and now here you are, quite the young lady. Time truly does fly, does it not, Edith?" Lady Crosby gave Lady Silvester a misty smile. "Oh, but pardon me, such a peahen I am! May I present my granddaughter, Lady Emma Crosby, to you both? Come here, dear, and make your curtsies."

"How do you do, Lady Silvester, and Lady Flora?" Emma offered them each a pretty curtsy.

"It's a pleasure, Lady Emma." Lady Silvester beamed at her.

"Lady Emma." Lady Flora gave Emma a shy smile, and opened her mouth to say something else, but a tall, fair-haired gentleman approached her, and claimed her for a dance.

Lord Lovell's dark eyes followed Lady Flora as her partner led her away, but then he seemed to shake himself, and offered Lord Dunn a careless bow. "How do you do, Dunn? Pleasure to see you."

But he wasn't looking at Lord Dunn. He was looking at Emma.

"You don't appear to see *me* at all, Lovell." Lord Dunn chuckled. "Not one to dally, are you? Very well. Lady Emma Crosby, this eager gentleman is Lord Lovell."

"My lord." Emma curtsied.

"Lady Emma." Lord Lovell bowed over her hand, his lips a mere hair's breadth from touching her glove. "It's a plea—" Before he could say anything more, however, a thin, dark-haired lady approached and took his arm. He was obliged to turn away, and Lady Crosby seized the opportunity to whisper in Emma's ear. "My goodness. That's Lady Lymington. I didn't expect to see *her* in London this season."

"*That*'s Lady Lymington?" Emma whispered back. "But where's the rest—"

"Emma, my love, I beg you not to inquire as to the whereabouts of the rest of Lady Lymington."

Emma watched as Lady Lymington moved among the company, clutching at Lord Lovell's arm. Her ladyship nodded graciously to various acquaintances, but didn't speak much. "What's she like?"

Lady Crosby shook her head. "I don't know her well, but the *ton* regards her as a sweet lady, if rather timid."

Lady Lymington looked nothing like her sister-in-law. She was fragile and pale, her shoulders slightly rounded, as if she were doing her best to shrink into the background. To Emma's disgust, she couldn't quell a pang of sympathy for the lady, who put her in mind more of a frightened rabbit than a haughty marchioness.

A frightened rabbit with two missing housemaids on her conscience, that is, both of whom had seemingly vanished into thin air without Lady Lymington expressing a single public word of concern for their whereabouts.

But Emma didn't have time to dwell on Lady Lymington's sins, because Lord Lovell had turned back to her and taken possession of her hand. "Lady Emma, I beg your pardon. It's a pleasure to meet you."

"Lady Emma isn't accustomed to your extravagant gallantry, Lovell," Lord Dunn warned. "This is her first visit to London."

"Well, of course it is." Lord Lovell released her hand, a boyish grin on his lips. "If Lady Emma had ever appeared at Almack's before, I'd remember her lovely blue eyes."

Oh, but he was a gallant, wasn't he? Why, one could almost hear the chorus of yearning sighs that arose from the young ladies gathered around them.

To her horror, a laugh tried to tear loose from Emma's lips. No, a laugh wouldn't do at all. An innocent young lady on her first appearance at Almack's didn't burst into laughter when the most sought-after gentleman in the room paid her a compliment, no matter how ridiculous it was.

She managed a demure smile instead. "I'm pleased to make your acquaintance, Lord Lovell."

"Are you, indeed?" Lord Lovell returned her smile with a flirtatious one of his own. "Then you'll indulge me with your hand for the next two dances, Lady Emma?"

Emma was half-tempted to refuse him, just to teach him some humility, but if she danced with Lord Lovell now, then he'd be obliged to take her into supper, as well.

The timing was perfect.

Emma opened her mouth, but before she could murmur her assent, a gentleman behind Lord Dunn's shoulder caught her attention. She gaped at him, forgetting herself entirely before gathering her wits enough to turn aside and whisper to Lady Crosby. "Dear God. Who is *that*?"

Lady Crosby turned, and sucked in a breath. "Oh, my. *That*, my dear Emma, is the Marquess of Lymington, Lady Lymington's son, and Lord Lovell's cousin. Rather a lot to take in at once, isn't he?"

Emma's mouth dropped open. "That scowling giant is that tiny, dainty lady's *son?*"

"Indeed. Rather a mystery, but it's said the marquess resembles his late father."

He was the tallest man Emma had ever seen, and the wide, powerful breadth of his shoulders exaggerated the effect of his height, making him look positively massive. It wasn't his size that arrested Emma's attention, though.

It was everything else.

He had none of his cousin's fashionable prettiness. Everything about him was hard, dark, forbidding, and excessively masculine. His clothing was impeccably tailored, yet somehow every seam appeared on the edge of bursting with the effort to contain him.

Like Lady Lovell, Lord Lymington appeared displeased with the company on offer at Almack's, or perhaps he was just displeased in general. One might be forgiven for assuming so, given that scowl on his face.

It took another moment before Emma noticed it wasn't just a random scowl intended for the company in general, but seemed to be directed right at *her*.

No, surely not.

She glanced over her shoulder, expecting to find someone looming behind her with a matching glare for Lord Lymington.

But there was no one. Emma turned around to face him again, eyes wide.

It *was* directed at her.

It wasn't a passing glance, nor was it a friendly one. The Marquess of Lymington was glowering at her as if he'd like to leap across the space between them and devour her.

For a single instant Emma's gaze met a pair of cool gray eyes. She stared back at him, her own eyes narrowing before she recalled she was meant to be a shy debutante. She dropped her gaze and gave a mental shrug, doing her best to dismiss him.

Let him glower all he liked.

The Marquess of Lymington was not, thankfully, her problem.

Chapter Three

The fair-haired, blue-eyed chit was going to be a problem.

Soft, silky gold hair gleaming under the chandeliers, creamy skin, and a slender, graceful form displayed to distracting advantage in a blue silk gown—a shade of blue too bright to be strictly proper for a debutante, but just shy of unseemly. If all that wasn't tempting enough, she also happened to be graced with eyes the startling blue of perfect summer skies, or sparkling sapphires, or sunlit oceans, or some other similar nonsense.

Lovell was already flirting with the girl, and carefully ignoring Lady Flora. She was dancing with a slack-jawed Lord Barrett, who was gazing down into her pretty face and looking as if he'd been struck by lightning.

Samuel muttered a curse under his breath. Dear God, what a fool Lovell was—

"That scowl doesn't become you, Lymington."

Samuel turned at the deep rumble beside him, and found Lord Dunn at his elbow. "That fair-haired chit. Who is she?"

"Ah. That bewitching creature, Lymington, is Lady Emma Crosby, Lady Crosby's granddaughter. This is her first visit to Almack's, and her first time in London."

Samuel's eyes narrowed on her, his brow creasing. No bashful smile graced those lips, nor were those blue eyes opened wide in awe at the splendor of the rooms and the company. For a young lady who'd never set foot in London, Lady Emma Crosby appeared remarkably self-possessed. "She doesn't behave like a debutante."

"No? How is a debutante meant to behave, then?"

"Terrified, and trying to hide it."

Dunn chuckled. "Well, don't despair yet, Lymington. There's every chance she'll find your scowl terrifying. Not that it will damage her prospects much. That girl is well on her way to becoming the undisputed belle of the season."

"My cousin seems to think so." Lovell looked as if he were already composing odes to the girl's beauty in his head.

"Yes, well, Lovell has a gift for finding the loveliest lady in every ballroom."

Samuel grunted. "It's not a gift, Dunn, it's a curse. The loveliest lady in any ballroom is invariably the most troublesome."

"Really, Lymington, you might at least wait until you've been introduced to Lady Emma before you decide she's more trouble than she's worth."

"It's nothing to do with *her*. The fault lies with Lovell. Lovely young ladies addle his wits." When Lovell became addled, trouble was sure to follow. Indeed, it already was.

Lovell had been madly in love with Lady Flora for years, but it had taken a duel and long, lonely weeks in a sick bed for him to realize it. Of course, love being the fickle thing it was, no sooner had Lovell prepared to declare himself than Lady Flora, disgusted with his antics, had fled to London for the season in search of the sort of gentleman who'd make a proper husband.

A gentleman like Lord Barrett, for instance.

"It's not Lady Emma who offends you then, Lymington, but lovely young ladies as a whole?"

"Why should I find Lady Emma offensive? I don't even know the girl." But the truth was, she did offend Samuel, for the same reason Lord Barrett did.

She was *in the way*.

To be fair, she wasn't the only one casting her lures at Lovell. If Samuel could judge by the whispering and the coquettish glances, nearly every young lady on this side of the ballroom was doing the same. Lady Emma's only sin was in having a prettier face than all the others.

No other lady, no matter how lovely her face, how blue her eyes, could ever take Lady Flora's place in Lovell's heart, but Lovell was already half in despair over his chances of winning back Flora. Now here was Lady Emma, the perfect distraction.

Samuel couldn't let some blue-eyed chit turn his cousin's head now, when Lovell was at last well enough to beg Lady Flora's forgiveness, and win the lady who'd stolen his heart.

"Well, I doubt you'll have any quarrel with Lady Emma," Dunn said. "She's a charming young lady."

Charming. Damn it. In addition to that face, she was also charming? "If she's so charming, why don't you court her, Dunn?"

That would keep her out of Lovell's way.

"I'm not looking for a wife, Lymington. It's a pity, really, as I can't say I'd mind being caught on the end of Lady Emma's hook."

Samuel snorted. "I daresay she'd be delighted to hear it, Dunn. Young ladies are always charmed by fishing analogies."

Nearly as charmed as they were by naval battle analogies.

Dunn smirked. "Perhaps you'll fall victim to Lady Emma's allure yourself. I'd quite like to see that."

"Unlikely, Dunn." Samuel's heart was made of sterner stuff than Lovell's. Near impenetrable, really—

A sweet, light sound drifted over to him, and Samuel jerked his head toward it. It was Lady Emma, laughing at some nonsense of Lovell's, her lovely red lips curved in a breathtaking smile.

Damn it. Even the girl's laugh was enchanting. It sounded like tinkling bells.

Abruptly, Samuel had seen enough. "Make yourself useful, Dunn, and invite Lady Flora to dance once she's finished with Barrett, will you? Two dances, if you would, then escort her into supper."

"My pleasure, Lymington."

Dunn could be trusted not to press a suit of his own with Lady Flora, but Samuel couldn't say the same for the rest of the gentlemen in the ballroom this evening. Flora had no fortune, but the gentlemen here who needn't worry about money would rush to court her soon enough, and Lovell would be out for good.

Samuel strode forward. A quick glance revealed his mother was deep in a conversation with Lady Crosby, so he made his way toward Lovell, and overheard him murmur in Lady Emma's ear.

"...indulge me with your hand for the next two—"

"There you are, Lovell." Samuel cut his cousin off just in time to prevent him from asking Lady Emma to dance.

Lovell looked up, his face darkening. "Lymington. Where did you come from?"

"I was dancing with Lady Jane Townsley. It *is* a ball, after all."

Samuel glanced from Lovell to Lady Emma, then back to Lovell, and raised an eyebrow. Lovell wasn't pleased at the interruption, but he could hardly refuse to make the introductions.

Lovell scowled, but bowed to the inevitable. "Lady Emma Crosby, this is my cousin, the Marquess of Lymington."

Lady Emma sank into a dainty curtsy. "How do you do, Lord Lymington?"

Samuel frowned. Her voice…had he heard it before?

There was something familiar about it, but he couldn't quite place it. It hovered just at the edges of his consciousness, teasing him. Smooth, a trifle husky, it conjured up images of—

He froze.

A lady, silhouetted in a pair of glass doors, then drifting across a darkened library, her movements fluid, silent. A lovely, sylphlike creature, floating inches above the ground, mysterious and ethereal.

Yes, he'd heard her speak before, a whisper in the darkness.

The dainty wraith, her pale hair limned in moonlight.

And that *voice*.

It had been *her* he'd seen last night at the Pink Pearl, that extraordinary face hidden under her hood, that distracting figure concealed under a bulky cloak.

But there was no mistaking that voice, no disguising it.

Samuel stared at her in astonishment. What had Lady Crosby's pure, sweet granddaughter been doing sneaking into a notorious brothel after dark? What sort of sheltered young innocent who'd never before set foot in London had a secret meeting with an infamous courtesan?

Lovell cleared his throat. "Lady Emma was just about to grant me the favor of—"

"Will you dance, Lady Emma?" Samuel didn't dare look at Lovell as he held out his hand to her. It was inexcusably rude to cut another gentleman out, and God knew he'd done it clumsily enough, but he didn't have any intention of turning his vulnerable cousin over to a lady who roamed London's brothels at night.

"For God's sake, Lymington," Lovell sputtered, outraged. "What do you think you're doing?"

"Inviting Lady Emma to dance." If he didn't dance with her, his cousin *would*, and by the time Lovell returned her to her grandmother, he'd have persuaded himself he was besotted with her.

"You know very well I was about to—"

"It's quite all right, Lord Lovell." Lady Emma's curious gaze rested on Samuel's face. "I'm perfectly happy to dance with Lord Lymington."

Lovell was still fuming. "Nonsense, Lady Emma. You don't have to—"

"Oh, but I think I must, my lord. Lord Lymington didn't so much invite me to dance as *command* me. Did it not sound like a command to you?"

"Every word out of Lymington's mouth sounds like a command." Lovell glared at Samuel before returning Lady Emma's smile. "It's gracious of you to indulge him, my lady."

Lady Emma curtsied to Lovell, then with a dazzling smile Samuel deemed far too sophisticated for an innocent debutante, she accepted his hand, and let him escort her to the floor.

Once Samuel had Lady Emma alone, however, he hadn't the faintest idea what to say to her. He opened his mouth, then closed it again, biting back an impatient grunt.

He'd have liked nothing more than to deliver Lady Emma a blunt warning to stay away from his cousin, and advise her to avoid London's brothels while she was at it, but a gentleman couldn't speak plainly to a lady. No, he must tiptoe his way around it, come at it from the side, hide it under flowery compliments and charming chatter, all of which he was hopeless at—

"I'm afraid you're uncomfortable, Lord Lymington. Would you prefer not to talk?"

"I *would* prefer it," Samuel snapped, before he could think better of it. "But we can't remain silent for an entire cotillion. It might have been all right, if it were a shorter dance."

It wasn't at all the thing to say, but Lady Emma's smile never faltered. "Very well, if you like. Tell me, Lord Lymington. Have you any particular plans for your stay in London?"

"No. Nothing out of the ordinary. Drury Lane, the Royal Academy, Rotten Row, and whatever card parties and suppers I'm unable to avoid." He waved an impatient hand, as if it was all very tedious.

Which, of course, it *was*.

"I'm afraid I'm rather hopeless at cards." Lady Emma peeked up at him from under thick, dark eyelashes. "I do long to visit the Royal Academy, however. My grandmother and I plan to go tomorrow, to see the Reynolds exhibit. Do you admire Reynolds, Lord Lymington?"

"Only his military portraits."

"Indeed. His portrait of Augustus, First Viscount Keppel, is, I believe, considered particularly fine."

Viscount Keppel? Samuel stared down at her in amazement. He didn't know of many young ladies with an interest in military portraiture. All at once, Samuel was tempted to bring up frontal assaults, just to see what she'd say.

No, he'd better not. Lovell would be horrified if he knew Samuel was even considering it. "Er, Lord Dunn tells me this is your first visit to Almack's, Lady Emma. What are your impressions?"

Yes, that was better. A man couldn't go wrong with Almack's.

He braced himself for the gushing praise and sighs of delight Almack's so often inspired in young ladies, but they didn't come. Instead, Lady Emma glanced about her as if just now noticing her surroundings.

"It's well enough, I suppose, though I confess I imagined something grander."

Samuel blinked down at her. "*Grander* than Almack's?"

A flush rose to Lady Emma's cheeks, as if she realized she'd said the wrong thing. "Er, perhaps that's not quite the right word. It's just, well... young ladies hear so much about Almack's, you see. It takes on a mythical significance in one's mind. In the end, it's just a ballroom, isn't it?"

Dear God, was the girl disparaging *Almack's*? Samuel couldn't say whether he was amused or shocked. "Best not let any of the patronesses hear you say so, Lady Emma. They'll take back your voucher."

Such a threat would have reduced most young ladies to a flood of tears, but Lady Emma only smiled. "If they choose to do so, they're welcome to it."

"Without a voucher to Almack's, you'll find it difficult to make a suitable match. I assume that is why you're in London for the season, Lady Emma. To make a suitable match? Or did you come to London for some other reason?"

A tour of London's bawdy houses, perhaps?

No, he couldn't say *that*. It was altogether too blunt, but the girl's complacency made him want to startle a reaction out of her. Her calm manner, her utter self-possession struck him as simply *wrong*.

Lady Emma's red lips pursed in a prim line. "It's kind of you to concern yourself with my matrimonial prospects, Lord Lymington. I do hope you'll forgive me if I decline to discuss them with you."

Despite himself, Samuel felt a reluctant tug of admiration. As setdowns went, it was a good one. Direct, but politely delivered, and he appreciated the succinctness of it. "Your matrimonial prospects don't interest me, Lady Emma, beyond your leaving my cousin out of them."

There. That was plain enough.

Her eyes went wide. Ah, good. He'd intended to startle her.

But the horrified expression he expected never appeared on her face. Instead, Lady Emma bit her lip, as if she were trying to smother a grin. "I beg your pardon, Lord Lymington, but I believe you misunderstood your cousin's intentions this evening. Lord Lovell proposed a *dance*, not a betrothal."

Good Lord, was the girl *laughing* at him? She certainly looked as if she were enjoying herself. "Let's dispense with the pleasantries, shall we, Lady Emma?"

"Was this you being pleasant, Lord Lymington? Forgive me. I didn't realize. I believe one generally does rely on pleasantries in these situations. What shall we talk about, if not the sights in London and the weakness of Almack's tea?"

He gazed into blue eyes sparkling with humor and reminded himself he was meant to be frightening her away from Lovell. "You have a distinctive voice, Lady Emma. Has anyone ever told you that before?"

"No, I don't believe they have. I find it curious *you'd* say so, Lord Lymington. I doubt I've said more than three dozen words to you tonight."

"No, but I've heard your voice before. Even if I hadn't, a single word would be sufficient. Yours is not a voice a man easily forgets." Samuel studied her face, but there wasn't a flicker of consciousness there, not even a hint of a blush. If Lady Emma had any inkling he knew about her secret visit to the Pink Pearl, she hid it well.

"Indeed? Well, er...thank you, Lord Lymington." She looked faintly puzzled, but there wasn't so much as a tremor in her voice, and she met his gaze without flinching.

Such big, innocent blue eyes...

Was it possible he'd made a mistake, and it *hadn't* been her voice he'd heard? Voices were easily mistaken for each other, even distinctive ones. He'd only heard her speak a few words aloud—the rest had been in whispers.

But the effect that voice had on him, the prickling of awareness over every inch of his skin, the deep tug in his belly—he'd never been so aroused by a lady's voice in his life. Samuel had known that voice as soon as the first word of greeting left her lips this evening.

Lady Emma was lying to him right now. Boldly, without a blush, while looking him directly in the eyes.

It *had* been her at the Pink Pearl last night. He was certain of it.

Samuel didn't know what sort of mischief she was engaged in, and he didn't care. She might visit every brothel and befriend every courtesan in London, with his blessing, as long as she stayed away from Lovell. "I advise you to deploy your charms on someone other than my cousin, Lady Emma."

"*Deploy* my charms? I don't—"

"You'll get nowhere with Lovell. His affections are already engaged, but I shouldn't worry, if I were you."

Her blue eyes went wide. "Worry?"

She truly did have extraordinary eyes. They were a darker blue than he'd thought at first, nearly cobalt. Not summer skies at all, but a midnight blue. Remarkable, even if she was staring at him as if he'd just escaped from Bedlam. "There are plenty of gentlemen in London who will be thrilled to be on the receiving end of flirtatious glances from your blue eyes."

She choked back what sounded, amazingly, like a laugh. "It's, ah, kind of you to say so, Lord Lymington. I'll endeavor not to despair of my matrimonial prospects *quite* yet, then."

The music ended, and he released her hand. He expected her to flee, as any other young lady should do after such a disastrous dance, but before she could stir a step, Samuel did something he hadn't intended to do.

He raised her hand to his mouth and touched his lips to her glove.

"Thank you for the dance, Lord Lymington. I believe I'll return to my grandmother now." Lady Emma sank into a perfect curtsey, and without another word she turned and strode away.

Samuel might have chased her, insisted on escorting her back to her grandmother, as was proper, but instead he remained where he was, watching her go, and wondering...

But Lady Emma's secrets were just that—*hers.* Let her keep them.

He'd made himself perfectly clear to her tonight.

Lady Emma Crosby wouldn't dare encourage Lovell's misguided attentions now.

* * * *

Emma didn't return to Lady Crosby, but instead slipped from the ballroom and made her way to the ladies' retiring room. She plopped down onto a settee, not sure if she should laugh, or fall into a temper, or burst into a flood of tears.

That was, without a doubt, the strangest half hour she'd ever passed. Lord Lymington wasn't like any other lord she'd ever known, and until tonight, she would have sworn she'd known them all.

It hadn't been a spontaneous decision, refusing Lord Lovell in favor of a dance with Lord Lymington. She hadn't fancied a scene in the middle of Almack's, but it hadn't been only that. That glare he'd cast her way when he'd first caught sight of her, then his strange insistence on a dance, had aroused her suspicions.

Very few people in London would recognize her as one of Madame Marchand's former courtesans. She'd never been one of the ladies who entertained whatever gentlemen happened to stroll through the front door of an evening. No, she'd been *special*, reserved for a single gentleman who'd paid Madame dearly for the privilege of being the first and only gentleman to enjoy her favors.

Given how *that* liaison had ended, Madame Marchand wasn't likely to tell Emma's secrets, either, as much as she might wish to. Madame bore her a bitter grudge, but she was as eager to hide Emma's past as Emma was.

Not many bawds wanted to lay claim to a murderous courtesan.

But when Emma saw Lord Lymington's baleful glare, she'd thought, in an instant of blind panic, that she'd come face to face with someone who knew who she was.

Or who she'd been.

Whether her suspicions were justified or not remained a mystery. She couldn't make heads or tails of Lord Lymington, or decide whether she was amused by him, or frightened of him, or if she simply despised him, as she did so many noblemen.

Loathing made the most sense, certainly.

He was grim, arrogant, suspicious, and far too large for a proper lord. He rivaled even Daniel Brixton for sheer muscular immensity.

He was dreadfully high-handed, too. Why, the cheek of the man, to cut his cousin out so shamelessly. No gentleman wanted a cotillion as badly as that. Then again, no gentleman wanted his cousin to dance a cotillion at Almack's with a courtesan, either.

Former courtesan.

Oh, blast Lord Lymington, anyway. The man had thrown everything into disarray tonight. Poor Lord Lovell, to be cursed with such an overbearing cousin. Emma had no sympathy for rakes, but Lord Lymington was enough to drive any man into rakishness.

Well then, it seemed as if she *did* despise him, after all. That should be reason enough to banish him from her mind at once. And so she would, only…

He'd startled her with that droll remark about their being silent for an entire cotillion, though she doubted he'd intended to amuse her. Then there'd been that ludicrous conversation about her matrimonial prospects. Charm seemed to wither and die in Lord Lymington's presence, but he'd been…honest.

He hadn't been the least charmed by *her*, that much was certain. She'd given him her widest eyes, her best smiles, and he'd scowled back at her as if he'd caught her picking his pocket.

That was unexpected, and…disarming, somehow.

Emma braced her elbows on the dressing table and pressed her fingers to her temples, trying to recall what he'd said. Something about deploying her charms on Lord Lovell. He'd actually used the word *deploy*, of all absurd things. Then he'd made that inexplicable observation about her voice, or flirtatious glances, or some such nonsense, and then he'd warned her to keep away from his cousin.

Emma sat up, her gaze meeting her own reflection in the glass. Lord Lymington had actually *warned* her away from Lord Lovell.

But why? What objection could he possibly have to Lady Emma Crosby? She was the daughter of an earl, for pity's sake, and possessed of an impressive fortune.

It didn't make any sense. Emma hadn't even had a chance to single Lord Lovell out for any particular attention this evening—

"Oh, dear. You don't look pleased, Lady Emma. Was your dance with Lord Lymington really as unpleasant as that?"

Emma's head jerked up, and she found Lady Flora Silvester hovering in the doorway to the lady's retiring room. "It wasn't unpleasant, precisely, but, well…not precisely *pleasant*, either. I've just been sitting here wondering whether I should have danced with him at all."

"He can be rather terrifying. That is, I don't mean one has a *reason* be terrified of him," Lady Flora hastened to correct herself. "Only that, well…one *is*, isn't one?"

Emma hadn't been at all terrified of Lord Lymington, but Lady Emma Crosby likely would have been, so she nodded in agreement. "A bit, yes."

Lady Flora ventured closer, a hesitant smile on her lips. "He's not nearly so bad as he seems upon first acquaintance. He rather grows on one, you see."

"Indeed? I'll keep that in mind." Not that she anticipated sharing another dance with Lord Lymington. Emma patted the empty space beside her on the settee. "Will you sit with me?"

"Oh, I don't wish to bother you. My grandmother and Lady Crosby sent me in search of you, and bid me bring you to supper. Have you ever had Almack's supper, Lady Emma?"

"No. Is it dreadfully elegant?"

"No, just dreadful."

Emma laughed. "Truly?"

"I'm afraid so. I rather despise Almack's, on the whole. Everyone smirking and staring, and gossiping behind your back." Lady Flora shuddered. "They all complain about the dry cake and sour lemonade, but the *ton* is much more distasteful than any cake I've ever tasted."

Emma laughed again, the comparison striking her fancy. "How are you so familiar with Almack's, Lady Flora? Didn't your grandmother say this is your first season?"

"Oh, it is, but I daresay it won't be my last."

"I'm certain that's not true." Lady Flora was the daughter of an earl, and such a pretty, engaging young lady, with her sweet smile. Were London's aristocratic gentlemen so foolish they couldn't see that?

"I'm afraid it is." Lady Flora sighed. "I have no money, you see. My father was a devotee of the hazard tables, and my elder brother followed in his footsteps. Now they're both dead, and my grandmother and I are left as poor as church mice."

"But that's awful!" Emma had heard such stories before, and they never failed to make her furious.

"Yes, isn't it? But I didn't come here to bemoan my fate. I only came to assure you Lord Lymington isn't as awful as he appears, in case he asks you to dance again." Lady Flora wandered across the room and perched on the settee at Emma's side. "He's really a kind gentleman, if a trifle blunt."

"Do you know the family well, then?" Emma leaned closer, half-ashamed of herself for attempting to pry secrets from Lady Flora's innocent lips, but not ashamed enough to keep her from doing it.

"Very well, yes. My father's estate in Kent is in the same neighborhood as Lymington House. My grandmother is friends with Lady Lymington, and I grew up with Lancelot—that is, Lord Lovell."

"But not with Lord Lymington?" Emma did her best to hide how interested she was in Lady Flora's answer.

"No. Lord Lovell is eight years his cousin's junior." Lady Flora smiled, her dark eyes lighting up. "Lancelot used to follow Samuel about like a devoted, adoring shadow when they were boys. They were like brothers then, but Lord Lymington's been gone these past eight years. He was a captain in the Royal Navy, on board the *HMS Nymphe*."

Emma frowned. "A marquess, risking his life on board a Navy ship? That's rather unusual."

"It is, yes. Lord Lymington's father died when he was very young, and his Uncle Lovell came to Lymington House to see to the estates. He and Lord Lymington never got on. The previous Lord Lovell was...rather a difficult man."

"He must have been difficult indeed, to chase Lord Lymington from his own estate," Emma said, eager to hear more.

But Lady Flora seemed to realize she'd said too much, and changed the subject. "Well, Lord Lymington is back now, in any case. He resigned his commission upon his uncle's death, but he was meant to be quite good at it. Captaining, I mean. He's very brave, by all accounts."

A captain, was he? Well, no wonder he was so curt, so presumptuous. Such a man would be accustomed to giving orders, and having them obeyed. No wonder he'd taken an immediate dislike to her. She'd never been good at following orders.

"What of Lord Lovell, Lady Flora? You must know him well, if you were childhood friends. Is he as charming as everyone says?"

"He's, ah…he's a charming gentleman, yes. Rather like a brother to me, you know." Lady Flora dropped her gaze. "My grandmother is fond of Lord Lovell, and won't hear a single word against him."

Lady Silvester must be partial to Lovell, indeed. Even leaving aside the thorny questions of kidnapping and murder, there was plenty to say about Lord Lovell that was less than flattering. His family had gone to a great deal of trouble to bury his scandals, but you couldn't hide everything.

From some people, you couldn't hide *anything*.

People like Lady Clifford, for instance.

England was full of sinners, and Lady Clifford knew all their ugliest, filthiest sins. Adultery, bastard children, ruined daughters, clandestine lovers and their secret sexual proclivities…

Seductions, ruinations, kidnappings, murder…

"I'm certain Lord Lovell is every bit as charming as you say." Emma rose to her feet. "He must have got the lion's share of charm in his family, because there doesn't seem to have been any left over for Lord Lymington."

Lady Flora slapped a hand over her mouth, but not before a giggle escaped. "Oh, dear. Poor Lord Lymington. That's quite wicked of you to say, Lady Emma."

Wicked, yes, and only the merest ripple on the surface of the deep, dark pool of Emma's wickedness. If Lady Flora knew how awful she really was, she'd fall into a swoon.

But until then…

Emma held out her hand to Lady Flora. "Shall we go into supper? I fancy a plate of dry cake, and a glass of sour lemonade."

Chapter Four

"How long do you intend to keep us wandering about this dreary old place, Lymington? I've never known you to give a bloody damn about Sir Joshua Reynolds before today."

"My goodness, Lancelot." Lady Lymington turned on her nephew, her eyes wide with reproach. "I can't think what poor Sir Joshua's ever done to make you curse so wickedly. Do guard your tongue, won't you?"

"I beg your pardon, Aunt Sophronia." Lovell cast a guilty look at his aunt, then pressed his lips together, as if the only reason he'd spoken at all was to curse, and he might as well remain silent now.

And he did remain so—for precisely four minutes, when he let out a heavy sigh. "You may stand there gaping up at that monstrosity for as long as you like, Lymington, but you'll never convince me you admire it."

"Certainly, I admire it." Samuel clasped his hands behind his back and adopted an appreciative pose. "The, ah…richness of the colors, and the, ah…the subjects. Very vigorous, indeed."

"Vigorous!" Lovell snorted. "Do you call the Ladies Waldegrave vigorous?"

"The Ladies Waldegrave?" Samuel focused on the portrait he'd been pretending to admire and stifled a groan. Damn it, when had they moved on from Sir Tarleton? There was nothing vigorous about three ladies gathered around a table doing…what *were* they doing? Tatting lace? Spinning skeins of silk? "Did I say vigorous? I meant domestic. Er, an impressive representation of domestic bliss."

Behind him, Lovell snickered. "Do try and keep up, eh, Lymington?"

Samuel smothered a sigh. In truth, he couldn't work up any more enthusiasm for Reynolds's portraits than Lovell could. He'd suggested they visit the Royal Academy because Lady Flora had mentioned she intended to attend the exhibit today.

Not because Lady Emma had mentioned she might visit, as well.

He'd dragged Lovell through nearly every room in the place this afternoon, hoping for a chance meeting with Lady Flora, but when they'd come across her at last, she and her grandmother hadn't been alone. Lord Barrett and his sister had been with them, his lordship with Lady Flora on his arm, casting openly admiring glances at her.

Lovell had stared at them in confusion for a moment, then his face had gone darker than a thundercloud. Since then, he'd been muttering to himself about upstart lords, and capricious young ladies who'd do well to be more particular about their escorts.

Samuel might have been cheered at this sign of Lovell's attachment to Lady Flora if Barrett had been a less desirable suitor, but he was a pleasant, handsome young gentleman, just the sort any young lady would be thrilled to have courting her.

"Would you call this one vigorous as well?" Lovell paused in front of Reynolds's sedate portrait of the Countess of Warwick. "Perhaps her hat might be referred to as vigorous. What do you think, Lymington?"

Samuel gave his cousin a dark look, but he bit back the ill-humored retort on his tongue. Lovell was still annoyed with him over the scene at Almack's with Lady Emma last night, and Samuel, knowing he deserved some of Lovell's ire, wasn't inclined to defend his behavior.

The rest of the ball hadn't gone as Lovell had hoped. Lady Flora had been claimed by one eager gentleman after another, and had hardly spared Lovell a glance all evening. That alone had been enough to put Lovell into a mood, but then he'd also never gotten his two dances with Lady Emma, who'd left Almack's with her grandmother soon after the supper was finished.

For his part, Samuel was relieved at their abrupt departure, as it seemed to indicate his warning to Lady Emma had had the desired effect. Yes, he was certainly relieved at it—of *course* he was—except now he'd succeeded in chasing her off, just the merest sliver of doubt over his behavior had begun to plague him.

Perhaps he hadn't needed to be *quite* so blunt with her. It wasn't as if she'd done anything wrong. Hers hadn't been the only pair of blue eyes that looked upon Lovell with admiration.

Just the prettiest pair.

Still, she certainly had been the lady he'd overhead at the Pink Pearl the other night. He couldn't think of a single innocent explanation for her presence at an infamous brothel, but he also couldn't banish the memory of her wide eyes gazing up at him. For a lady engaged in some sort of mischief, Lady Emma contrived to look as guileless as a newborn fawn.

That, more than anything else, made him wonder about her.

Samuel paused, frowning at the Countess of Warwick in her monstrous hat. Lady Emma was…intriguing. Of all the young ladies he'd danced with last night, she was the only one of them who hadn't scurried away after their dance as if rabid hounds were nipping at her heels.

Which was curious indeed, given she was the only one who had reason to.

She hadn't appeared alarmed by him at all. He'd caught her watching him more than once throughout the remainder of the evening, her expression speculative rather than terrified. He couldn't make sense of the girl, but then he couldn't make sense of most ladies.

Why Lady Emma's reaction mattered to him one way or the other, Samuel couldn't say. All that *should* matter was that she stay away from Lovell for the rest of the season, so he could get on with the business of capturing Lady Flora's heart.

Really, there was no reason for Samuel to spare Lady Emma another thought. He drew in a calming breath, and vowed for the fourth time since he'd woken this morning to forget about Lady Emma.

The trouble was, he'd kissed her hand.

He shouldn't have kissed her hand. Why had he kissed her hand? He'd lain awake half the night trying to explain it to himself, but he couldn't come up with anything satisfactory.

He was only certain of one thing.

It would be madness to touch her again. Whatever else he did, he had to remember that.

Don't bloody touch her again.

The kiss had been an impulse, a momentary lapse in logical reasoning. He wasn't a reckless man, or a spontaneous one, but one moment he'd been warning her away from Lovell, and the next thing he knew he'd been kissing her hand. If he'd managed to show even the slightest hint of restraint last night, he wouldn't be cursed with the memory of the warmth of her fingers under her smooth kid gloves—

"If you've quite finished with Lady Warwick, Lymington, might we move along? It makes perfect sense that you'd find a portrait of a lady lounging in a chair beside a window fascinating, but since we're here, I'd like to see the rest of the military portraits, if we may."

"Yes, do move on, Lymington," Lady Lovell echoed, with an indulgent look at her son. "You can hardly blame Lovell for finding it tedious. Don't you agree, Mr. Humphries?"

"Of course." Felix Humphries, his aunt's new favorite companion, patted her hand. "I always agree with you, my lady."

Samuel resisted the urge to roll his eyes. Humphries had been a friend of his Uncle Lovell's, and had been hanging about since his death to comfort Lady Lovell. Samuel didn't know Humphries well, but he seemed a sluggish, dull-witted creature. As for his Aunt Adelaide, she appeared to be perfectly reconciled to her husband's death, and not in much need of comforting.

Together, they were the greatest pair of fools Samuel had ever encountered. He'd never been fond of his Aunt Adelaide, and he did his best to pretend Humphries wasn't there.

Lovell made an impatient noise, and Samuel turned back to him with an irritable sigh. "For God's sake, Lovell. What have you got against the Countess of Warwick?"

"She's the dullest countess imaginable, that's what. Who wants to look at a fusty portrait of a countess half smothered in blue ribbons? You may as well stop pretending you find it engrossing, Lymington. You're not fooling anyone."

Another retort threatened, but a light touch on Samuel's arm caught his attention, and he looked down to find his mother gazing up at him with an anxious expression. "Why not let Lancelot move on as he chooses? I'll remain here with you as long as you like."

Samuel managed a smile for his mother. "Never mind. I'm perfectly willing to move on."

They wandered through the exhibit, pausing here and there as Lady Lovell and Humphries held forth on the merits of one painting or another, without having the faintest idea what they were talking about. Lady Lymington ventured a hesitant question or two about Reynolds's naval heroes, but despite Lovell's insistence on seeing them, he hardly spared the paintings a glance.

"Might we go see the portrait of the Duchess of Devonshire and Lady Georgiana?" Lady Sophronia asked, once they'd made their way through the military paintings. "I haven't had the pleasure of viewing it before."

"Of course, if you wish it."

Samuel turned to tell Lovell, but Lady Adelaide had stopped to chat with an acquaintance, and Humphries was snoozing on a bench in the corner.

"Go on. We'll catch up to you in a moment." Lovell waved them on, dropping limply onto another bench, his bad leg stretched out in front of him, muttering that he'd seen enough portraits to last him a lifetime.

So Samuel escorted his mother to the other end of the hallway, where Reynolds's portraits of the Duchess of Devonshire were hung.

"Why, how charming!" Lady Sophronia exclaimed over the portrait of the duchess with her infant daughter on her knee. "Lady Georgiana Cavendish is such a lovely child! Don't you think so, Samuel?"

Samuel could hardly tell one child from another, but he smiled at his mother's pleasure. "She's very pretty, yes."

They went down the row, and after a while some of the tension eased from Samuel's shoulders. He'd hardly seen his mother smile at all since his return to England, but she seemed to be taking great pleasure in their outing today.

It had been her idea to come to London for the season. She had great hopes of restoring Lovell to Lady Flora's good graces, but she'd also delicately hinted that Samuel might pay a visit to Caroline Francis at the Pink Pearl while they were in town. That particular task had yet to bear fruit, but it would, and soon.

He would make certain of it.

Samuel listened to his mother's cheerful chatter and the moments slid by without his noticing, until nearly half an hour had elapsed without any sign of Lovell.

When it came to Lovell, half an hour was a lifetime. If he'd been seized with one of his freaks or whims, there was no telling what he might have gotten up to in that time.

"You must be fatigued." Samuel tucked his mother's hand through his arm and started down the hallway. "Shall we fetch Lovell, and have tea?"

They strolled back down the hallway, and found Humphries and Lady Adelaide lounging on the bench, whispering to each other, but Lovell...

Samuel's gaze swept from one end of the room to the other, his jaw tightening.

Lovell was gone.

* * * *

"Lord Lovell's been at the Pink Pearl."

Emma had been toying with the ribbons on her hat, waiting for Lady Crosby to appear so they might be on their way to the Royal Academy, but her fingers stilled at Daniel Brixton's words, her heart crowding into her throat. "Lord Lovell?"

"Aye, lass." Daniel held out a note with Lady Crosby's direction written on the front in Helena's familiar scrawl. "Read this."

Emma eyed the note, unease coiling in her stomach. "We're a single day into the season, and something's gone amiss already?"

"Read it, lass." Daniel pressed the note into her hand.

Emma was just unfolding it when Lady Crosby appeared in the drawing room. "Here I am, ready at last. Good afternoon, Daniel. Shall we…oh, Emma, my dear, don't furrow your brow with such ferocity. It's not good for your complexion. What have you got there in your hand?"

"It's a note from Helena. It seems Lord Lovell paid a visit to the Pink Pearl two nights ago." That in itself wasn't so surprising. Gentlemen with the means to do so did tend to turn up at the Pink Pearl sooner or later, but Lord Lovell had hardly set foot in London before he was darkening Madame Marchand's doorstep.

Lady Crosby's eyes widened. "Oh, dear. He's after Caroline Francis, already?"

Emma scanned the rest of the note. "It's curious, but Helena doesn't mention that. She says only that Lord Lovell is as pretty as rumor claims—"

Daniel snorted.

"—and that he behaved like a perfect gentleman." Emma let the note drop into her lap.

"Hmm. Well, perhaps we'll find out more at the Royal Academy. All the *ton* will be there, and where the *ton* is, there's sure to be gossip." Lady Crosby drew on her gloves. "Shall we go?"

"Yes, but first I want to write a quick note to Helena, and ask her if anyone heard Lord Lovell mention Caroline last night." Emma went to a desk in the corner, wrote a few hasty lines, then folded it and offered it to Daniel. "You'll see Helena gets this?"

"Aye." Daniel took the note and stuffed it into his pocket.

"Thank you. I'm ready now, my lady." Emma snatched up her hat, and followed Lady Crosby out to the carriage.

It was the opening day of the exhibit. Lord Lovell would almost certainly be there, and his odious cousin likely with him, but this time Emma wouldn't let Lord Lymington interfere with her plans.

It was all a matter of proper coordination.

She spent the carriage ride from Mayfair to the Royal Academy coming up with various schemes to lure Lord Lovell away from his cousin, but in the end, it was the easiest thing in the world. She found Lord Lovell sitting on a bench, alone. All it took was a half-smile and an inviting glance over her shoulder, and he'd followed her down the hallway.

"Good afternoon, Lady Emma, and Lady Crosby! Such a pleasure to see you both again so soon." He bowed over Emma's hand, his blue eyes moving over her face with frank appreciation.

"How do you do, Lord Lovell?" Lady Crosby inclined her head, and Emma distracted him with her sweetest smile while she glanced subtly about for any signs of Lord Lymington. She didn't see him, but he'd appear soon enough.

He wasn't going to be pleased to find her with his cousin. The thought made Emma's stomach clench with nervousness, but she couldn't deny there was a thread of anticipation there, as well. She did so love a challenge.

"Will you come and join my party?" Lord Lovell asked, offering Emma and Lady Crosby each an arm. "They're viewing the Duchess of Devonshire's portrait in the next room."

"Oh, how kind you are, Lord Lovell, but I'm afraid we've been here for some time already, and my grandmother is fatigued. We're just going to see Reynolds's portraits of Kitty Fisher before taking our leave for the day."

"Er...Kitty Fisher?" Lovell asked, a flush sweeping up his neck.

"Yes." Emma regarded him with wide, innocent eyes, but she couldn't prevent a twitch at the corner of her lip. The exhibit was arranged by theme, which meant Kitty Fisher's portrait was hanging with Reynolds's other portraits of scandalous courtesans and actresses.

It wasn't at all the thing for a young, unmarried lady to gape at portraits of harlots, not least because gentlemen tended to be more frequent visitors to that part of the exhibit, and it was tucked into rather a remote corner of the museum, so as not to offend the virtuous.

Emma wasn't, alas, one of the virtuous, nor was she shy of harlots.

Poor Lord Lovell, however, looked as if he was about to swallow his tongue. "Are you all right, my lord? You seem a trifle warm."

"Yes, yes, indeed." Lord Lovell ran a finger under the edge of his cravat. "But are you certain you wouldn't rather see the duchess's portrait, Lady Emma, or the military portraits? The one of General Burgoyne is an especially good likeness."

"Oh no, my lord. Military portraits are rather dull, and I've been longing to see Mrs. Fisher, and the portrait of Emma Hamilton as Bacchante."

Lord Lovell's blush deepened at mention of Emma Hamilton. Goodness, how singular. Emma had never seen a notorious rake *blush* before, but Lord Lovell didn't seem much like any of the rakes she'd known, any more than his cousin was like other lords.

Emma didn't care for rakes. She was too well acquainted with the damage they could do to find them intriguing, but there was something sweetly boyish about Lord Lovell, a vulnerability that made him seem younger than he was.

Younger, and very unlike a hardened villain.

Certainly, a man might look a picture of gentlemanliness when a monster was lurking just under the surface, but as far as she could tell, the only thing lurking under Lord Lovell's surface was more tender skin.

He didn't seem at all the sort of despicable fiend who'd hurt a young lady, but Caroline Francis swore he had. Caroline's word was all they had so far regarding Amy and Kitty's disappearances, so until Emma knew better, she'd follow where it led.

"You're welcome to accompany us, my lord." Emma smiled and fluttered her eyelashes at him, hoping to hurry him along before his enormous cousin emerged from whatever corner he was lurking behind. Lord Lymington might have prevented her from dancing with Lord Lovell last night, but she'd have her way this afternoon.

"I think I must, yes, as I don't like to send you there without an escort."

"Why, how chivalrous you are, Lord Lovell." Lady Crosby took the arm he offered, beaming at him, but as soon as they reached the exhibit, she announced herself much too fatigued to take another step, and waved them off to admire the paintings while she sank onto a stone bench in the corner.

Emma hid her smile. For all her fluffy white hair and grandmotherly charm, Lady Crosby had taken to subterfuge as if she'd emerged from the womb with a dagger in her hand and a secret on her lips.

"Did you enjoy yourself at Almack's last night, Lord Lovell?" Emma didn't pause to allow him to answer, but rushed on with a gasp. "Oh, look, my lord! It's Nelly O'Brien's portrait. My goodness, she looks rather prim, doesn't she? Nothing like I'd imagine a courtesan would look. She bore the Earl of Thanet three illegitimate sons, you know."

Lord Lovell made a faint choking sound. "Yes, I, ah…I do believe I heard that. But to answer your question, Lady Emma, I found Almack's a bit disappointing, as I didn't share even one dance with you. I do hope you and Lady Crosby are attending Lady Swinton's ball this evening, so I might have another chance."

"I believe my grandmother intends it, yes."

"May I solicit your hand for the first two dances, Lady Emma?"

Emma cast him a sidelong glance. Unlike his cousin, Lord Lovell knew very well how to play the gallant. "You're not flirting with me, are you, Lord Lovell?"

"Flirting? Certainly not. That would be improper." Lovell grinned at her and pressed a hand over hers. "But you won't be so hard-hearted as to refuse me?"

"Oh, very well. I'll dance with you, my lord, though I daresay I'll regret it when all the other young ladies are shooting daggers at me with their eyes."

He raised her hand to his lips, but stopped short of touching them to her glove. "Are there any other young ladies in London aside from you, Lady Emma? If so, I didn't notice them."

Emma laughed, the bright sound ringing in the close chamber. Goodness, he *was* a practiced flirt, wasn't he? If she were the sweet young innocent she was pretending to be, it would never occur to her this was merely a game to him, and her heart would be in his possession already.

But she wasn't an innocent. She was a performer, just as Lord Lovell was. Emma gave him a prim look, and withdrew her hand from his. "Hush, Lord Lovell. You're a dreadful liar."

"How can you say so?" He pressed a hand to his chest. "Such cruelty, Lady Emma! Your accusations wound me."

"Nonsense. You'll be betrothed to some young lady or other before the end of the season, and won't spare me another glance." My, how the young ladies' tears would flow when Lord Lovell's heart was taken. London would be drowned in them.

"*Betrothed?* Heavens, what an accusation. I assure you, I'm not seeking any such thing. Why, the season's only just begun, my lady, and already you have me caught in the parson's mousetrap." Lord Lovell laughed, but it rang a bit hollow. "I demand to know which lady I'm meant to be marrying, and where you heard such a scandalous falsehood."

Emma blinked. Well, there was nothing rehearsed about *that* reaction. "Never, my lord. I know when to hold my tongue."

Such a vehement protest against the parson's mousetrap made Emma wonder if Lord Lovell had one foot caught in it already. Perhaps Lord Lymington was telling the truth about his cousin's affections being already engaged.

She couldn't ask, of course. Proper young ladies didn't quiz gentlemen about courtships, betrothals, or their mistresses. Though that *was* rather splitting hairs, since she did intend to quiz him about ruining, kidnapping, and possibly murdering his aunt's housemaids.

But not today.

"If I were to have my own portrait painted, I'd like it to be done like this one." Emma paused in front of Reynolds's portrait of the courtesan Emily Warren as Thaïs. "See how commanding she looks with her torch?

I believe I'd like to carry a torch and stride triumphantly through the flames, as she does here."

"You must—nay, you *will* be painted, Lady Emma, for what artist could resist a face as perfect as yours? You must be painted as Aphrodite, the goddess of love and beauty—"

"Not Aphrodite, Lovell," said a deep voice from behind them. "I think Lady Emma is more like Athena, the goddess of warcraft."

Lord Lovell whirled around. "Lymington! I, ah…was just on my way to come find you."

"I've no doubt of it, cousin."

Lovell was flustered at Lord Lymington's sudden appearance, but Emma wasn't. She'd known all along he'd sniff them out sooner or later. "Good afternoon, Lord Lymington. I thought you must be here somewhere."

Lord Lymington offered her a polite bow, not taking his eyes off her, even as he addressed his cousin. "Your mother is fatigued, Lovell, and ready to return home."

"Yes, of course." A guilty flush rose to Lord Lovell's cheeks, but he took a moment to raise Emma's hand to his lips. "Remember your promise, Lady Emma, about the first two dances at tonight's ball." With that, he went off to do his cousin's bidding.

"Emma, my dear?" Lady Crosby had kept to her bench while Emma flirted with Lovell, but at Lord Lymington's appearance her brows furrowed with concern, and she half rose from her seat.

As well she might. Lord Lymington was a good deal more concerning than his cousin—it was rather like the difference between a playful kitten and a ravenous lion.

"It's all right, Grandmother." Emma's gaze remained fixed on the painting before her. "Do keep resting. I'll fetch you once I've finished with the portraits."

Lord Lymington didn't follow his cousin, but kept his place beside Emma. She could feel his dark gaze on the side of her face like a touch, but she remained silent, studying the painting before them, and waiting.

"Do you have an interest in courtesans, Lady Emma?" Lord Lymington drawled, once Lord Lovell's footsteps had faded to silence.

And just like that, all of Emma's careful schemes to manage Lord Lymington vanished in a burst of annoyance. "Do you have a *quarrel* with courtesans, Lord Lymington?"

Naturally, he had a quarrel with courtesans, just like every other gentleman did. Once they'd finished with them, that is. Such was the hypocrisy of England's privileged class. One would think she'd be used to it by now, but perhaps she never would be.

He shrugged. "Not with courtesans, no, though I do have a quarrel with the men who turn into brutes the moment they step foot inside a brothel."

Emma had been studying the portrait of Emily Warren, but she jerked her attention to Lord Lymington, and was taken aback to see his face had darkened with a scowl. "I'm surprised to hear you say so, my lord. Gentlemen tend to overlook their own culpability in their dealings with bawds and brothels."

"Some gentlemen overlook their culpability in all their dealings, Lady Emma, but not every gentleman. A gentleman may choose not to visit a courtesan, whereas most courtesans don't choose to become one. If there *is* any wrongdoing in the practice, it lies with those who have the choice."

Choice. Yes, that was a luxury, indeed.

Emma thought of Helena, and Madame Marchand and Lord Peabody, and bitterness swelled in her chest, the taste of it coating her tongue, and she turned back to the portrait to hide her expression from Lord Lymington. "Nearly every gentleman in London frequents courtesans, my lord. None of them are much inclined to chastise themselves for it."

"Indeed. But you never answered my question, Lady Emma."

"Your question, my lord?"

"I asked if you take an interest in courtesans." He nodded at the portrait of Emily Warren, her flaming torch held high, an avenging angel setting everything in her path ablaze.

"It's an impertinent question, Lord Lymington. I don't feel obligated to answer it."

"I beg your pardon. I meant no offense. It's just that I couldn't think of any reason why you'd wish to visit *this* exhibit, particularly in company with my cousin."

Emma made herself look directly into those glittering gray eyes, and smiled. "Perhaps I'm merely interested in Reynolds's portraiture, my lord."

"Ah." One corner of his lip twitched in what might have been a smile on another man. "You do recall our conversation regarding Lord Lovell, do you not, Lady Emma?"

"I do recall it, yes. It was last night, my lord."

There was a brief pause, then, "Did I not make myself clear?"

"On the contrary, Lord Lymington. You made yourself perfectly clear."

"Yet here we are. Why is that, Lady Emma?"

Emma paused, studying him. It was a pleasant spring day in London, and the rays of sun shining through a nearby window illuminated his face.

In this light his resemblance to his cousin was more pronounced. They had the same angular jaw, the same prominent cheekbones and straight, proud noses, but Lord Lymington's hair was darker, his eyes a stormy gray instead of Lovell's lively blue.

Lord Lymington was handsome, Emma noticed with vague surprise, though he had none of his cousin's boyish charm. "I believe it's Lord Lovell's business to decide who he wishes to honor with his company, Lord Lymington. He's not a child."

"I'm aware that he is not, Lady Emma."

"Are you? I would have said otherwise."

Lord Lymington's expression didn't change, but his fingers tightened around the silver head of his walking stick. "Explain yourself, please."

"Forgive me, my lord, but if you were aware of it, you wouldn't feel the need to follow after him as if he were a naughty schoolboy. I wonder what Lord Lovell would think, if he knew you were chasing the young ladies at Almack's away from him."

He took a step toward her, his jaw tight. "Are you *threatening* me, Lady Emma?"

Oh, dear. He didn't care for *that* at all. It was a pity Sir Joshua Reynolds was dead, because the expression on Lord Lymington's face was worthy of the efforts of the finest artist. "Me, threaten *you*, my lord? Certainly not."

"It sounds as if you are."

"I wouldn't dream of it, Lord Lymington."

"It isn't your place to wonder anything about Lord Lovell, Lady Emma." Lord Lymington's tone was clipped, every syllable resonant with authority.

Goodness. Lord Lovell had the right of it, when he said all of his cousin's words sounded like commands.

No, there was nothing of the boy in Lord Lymington. No guile, either, and no mercy.

And now all of his doggedness, his extraordinary persistence was focused on being rid of *her*, and it didn't appear to Emma to be a simple matter of his preferring a different lady for his cousin.

No, he seemed to object to *her*, specifically. Or, not *her*, but Lady Emma Crosby.

Unless he'd somehow discovered who she really was?

If he'd been anyone else, she'd have scoffed at the idea, but Emma's instincts warned her not to underestimate Lord Lymington. No secrets were safe from a man like him. If she was obliged to tangle with him—and it looked as if she would be—he'd prove a fierce adversary.

Under cover of her skirts, Emma's knees were wobbling, but she raised her chin and met his eyes. "I won't be commanded by you, Lord Lymington. If you imagine I'll scurry out of your way like a timid schoolgirl just out of pinafores, you're very much mistaken."

"Am I, indeed?" One dark eyebrow rose. "How refreshing."

Dear God, that glower. "I imagine most young ladies quiver in their slippers at a single glare from you, but I'm not one of them."

"No?" He caught her upraised chin between his fingers. "What *does* make you quiver, Lady Emma?"

Emma sucked in a breath, unable to hide her shock. Not at the innuendo—she'd heard far worse—but that he'd say it to Lady Emma Crosby, daughter of an earl, a sweet young innocent who'd never set foot outside of Somerset.

He must know who she really was. He *must*, or he'd never dare—

"Forgive me." Lord Lymington released her, his hand dropping away from her face as if her skin had burned him. "Whatever your game is, I'd advise you to think carefully before you choose to play it with me."

"Game? I don't know what you mean."

"I think you do, my lady. I think you know precisely what I mean."

Uneasiness tightened Emma's stomach, but she held her ground, chin still raised. "I haven't the faintest idea, my lord, but you'll have to enlighten me at some other time. My grandmother is fatigued, and must rest before our engagement tonight."

Lord Lymington offered her a polite bow, but his narrowed gray eyes seemed to see right through her. "Of course, Lady Emma."

Emma couldn't quite suppress a flinch at the cold edge with which he said her name, and didn't wait to hear any more, but hurried back to Lady Crosby.

When they reached the carriage, they found Daniel standing beside it, a note from Helena in his hand, which he handed over to Emma. "Here ye are, lass."

Emma waited until they were settled in the carriage and on their way to Mayfair before she tore it open and read the few lines Helena had scrawled. "She says as far as she can tell, Lord Lovell didn't mention a word to anyone about Caroline Francis."

"Do you suppose he doesn't yet realize she's there?" Lady Crosby asked. "Perhaps that isn't so surprising. The family has been in mourning since the previous Lord Lovell passed."

Emma considered it, then shook her head. "Perhaps, but that would be strange, wouldn't it? If you were Lord Lovell, and you'd committed a crime, wouldn't you make it your business to keep track of the one lady who could expose you?"

Lady Crosby frowned. "Perhaps Lord Lovell didn't commit the crimes Caroline's accused him of, after all. Then he'd have no reason to worry about where she is."

"But why would Caroline lie about it?"

"I don't know. What else does Helena say?" Lady Crosby peered over Emma's shoulder at the letter. "I can't make out a word of her scrawl."

"Only that the ladies at the Pink Pearl were all atwitter at Lord Lovell's appearance, and that all of them were vying for his attention before he led his chosen companion to a bedchamber upstairs—" Emma glanced at Lady Crosby. "I beg your pardon, my lady."

Lady Crosby waved a dismissive hand. "My dear Emma, by the time you reach my age, nothing shocks you."

"Well, that's something to look forward to." Emma grinned at her, then glanced back down at the note in her hands. "It may be that Lord Lovell *does* know Caroline is at the Pink Pearl, and he wants her to be aware he knows. He must have realized the entire brothel would be in an uproar when *Lord Lovely* appeared at the Pink Pearl. Caroline couldn't have failed to hear of it, despite not being there that night."

Lady Crosby patted Emma's hand. "It's all quite peculiar, but I have utter faith in you, Emma. Until you sort it out, however, we'll have to bear with there being a great many questions, and not many answers."

Emma settled against the squabs and closed her eyes, but behind her eyelids, her head was spinning. A potentially murderous viscount, a marchioness who hadn't breathed a single word about her missing servants, and a marquess who was determined to frighten away his cousin's admirers.

Peculiar, indeed.

Under cover of the darkness in the carriage, she reached up and trailed her fingertips over her chin. She could still feel the imprint of Lord Lymington's fingers there, warm and firm against her skin.

Chapter Five

"Lord Barrett hasn't left Flora's side all night."

"Hmmm?" Samuel was distracted by the couples twirling around Lady Swinton's ballroom. Lord Dunn had taken Lady Emma to the floor, and Samuel couldn't seem to tear his gaze away from her.

His heart quickened each time he caught a glimpse of her creamy skin peeking from the delicate lace sleeves of her gown, so perfect against the vibrant green.

Not blue tonight, but green.

The color of her gown made no difference. She was tempting, no matter what she wore.

No doubt she was even more tempting *out* of it.

Silk or satin, lace or linen, her fair hair half-hidden under a deep hood, or with ribbons woven through the golden strands as they were tonight— Lady Emma was as enticing as a bit of sweet, ripe fruit drowning in fresh cream, the juice lingering on his tongue.

Samuel stifled a groan. Just the thought of it made his heart pound, sending a hot rush of blood to some very inconvenient places.

Damn her.

"Are you listening to me, Lymington?" Lovell let out a fretful sigh. "They've danced together twice already. Before that, she danced twice with Dunn, and twice with Tarrington before *that*. I'm surprised she hasn't worn holes in her slippers by now."

Lady Emma wasn't wearing the pale green favored by the other young ladies this season. No, hers was a deeper, more vibrant green—a green that complemented the mass of thick, golden curls gathered at the back of her neck. The ends of her green ribbons fluttered madly as Dunn swept her across the floor, mocking Samuel with their wild abandon.

"Flora may do as she pleases, of course. Perhaps I'll dance with Lady Jane Townsley instead. Lady Jane has such lovely eyes. Have I mentioned, Lymington, that I prefer blue eyes to dark now? Blue eyes, and fair hair."

Samuel had hardly been able to take his eyes off that damned green ribbon all night—

"Another thing, Lymington. Flora and Barrett may announce their betrothal, and welcome. Why, I'll be the first to wish them joy. It's no longer *my* concern what Flora does, though I will say I credited her with better taste."

Samuel dragged his attention from the green ribbons to his cousin, who was glowering at the dance floor, his expression lost somewhere between anger and despair. "Who's betrothed?"

"Flora and Barrett, of course! Who else?" Lovell turned such a fierce frown on Lord Barrett it was a wonder the man didn't burst into flames on the spot.

"*Betrothed*? For God's sake, Lovell. Flora's only just met Barrett this season. She isn't the sort to enter into a betrothal on so short an acquaintance as that." Still, a pang of apprehension jolted him as Lady Flora laughed at some nonsense of Barrett's, her dark eyes bright as she gazed up at him.

Lovell cursed. "She's in love with him, Lymington! Why, anyone can see she's fallen madly in love with him. With *Barrett*, for God's sake. It's bad enough she sneaked off to London for the season without saying a word about it to me, but if she's so determined to fall in love, she might have chosen better than Barrett."

"Lady Flora is *not* in love with Lord Barrett. She's simply being polite." Then again, a man couldn't be too careful when it came to the lady he loved. "Still, I don't know why you're yielding the field to Barrett, Lovell. If you want Lady Flora's attention, go and engage her for the next two dances instead of standing here pining hopelessly after her."

"Pining! You're mad, Lymington. I'm not pining for Flora. It makes no difference to me if she flirts with every lord in London. I'm merely noting that Barrett is as dull as a church sermon."

Samuel said nothing, but waited while Lovell huffed and muttered to himself.

Any moment now—

"Even if I *did* want to dance with her—and I'm not saying I *do*—Flora hasn't looked at me once this entire evening, Lymington. She seems to have forgotten all about me."

"I doubt that, Lovell." Samuel had kept a close eye on Flora, and he'd seen her cast more than one furtive glance in his cousin's direction. Samuel was far from being a romantic, but he couldn't make himself believe Lady Flora's feelings for Lovell had faded so quickly.

Lovell grunted, his gaze following Barrett as the dance ended, and he led Lady Flora back to her grandmother.

"Lady Flora can't refuse to dance with you, Lovell. Not after she's danced twice with Barrett." Samuel nodded toward the other side of the ballroom, where Lord Barrett still stood with Flora, the two of them laughing over something.

"A courtesy dance, Lymington?" Lovell huffed. "You want me to gain Flora's hand for a dance on a rule of propriety?"

Samuel shrugged. "I suppose you could stand about and scowl while some other gentleman steals your lady right out from under your nose instead."

And steal her he would. Barrett had wasted no time indicating his interest in Flora. His attentions were marked enough that the *ton* had noticed, and they were already whispering about a match. There was no time for Lovell to stand about agonizing over it.

"She isn't my lady, Lymington." Lovell's pique had vanished, and in its place was a hopelessness Samuel had never heard in his cousin's voice before. It was the voice of a man who'd realized the bliss he longed for had been in front of his eyes all along and had reached out to seize it, only to watch it disintegrate into dust in his hands.

"She can still be yours, Lovell." Samuel braced a hand on his cousin's shoulder. "But you'll have to fight for her this time."

Lovell gave him an uncertain look. "Do you really think so, Lymington?"

"I do." Samuel nodded toward Lady Flora. "Go and claim her."

Lovell pressed his lips into a determined line, and marched off toward the other side of the ballroom without another word. Quite a number of female heads turned to watch his progress with hopeful smiles, but Lovell didn't seem to notice them.

Lady Flora hesitated when he held his hand out to her, her pretty lips turned down in a frown, but as Samuel had predicted, she was too polite to refuse him. An instant later she accepted Lovell's hand and let him lead her to the floor.

There, that was one problem solved. Now for the other.

Lady Emma and her grandmother were propped on the gilt chairs lined up at the edges of the ballroom, Lord Dunn with them. Samuel narrowed his eyes, his gaze once again caught by that damnable green ribbon peeking through the locks of her hair.

Dunn remained to exchange pleasantries, keeping the half-dozen swains who were waiting to pounce on her at bay, each of them more determined than the last to write his name on her dance card the moment Dunn was gone.

But none of them were more determined than Samuel.

He might have gone to her then, to finish the business they'd begun at the Royal Academy this afternoon. He might have marched across the ballroom as Lovell had done, scattering the swains surrounding her, all of them giving way by instinct to the fiercest competitor.

He'd been biding his time all evening, waiting for the right moment to approach her, but this wasn't it. No, he'd need privacy for his next skirmish with Lady Emma.

Or was it an ambush?

Samuel tried to ignore a thrill of anticipation as he made his way across the ballroom, and bowed before Lady Mary Worthington.

Soon, but not yet.

* * * *

"As you can imagine, Lady Emma, I'm quite relieved to be back in London at last, after such a prolonged absence."

Emma nodded politely to Lord Dunn, one half of her attention on his conversation, and the other half on Lord Lymington, whom she was peeking at over Lord Dunn's shoulder.

"I do prefer the town to the country, don't you?"

Emma pasted a bright smile on her lips. "Yes, indeed. Do you spend a great deal of time in, ah…in Cumbria?"

"*Cornwall*," Lady Crosby hissed in Emma's ear, under cover of her fluttering fan.

"Er, Cornwall, that is."

Had he truly said Cornwall? She would have sworn it was Cumbria. It was a place that began with a "C," at any rate.

In truth, she couldn't recall more than a half dozen words. She was being driven to distraction trying to keep an eye on Lord Lovell and Lord Lymington at once. They'd been hovering on the other side of the ballroom for the past half hour, looking as thick as two thieves conspiring to commit a crime, with Lord Lovell glaring at Lord Barrett while Lord Lymington muttered earnestly to him.

Lord Dunn smiled down at her. "Cornwall, yes. I returned to London in late March, just before the start of the season."

There would be another confrontation with Lord Lymington tonight—it was simply a matter of when. He'd been watching her all evening, like a predator circling its prey. Every time she turned around his glittering dark eyes were upon her.

Emma had been awaiting his approach for hours, practicing her denials and disdainful sniffs, her frowns and haughty head tosses, and cursing Lord Lymington all the while for being the only aristocratic gentleman in London she couldn't charm.

But there was a problem, an unforeseen complication.

For all his glowering, Lord Lymington hadn't approached her all evening.

Emma had danced her two dances with Lord Lovell as she'd promised she would, all the while expecting Lord Lymington to march into the middle of the ballroom and wrench his innocent cousin free of her sinister clutches.

But he hadn't. Instead, he'd kept his distance.

It was maddening, like a tormenting itch that was just out of reach. He was the most infuriating, vexing man alive—

"My sister, the Countess of Addington, rarely leaves her estate there," Lord Dunn was saying. "I make the journey every other year and remain for some months."

Emma jerked her attention guiltily back to him. "How lovely, my lord. I daresay it's very pleasant there."

"Not at all, Lady Emma. It's as dull as a tomb."

Lady Crosby laughed. "Somerset is much the same, I'm afraid. Isn't it, Emma?"

She nudged Emma, who belatedly returned Lord Dunn's smile. "Yes, indeed."

"It's not as dull as it might be, however, as I have three young nephews in Cornwall who keep me entertained."

Emma stifled a sigh. Lord Dunn was such a charming, easygoing gentleman. Why couldn't *he* be Lord Lovell's cousin? But no, she must be cursed with Lord Lymington, who was about as charming as a block of ice—

"...so you see, all is not lost, Lady Emma."

"I daresay Lady Addington was distraught to lose you to the London season," Emma said quickly, doing her best to look interested.

"Not at all. She ordered me gone, and bade me not to return until I'd found a wife." Lord Dunn's deep, smooth voice lingered on the last word, his eyebrows raised over pale blue eyes.

Emma stared dumbly back at him until Lady Crosby's sharp elbow to her ribs recalled her to the fact she was meant to be on the hunt for a husband, and that any reasonable young lady would be thrilled to receive such a hint from a wealthy, handsome gentleman like Lord Dunn.

But Lord Dunn seemed a decent fellow, at least as far as aristocrats went, and Emma didn't like to give him false hopes. "Nonsense. I can't think why you'd want such a troublesome thing as a wife, my lord."

Lady Crosby made a choking sound, and Lord Dunn gaped at her for a moment before throwing his head back in a laugh. "You astound me, Lady Emma."

Oh, dear. That had been the wrong thing to say, then. For a lady whose masque was usually so firmly in place, she'd made a number of alarming missteps recently. She couldn't quite work out why she'd become so scattered, but she was certain it was all Lord Lymington's fault.

"You're uniformly charming, Lady Emma." Lord Dunn swept her an elegant bow. "I'll endeavor not to expire of a broken heart as I'm forced to watch every other gentleman here tonight partner you."

"There's a good bit of the rogue in you, Lord Dunn." Emma gave him an admonishing tap on the arm with her fan, but her attention had already wandered to Lord Lovell, who'd just claimed Lady Flora for a dance.

Meanwhile, Lord Lymington was still hovering at the edges of the ballroom, considering her with cool calculation, as if she were a thorny maths problem he hadn't yet solved.

Emma laid a hand on her stomach, over the tight green silk of her bodice, and drew in a long, slow breath. Her heart took up a nervous fluttering as Lord Dunn departed, clearing the way for Lord Lymington to approach.

Surely, he'd come now—

But no. The blasted man turned away. *Again.*

A moment later he bowed to Lady Mary Worthington, and led her to the floor.

"Dear me, Lord Lymington is making himself elusive this evening, is he not?" Lady Crosby peered at him over the top of her fan. "My dear Emma, you could charm a bird from a tree, but Lord Lymington doesn't seem the sort to be much moved by charm."

"Not in the least, no." Not charm, or flirtation, or teasing, or any of Emma's other tricks. She'd never come across a man less inclined to beguilement than Lord Lymington. "He glares at me as if I'm a servant sneaking from his house with a pocketful of silver spoons."

Lady Crosby laughed. "He is rather stern, isn't he? He doesn't have his cousin's pretty manners. There's a similarity in their features, of course, but I've never seen two gentlemen less alike. I find Lord Lymington rather handsome, though perhaps not in the conventional way." Lady Crosby cast her a sidelong glance. "Do you think he's handsome, Emma?"

"Lord Lymington, handsome!" Emma couldn't imagine why Lady Crosby would ask her such a question, when it must be obvious that she *didn't* find him handsome or alluring in the least.

Quite the opposite, in fact.

Lady Crosby chuckled. "You didn't answer my question, dear."

Emma sniffed. "I find him arrogant and presumptuous, my lady. He's quite the most ill-tempered gentleman I've ever met."

"Indeed. Well, at least Lady Flora is having a pleasant evening. She looks pretty tonight. That shade of pink flatters her, doesn't it?"

Lady Crosby tilted her fan toward the dance floor. Emma followed the gesture, brightening at mention of Lady Flora. She hadn't dared hope she'd make a friend this season, but Lady Flora's heart was every bit as sweet as her face, and Emma grew fonder of her every day.

But Emma's smile faded as she peered into the sea of pink silk gowns. "Where is she? I don't see her."

"That's odd. She was just there a moment ago, dancing with Lord Lovell."

Emma searched the ballroom, but she didn't see either Lady Flora or Lord Lovell. "Do you suppose she's gone to the ladies' retiring room?"

Lady Crosby frowned. "Perhaps you'd better check, Emma, dear."

Emma was already on her feet. "Yes, I think so."

But the ladies' retiring room was deserted, and the tiny knot of worry lodged in Emma's stomach pulled tighter.

She hesitated in the hallway, unsure whether to return to the ballroom or wander further, but then she heard a soft echo of footsteps at the opposite end of the corridor. Emma hurried after the sound, down the dimly lit corridor. It ended in a pair of glass doors, the darkness swallowing whatever was on the other side of them.

A cool breeze drifted down the hallway, raising goosebumps on Emma's arms. Moonlight glinted on the glass, and just beyond it, Emma caught a flash of pale pink skirts before a gentleman in dark evening dress closed the door behind him. He was turned away from her, so Emma couldn't see his face, but she'd recognize those pretty dark curls anywhere.

Lord Lovell.

She hurried after them, anxiety quickening her steps.

Surely, Lord Lovell would never dream of harming Lady Flora? Even if he *was* the villain Caroline Francis accused him of being, Flora herself had told Emma she and Lord Lovell were dear friends, as close as a brother and sister. And they were at a ball, steps away from a gathering of a hundred or more guests. No villain, no matter how bold, how vicious, would dare to harm a young lady *here*.

But it was dark, so dark and quiet....

Emma flew down the corridor to the door, wrenched it open, and ran outside, heedless of the open door behind her, and stepped out onto a narrow stone terrace. There was just enough light for her to see that it let out into a small but lush garden with a series of gravel pathways that seemed to converge at an enormous tree in the center, its leafy, flowing branches dark against the moonlit sky.

Under those spreading branches were a dozen hiding places for a pair of lovers, a rake intent on seduction, or another kind of rake entirely, a rake turned villain, his intent unspeakable, unthinkable....

Further, a little further and she'd find them—

A faint sound met Emma's ear, a whisper in the darkness. She froze, listening, then crept forward, peering ahead of her into the gloom. A man's voice, was it? Low and familiar, and his shadow, nearly invisible, just an outline of a man, but there was enough light for Emma to see him raise his arm, his hand moving toward Flora's face—

Emma stifled a gasp. Her stomach dropped, and she tensed to run, to leap on his back, and—

Lord Lovell cradled Flora's cheek, his touch infinitely gentle as he murmured earnestly to her, his tone pleading.

Oh. Not brother and sister, then.

His voice was too low for Emma to hear his words, and she drew closer, the invisible fist around her throat easing its grip when she saw the tender expression on his face.

All of Lord Lovell's legendary charm had deserted him. There was nothing of the rake about him, nothing of the practiced flirt. His handsome face was somber, the hand on Flora's cheek trembling slightly. He hadn't brought Flora out here to harm her, or even to steal a few forbidden kisses in a moonlit garden.

Whatever it was he was whispering to Flora, he meant it with all his heart.

And she—oh, the expression on Flora's face as she listened to him! It was hope and doubt at once, as if her every wish had come true only for her to wake and discover it had been nothing more than a dream.

Emma lingered for a moment, but then quietly withdrew, and crept back down the pathway in the direction she'd come, unwilling to intrude on such a tender moment. Flora was her friend, and such a violation would be unforgiveable.

No, she'd return to the ladies' retiring room, and wait for Flora to pass by on her way back to the ballroom, and—

"Are you going somewhere, Lady Emma?"

Emma gasped as a gloved hand landed on her wrist and tugged her into a remote corner of the garden. Only the faintest glimmer of moonlight filtered through the thick branches here, but Emma knew at once who'd waylaid her. Lord Lymington was much too large to be mistaken for any of the other, punier lords in London.

She looked up into that severe face, and her mouth went dry. He was intimidating enough in broad daylight, but far more so here in a lonely garden, his face in darkness but for a hint of the stern line of his lips. For an instant Emma considered fleeing, as she was much smaller than he was and could make her way through the branches more quickly, but if she cowered from him now, she'd spend the rest of the season running from him.

"You didn't answer my question, my lady. I asked where you're going."

"I *was* going to the ladies' retiring room, Lord Lymington. Fortunately, you've caught me out before I did something shocking, like *retire*."

"You're strolling through a hidden garden, alone in the dark, on your way to the ladies' retiring room? Strange, but I would have thought the ladies' retiring room was *inside* Lady Swinton's townhouse."

Emma glanced nervously behind her, toward the tree in the center of the garden. She *wasn't* alone, but she had no intention of setting Lord Lymington on poor Lady Flora, who already had her hands full. "Yes, er…I needed a breath of fresh air, and then I got lost. Thank goodness you found me. Well, if that's all, my lord, then—"

"You do turn up in the strangest places, don't you? Tell me, my lady. Does your grandmother know about your midnight frolics?"

Emma went still, her heart giving a sudden lurch in her chest. It wasn't his words that disturbed her, but a thread of something in his voice. Not a threat, and not his usual commanding arrogance, but something else that made her tingle with foreboding. "Midnight frolics? I don't understand you, Lord Lymington."

"No?" He traced the bones of her wrist with his thumb. "I beg your pardon, my lady. I'm referring to the Pink Pearl."

For one frozen moment Emma didn't move, didn't breathe, but then she snatched her hand free of Lord Lymington's grasp. "I-I don't know what you're—"

"Do you think I don't know about your bawdy house romp, Lady Emma?" He caught her chin between his fingers. "I did warn you not to play games with me."

That was all it took—those few words from his lips, and Emma's past came racing headlong into her present with a deafening roar, sweeping all before it. How had she imagined she could ever escape it? You could never be free of a thing that lived inside of you.

He wasn't hurting her. His touch on her face was careful, gentle even, but Emma's breath froze in her lungs as surely as if he'd seized her throat. She tried to gasp, but she couldn't get a breath.

"Lady Emma?" Lord Lymington released her at once, his jaw tensed, something like regret in his expression.

But by then, it was too late. Helena's face flashed behind Emma's eyes, and Amy Townshend and Kitty Yardley, both faceless, but no less real to Emma for it, and then…she saw herself as she'd been five years ago, the night she'd tried to leave the Pink Pearl behind forever, a terrified girl of fifteen with blood gushing from the slashes on her hands, so much blood, but not all of it hers.…

"Emma!" Lord Lymington muttered a curse. His voice was faint, as if he were a great distance away from her, but his hands were warm and strong on her shoulders, holding her almost protectively, until at last Emma was able to gulp in a desperate breath, then another.

The haze of panic receded then, just enough for Emma to whisper, "M-my grandmother is waiting for me in the ballroom, Lord Lymington."

He hesitated, his dark gaze moving over her, as palpable as a touch, tracking her every move, her every labored breath. Emma's heart began to race again, and his gaze darted to the pulse fluttering at the base of her throat.

He dragged a hand through his hair, then stepped back. "Tomorrow, then. I'll call in the morning. And Lady Emma? Don't think about trying to evade me."

Emma was shaking, but she drew herself up and raised her chin. "I don't run away from anyone, my lord."

He stared down at her, a strange look on his face, then without warning he gently brushed his thumb across her lower lip. "No, I don't imagine you do."

They stared at each other, the air thick with tension, then he let his hand drop. "Until tomorrow, then."

Emma didn't wait for him to say any more, but fled down the pathway, through the corridor and back to the ballroom, where she found Lady Crosby waiting for her.

"Lady Flora has returned to—" Lady Crosby began, but Emma interrupted her.

"Forgive me, my lady, but we must leave at once."

Lady Crosby's eyes went wide, but she didn't argue. She followed Emma to the entrance of Lady Swinton's townhouse without a word, where they waited for what felt like years for Daniel to arrive with the carriage.

He handed them in, but lingered by the open door, his sharp gaze on Emma's face. "All right, lass?"

"Yes, I…yes. I'm well, Daniel."

Daniel didn't look convinced, but he closed the carriage door and leapt onto the box. Emma went limp against the squabs, one hand cradling her aching head, and closed her eyes to ease the throbbing.

"There, dear, that's better. You rest now." Lady Crosby said no more, but she lay her hand over Emma's, and kept it there as they made their way through the streets of London.

At the Royal Academy this afternoon, Emma had lied to Lord Lymington.

She'd told him she wasn't playing a game, but she was. She'd been playing it since she first set foot in Madame Marchand's library.

Her mistake was in thinking she was playing it with Lord Lovell.

She wasn't. She was playing with Lord Lymington.

Chapter Six

Samuel wasn't certain what to expect when he called on Lady Emma the following day.

He hesitated in the hallway outside Lady Crosby's drawing room door, bracing himself for anything from the unexpectedly painful sight of Lady Emma pale and lost, as she'd been last night, to the scandalous—intrigue, flirtation, a dozen gentleman callers on their knees at her feet, all of them vying for the merest flutter from her wide blue eyes.

What he found was Lady Emma sitting quietly on a settee, alone, wearing a modest gray gown—no vibrant blue today—her fair hair bound back into a severe knot, her fingers working at...

Embroidery? Samuel glanced at the frilly white scraps in her lap.

Lace. Lady Emma was tatting lace.

Well. He hadn't expected *that*.

"Good afternoon, Lord Lymington." Lady Emma set aside her busywork and gestured gracefully to the chair across from the settee on which she sat.

Samuel's eyes narrowed on her, but her expression gave nothing away. The panic he'd seen in her face last night was gone, hidden once again under the smooth masque she wore, the surface so exquisite no one bothered to look underneath it.

Disappointment, sharp and unexpected, squeezed his chest.

"Lord Lymington?" Lady Emma raised an eyebrow at his silence.

Samuel offered her a belated bow. "Good afternoon, Lady Emma."

"I beg your pardon for receiving you alone, my lord. My grandmother's exertions at Lady Swinton's ball last night caught up with her, I'm afraid. She's retired to her bedchamber with a headache." Lady Emma offered him a serene smile. "I daresay she would rather have remained downstairs for your call this morning, but here we are. Won't you sit down?"

Samuel took a seat and met that cool, blue gaze, a humorless smile on his lips. She might pretend all she liked, but Lady Emma knew what they had to say to each other was best said in private.

Still, if she wished to act as though this was an ordinary call, he'd oblige her. "I came to enquire after your health and your grandmother's. It's customary for a gentleman to do so, I believe."

"How kind. As I said, my grandmother is a trifle fatigued, but I'm very well today."

Samuel let his gaze rove over her, not bothering to hide the way he lingered on her lips and the curve of her neck, the flutter of her pulse just visible above the modest cut of her gown. An unwelcome heat surged through him, and he dragged his gaze back to her face. "You look very well, but then I think you always look well, don't you, Lady Emma?"

With her prim bodice, the restrained hairstyle, that sweet scrap of lace that drew attention to her long, elegant fingers, she was every inch the sweet, demure young innocent.

So ladylike, untouchable.

It only made him want to touch her more.

His lips twisted as they took each other's measure, neither of them speaking as they searched for chinks in the other's armor, and planned their strikes accordingly. The tension crackled between them, tightening and lengthening, until inexplicably Samuel's cock began to thicken, pulsing with every thundering beat of his heart.

Oh, she was dangerous. Even *he* found it difficult to tear his eyes away from her. How had he ever imagined she was only a danger to Lovell?

"I recall from our dance at Almack's, Lord Lymington, that you're not fond of aimless chatter. Shall we get to the purpose of your visit?"

So cool, so composed, the tiny tears he'd seen in her façade last night carefully patched and smoothed over. "My purpose, Lady Emma, is to find out what you were doing at the Pink Pearl three nights ago."

It was a swift, brutal strike, a frontal assault designed to leave her shuddering, so the real Lady Emma he'd glimpsed last night would appear again, seeping through the cracks.

But she gave no sign she'd been hit. Samuel searched for any change in her expression, but she merely cocked her head to the side, a faint crease in her brow. "The Pink Pearl? Yes, I believe you mentioned that place last night. I beg your pardon, my lord, but I don't know what that is."

"On the contrary, Lady Emma. You do know it, and rather well. You sneaked into the library at the Pink Pearl three nights ago, to meet with a courtesan called Letty. I'm afraid I didn't get her surname."

She blinked, and there it was, the shift in her expression he'd been waiting for, but it was there and gone again in an instant. "A courtesan? My goodness, Lord Lymington. You think me wicked, indeed. I wouldn't have suspected you of entertaining such intrigue. But tell me, what do you base your suspicions on?"

"You'll recall that when we danced at Almack's I mentioned you had a distinctive voice, my lady. As soon as I heard it again, I knew it at once."

She let out an amused laugh, but Samuel was watching her closely, and he saw her knuckles go white as her fingers tightened around the scrap of lace. "My *voice*? Rather flimsy evidence, isn't it? Tell me, Lord Lymington. This lady at the Pink Pearl, who had my voice. Did she also have my face?"

"Alas, my lady, your face was hidden by a hood."

"You mean to say you came here today to accuse me of sneaking into a London brothel because you caught a fleeting glimpse of a lady in a hood, and you've decided that lady was me?"

"I caught a glimpse of a lock of your hair, as well. A fleeting glimpse, admittedly, but that honey gold shade is as distinctive as your voice."

"On the contrary, Lord Lymington. Dozens of young ladies in London have fair hair."

"Not like yours. Come, Lady Emma. We both know it was you. Tell me, what sort of business can a naïve young innocent like yourself have with a notorious courtesan?"

Lady Emma's fingers twitched in her lap. "Why, no business at all, my lord."

Samuel studied the tip of one of his flawlessly shined boots, letting the silence stretch between them before he turned his attention back to her. "Is that all, then? Nothing else to say? No furious arguments, no outraged denials?"

She shrugged. "I daresay it won't make much difference to you what I say. You seem to have made up your mind about me already."

"I've wondered about you from the first moment I laid eyes on you." Samuel leaned forward, his gaze holding hers. "For all your sweet, guileless smiles, you don't strike me as a sheltered young innocent making her first foray into London society."

"I see. Dare I ask what I do strike you as, my lord? A female adventurer, perhaps? A spy, or a thief, or some other sort of criminal?"

"You strike me as a bewitching young lady with a face that scatters a gentleman's wits before he's even aware he's said a word."

"Ah, yes, the poor, helpless gentlemen." She gave him a thin smile, her blue eyes cold.

"I don't pretend to know what you want with my cousin, but you may reconcile yourself to not getting it. As I told you before, Lord Lovell's affections are already engaged. Even if his heart *was* free, I'd object to his giving it to a young lady with so many secrets. Do we understand each other?"

She was quiet for a moment as she considered his question, then she shook her head. "Not entirely, no. I'm not certain what it is you're threatening me with, Lord Lymington. Are you saying you'll expose my alleged brothel escapade to the *ton*?"

"I've no wish to reveal your scandals, Lady Emma. Play your games, if you must. It's no business of mine, as long as you keep Lovell out of it."

"Why, how generous you are, my lord. But I confess I'm almost inclined to take my chances, if only to see what comes of it."

It wasn't until he saw that hint of challenge in her eyes that Samuel realized a part of him had been hoping she'd defy him. "Do you really want me digging into your scandals? Because if I start, I won't stop until I know them all. I wonder, Lady Emma. How many secrets do you have?"

A slow, sly smile curved her lips. "I could ask you the same thing, Lord Lymington."

Samuel was still as hard as stone, his cock never having once subsided during the whole of his skirmish with her, but it wasn't just the desire pounding through his veins that urged him on.

Hidden beneath that fetching smile and that soft voice, that long, delicate neck and those distracting curves was a woman with nerves of iron, one who'd struggle against him every step of the way. She'd fight him, she'd brawl and claw and scratch. He sensed that courage in her, felt it down to the very depths of his bones.

God help him, he wanted it. He wanted to match wits with her, to scheme and battle and scrap until he overcame her, and then…then he wanted to take her to his bed and hold her breathless body in his arms until she begged him to sink into her heat, to take her and claim her.

He wanted her, but Lady Emma was as far out of his reach as a star in the midnight sky.

Lovell was at last waking up to his love for Lady Flora. He was poised on the edge of happiness, and whatever dubious business Lady Emma was tangled up in, he didn't want his cousin anywhere near it.

Samuel took in Lady Emma's soft red lips, the flush of color on her cheeks, the blue eyes now darkened with emotion, and he saw a lady who tempted him unlike any he'd ever known before.

Yet it didn't make the least bit of difference.

"Tell me, my lady," he drawled, his tone deceptively bland. "Why are you and your friend Letty so interested in Caroline Francis?"

Ah, now that got a reaction. Lady Emma's entire body went still for an instant, then she rose from the settee, went to the window and gazed out for a long moment, her back to him.

Samuel waited, his heated gaze trailing from her narrow shoulders to her curved hips. The back of her gown was just as prim as the front, and just as maddening, with tiny buttons marching in a perfect row down her spine. She drew in a deep breath, her back rising, then falling again as she exhaled.

"I don't know if you're aware, Lady Emma, but until she went missing six weeks ago, Caroline Francis was a housemaid at Lymington House, my country estate in Kent."

Caroline wasn't the first to go missing, but she was the only one who'd since reappeared, and Samuel's hopes that the other two missing housemaids would be found were fading. He wanted the name of the man who'd trifled with Caroline, and God help the scoundrel when Samuel caught up with him.

"I was not aware, my lord." Lady Emma turned to face him again.

There wasn't a tremor in that husky voice, but somehow, Samuel knew she was lying to him. "I'm anxious to speak to Caroline, but she's proved strangely elusive. I don't suppose you'd know anything about that, would you, Lady Emma?"

"I don't know why I would, Lord Lymington."

"No? I wonder if your friend Letty does." He held her gaze. "I'll have to pay her a visit, and find out for myself."

Lady Emma remained perfectly composed, her head high, but she couldn't disguise the rapid rise and fall of her chest. "Forgive me, my lord, but I must go and check on my grandmother now. It was kind of you to call on me this morning."

With that, she was gone. Her retreat was so graceful, Samuel wasn't certain if it was a retreat at all, and he couldn't help but notice he was once again left speechless, breathless, staring at her back as she disappeared.

* * * *

This was a disaster, a nightmare.

Emma hurried down the corridor, ducked into a small closet, closed the door behind her, and fell back against it, her heart thundering in her chest.

A nightmare, yes, but not the nightmare she'd thought it was. Lord Lymington didn't seem to know anything about her past at the Pink Pearl, as she'd feared. That was a stroke of good fortune she hadn't dared hope for.

No, this was a different nightmare altogether.

He'd been lurking in the shadows the night she'd met Helena in Madame Marchand's library. He knew all about her conversation with Letty. Worse, he'd heard them mention Caroline's name.

Lady Clifford had warned Emma not to go near the Pink Pearl, but she'd gone anyway, and now she'd made a dreadful mess of things. This after she'd taken such care not to attract any notice so she might appear in London as Lady Crosby's granddaughter.

She hadn't seen her friends in *weeks*. Why, it had been so long she could hardly recall the faces of Sophia, Cecilia, and Georgiana.

Now, because of one tiny misstep, all her efforts lay in ruins.

Good Lord, but Lord Lymington was a sly one.

Why, oh *why*, had he been at the Pink Pearl that night? If he *had* to be there, why couldn't he have spent his evening chasing courtesans in the usual way, rather than sneaking off to a cold library to sit there in the dark, alone? What sort of gentleman went to a brothel to *read*?

Now he knew everything, had heard everything—

No. Not everything. He didn't know who she really was, and that meant there was still hope, some chance to salvage this. It would simply require a different approach, that was all.

Emma closed her eyes and tried to think, but they popped back open again at once, a shaky breath on her lips. Those penetrating gray eyes of his saw *everything*. If she blinked, Lord Lymington's gaze darted to her eyes. If she smiled, he focused on her mouth.

He saw it all, assessed it, and drew his conclusions, all without giving away a thing.

God in heaven. Of all the gentlemen who might have been lurking in the library, why did it have to be *him*? He was the last man in the world she wanted knowing her secrets.

Presumptuous, infuriating marquess.

Clever, too. Don't forget clever, Emma.

Yes, he was clever, damn him. Downright diabolical, even, creeping about the Pink Pearl as he'd done. That sneakiness made him dangerous, and that was to say nothing of those enormous hands, that slow, predatory smile.

Couldn't any of the other dozens of brothels in London have done for Lord Lymington that night? Of all the choices he had at his fingertips, why did he have to choose the Pink Pearl?

But she already knew the answer. Because he hadn't gone there to dally with a courtesan. Why should he? There must be dozens of ladies in London willing to warm *his* bed. It was no coincidence he'd ended up at the Pink Pearl rather than some other brothel.

No, Lord Lymington had gone to the Pink Pearl that night to find Caroline Francis.

His interest in her might be perfectly innocent, of course. He might have found out she was there, and gone on Lady Lymington's behalf to enquire into Caroline's well-being, or to offer to restore her to her place as a housemaid, all her sins forgiven.

But in Emma's experience, few things were perfect, even fewer of them innocent, and forgiveness was as elusive as a virgin courtesan. No, it was far more likely Lord Lymington had gone to find out just how many of his family's ugly secrets Caroline knew.

Ugly, potentially deadly secrets.

That he'd gone there to uncover them, or…

Or bury them. Bury them so deeply they'd never again see the light of day.

And now Emma had exposed Helena to him with her carelessness, and there was no telling what he'd do, or how far he'd go to get what he wanted.

Emma pressed her fingers into the hard, wooden door behind her, eyes squeezed closed, willing away the dread threatening to engulf her. She couldn't lose her wits now. They had one chance at this—a single chance to find out what had happened to Amy and Kitty, and discover who'd been responsible for their disappearances.

She drew in a deep breath, and tried to think.

One thing was certain. Lord Lymington would go to the Pink Pearl in search of Caroline again, and soon. He'd demand to see her, and Madame Marchand…well, Madame Marchand would do what she always did with every powerful, wealthy aristocrat.

She'd give him what he wanted. She'd hand Caroline over without hesitation, and without a qualm. But Caroline wasn't the only lady at the Pink Pearl who knew Lord Lovell's secrets.

Helena knew them, as well.

That made her as much a target for Lord Lymington as Caroline herself, and it wasn't as if Madame Marchand would lift a finger to defend Helena.

Emma let her head drop back against the door. What could *she* do to protect Helena? How she could possibly undo the damage she'd…

She raised her head, her scattered thoughts ceasing their frenzy.

She'd never spoken Helena's full name. That night, in the library at the Pink Pearl, she'd only ever referred to Helena as "Letty." It was a private nickname, known only to the two of them. No one else at the Pink Pearl would recognize it. When Lord Lymington went back to the Pink Pearl looking for "Letty," he wouldn't find her.

Not right away but he wasn't, alas, a fool.

It wouldn't be long before he'd work out that Letty was Helena, but aside from warning Helena to stay away from Lord Lymington for as long as possible, there wasn't much Emma could do for her. Helena was their only source of information to the goings-on at the Pink Pearl, and they needed her to remain where she was.

Emma would simply have to continue to deny knowing Helena, and trust that when the time came, Helena could hold her own with Lord Lymington—

"Emma?" A knock vibrated against Emma's back, and Lady Crosby's voice drifted through the door. "Emma, my dear child, why are you hiding in the closet?"

Emma let out a silent groan, but there was no use in delaying the inevitable. She had to tell Lady Crosby and Daniel about the mess she'd made, and hope Daniel wouldn't insist on telling Lady Clifford.

Good Lord, what a mess it was.

Another not-so-silent groan fell from Emma's lips as she threw open the door.

Lady Crosby's startled face was on the other side. "Emma, what are you…" She paused to take in Emma's agitated appearance. "Oh, dear. It doesn't look as if Lord Lymington's call went well."

"It did not. I, ah…I've made a terrible mistake, my lady."

"Oh, well, I'm certain it's not as bad as you imagine, dear." Lady Crosby gave Emma's hand a comforting pat.

"The night before Almack's ball I sneaked into the Pink Pearl at night, alone, so I could speak to Caroline Francis about Lord Lovell, but she wasn't there, so I spoke to Helena, and I've just found out Lord Lymington was lurking in the library that night like a thief, and he both heard and saw me there."

Lady Crosby blinked. "Well, that *is* rather bad, isn't it?"

"It's bad enough, yes, but perhaps not quite as bad as I thought."

"That *is* a relief, dear. But perhaps you'd better tell me over tea in the drawing room. You look a trifle…peaked."

Emma followed obediently after Lady Crosby. "We'd better summon Daniel, as well. He needs to hear this, too."

Once Emma and Lady Crosby were tucked into a settee with the tea tray on the table before them, and Daniel had taken up his usual place in front of the fireplace, Emma blurted out the humiliating truth about her misadventures at the Pink Pearl.

As she'd expected, Daniel wasn't pleased about it.

"What did ye think ye were doing, lass, sneaking about that bawdy house at night, alone? Ye might have been hurt. Ye know better than that, Miss Emma."

Emma grimaced. "I do, and I regret it. I wanted to hear Caroline's story for myself, but I never even got a chance to speak to her. She was away at a private engagement that night, which I suppose turned out to be a good thing, because if she had been there, Lord Lymington would have gotten ahold of her."

Daniel grunted. "Aye, that's so."

"Did Lord Lymington overhear what you and Helena discussed?" Lady Crosby asked. "If so, he must know of Caroline's accusations against his cousin, mustn't he?"

"Now I've had a chance to think on it, I don't think Helena said anything that would arouse Lord Lymington's suspicions against Caroline." Helena had mentioned something about Caroline having a lurid tale to tell, but neither she nor Emma had ever said Lord Lovell's name. "And we were whispering the entire time, so there's a chance Lord Lymington didn't hear much of what we said at all."

"The bawd will turn Caroline over to Lymington." Daniel couldn't abide Madame Marchand, and his lips pinched with disgust.

"Yes, there's little doubt of that." Emma glanced between Daniel and Lady Crosby. "But by the time Lord Lymington gets to Madame Marchand, Caroline will no longer be at the Pink Pearl."

Lady Crosby frowned. "Where will she be?"

"With Lady Clifford." Emma turned to Daniel. "I'm sorry to ask it, Daniel, but will you please go to the Pink Pearl, fetch Caroline Francis, and take her to Maddox Street?"

Lady Crosby touched Emma's hand. "Oh, dear. Do you really think that's necessary, Emma?"

"Yes, I think so." Even now Lord Lymington could be on his way to the Pink Pearl, where he'd demand to see Caroline Francis. It was only dumb luck he hadn't gotten to her two nights ago. "Please, Daniel?"

"Aye, I'll get her. Don't fret about that, lass."

Emma breathed a sigh of relief. "Thank you. Lady Crosby and I will wait here for your return. I'll worry until I know Caroline's safe at Lady Clifford's."

"Worry about yerself, lass. Lymington won't take it kindly when he can't get 'is hands on Caroline."

"I can handle Lord Lymington." Emma wasn't sure that was true, but she was responsible for this mess. If she hadn't gone to the Pink Pearl that night, none of this would have happened. Like it or not, Lord Lymington was now her problem to solve.

Lady Crosby abandoned her teacup to its saucer. "I daresay he won't, but why should he come after Emma?"

"He, ah…he *might* suspect I'm behind Caroline's leaving the Pink Pearl."

Lady Crosby paled. "I don't like this at all, Emma. Lord Lymington is a bit terrifying, and he's a great deal larger than you are."

"Her ladyship is right, lass. It's not safe, throwing yerself into Lymington's way like that."

No, it wasn't. When Caroline went missing from the Pink Pearl, Lord Lymington would suspect Emma at once, and those gray eyes would go as dark as thunderclouds. But he wouldn't hurt her. Emma wasn't sure how she knew this, but she did. "We don't have a choice, Daniel."

The first rule of intrigue was that plans could change in the blink of an eye. *The best laid schemes of mice and men…*

Robert Burns hadn't spared a word for the schemes of *women* in his famous poem, but Emma liked to think of it less as a careless omission than a testament to Scottish wisdom.

Once a lady settled on a scheme, it seldom went awry.

On the rare occasions Emma had been obliged to alter her plans, they hadn't turned out the better for it, but every now and then, fortune smiled on the wicked.

She could only hope this was one of those times.

Daniel left at once to fetch Caroline from the Pink Pearl. Emma paced back and forth in front of the fireplace, while Lady Crosby sat on the settee and urged her to calm down until Daniel returned.

It felt like years before he reappeared, but when he strode into the drawing room at last, he had a thick letter in his hand, which he held out to Emma.

Emma took it from his hand with a frown. "Is this from Caroline?"

"Nay, Helena sent it."

Emma tore it open. It was written in a hand she didn't recognize, but after she read the first few lines, she realized it was the letter she'd asked Caroline to write, detailing her affair with Lord Lovell. "Ah, yes. This is very good."

The rest of Daniel's news wasn't as promising, however. "I couldn't fetch the lass. She wasn't there. The little lad, Charles, says as she went off with some lord or other last night, and no telling when she'll be back."

"What, *again*?" Emma dropped down on the settee. "Who is this lord who's taking up all of Caroline's time? I don't like it."

"Do you suppose it could be Lord Lovell?" Lady Crosby asked.

Emma tapped a finger to her lips, thinking. Young ladies *did* seem to disappear with astonishing regularity whenever Lord Lovell was about, but he couldn't have taken Caroline anywhere last night. He'd been at Lady Swinton's ball.

He might have gone afterwards, though, or sent someone else to fetch her. A man of wealth and resources like Lord Lovell had any number of faithful servants who'd perform whatever task he demanded of them, no matter how questionable.

But then Emma recalled the expression on Lord Lovell's face in the garden last night when he'd looked at Flora, the tenderness with which he'd touched her face, and she shook her head. "No, I don't think it was Lord Lovell."

Emma went to the desk, scratched out a few quick lines to Helena, then held out the note to Daniel. "I've asked Helena to let us know the moment Caroline returns."

Daniel took the note and slipped it into his pocket. "I'll see to it."

Emma wasn't satisfied, but there wasn't much else she could do, and all thanks to Lord Lymington.

That man was slipperier than a fish wriggling on the end of a hook. Slipperier even than Emma herself, which made him the most maddening gentleman she'd ever met, or the most intriguing.

Either way, Emma intended to do just as Lord Lymington had ordered her to do.

She was going to stay away from Lord Lovell.

As for Lord Lymington…well, he was another matter, entirely.

Chapter Seven

Rotten Row was awash in flawlessly tailored coats, silver-tipped walking sticks, and gleaming Hessians. Aristocratic gentlemen crowded the pathway, posing and preening like a muster of peacocks on the strut.

That was always the case in London during the season, but never more so than when the weather was fine during the fashionable hour, as it was today. Emma took in the masculine display with an amused smile on her lips. It looked as if a giant hand had plucked up White's, turned it upside down, and shaken it like a salt cellar until every gentleman inside had come toppling out onto Rotten Row.

If a lady was on the hunt for a nobleman, she'd find him here.

Or he'd find *her*—

"Goodness, Lady Jane looks dashing today, doesn't she, Emma? Just look at her pelisse. It's the height of fashion, and that shade of yellow is so flattering on her!"

"It is, indeed." Emma drew Lady Flora's arm through hers and gave her hand an affectionate pat. She'd never known anyone more disposed to be pleased with people than Lady Flora. She had a kind word for everyone.

Such an open, generous heart was rare, in Emma's experience.

"I don't know that I've ever seen a London sky quite so blue as it is today." Lady Flora turned to Emma with a smile. "It's a lovely day for a walk."

"It might be lovelier still, Flora," Lady Silvester spoke up from behind them, where she was walking arm in arm with Lady Crosby. "Lord Lovell and Lord Lymington are behind us, and will surely overtake us if we proceed at a more sedate pace."

Lady Flora's sunny smile vanished. "Lord Lovell might do as he pleases. I've no idea what he's even doing in London. His family hadn't any plans to come for the season. You may be sure I won't trouble myself to accommodate his sudden appearance. No gentleman is worth such a fuss, no matter how handsome or charming he is."

A brief, shocked silence fell, then Lady Silvester sputtered, "Why, what an unkind thing to say. Shame on you, Flora!"

"Unkind, but true all the same."

Lady Silvester was gaping at Lady Flora's back. "That's no way to speak of a gentleman who's been your friend all these years. He's always been kind to you, Flora—"

"He's kind to all the young ladies." Lady Flora thrust her chin up in the air. "Lord Lovell is a rake. You know it as well as I do, Grandmother, and there's no sense in pretending otherwise. Any young lady of sense won't give any credit to his flirtations."

Emma's wide-eyed gaze swung between Lady Silvester and Lady Flora. If what she'd seen in the garden last night wasn't enough to convince her there was more than just friendship between Lady Flora and Lord Lovell, *this* certainly was.

For Lady Flora to unleash such a flurry of barbs on Lord Lovell was a sure sign she was nursing a secret affection for him. Or perhaps a not-so-secret affection, nor an unrequited one, from what Emma had witnessed last night.

"I won't be such a fool as to listen to his nonsense," Lady Flora muttered, more to herself than to Emma. She was marching down the pathway, as if determined to leave Lord Lovell choking on her dust.

Emma scurried after her, cursing herself for not seeing how it was at once. *Of course*, Lady Flora was besotted with Lord Lovell. Why shouldn't she be? Every other young lady in London was besotted with him.

Well, not *every* lady. Emma wasn't, but then she'd never been susceptible to handsome faces. She knew too well how often they hid an ugly heart.

Still, perhaps it wasn't as dire as it seemed. Lady Flora was a soft-hearted young lady, but even if she did have a *tendre* for Lord Lovell, that didn't mean she was in love with—

"For pity's sake, Flora," Lady Silvester began again, exasperated. "If you'd only talk to him—"

"No." Flora, who'd never treated her grandmother with anything but tender affection, cut Lady Silvester off with an impatient exclamation. "I'm sorry, Grandmother, but I won't let Lord Lovell spoil my pleasure in the day. Come along, Emma."

Emma did as she was told, but her heart sank like a stone in her chest. It didn't sound like a mild *tendre*, and it hadn't looked that way in Lady

Swinton's garden last night, either. No, it had looked as if Lady Flora was desperately in love with Lord Lovell, and he with her.

Lord Lovell who, under that handsome face of his, might very well be a fiend.

Dash it, how had everything become so complicated, and so quickly? What a fool she'd been, to suppose it would be a simple task to charm Lord Lovell into revealing enough of his secrets to incriminate himself.

She hadn't counted on a lovesick debutante, had she? Or on Lord Lymington, who'd do whatever he must to keep her away from his cousin, and whose penetrating gray gaze seemed to peel back her protective layers until he found the raw, tender skin underneath.

No gentleman had ever done that before. None had ever bothered, but as surely as she'd gotten a peek under Lord Lovell's masque, Lord Lymington had gotten a peek under *hers*.

Emma hurried to catch up to Flora. "Did, ah…did you and Lord Lovell have a falling out?" she asked, keeping her voice low.

Lady Flora bit her trembling lip. "No, nothing like that. It's just…well, can't anyone talk of anything but Lord Lovell? It seems as if some young lady or other is forever nattering in my ear about him. Why, there are plenty of gentlemen here in London as handsome as he is."

"Well, of course there are—"

"Lord Barrett is every bit as handsome as Lord Lovell. Handsomer, if you ask me."

Emma blinked at Lady Flora's vehemence. "Certainly, Lord Barrett is very—"

"Far more gentlemanly, too," Lady Flora declared with a toss of her head. "I could tell you any number of perfectly dreadful things about Lord Lovell, but I don't like to alarm you, Lady Emma."

"Does Lord Lovell have some shocking secrets, then?" Emma braced herself for lurid tales of wicked debaucheries, seductions, possible kidnappings—

"My, yes! Did you know, Lady Emma, that Lord Lovell was sent down from Oxford last year, for brawling?"

"Sent down?" *That* was Lord Lovell's shocking secret? Didn't every nobleman get sent down from Oxford?

"Yes, last September, and now he'll never finish." Lady Flora sighed, some of her anger draining out of her. "It's a great pity, really."

September? Emma frowned.

Caroline's letter claimed that Amy Townshend had gone missing from Lymington House in late August. If Lord Lovell hadn't been sent down until September, then he wouldn't have even been at Lymington House when Amy disappeared.

"Are you certain it was September, Flora?"

Emma didn't have any plausible reason for asking such a strange question, but Flora merely nodded. "Yes, quite sure."

That didn't absolve him of Kitty Yardley's disappearance, of course, but what were the odds there were *two* kidnappers at Lymington House?

Very slim, indeed, unless Lord Lovell had been home for a visit in August? "Did, ah…did Lord Lovell visit often at Lymington House while he was at Oxford? In the summer, perhaps?"

It was another risky question, and Emma held her breath, praying her friend wouldn't remark on it, but Flora was very much caught up in her indignation with Lord Lovell and didn't appear to notice it.

"He did at first, yes, but in his final year, he… well, you wouldn't know this, Lady Emma, not having spent any time in London, but Lord Lovell has a rather…unfortunate reputation as a rake."

Emma adopted a properly horrified expression. "A *rake*? How shocking."

"Yes. It broke all our hearts, particularly Lady Lymington's, as Lovell was always a most affectionate nephew to her. He was a dutiful son, as well." For all her professed pique with Lord Lovell, Lady Flora was eager to defend him.

"He does seem fond of Lady Lymington."

"Very fond, but then last year he started running about London with a crowd of spoiled nobleman, and they…they ruined him, Emma. Lord Dunn did his best to extricate Lovell, but it did no good. After that, we hardly ever saw him at Lymington House anymore."

Emma squeezed Lady Flora's hand. "That's dreadful, Flora. I'm truly sorry for it."

Lady Flora gave Emma a grateful glance, but her chin was wobbling, and she turned her face away.

* * * *

Samuel couldn't see her face. Her back was to him, and there were dozens of other fair-haired ladies in blue gowns on the promenade this afternoon, but he knew of only one lady who wore that particular shade of blue.

A deep, endless blue that matched the color of her eyes.

He quickened his gait, an unwelcome tug of anticipation in his belly. "Come along, Lovell. Lady Flora is just ahead of us. If we hurry, we can catch her."

"No, Lymington. You know damn well she doesn't want to see me."

Several ladies who were strolling nearby gasped at Lovell's curse, but he turned such a fierce scowl on them, they scurried off down the pathway, whispering to each other.

Samuel sighed. Last night when Lovell had returned to Lady Swinton's ballroom after his garden adventure, he'd been more downcast than Samuel had ever seen him. He hadn't said a word about Lady Flora, and Samuel hadn't asked, but it was as plain as day she'd sent Lovell on his way without a single word of encouragement.

"You give up too easily. Recall, Lovell, that you and Lady Flora have been friends for years. She cares very much for you."

"Not anymore. She despises me now." Lovell swiped a rock from the pathway with a vicious swing of his walking stick.

Samuel didn't care for lovesick dramatics, and he'd never coddled his cousin, but he couldn't ignore the misery in Lovell's eyes, the despairing twist of his lips. "She's angry with you, yes, but a friendship like yours doesn't wither and die because of a few mistakes. Stop sulking over it, and beg Flora's forgiveness."

Lovell's laugh was bitter. "It didn't *die*, Lymington. I murdered it, and there's not a reason in the world why Flora should forgive me for it."

Samuel glanced ahead of them at Lady Flora, who was getting farther away with every step, and decided this wasn't a moment for subtly. He tore his hat from his head and waved it in the air. "Lady Flora! Wait!"

"For God's sake, Lymington! Have you gone mad?"

Lovell snatched Samuel's hat from his hand, but it was already too late. Lady Flora and Lady Emma both turned at the sound of his voice.

Lady Flora's lips turned down into a dark frown, and Lovell blanched. "*No*, Lymington. I told you, I don't want—"

But Samuel was already striding down the pathway. "Hurry up, will you, before some other gentleman cuts us out."

"Just as well if they did," Lovell grumbled, but he trailed after Samuel, dragging his feet with every step.

"Lord Lovell, and Lord Lymington. How do you do?" Lady Silvester nodded politely, but she cast an uneasy glance at Lady Flora, who was looking everywhere but at Lovell's face.

Samuel frowned, doubt niggling at him. Perhaps this had been a mistake, but it was too late now. "Good afternoon, ladies. What luck that we should have run into you."

"Yes, extraordinary good luck," Lady Crosby offered, attempting to smooth over the awkwardness. "It's a lovely day, is it not?"

"Indeed. Even lovelier now." Lovell, flustered by Lady Flora's coldness, directed the full force of his charm at Lady Emma. "The heat has put such pretty color in your cheeks, Lady Emma. Do you care for a stroll around the Serpentine? Perhaps you'll find the breeze refreshing."

"Why, what a good idea, Lord Lovell. I'm certain the young ladies will be pleased to accompany you." Lady Silvester turned a bright smile on her granddaughter. "Doesn't that sound pleasant, Flora?"

Flora didn't answer. Lovell's tentative smile fell, and things might have become painful indeed, if Lady Emma hadn't stepped forward and taken Samuel's arm. "A walk sounds lovely."

Samuel blew out a relieved breath. "Very well, then. Lead the way, Lovell."

"Lady Flora?" Lovell turned hesitantly toward her, and offered his arm. She made no move to take it, but hung back, her eyes downcast until Lovell drew closer and murmured in a voice hoarse with pain, "Please, Flora?"

Samuel tensed as he waited for Lady Flora to make her decision. She hesitated, but as angry as she was, she'd never been able to bear Lovell's pain. She took his arm. "Thank you, my lord."

Lovell bore her off with exquisite care, and Samuel and Lady Emma followed after them, leaving the older ladies to pursue their sedate walk along Rotten Row.

"I paid at visit at the Pink Pearl this afternoon, Lady Emma," Samuel said, once they were out of earshot of the others. "Who do you suppose I saw there?"

"I don't dare hazard a guess, Lord Lymington."

"A very large, dark-haired fellow I recognized at once as Lady Crosby's coachman. He was just leaving as I arrived. No." Samuel held up a hand to quiet her when she opened her mouth to speak. "Don't try and persuade me it wasn't him. He's not the sort of man easily mistaken for another."

"I don't see what's so remarkable about him being at the Pink Pearl." Lady Emma gave him a chastising look. "A coachman has the same, er... needs as a nobleman, Lord Lymington."

Samuel gaped at her, a wild laugh threatening, but he bit it back, and settled for an incredulous glare instead. "There's no need for you to explain a man's needs to me, Lady Emma. Lady Crosby's man wasn't there to visit a courtesan."

"Well, I can't think of any other reason why he'd—"

"Can't you?" For an instant, Samuel wondered what it would be like to simply walk along the Serpentine with Lady Emma, without all this maneuvering between them.

He doubted he'd ever find out.

"I don't know what tortures you think I intend to inflict on Caroline Francis, my lady, but I can assure you, I only want to speak to her. There's no need to send your grandmother's coachman to hide her from me."

"I haven't the faintest idea what you're talking about, my lord."

"I think you do." He stopped, and turned her to face him. "From what I overheard in the library at the Pink Pearl, your friend Letty is in Caroline's confidence. Since you've secreted Caroline away, I may have to pose my questions to Letty instead."

"I wish you much success in finding her, but as I told you before, my lord, I've never been to the Pink Pearl, and I don't know any Letty."

The devil she didn't. Samuel was just about to say he didn't believe a word out of her mouth when Lady Emma added, "Your cousin and Lady Flora look well together, don't they?"

Samuel blinked at her, surprised, then followed her gaze to Lovell and Lady Flora, who had moved some distance ahead of them. "They do, yes. She's a lovely young lady."

"She is, indeed." Lady Emma was watching the two of them wandering along the pathway beside the Serpentine, her lower lip caught between her teeth. "Lady Flora knows him quite well, I think?"

"Yes. They've known each other since they were children. Lovell's fond of her." A small smile curved Samuel's lips as he watched his cousin. Lovell was gesturing wildly, and Lady Flora was smiling at his antics. It wasn't quite the doting smile with which she'd used to look at him, but whatever had caused her earlier ill-temper, Lovell had coaxed her out of it.

He was good at making people laugh—at making them happy. Certainly, charm flowed like wine through Lovell's veins, but there was nothing practiced about the way he spoke to Flora, or the way he looked at her. He'd never had to pretend with her.

"You don't appear at all concerned your friend will steal away your favorite," Samuel observed, with a sidelong glance at Lady Emma.

He wasn't sure what sort of response he expected, but Lady Emma only shrugged. "Lord Lovell isn't a toy to be squabbled over. He may do as he pleases."

Samuel had no reply to that. His had been an ill-natured comment, and such a rational, reasonable response was difficult to argue with.

Damn her.

"Or perhaps I should have said, he may do as *you* please." A sly smile drifted over her lips. "Yes, I believe that's more accurate. Don't you think so, my lord?"

Despite himself, Samuel's own lips twitched. "What do you imagine would please me, as far as my cousin is concerned?"

"I wouldn't dare speculate on what would please *you*, Lord Lymington."

"It's nothing so mysterious. My cousin is like a brother to me. I simply want what any brother would want for another. His happiness."

Lady Emma's brow furrowed, as if she were troubled by his words. She was quiet for a moment, watching the breeze ripple across the surface of the water, but just when Samuel thought she wouldn't answer, she said, "If you truly want his happiness, Lord Lymington, then why not let him do as he pleases?"

Because what pleases Lovell nearly killed him.

The words rose to Samuel's lips, hovered there—

"Or do you think you know best what would make him happy?" She turned to him, the sun flickering in her eyes, turning them a blue he'd never seen before, like the blue fire at the base of a candle's flame.

He looked away from her, dizzy with sudden longing, confusion, and desire. "I think I know better than you do, Lady Emma."

"Of course, you know better than *I* do. My question, Lord Lymington, is if you know better than *he* does."

Lady Emma looked troubled, as if she'd spent time considering the question of Lovell's happiness, as if she had a sincere interest in him, and was concerned about his future happiness.

And Samuel…didn't like it? Was that what the sudden clench of his fists meant, the tightness in his chest? He turned the strange reaction over inside himself, prodded and poked at it, and…

No. He didn't like it. Not because he was *jealous* of her attentions to his cousin, of course. The very idea was absurd. That is, he couldn't deny he'd been intrigued with her since the night he'd seen her at the Pink Pearl, but he was as wary of her as he was fascinated by her.

In any case, she was all wrong for Lovell. Even if he wasn't hopelessly besotted with Lady Flora, Samuel would never encourage a match between Lovell and Lady Emma. They'd flirt and charm each other to exhaustion, without ever exchanging an honest word between them.

He glanced at her. She'd turned her gaze back to the river, and he seized the rare moment to study her face—her creamy skin and pert nose, her full, sensuous lips and surprisingly firm chin, the wisps of golden hair at her temples—without her noticing.

Samuel had seen many lovely ladies in his time—ladies with faces lovelier than hers, even—but when she was like this, without her usual flirtations and wiles and artifice, her face touched him in a way no other face ever had.

He couldn't explain it, and he didn't care to dwell on it. He wasn't the sort of man who indulged in fanciful notions, and for all that Lady Emma bewitched him, he didn't trust her. "Come. It grows late. I'm certain your grandmother is wondering where you are."

"Yes, I daresay she is." Lady Emma let him hurry her along the pathway until they caught up to Lady Flora and Lovell. "Oh, Lady Emma, Lord Lovell was just telling me the most amusing story about a nonsensical wager over a footrace in Black Hawk Lane."

Lady Flora was flushed with laughter, and the elation on Lovell's face eased the tightness in Samuel's chest.

"Lady Emma, you look like a breath of fresh air, with the wind having put such color into your cheeks." Lovell gave her an admiring look, but he made no move to take her arm. "Or has my cousin been making you blush?"

"Nonsense, Lord Lovell. Lord Lymington is a perfect gentleman."

"It's time we returned the ladies to their grandmothers, Lovell." Samuel covered Lady Emma's gloved hand with his. "It's nearly time to dress for the evening."

"Is it so late as that? Why, the time flies with such company." Lovell gazed at Lady Flora with a look that made her cheeks color, then offered her his arm. They fell into step behind Samuel and Emma, and the four of them made their way back toward Rotten Row.

"The footrace was between the Earl of Barrymore and a butcher named Mr. Bullock," Lady Flora was telling Lady Emma, still laughing over it. "Lord Barrymore thought he had the best of it, as he's quite fit and Mr. Bullock rather stout, but Mr. Bullock demanded a head start, and to choose the course. Well, you know how narrow Black Hawk Lane is, and…Lady Emma? Are you coming?"

They'd reached Rotten Row, which was still crowded with people, despite the late hour. Some sort of commotion was unfolding on the far end of the pathway, and a dozen or more people had paused, craning their necks to get a glimpse of it.

"Lady Emma?" Lady Flora frowned at her friend. "What is it?"

Lady Emma had stopped on the pathway, her head turned toward the crowd of people squeezing past each other to get a look at a dashing, high-perch phaeton passing by on South Carriage Drive. It was done up to perfection in a shiny powder blue with gold-painted wheels, and carried along by a splendid matched pair of pure white horses.

But it wasn't the smartness of the equipage that had everyone gawking.

It was the lady at the ribbons, a spectacular dark-haired beauty, her charms set off to perfection by a pink gown in the latest fashion.

"Oh, my goodness," Lady Flora breathed, patting her chest. "Who is that lady? She's ever so elegant, isn't she?"

Lady Flora had addressed this question to Lady Emma, but Lady Emma seemed to be frozen in place as she watched the phaeton approach, and didn't answer.

"That lady is Helena Reeves." Samuel was the only person in the vicinity who wasn't watching Miss Reeves, and gasping over her expert handling of the ribbons.

He was watching Lady Emma.

Helena Reeves was a courtesan, and like many of London's courtesans, she'd begun her career under the tutelage of Madame Marchand.

Samuel kept his gaze on Lady Emma as the phaeton approached, his eyes narrowed. "She's with Viscount Wingate, driving his pair. It's rumored he's considering making her his mistress."

Lady Flora gasped, her cheeks flooding with color. "M-mistress?"

Samuel knew better than to discuss mistresses in front of an innocent young lady. If he'd been in his right mind, he would have steered Lady Flora and Lady Emma in the opposite direction down Rotten Row.

But he wasn't in his right mind, and neither, it seemed, was Lady Emma, who appeared to be rooted to the spot. The carriage drew closer, then closer still, the lady inside winking and grinning at the crowd, clearly enjoying every moment of the stir she was causing.

A half-dozen of the haughtier members of the *ton* turned away from the dazzling display, and Samuel was about to do the same when Helena Reeves's roving gaze paused as it moved over the crowd, catching on Lady Emma.

It happened so quickly, if Samuel had happened to blink, he would have missed it.

It was subtle, but unmistakable, just the tiniest nod of her head.

Lady Emma did not return the nod, nor did she give any outward sign she'd noticed it, but Samuel felt a nearly imperceptible stiffening in her body, a tightening of her fingers on his arm.

"There you are, Emma." Lady Crosby came hurrying down Rotten Row toward them. Her cheeks were pink and she was breathless, as if she'd been running. "Come along, dear. It grows late. Shall we go, Lady Silvester?"

Lady Crosby didn't wait for an answer, but took Lady Emma's arm and began hurrying her down the pathway.

"Thank you for the pleasant walk, Lord Lovell, and Lord Lymington." Lady Flora dipped into a polite curtsy, but her troubled gaze followed Lady Emma and Lady Crosby, who'd rushed off at a brisk pace without a backward glance, leaving Samuel and Lovell standing alone on the pathway, staring after them.

Lovell frowned. "That was strange."

Strange, indeed. Samuel stood in the middle of Rotten Row and watched as the crowd swallowed a young lady dressed in blue, her fair hair the color of sunflowers, and wondered how many secrets were hiding behind those perfect red lips.

Chapter Eight

"I don't think the season was ever so pleasant as this when we were girls, do you, Edith?" Lady Crosby turned an enquiring gaze on Lady Silvester, who was seated beside her in the carriage. "If I ever attended a supper picnic among the roses, I don't recall it."

"No, it was all formal balls and tedious, stuffy dinners then, and all of us strapped into those enormous panniers, and our hair covered with lace caps."

"Don't forget the hoop petticoat and underpetticoats, Edith. Goodness, it's a wonder we could dance with all that heavy silk dragging behind us."

Lady Silvester laughed at the memory. "It's a great deal more pleasant for the young ladies now."

"I'm certain I don't recall the weather ever being so cooperative, either. I'm sure it rained on us every day." Lady Crosby peered out the window, then gasped as the carriage crested the hill and the south-facing view of Tremaine House appeared. "My goodness, so elegant! Don't you think so, Emma?"

Emma thought it looked rather grim. Or perhaps the house was very well, and it was *she* who was grim. Either way, she didn't like to put a damper on everyone's mood by saying so. "It has, er...elegant proportions."

By that, she meant it was square. Two enormous squares with towers at each of the four corners, and a long, low rectangle with dozens of rows of windows along the front between them, the whole of it faced with a dark red brick.

Lady Flora had her nose pressed to the glass as the carriage approached the house. "The gardens are meant to be lovely, as well, aren't they, Grandmother?"

"It's been some years since I've been to Tremaine House, dear, but I remember being delighted with them. There are quite a lot of fountains and dear little rose arbors tucked into every corner, if I recall correctly. I daresay they've only improved since then."

Emma peered at the approaching house over Lady Flora's shoulder, still not quite able to believe she and Lady Crosby had received an invitation to Lord and Lady Tremaine's picnic. All the *ton* were panting for one, but only a select few had been invited.

Among them, Lord Lovell, his mother and his aunt, Mr. Humphries, and with them…

Lord Lymington, who'd pounce on Emma like an ill-tempered cat the moment she stepped out of the carriage, his massive paws at the ready to bat her about like a hapless mouse.

Emma turned away from the window to hide her expression from the others, a defeated sigh on her lips. She'd done her best to banish him from her thoughts, but after his morning call and their walk in Hyde Park yesterday, his every word, his every glance had been plaguing her like dozens of buzzing insects.

This was *not* how she'd imagined this business would unfold.

Lady Flora was infatuated with Lord Lovell, and Lord Lovell spent every moment with Lady Flora casting hopeful, yearning glances at her. Then there was Lord Lymington, who listened to every word Emma said, and somehow also heard all those she didn't.

Lord Lymington, with his sharp gray gaze, and a touch that made her quiver.

After what he'd seen at Hyde Park yesterday, he must have realized the mysterious "Letty" was Helena Reeves. He was too clever not to have done.

With Helena's one little nod, any hopes Emma had had of keeping their acquaintance a secret had been obliterated. What dreadful luck, that she and Helena should happen to cross paths just then, right under Lord Lymington's nose!

Anyone else wouldn't have even noticed Letty's nod, but *he* had.

He noticed everything, blast him. Emma could hardly deny knowing Helena *now*, nor could she continue to insist that she'd never set foot inside the Pink Pearl.

With all these distractions plaguing her, Emma was being driven half mad, and she couldn't afford a bout of insanity just now. She had an obligation to Lady Clifford, to Amy Townshend and Kitty Yardley, and to Caroline Francis.

And what of all the silent promises she'd made to the nameless, faceless young girls who'd met their fates at the hands of aristocrats who seduced them, and then discarded them when they grew bored, as if they were soiled gloves? Girls like Helena, and like Emma herself, who'd only escaped Helena's fate by mere chance.

"Lord Lovell and his party are here." Lady Silvester leaned over Lady Crosby to get a better look out the window as the carriage made its way up the drive. "Goodness, Lord Lovell looks well today, doesn't he, Flora? I've never seen a more handsome man in my life."

Lady Flora didn't reply, but Emma cast a sidelong glance at her friend, and cringed at the longing she saw in her face. Flora might protest that she didn't care a whit for Lord Lovell, but anyone could see he held her heart in the palm of his hand. One careless move, and he'd shatter it into thousands of tiny pieces that could never be put right again.

"Lord Lymington looks somber, doesn't he?" Lady Flora wrinkled her forehead. "I can't think how he can be cross on such a beautiful day."

Unable to help herself, Emma peered over Lady Flora's shoulder again, her heart leaping in her chest at the sight of an unsmiling Lord Lymington, his broad shoulders outlined against the blue sky, the wind tousling his dark hair. "He looks as if he's going to an execution instead of a picnic."

Lady Flora, always ready to defend the indefensible, gave Emma a chastising look. "Perhaps he's simply not fond of picnics. Not everyone is, I suppose."

Emma snorted. "He's not fond of balls, or dancing, or company, or art, and now he has a quarrel with picnics, sunny skies, and rose gardens? I've yet to find a single thing Lord Lymington approves of."

"Oh, hush. I'm sure that's not the case," Lady Flora scolded, but her lips were twitching.

"One can't say the same of his cousin." Lady Silvester gave an approving nod as a smile lit Lord Lovell's handsome face. "I've never known a gentleman more inclined to be pleased with everything than Lord Lovell. Don't you agree, Flora?"

"Rather too inclined, perhaps," Lady Flora muttered, but she let out a resigned sigh after a glance at her grandmother's anxious face. "I don't deny Lord Lovell is gifted with a charming temperament, grandmother, but charm isn't proof of a gentleman's honor. Don't you agree, Emma?"

"I do, indeed." The most charming gentlemen were invariably the least honorable, which, ironically, meant Lord Lymington was the most honorable man she'd ever encountered.

"Still, Lovell has always had a good heart." Lady Flora was still gazing out the window, as if unable to tear her eyes away from Lord Lovell's face. "Don't you think he has a good heart, Emma?"

As good a heart as any other wicked rake.

Emma bit down hard on her lip before the words could tumble out. "Er...I imagine his heart is very...that is, I'm sure it's as good as...any other gentleman's."

Faint praise, indeed. Emma cast Lady Crosby a despairing look, and sank down further in her seat, wishing she could disappear entirely—wishing herself anywhere but here.

Lady Flora gave Emma a curious look, but a shout pulled her attention back to the window. "Here comes Lord Lovell now." She patted at her hair, and gave her skirts a nervous twitch.

Emma peeked out the window as Lord Lovell strode toward their carriage. A gust of cool, fresh air rushed inside as he pulled the door open. "Good afternoon, ladies!" He offered them all a polite bow, and reached a hand out to Emma, who was closest to the door.

Her smile felt stiff on her lips as she slipped the tips of her fingers into his hand and allowed him to assist her from the carriage. "How do you do, Lord Lovell?"

"You look lovely this afternoon, Lady Emma." Lovell pressed a playful kiss to her gloved hand. "As bright at the sun itself."

"You're a shameless flirt, my lord." Emma intended the words as a tease, but they emerged from her lips as a scold, even as the irony of *her* scolding anyone for flirting made her cheeks burn with shame.

Lovell didn't seem to notice. He pressed a hand over his heart, but his pretty dark eyes were filled with laughter. "You wound me, my lady."

"A hand for Lady Flora, if you would, Lord Lovell?" Lady Silvester prodded gently, recalling him to his duty. Lovell turned his attention back to the carriage at once, his cheeks coloring. "Yes, of course. Forgive me. Lady Flora, you're as fresh and pretty as Lady Tremaine's roses."

Lord Lovell forgot Emma in an instant, and handed Flora down as if she were a precious object, his adoring gaze devouring every curve of her face.

But like so many ladies in love, Lady Flora's feelings were easily hurt. Her smile faded, her joy in the lovely day dimming in an instant. She managed a brief nod for Lovell, but she didn't meet either his or Emma's eyes as she stepped down from the carriage.

Emma dragged her gaze away from Flora's crestfallen face and looked down at her feet, kicking a loose stone aside with the toe of her shoe and cursing love and lovers alike with every breath in her body. From what she'd seen of it—which was, thankfully, blessedly little—love seemed to cause a great deal more misery than happiness.

She bit her lip to hold in a sigh, joined arms with Lady Flora, and painted a bright smile on her face. "Is there a room where Lady Flora and I might tidy ourselves before greeting the rest of the company, Lord Lovell?"

Lovell bowed. "Certainly. You'll escort the other ladies, Lymington?"

Emma glanced up, and found Lord Lymington standing in the drive. He scowled at Lovell's request, but Lady Silvester and Lady Crosby had already taken possession of Lady Lymington, and Mr. Humphries appeared to be asleep in the carriage. That left Lady Lovell on her own, leaving Lord Lymington no choice but to offer her his arm.

Emma breathed out a sigh of relief. It was a brief reprieve only, but that frown on Lord Lymington's hard lips didn't bode well. She needed a moment to gather herself together before she crossed swords with him again.

"Come with me, if you would, ladies." Lord Lovell led them into the house and showed them to a pretty little parlor papered in figured yellow silk, then withdrew with another bow. Lady Flora didn't speak to Emma, but went straight to a looking glass and began to tidy her hair.

Emma swallowed the lump in her throat and joined her friend at the glass, brushing Flora's hands gently aside to remove a few tangled hairpins. "You might have told me, Flora."

A flush rose to Lady Flora's cheeks. "I…tell you what?"

Emma smoothed the long, dark curl in her hand before meeting Lady Flora's gaze in the mirror. "That you're in love with Lord Lovell."

Lady Flora's eyes went as round as tea saucers. "I'm not…I don't…" she began, then her shoulders drooped and she turned to face Emma, her lower lip trembling. "Is it that obvious?"

"To me, yes. It's difficult to say with Lord Lovell. Gentlemen are dense about such things."

"Are you…don't you love him, too?" Lady Flora's dark eyes shimmered with unshed tears, but she appeared resigned, as if she expected to hear Emma say she was deeply, madly in love with Lord Lovell.

Emma couldn't help but press her palm to Lady Flora's cheek. "No, Flora, I don't. I don't deny flirting with him, but only as a pleasant diversion. Nothing more than that." That, and because he was her best chance to get to the heart of the mystery that surrounded the Lymington family.

Dear God, what am I doing?

"But how can you *not* be in love with him?" Lady Flora's brow wrinkled in confusion, as if she couldn't imagine the entire world wasn't in love with the object of her affection. "He's so handsome and lively and kind, and…well, he's Lord Lovely, isn't he?"

Emma sent up a quick prayer that Lord Lovell was in fact Lord Lovely, and not Lord Lecherous, or worse. "I have no wish to fall in love with anyone. I'm content as I am."

She attempted a laugh, but to her horror a sad, forlorn little squeak emerged in its place. She'd hoped for love once, like all young girls did, but her girlish fancies of love and romance had been bled out of her long ago.

But this was hardly the time to indulge in the megrims. "Why didn't you simply tell me how you feel about him, Flora?" She gave one of Flora's pretty curls a gentle tug. "There are dozens of gentlemen I might flirt with besides Lord Lovell."

And not one of them of any use to me.

"It wouldn't have been fair of me to do so. It isn't your fault if Lovell prefers you to me. He never flirts with *me*," she added morosely.

Emma secured Flora's curl with a hairpin. "That's how you know he has true feelings for you, Flora. He doesn't pretend with you. Flirting means nothing, you know, whereas honesty means everything."

No one knew better than Emma how hollow flirting was, how meaningless, and how exhausting. Dangerous, as well. There were times when she spent so much effort performing, she couldn't remember who she really was.

Lady Flora's lower lip was wobbling. "It's just that…well, it's all become so complicated."

"I don't see how. You're in love with Lord Lovell, and he appears to me to be well aware of how fortunate he'd be to have you. You're a delight, Flora."

"Well, there's a bit more to it than that." Lady Flora shot Emma a glance from under her lashes, then looked guiltily away. "I think I've made a terrible mistake."

Emma frowned, puzzled. "I don't understand."

"Oh, dear. It's not known, and I really shouldn't tell anyone, but…"

"We're friends, Flora, and friends may tell each other anything."

Well, nearly anything. Or, in Emma's case, almost nothing, but whatever Lady Flora's sins might be, she couldn't possibly be as wicked as she thought she was.

Certainly not as wicked as Emma.

Lady Flora squirmed under Emma's gaze. "I, ah…I did something I shouldn't…well, to be fair, it seemed the right decision at the time, but I broke a promise, and now I can't help but think I've been dreadfully unfair to him."

Emma raised an eyebrow. "Unfair to whom? What sort of promise?"

"It didn't feel as if I had any other choice at the time, but now the season's begun and Lovell's here, and despite it all he's...well, he seems to be very much as he used to be, when we were..." Lady Flora trailed off with a sniffle, but then she seized Emma's hands, her eyes pleading. "You'll help me, won't you?"

Goodness. This was getting more interesting by the moment.

"Forgive me, Flora, but you haven't told me what you've done yet. Help you with *what?*" Emma felt as she did when she eavesdropped, and could only hear one side of the conversation.

Lady Flora was on the edge of tears. "Help me make Lord Lovell fall in love with me! If he did fall in love with me, all might yet be well."

Emma tried to patch all of Flora's strange comments into some sort of coherent whole, but the puzzle was missing some pieces. "I can't help you if you don't tell me what you're on about, Flora."

"I'm buht...buhrowdtolrdlovell," Lady Flora mumbled.

"I beg your pardon?"

Lady Flora drew in a shaky breath. "Lord Lovell. I, ah... heandiarebuhtrowd."

Emma frowned, and bent down to catch Flora's eye. "I didn't understand you."

Lady Flora huffed out a breath, met Emma's eyes, and blurted. "I said, I'm betrothed to Lord Lovell!"

Emma gaped at her, speechless.

Betrothed? No, she must have misunderstood. "Did you just say you're *betrothed* to Lord Lovell?"

"Well, not really *betrothed*, betrothed, but..." Lady Flora gave a miserable nod. "Yes."

"But how can you be *betrothed* to him?" A secret passion, yes—Emma had already guessed as much. But a betrothal? It didn't make any sense.

"Well, to be perfectly truthful, Lady Emma, it was never a real betrothal—not in the strictest sense of the word, and it's not quite right to say I'm betrothed to him *now*, not since I...oh, dear. I can't say it."

"Oh, yes, you can. You must, Flora." Emma, who was about to explode with curiosity, grasped Flora's hand. "Just say it quickly."

"I jilted him!" Lady Flora wailed, then slapped a hand over her mouth, appalled.

"*Jilted* him!" Emma staggered backward in shock.

"Oh, dear. You've gone white, Emma." Flora clutched at Emma's hands. "I shouldn't have said it *quite* so quickly."

"No, no, I just…perhaps we'd better sit down." Emma tugged Flora over to a settee in the corner of the parlor. "Tell it to me from the beginning."

Flora drew in several deep breaths to calm herself. "Lord Lovell and I have been meant for each other since we were infants. A marriage between us was my mother's dearest wish. It was always expected we'd marry, and I…" Flora raised her eyes to Emma's. "I've loved him for as long as I can remember. We were dear friends growing up, and…"

"As you grew older, friendship turned to love." Emma had heard similar stories before, and could credit a love grown over years more easily than the sudden, explosive burst of adoration one read about in romantic novels.

"On my part, yes, and I used to think he returned my affections. Lord Lovell and I were very much alike at one time, you see. Lovell used to be…oh, so tenderhearted, Emma! Fanciful, even, and romantic."

Emma smiled. If that was true, then Lovell and Flora had been well suited. If she hadn't met Flora for herself, Emma wouldn't have believed anyone with such trust in the goodness of others could exist.

"But he's changed so much over this past year." Flora wiped her hand over her damp cheek. "I hardly recognize him anymore."

Emma stiffened. Amy and Kitty had gone missing from Lymington House during the past year, and God knew a guilty conscience could wreak havoc on a man.

"In what way has he changed, Flora?" Emma asked, taking care to keep her tone neutral.

"Well, I already told you he got ensnared by a wild crowd of fashionable young noblemen, and took up wagering and drinking and…the usual sorts of trouble young gentlemen tend to get up to."

Lady Flora's cheeks turned so red Emma could well guess what sort of "trouble" her friend meant. "I see. He must have behaved badly indeed, Flora, if it came to a jilting. That's not a thing I imagine you'd do lightly."

"Not at all. Indeed, I'm ashamed to say I excused his behavior for far longer than I should have, but then he…he did something I couldn't overlook, and I realized I-I didn't even know him anymore, Emma."

"What did he do?"

"He got into a duel over a wager he made in a card game in London. I don't know the whole story, but it seems Lovell had wagered his father's pocket watch—which he should *never* have done—but then he caught the other gentleman cheating, and…well, it ended in a duel."

"Dear God."

"It wasn't just the wagering, Emma, though I don't approve of cards. It was the duel as well. I despise duels!"

Flora swiped the back of her hand across her eyes, but when she looked up at Emma, her gaze was fierce. "To engage in something so shameful as that, to risk life and limb without the least consideration for me, or his mother or aunt, or indeed for himself, Emma! I just, I couldn't overlook such a thing."

"Of course, you couldn't, Flora! Nor should you have done." Flora was such a tenderhearted lady Emma was rather stunned she'd had the courage to jilt a gentleman she loved.

Because, for all Lovell's bad behavior, it was plain to see Flora loved him still.

"What was the outcome of the duel? Did they elope?" They must have done. If an aristocrat had been shot in a duel in London, Lady Clifford surely would have heard of it.

Flora took a shaky breath. "No. Lovell was shot in the leg, and it turned...rather bad."

"Shot! How is it I never heard of this, Flora?" A nobleman being shot in London over a squabble over a wager was not the sort of titillating story the *ton* generally ignored.

"You would have, I'm certain, but Lord Lymington returned to England shortly after Lovell's duel, and he made certain the matter was kept absolutely quiet."

"Lord Lymington must have kept it quiet, indeed." If Lady Clifford didn't know of it, no one did.

"He did. No one outside the family knew of it, aside from my grandmother and myself, and even we didn't learn of his illness until months later. My grandmother and I were away when it happened, visiting a dear friend of hers in Herefordshire for the holidays, so I might get away from Kent."

Away from Lovell, Flora meant, so she might nurse her broken heart in peace.

"I've no idea how Lord Lymington kept it a secret, but he isn't the sort of gentleman one dismisses, is he? He and Lovell remained in London after Lovell's injury, then when things became dire, Lady Lovell and Lady Lymington joined them there."

"Dire? Did the wound become infected, then?"

"Yes. A fever set in, and he..." Lady Flora's voice broke. "He nearly died, Emma. He was bedridden for weeks."

Emma's head jerked up. "*Weeks*?"

"Yes. He only just recovered in time for the season."

Emma stared. "What, was the duel so recent as *that*?"

Her tone must have been too urgent, because Lady Flora blinked at her in surprise. "It happened near the end of January."

"That, ah…that's truly dreadful, Flora. It sounds as if Lord Lovell was fortunate to survive." Emma hardly knew what she said, as her mind raced to compare Flora's dates to Caroline Francis's.

If Lord Lovell had been bedridden from January until the start of the season, how had he managed to seduce, ruin, and abandon Caroline Francis at the Pink Pearl in February? The timeline in which Lovell was meant to have committed all his wicked crimes was falling apart with astonishing rapidity.

Unless Flora had mixed up the dates, but what were the odds she'd have mistaken the dates of both Lovell's duel, and his being sent down from Oxford? Unlikely, indeed—

"Lovell still walks with a slight limp, but even that's not the worst of it, Emma."

Emma shook her head to clear it. "I'd say that's quite bad enough, Flora."

"It's dreadful, but the jilting, Emma! I sent Lovell a letter from Herefordshire after I learned of the duel, ending our betrothal. I didn't know then that his life was in danger. Indeed, I didn't find it out until much later, after my grandmother and I arrived in London for the season."

Lady Flora dropped her face into her hands, her shoulders shaking.

Emma pressed a soothing hand to her back. "There now, Flora, it's all right. You didn't do a single thing you need be ashamed of."

"If I hadn't jilted Lovell, then perhaps he might not have suffered—"

"No, that's not so, Flora." Emma's voice was firm. "No one is to blame for Lord Lovell's behavior but Lord Lovell, himself."

Lady Flora gripped Emma's hand. "You don't think me dreadful?"

Emma's heart softened at the misery on Lady Flora's pretty face. "No, I don't think you're dreadful, Flora. How could I? Duels are appalling, ghastly things. You did what you must to protect your heart. You couldn't have known Lord Lovell would become so ill."

"*I* think I'm dreadful. Dreadful and selfish. Oh, not for the jilting—I don't know what else I could have done there—but I do regret turning my back on Lovell when that shameful mob of wicked London rakes turned his head, for he needed me most then, and we've always been dear friends, Emma."

"You're the furthest thing from selfish." Emma was quiet for a bit as she considered all Flora had told her. There was one thing that didn't make sense.

Why had Lord Lovell stayed in London for the season? He was madly in love with Flora still—that was plain to see—so why should he wish to stand by and watch while she secured another betrothal? Because she would do, and quickly. Flora was sweet and lovely and kind, and the gentlemen had taken notice of it.

Unless…

"Why, Flora! Lord Lovell is in London for the season to prevent you from becoming betrothed to another gentleman, isn't he?"

Flora let out a forlorn little laugh. "I think so, yes, but I suspect that was Lord Lymington's idea, not Lovell's."

"Lord Lymington! But why should *he* wish to chase you to London and keep you from marrying?"

Lady Flora looked surprised at the question. "Why, for his cousin's sake, Emma. He's only ever wanted Lovell to be happy, and I suppose… well, I suppose he thinks Lovell won't be happy without me."

"I think Lord Lymington is right." Emma hadn't expected to ever have occasion to utter *those* words, but she couldn't help but think of the sweetness with which Lord Lovell had touched Flora's cheek that night in Lady Swinton's garden.

He was as besotted with Flora as she was with him. Indeed, there was nothing standing between the two of them and a rather impressive happily-ever-after, other than…

Well, Emma herself. At least, she had been, at first.

Was that why Lord Lymington had been chasing her away from Lovell with such determination? She'd conjured any number of dark reasons for his behavior, but mightn't it simply have started because he wanted his cousin to win back the lady he loved, and Emma was in the way?

She would have said Lord Lymington was the last gentleman in the world to nurture a fledging romance. Was it possible he hid a tender heart under all that gruff ill temper?

The thought made Emma's chest ache in a way it never had before.

She didn't like it, really—

"I don't know how to make a man fall in love with me, Emma."

Emma dragged her attention back to Flora. "I don't think you need to worry about—"

"But *you* know how, Emma," Lady Flora interrupted, as if Emma hadn't spoken. "Half the gentlemen in London are in love with you. You *will* help me, won't you?"

Emma stared at Flora in shock. If Flora had asked her to seduce Lord Lovell, Emma might have been of some use to her, but *love*? What did a courtesan know about love?

Former courtesan, that is.

Still, she didn't have the first idea how people fell in love, or why.

Or if they ever truly did so at all.

She'd never seen any evidence of the exalted love described in novels. Desire, yes. Attraction, passion, and lust—those were real enough. She'd seen those things many times, in all their ugliest permutations.

But love—true, unselfish love, like what Lady Flora felt for Lord Lovell? For a long time, Emma hadn't believed such a thing existed. She'd scoffed at those who believed in pure, selfless love, thinking them tragically naïve.

But then, one by one her friends Sophia, Cecilia, and Georgiana—yes, even rational, practical Georgiana—had fallen head over heels into…well, something that looked very much like real love.

That is, it did from the outside looking in, which was as close as Emma would ever get to it. Even if she'd wished for something more, something better, something of her own, it wouldn't have made any difference.

She was broken inside, her heart disfigured by scars as surely as her hands were.

But the same wasn't true of Lady Flora. Didn't a sweet, starry-eyed optimist like Flora deserve her chance at love? And what of Lord Lovell? If he was innocent of the crimes Caroline Francis had accused him of, didn't he deserve love, too?

Emma thought of the light in Lady Flora's eyes when Lord Lovell smiled at her as he'd done yesterday in Hyde Park, and then of Lovell himself, with his easy laughter, and the unmistakable joy in his face when he gazed at Flora as they'd wandered beside the Serpentine.

Emma wouldn't give up until she'd found justice for Amy, Kitty, and Caroline, but it looked increasingly like Lord Lovell wasn't the key that would unlock the mysteries of Lymington House.

Lord Lymington, on the other hand…

Fate certainly had a wicked sense of humor, didn't she?

Because Lord Lymington wasn't the easygoing rogue his cousin was. He was a *man*, and a formidable one—

"Lady Emma?"

Emma glanced down at her gloved hands, the soft, fine kid hiding the web of silvery scars there, then back up at Lady Flora's hopeful face. "Of course, I'll help you."

Really, hadn't she known all along this would end in a confrontation with Lord Lymington? They'd been drawing their battle lines since their first dance together at Almack's.

It had been coming to this from the very start.

And so Emma wasn't surprised when she emerged from the little parlor, and found Lord Lymington waiting for her.

Chapter Nine

After Samuel's walk with Lady Emma yesterday, time had slowed to an excruciating crawl. He'd spent an interminable evening at White's with Lovell and Lord Dunn, followed by an endless night tossing in his bed, playing that strange interaction between Emma and Helena Reeves over and over in his mind.

When he'd finally fallen into a fitful sleep, his dreams were haunted with hazy visions of a tinkling laugh and smiling red lips. He'd woken with stinging eyes and an erect cock, and neither condition had been resolved to his satisfaction.

By the time Lady Emma emerged from the parlor, the hours since he'd last seen her seemed to have spun into days, and his patience was worn down to the merest sliver.

"Lady Emma," he barked, rushing forward. "Here you are, at last."

Lady Flora startled, then gave a delicate little cough. "Er, good afternoon, my lord."

"My goodness, Lord Lymington." Lady Emma turned cool blue eyes on him. "Where did you come from? Not hiding in the shrubbery, were you?"

"No, I…no." Samuel shifted from one foot to the other, amazed to feel heat rising in his cheeks. Perhaps a *bit* more decorum wouldn't go amiss. "I've come to take you for a walk through the rose gardens."

"How kind." Lady Emma's lips twitched, as if she were enjoying his discomfiture. "A walk sounds lovely after being confined to the carriage."

She accepted Samuel's arm, but before he could hurry her off into the gardens, Lady Flora snatched up her other arm. For one ludicrous moment Lady Emma stood suspended between them, each of them unwilling to relinquish their hold.

Lady Emma tried to gently disengage herself from Lady Flora's grip. "Lady Silvester must be wondering where you are by now."

But Lady Flora held on. "Oh, but I long for a walk! I'll accompany you, shall I?"

Samuel smothered a curse. A solitary walk was pushing the bounds of propriety as it was, and now Flora had gone and offered Lady Emma just the excuse she needed to refuse him—

"Nonsense, Flora. We won't be gone for long. Isn't that so, Lord Lymington?"

"No, indeed." Not any longer than it took to get what he wanted. Whatever *that* was. Samuel's wits were so addled he was no longer sure.

"Yesterday when we were walking by the Serpentine, Lord Lymington promised he'd take me for a stroll in Lady Tremaine's gardens."

"A *private* stroll," Samuel added.

"P-private?" An anxious pucker appeared between Flora's brows. "Oh, but a walk in the sun will only aggravate your headache. If you recall, Emma, you *did* just tell me you had a headache."

Samuel drew Lady Emma toward him, his grip firm. "There's no need for you to worry for your friend, Lady Flora. I promise you I'll be careful with her. We'll keep to the shady gardens on the western side of the house."

"But your *headache*, Emma." Lady Flora stared meaningfully at Emma with wide-open eyes.

"It's nearly gone." Emma took Lady Flora by the shoulders and turned her in the direction of the terrace, where the rest of the party was assembled. "Lord Lovell is waiting for you, Flora, and I'm certain you must be parched. I daresay Lady Tremaine has lemonade."

Lady Flora didn't look pleased, but at Lady Emma's urging she went off toward the picnickers on the other side of the terrace. Samuel took Lady Emma's arm and hurried her toward the west side of the house, before anyone noticed she wasn't with Flora, and came after them.

What he had to say was for her ears alone.

He hadn't imagined that cryptic little nod at Hyde Park yesterday. "Letty" was Helena Reeves, of course. He'd realized it as soon as he'd seen that subtle exchange between them yesterday. Emma and Helena Reeves knew each other, and it was no passing acquaintance. They were close enough that Lady Emma had risked her reputation to sneak into the Pink Pearl to see Helena that night.

Samuel was determined to discover how one of London's most notorious courtesans could possibly be acquainted with Lady Emma Crosby.

Samuel led her down a quiet pathway to a nook hidden behind a rose arbor, and shaded by a cascade of heavy roses. "Tell me about Helena Reeves, Lady Emma."

Tears, denials, loud recriminations, even a swoon—Samuel was prepared for one or all of these reactions, but Lady Emma merely stroked a gentle fingertip over one of the rose blossoms. A few of the petals dropped into her palm, their pink color deeper against the soft white of her glove. "How pretty."

"I saw Helena Reeves nod to you at Hyde Park yesterday." Samuel took a step closer, but resisted the urge to touch her. "It makes no sense an innocent young lady—the naïve, virtuous daughter of an earl—should be acquainted with an infamous Cyprian, Lady Emma."

Lady Emma was clever, but even she couldn't invent a plausible explanation for that.

She didn't turn to face him, but instead rose to her tiptoes to inhale the scent of the climbing rose just above her head. "I'd heard Lady Tremaine's gardens were lovely."

Samuel looked around them with a frown. Lovely, yes, and extravagantly romantic. This little nook was the sort of place a gentleman took a young lady to steal a kiss, not accuse her of…what *was* he accusing her of? Cavorting with courtesans?

But Lady Emma wasn't just any young lady. She never had been.

He'd known that since he'd watched her float from a windswept terrace through a pair of glass doors,—since he'd first heard that sweet, sultry voice in the deserted library of the Pink Pearl.

Lady Emma sighed. "I did hope Lady Tremaine's picnic would be more enjoyable."

Samuel had the strangest urge to take her hand, but he said only, "I beg your pardon for ruining your afternoon."

"Ah, well. It can't be helped, I suppose," she murmured, turning to face him at last. She was smiling, but Samuel sensed a sadness in her, a sort of held breath, and all at once he wanted nothing more than to let this thing go—to send her back to her grandmother with the carefree smile every lovely young lady at an afternoon picnic should wear on her lips.

"Please do sit down, Lady Emma." Samuel led her to a stone bench in the center of the tiny, circular rose garden awash in pale pink roses. "I did promise Lady Flora I'd take care of you."

"You did, yes." Lady Emma sank down onto the bench as he'd bid her. "It's a promise you make often, I think."

Her voice was so soft, Samuel wondered if her words were for herself rather than for him, but he heard her. "Forgive me, Lady Emma, but I don't see how you can know anything about the promises I've made."

Or those I've broken.

"Not much, no, but perhaps more than you think. Lady Flora told me you've gone to great lengths to help Lord Lovell secure her hand. I confess I was surprised, my lord. I wouldn't have guessed you were such a romantic."

Romantic? Samuel gaped at her, his lips moving silently until at last he managed to say, "I assure you, Lady Emma, that is the last word that can be applied to me."

"Not the very last, I don't think. I'd rather say *subtle*, or perhaps *accommodating* are the very last. I can't make up my mind which I'd choose."

Her gentle teasing startled a laugh out of Samuel. "*Charming* is the very last."

Lady Emma's red lips quirked in a wry smile. "But I can't think of anything more romantic than your conviction Lord Lovell can never be truly happy without Lady Flora."

"I wouldn't put it quite like—"

"I don't know why you'd wish to deny it. It's one of the loveliest things I've heard in a long time. You told me yesterday you only wanted Lord Lovell's happiness. It seems you were telling the truth."

A dozen protests rose to Samuel's lips, but he bit them back, and said only, "My cousin has always been good to me, and I haven't always... appreciated it as I ought to have done."

The truth was, he *had* gone to extraordinary lengths to restore Lady Flora to Lovell's arms, and for the very reason Lady Emma thought he had. Because Lovell would never be happy without Lady Flora, and Samuel couldn't bear to see his cousin unhappy.

It had been Lovell who'd seen Samuel through those long, lonely years after his father's death. His mother had done her best, but her timid protests hadn't done much to protect him from his uncle's cruelty.

But Lovell's sincere affection, his steadfast devotion to Samuel had never wavered. As bad as it had been after his father died, it would have been a great deal worse without Lovell there.

Samuel had no excuse for abandoning Lovell as he'd done. It was mere chance only that he hadn't returned to England to find his cousin a corpse.

"Lady Flora told me about their betrothal. Their betrothal, and her jilting him." For the first time since she'd sat down, Emma turned to face him. "You didn't follow Lady Flora to London to coerce her into honoring their betrothal, I hope."

Samuel stared at her, incredulous. Did she truly believe he was the sort of man who'd attempt to force a young lady to marry against her will? He wasn't accustomed to explaining himself to anyone, least of all to a lady who crept about brothels under cover of darkness, but he found himself doing just that. "I would never do anything to hurt Lady Flora. I've only ever wanted her happiness, and Lovell is her happiness."

"Presumption indeed, Lord Lymington," Lady Emma murmured, but a smile took the bite out of her words. "I suppose it's not entirely out of your character to suppose yourself much wiser than your cousin, and thus better able than he is to choose his wife."

"If I am presumptuous, it's because I wish to protect my cousin. If there's trouble about, Lovell will find it."

Samuel expected her to scoff—to remind him, as she'd done once before—that Lovell was an adult, and might make his own decisions, but Lady Emma remained quiet, an expression Samuel couldn't read on her face.

They both fell silent, each of them lost in their own thoughts. Samuel's chest had tightened when he recalled the state in which he'd found Lovell when he returned to England, and Lady Emma was still toying with the petals of the rose, as if mesmerized by the drift of them between her fingertips.

Finally, Samuel cleared his throat. "Lord Lovell is…impetuous when it comes to matters of the heart. Passionate, even reckless."

"Indeed? How foolish of him. What has passion to do with matters of the heart, after all?"

An ill-tempered retort threatened, but then Samuel noticed the spark of humor in her eyes, and the hard, tight thing in his chest loosened. "I only mean that Lovell's apt to leap first and regret it later, and I don't wish to see him endure a lifetime of suffering because of one foolish choice."

"It *is* far better to approach love *practically*, isn't it? I'm certain some romantic poet or other has written verses lauding the rationality of lovers."

A reluctant grin tugged at Samuel's lips. "Are you laughing at me, my lady?"

Lady Emma's lips quirked. "Certainly not, Lord Lymington. I wouldn't dare."

No other lady in London had a smile like hers. It was as if it had some magical quality to loosen his tongue, because the words kept pouring from Samuel's lips. "If Lovell had kept on the way he was going, it was only a matter of time before he paid for his scandals with a pistol ball to the head."

Lady Emma went strangely still, but all she said was, "That would have been a very great tragedy, Lord Lymington."

Greater than she could ever imagine, and so close—so very close—to being a reality. All at once, Samuel's throat was too dry to speak.

Lady Emma seemed to realize it, and hurried to fill the silence. "It's fashionable for handsome young gentlemen to affect romantic sensibilities, but Lord Lovell truly is a romantic, isn't he?"

Despite the ache in his chest, Samuel smiled. "He's a genuine fool for love, yes."

"Rather like Lady Flora. I can't say I approve of your high-handed tactics, my lord, but there's no denying you chose well for Lord Lovell. He and Flora are enchanting together."

"I didn't choose for him. He chose for himself, years ago, just as Flora did. They chose each other."

Lady Emma's brow creased, and she shook her head. "But…I don't understand. How did they *know*?"

Samuel gazed at her, so still, sitting amidst a wild profusion of pink roses. "Know what?" he asked, crossing the tiny courtyard to seat himself beside her on the bench.

"How did they know they were in love with each other?" She swallowed. "I don't…it doesn't make sense."

Samuel frowned. "What doesn't make sense? Love at first sight?"

"No, just…" She gave a helpless shrug. "Just *love*."

He'd spent more time than he should have gazing at Lady Emma's face, but he'd never before seen her look as lost as she did now, her blue eyes dark with shadows, her mouth soft and vulnerable, and all at once, he realized he was seeing *her*.

Not just a fleeting glimpse this time, but all of her—the whole of who she was.

The lady beside him wasn't the dazzling, beautiful Lady Emma, with her flirtatious smile and flashing blue eyes, but who she was underneath the masque. He'd thought her beautiful before, but no glittering masque could *ever* compare to the truth of her face.

His gaze lingered on those plump, rosy lips, and he imagined how they would feel beneath his—how it would feel to hold her so close against him every one of her breaths felt like his own.

She gazed at him, puzzled. "My lord? You look…are you unwell?"

Samuel gazed at her, at her deep blue eyes dark with secrets, at that sweet, red mouth, and he knew he wasn't well.

There was no way he could see the truths she hid under her masque, and in the next moment forget he'd ever seen them. He wanted to crawl inside her, see everything, all she hid, and all she was—to touch every part of her with his hands and his mouth until she couldn't remember a time when he hadn't been there.

He *wasn't* well, and he didn't give a damn.

"Haven't you ever been in love, Lady Emma?"

"No." She laughed, but it was a broken, forlorn sound, without joy. "The devotion Lord Lovell and Lady Flora feel, their happiness in each other seems…very far away from me."

"How can it be that a lady with a face like yours, a lady of such charm and allure, has never stolen a gentleman's heart?"

"How? It's the easiest thing in the world, Lord Lymington." Lady Emma's gaze had returned to the loose rose petals in her hand, but when she looked up at him, they slipped through her fingers and fluttered to the ground. "Desire isn't love."

Something swelled inside Samuel's chest then—confusion, yes, and desire, too, but there was something else, something deeper and wild, an uncontrollable longing he was helpless to resist. There was no explanation for it, no reason why it should be *she* who moved him, when others had failed.

It just *was*.

Samuel hadn't brought her here to kiss her, but he didn't think of that— he didn't think of anything at all. He simply brushed his fingers across the soft skin of her cheek, turning her toward him. When she didn't move away, he cradled her face in his hands, leaned toward her, and here, in this place with fragrant roses dripping in lush petals from the arbor above them, he brought his lips down on hers.

His mouth was as soft as a whisper, the touch of his lips careful at first, as gentle and tentative as his fingers against her skin. It wasn't until she parted her lips for him and the sweet taste of her flooded through him that Samuel understood the enormity of the risk he was taking.

By then, it was already too late.

By then her taste—vanilla, smooth and smoky at once, like the finest whiskey—was rushing through his veins with wild abandon. Then he was taking her mouth over and over again, his gentle kisses growing desperate.

He'd known she'd be delicious, addictive, but *this*…he'd never known a kiss could steal your reason, could make you dizzy with want. He traced his tongue over her bottom lip. She gasped, and the soft, surprised sound went straight to his cock, shattering his control.

"*Emma.*" Samuel sank his hands into her hair, groaning as one pale, silky lock came loose from its pins and tickled the back of his hand, a shockingly sweet caress. "Touch me."

He caught her hands in shaking fingers and twined them around his neck, and a tiny sigh fell from her lips as she sifted through the hair at the back of his neck with her fingers.

"So soft," she whispered, as if stunned.

Dear God. He'd never felt anything as tempting as her kiss, never tasted anything sweeter than her mouth. He traced her bottom lip, his tongue eager, and a soft, choked whimper caught in her throat. He thought she'd pull away from him then—hoped she would—that one of them would put an end to this madness—but instead she urged him closer, her fingers tightening in his hair.

"Emma, let me…" *Let me touch you.*

Samuel dragged his palm down her neck, over that impossibly soft skin, his lips following the trail of goosebumps left in the wake of his stroking hand.

Emma's breath caught, and her head fell back as she bared her neck to him. Samuel touched his fingertip to the hollow of her throat, and felt her pulse fluttering madly there. Her scent was stronger here, over her pulse point, and Samuel found himself inhaling, hungry for more of that vanilla-scented skin. "So sweet, Emma."

Her fingers closed around his wrist, and she raised his hand to her lips and kissed his fingertip.

Samuel gazed down at their hands, mesmerized by the sight of her gloved fingers holding his wrist, her hand so small next to his, and a wave of tenderness swept over him, leaving him shaking in its wake.

It was *right*, somehow, kissing her, perfect, in a way it never had been before, and Samuel couldn't resist the pull between them—didn't want to resist it.

"Emma." He cupped her face gently in his palms, and then he was kissing her everywhere, her lips and her neck, the secret place behind her ear, so impossibly soft, her pulse quickening under his tongue, the arch of her cheekbone, flushed with passion, and her full, red lips, now swollen from his ardent kisses.

Her warm breath drifted over his lips, and dear God, her soft sighs, the scent of her all over him, drowning him, drove him mad. He gathered the loose locks of her hair into his hands and pressed them to his lips. He nuzzled her temple, trailed a chain of kisses from her throat to the delicious arch of her neck.

I have to stop, have to—

But she was panting for him, her fingers tangled in his hair, tugging, and he couldn't stop, couldn't make himself release her. "Samuel, please."

Samuel's hands flexed, his fingers itching to loosen her gown until inches of bare, creamy skin were revealed, to pluck the rest of the pins from her hair so the heavy locks tumbled over her shoulders and he might sink his hands into it, stilling her for his mouth. He burned to slide his fingers under her skirts and up the outside of her thigh, and his cock thickened, pressing insistently against the tight confines of his falls.

"My lord." Her small, gloved hand landed on his chest. "Samuel."

Samuel allowed himself one final kiss, just the briefest brush of his lips over hers before he pulled away with a low groan, setting her away from him before he could kiss her again, before he couldn't stop. Releasing her was torture, a severing, as if he'd lost a piece of himself once she was no longer in his arms.

"I…I beg your pardon." Samuel shot to his feet, desperate to put some distance between them before he snatched her into his arms again. "I shouldn't have…"

I shouldn't have kissed you, touched you.

But he couldn't make himself say it, couldn't breathe those words into being, because they were lies. He turned away from her, dragging one long, deep breath after another into his lungs until he'd calmed the demands of his body, and could face her again.

"Lady Emma, I—"

She hadn't moved. She was sitting on the stone bench where he'd left her, the long locks of hair he'd loosened in disheveled curls on her shoulders, her fingertips pressed to her reddened lips, the usual spark of mischief in her blue eyes gone, and in its place…

Confusion. Distress.

Dear God, what had he done?

A dull, throbbing ache lodged under his breastbone. He wasn't aware of moving, but the next thing he knew he was seated on the bench beside her again, her slender hand caught in his. "You're very pale, my lady."

"Am I?" A shaky smile crossed her lips, but she looked lost, all her usual playful confidence vanished.

"You're unwell. Please permit me to take you to your grandmother."

She nodded. "I…yes. Perhaps that would be best." Samuel waited while she tidied her hair and straightened her skirts. They didn't speak as he led her from the private rose garden back toward the terrace. The picknickers were frolicking on the lawn beyond it, seated on cushions with white cloths spread before them.

Samuel wasn't certain how long they'd been gone, but long enough so Lady Crosby was waiting for them. When she saw Lady Emma's face she shot to her feet, her own cheeks going pale. "Emma? My dear child, what's the matter?"

Samuel released Emma's arm, and turned her over to her grandmother. "Too much sun, perhaps."

Too much of something, certainly.

"Come, dearest. Some lemonade will set you to rights again, or perhaps a rest in Lady Tremaine's drawing room." Lady Crosby led her granddaughter away, still fussing and fretting over her.

Samuel watched them go, a strange heaviness near his heart. He spent the next hour waiting on his mother and aunt and trying to put the memory of Lady Emma's swollen lips and pale face from his mind.

When he could no longer help himself, and did look for her again, she was gone.

Chapter Ten

"Someone's been telling lies," Emma announced, as soon as she and Lady Crosby were settled in the carriage and on their way to the Pink Pearl.

Lady Crosby had looked inclined to doze, but her ladyship did love intrigue, and she perked up at once at Emma's words. "Have they indeed, dear? Who?"

"I'm…not certain yet." Not *entirely* certain, no, but it was either Lady Flora or Caroline Francis, and she was inclined to suspect the latter. What reason did Flora have to lie? She didn't know Caroline had accused Lord Lovell of a heinous crime, so she had no reason to lie to protect him.

Of course, memory could be a tricky, deceptive thing, but a lady as in love as Flora was with Lord Lovell didn't mistake the month, or even the day he'd been shot in a duel, or miscalculate the weeks he'd spent lying in his bed, fighting for his life.

No, it was much more likely it was Caroline who was lying, or at the very least, been careless with her dates, though it would seem a lady who'd accused a man of kidnapping two of her fellow servants before he seduced and ruined her might be relied upon to be certain about when those events had taken place.

It was all very strange.

If Caroline *had* lied, the question was, why had she done it, and who stood to benefit from that lie? Whoever it was, they seemed to be going to great lengths to implicate Lord Lovell in the crime, and it looked as if Caroline was helping them do it.

Caroline Francis owed her an explanation, and Emma would have it, tonight.

"You appear to have recovered from your fatigue, at any rate." Lady Crosby cast her a shrewd glance. "You were quite feeble when you returned from your walk with Lord Lymington, but you look to be in the pink of health now."

"I wouldn't say *pink*, precisely." Emma squirmed under Lady Crosby's knowing gaze. "I, ah, I do feel better, however." And if she could keep herself from dwelling on that kiss, she'd be better still.

"Such a miraculous recovery." Lady Crosby's eyes were twinkling.

Emma's face heated. She hadn't been feigning her indisposition when she returned from the rose garden with Lord Lymington. His kiss had scattered her wits like leaves in an autumn breeze, and left her reeling.

She didn't trust herself to speak, and after brief silence, Lady Crosby added, "I can only hope Lord Lymington recovers as swiftly from whatever aches your stroll together might have caused him."

"Can we please not talk about Lord Lymington, my lady?" Emma didn't want to think about his aches, or his mouth, or the moment his lips had touched hers. It was altogether too warm in the carriage already, without dragging Lord Lymington into it.

"Certainly, if you wish it, dear, but you look a trifle flushed."

"I'm not flushed." But even as the denial left her lips, Emma was stripping off her gloves and wriggling out of her cloak.

"Oh, I beg your pardon. It's just that your cheeks have gone very red."

Not *just* her cheeks. Her neck and chest felt as if they were on fire. Emma plucked at the neckline of her gown, which suddenly felt much too tight, and turned a sour look on Lady Crosby. "You're a dreadful tease, my lady."

Lady Crosby let out a gleeful chortle. "Forgive me dear, but I couldn't resist. Oh, come now, there's no reason for you to blush as pink as a peony, Emma. Lord Lymington is rather devastating, taken altogether."

"Nonsense. I'm not blushing." Emma wouldn't permit such a thing, particularly not over Lord Lymington, no matter if his kiss had turned her knees to water.

Especially then.

"Of course not, dear." Lady Crosby was still smiling, but she patted Emma's hand and ceased her torment for the remainder of the drive.

It gave Emma far too much time to dwell on the memory of that kiss, but after a struggle and a hesitant stroke of her fingertips across her swollen lips, Emma wrenched her wayward thoughts back to the matter at hand.

One thing was certain. It was past time for Caroline to be gone from the Pink Pearl, and Helena with her. Now that Emma understood how, er...*persuasive* Lord Lymington could be, she'd just as soon keep Helena out of his way.

Her first problem would be getting them away tonight without Madame Marchand catching them. She couldn't simply stroll through the front door and demand them. She could send Daniel in, but Caroline Francis had never laid eyes on Daniel, and he was...well, a trifle intimidating at first glance. Emma wasn't certain Caroline would go with him. Even Helena was a bit skittish of him.

And it wasn't as if Madame Marchand wouldn't recognize Daniel.

"Do be careful, dear," Lady Crosby said, leaning over to kiss Emma's cheek once they'd reached Audley Square. "Don't let that wicked woman see you."

"I won't, my lady." Emma waited as Daniel handed her ladyship from the carriage, wishing she was as confident as she sounded. It was madness, venturing into the library tonight, but something was dreadfully amiss with this business, and she needed answers at once.

After they'd left Lady Crosby safely ensconced in her townhouse, Daniel drove them to St. James, and brought the carriage to a stop in one of the darker side streets near the Pink Pearl. "All right then, lass. How do ye want to manage it this time?"

"Fate does seem to keep leading us back to the Pink Pearl, doesn't it, Daniel?" Emma let out a short, humorless laugh. "I think we'll have to rely on Charles again. Once you find him, tell him Miss Emma needs to see Helena and Caroline in the library. It's best if you go in through the mews, as he'll likely be near the kitchens. I'll wait here until you return, then I'll sneak in the terrace door again."

"Aye." Daniel's nod was reluctant, as if he didn't entirely approve of this plan, but he did as she asked.

It felt as if years had passed by the time Daniel returned, but it likely wasn't more than ten minutes or so before he appeared at the carriage door. "Wait a bit longer to give the boy a moment to fetch the girls and unlock the library door, then ye can go."

Emma waited until she couldn't make herself sit still a moment longer, then she crept down the street, blending seamlessly with the shadows, and slipped through the gate leading to the back garden. With a quick glance around to make certain no one was about, she darted up the shallow stone steps that led to the library doors.

The wrought iron latch under her bare palm was cold to the touch, despite it having been a warm spring day today. Or was it just Emma's hands that were cold? All this sneaking about couldn't be good for her circulation.

The latch turned easily—thank goodness for Charles—and she slipped silently through the doors. She paused when she was inside, half-expecting Lord Lymington to leap from the shadows, clamp one of his enormous paws on her shoulder, and demand to know what business she had at the Pink Pearl in the middle of the night.

She didn't fancy another clandestine meeting in this library after the last one had gone so disastrously wrong, but Lord Lymington had been trapped in a conversation with Felix Humphries when Emma left Lady Tremaine's, after pleading fatigue and begging her ladyship's pardon for leaving her picnic supper early.

Lord Lymington hadn't seen them leave, yet Emma still imagined she felt his glare following her from the garden, that hot gaze boring into her back all the way to the carriage. He wouldn't be a bit pleased when he discovered she'd sneaked off while he wasn't looking. Those stern lips would press into a grim line, his gray eyes would darken, and he'd reach for her, growling low into her ear, and…

Emma sucked in a tremulous breath, and shook her head to clear it.

That was quite enough of *that*.

This would all be a great deal easier if Lord Lymington were far less attractive, and better yet, as dim as a sputtering candle, but instead he was as distracting a man as she'd ever met, and worse, he was as shrewd and wily as Emma herself.

He was sure to realize at once where she'd gone, and would be right on her heels, but unfortunately for him, he'd be just a touch too late. By the time he reached the Pink Pearl, Helena and Caroline would be gone.

Unless he'd somehow gotten past her? It would be just like the man to find a way to get here before she did. He was distressingly resourceful. Emma peered into the shadows, biting her lip. The library appeared to be deserted, but it had appeared so the last time as well.

Just in case, Emma searched the shadows cast by the tall bookcases, and behind the drapes. She was just sneaking a look behind the pillows— because of course a man Lord Lymington's size must be lurking behind *a pillow*—when the door opened.

The glow of light from the hallway illuminated the darkness for an instant before Helena closed the door behind her again. "Emma?"

"Here, Letty."

There was a rustle of silk skirts and the soft drag of slippers over the thick carpets, then Helena appeared, her brows drawing together when she caught sight of Emma. "Why are you tossing the pillows about? Is there something under there?"

"No one is under—that is, nothing is under there." Emma turned to Helena, but her heart sank when she saw she was standing there alone. "Where's Caroline?"

Helena bit her lip. "Gone for the evening again."

Emma blew out a frustrated breath. Caroline Francis had been at the Pink Pearl for several months, and Emma had yet to lay eyes on the girl. "You're quite sure she's not a figment of your imagination, aren't you, Letty?"

"Oh, she's real enough, if elusive. This is her fourth engagement this week." A troubled frown creased Helena's forehead. "That *is* rather a lot, isn't it?"

"Often enough to arouse my suspicions, yes." It wasn't unusual for a gentleman to request a courtesan attend him at a private location, but everything to do with this business had taken on a sinister cast since the season started. "Is it the same gentleman, each time?"

Helena nodded. "Yes. Caroline says so, at least."

Emma sank down onto a settee. It was a lovely blue velvet, costly and plush. The desk beside it and the chair opposite were equally beautiful.

Everything at the Pink Pearl was beautiful, on the surface.

Emma braced her elbows on her knees. "Have you ever seen him?"

Helena dropped into the chair opposite Emma, her frown deepening. "No. He fetches Caroline in his carriage each time, but she runs out to meet him. He never comes inside."

"What sort of carriage does he have?" A description of his carriage wasn't likely to help much, unless… "Does it bear a crest?"

"No. It's just a plain black carriage, unmarked."

Indistinguishable from any other carriage in London, then. "I suppose Caroline is smitten with him?" Smitten enough to tell lies for him, even if those lies led to an innocent man dangling from a noose.

"She was at first," Helena said slowly. "When she returned to the Pink Pearl after that first time, she was positively giddy. But lately she seems… almost afraid of him."

"Afraid?" Emma said sharply, leaning forward. "What makes you think that?"

"I could tell she didn't want to go with him tonight. Madame Marchand made her, of course, but before she left, she…she gave me something." Helena was twisting the fringe on the pillow, her knuckles white. "I have it with me."

Emma's heart started to pound. "May I see it?"

Helena reached into the bodice of her gown, withdrew a round object, and placed it in Emma's outstretched palm.

"It's a pendant." A very fine gold one, surrounded by diamonds and with a tiny, perfect enameled portrait of a handsome, dark-haired little boy inside. "Where did she get this?"

"She had it from him. Took it, I mean, without his knowing it."

She'd stolen it, then. Emma held the pendant up, studying the dull sparkle of the diamonds in the weak light. What would a gentleman be doing with a lady's pendant? It seemed a strange thing for him to carry about, unless...

Emma's fingers froze on the pendant. What if this secret paramour of Caroline's wasn't her lover? What reason did they have to assume it was even a *man,* at all? One need only look at Madame Marchand for proof that a woman could be as cruel and wicked as a man.

The truth was, they knew next to nothing about Caroline's mysterious visitor, including whether he—or she—was the same person attempting to implicate Lord Lovell in the crimes.

Still, it stood to reason it *was* the same person. Odds were whoever had persuaded Caroline to lie had followed her to London to see to it she kept her promise.

"Did Caroline say who the boy in the portrait is?"

"No. I don't think she knows. Even if she did, I doubt she would have told me. She wouldn't say anything about it, except that I must take it, and keep it safe. I think..."

Emma jerked her gaze to Helena's face. "What, Letty?"

"I think she was afraid something might happen to her," Helena whispered.

Emma's hand closed into a tight fist around the pendant. The boy in the portrait must somehow reveal the identity of the culprit, then, or else Caroline would never have risked stealing it.

It was also proof of a connection between him and Caroline.

Or *her.*

Perhaps it was the *only* proof.

Emma slipped the pendant into her pocket, tossed the pillow aside, and got to her feet. "I need you to come with me tonight, Letty. Right now."

Helena blinked up at her. "Come with you where?"

"To Lady Clifford's. Daniel is outside with the carriage, and Lady Clifford is expecting you." That wasn't quite true, but Emma wanted Helena gone from this place, before something awful happened.

The sooner Emma could coax her to leave here, the better.

"I can't simply walk out the door, Emma. You know as well as I do Madame Marchand will come after me. I owe her for board and clothing." Helena snatched up the folds of her gown. "This gown on my back belongs to her. She'll have me taken up for theft!"

Emma's hands tightened into fists as a strange emotion, something between fury and despair swept through her. This was how the bawds made courtesans of the young, friendless girls who came to London looking for employment. They coaxed them into the brothel with false promises, offered them shelter and fancy clothes, then threatened to have them taken up for theft when the girls balked at earning a living on their backs.

"Lady Clifford will see to it your debt to Madame Marchand is settled. You can't stay here, Helena. Lord Lymington saw you nod to me at Hyde Park yesterday. He knows who you are, and he knows you're Caroline's friend. He'll come here looking for Caroline, and when he can't find her, he'll ask for you. He's likely on his way here even now."

If he wasn't here already.

Helena didn't move.

"Come, Letty," Emma bit out. "Before Daniel comes searching for us."

"No. I can't leave without Caroline."

"You can, Letty, and you will." Emma, who recognized the familiar stubborn expression on Helena's face, was ready to tear her hair out. "If you think I'm leaving you here, you're mad."

Helena crossed her arms over her chest. "Lord Lymington can ask me whatever he likes. I'm not obliged to answer him. If I can manage a blackguard like Lord Peabody, then I can daresay can manage Lord Lymington."

"It's not Lord Lymington I'm worried about. He's the least of our problems." Lord Lymington might scowl and seethe a bit, but there was no cruelty in him, no violence. He was everything so many other men claimed to be, but weren't.

A true gentleman.

He'd never hurt Helena, or anyone else, but that was the only thing Emma could be certain of at this point. With every day that passed, more worrying questions arose, and she didn't have any answers.

All she knew was that something was terribly, terribly wrong at Lymington House.

Someone had seduced and ruined Caroline, almost certainly the same person who'd taken Amy and Kitty, and was trying to shift the blame for it onto Lord Lovell by having Caroline come to London and lie about it. *That* was why Caroline was still alive—because the culprit needed her to point the finger at Lord Lovell.

And what better place to spread those lies than at the Pink Pearl?

But the culprit's plans had gone awry when Lovell and his family had appeared in London for the season. The culprit hadn't expected *that*—and then Lord Lymington had come to the Pink Pearl in search of Caroline

Francis on his first night in London. Caroline's private engagements had
begun that very same night, the first of them a *sudden* private engagement,
Helena had said.

Whoever the villain was, he—or *she*—was determined to keep Caroline
from speaking to Lord Lymington.

"Listen to me, Letty. Caroline believes her paramour is a threat to her,
or else she never would have given you that pendant to begin with. If he's
willing to hurt her, why should you think he'd hesitate to hurt *you*? It's
not safe here."

Letty's voice rose. "If it's as dangerous as you say it is, then how can
you think to leave Caroline here alone?"

"Hush, Letty! Someone will hear you. I don't like to leave Caroline. I came
here tonight to fetch you both, but it might be hours yet before she returns."

Helena huffed. "A few more hours won't make a difference."

"A few hours could make *all* the difference! In another few hours,
you could both be gone." Emma lowered her voice with an effort. "Once
Daniel's delivered you to Lady Clifford, he'll come back here and wait for
Caroline. I promise it, Letty."

Helena said nothing, but Emma could see wasn't convinced. Short of
dragging Helena out of here kicking and screaming, there wasn't a chance
Emma could get her to leave the Pink Pearl tonight.

"I'm sorry, Emma." Helena gave her a pleading look. "I'm Caroline's
only friend here. I can't simply abandon her. You can't ask it of me—you,
of all people, who are so protective of me."

"Not protective enough." Emma's jaw was tight. "If I were, I would
have persuaded you to leave this place years ago."

"One more night, Emma, I swear it, and if anything goes wrong, I'll
alert Daniel at once."

Emma's hands opened and closed at her sides, grasping at nothing.
She'd never felt more helpless in her life, but there was little she could
do. If she lingered any longer arguing with Helena, Madame Marchand
would be sure to discover them. "Go, then. Quickly, before Madame
Marchand misses you."

Helena rushed forward and pressed a kiss to Emma's cheek. "One more
night only, Emma. I promise it."

One more night.

Emma hardly had time to draw a breath before Helena was gone,
swallowed back into the depths of the Pink Pearl.

One more night that would last a lifetime.

* * * *

"What a pleasure to see you again, Lord Lymington. Are you interested in female companionship this evening, or have you returned to the Pink Pearl to tease us once again?"

Samuel had burst through the door of the Pink Pearl and started immediately for the library, scanning the entryway as he went. There was no sign of Helena Reeves, but the same redhead he'd offended last week was smiling up at him with pink, painted lips.

"Neither," he snapped, not bothering to hide his scowl. "I need to find Helena Reeves."

"Ah, so it's Helena this time, is it? Have you finished with Caroline already? Inconstant man!" She giggled, tapping his chest with her fan.

"Is Caroline here?" Samuel asked, ignoring her flirtation. "She'll do just as well."

"I'm certain both Caroline and Helena will be overjoyed to find you consider them interchangeable, my lord. Alas, Caroline is not here this evening. Helena is, though I haven't seen her for some time."

"Where did you see her last?" Samuel was trying to remain calm, but it had taken him ages to disentangle himself from the company at Lady Tremaine's. Lady Emma had at least a half hour's start on him, and God knew half an hour was more than enough time for her to wreak havoc.

In short, he was ready to squeeze the redhead until useful words spilled from her lips.

"Oh, here and there." She smirked up at him, clearly enjoying her game. "First, she was in the music room, then I believe she was upstairs for a time with Lord Dimmock, then I saw her wandering down the hallway outside the library—"

Samuel didn't wait to hear more, but strode across the drawing room and down the adjacent hallway, his boots ringing against the marble floors with every step. He passed the music room, then threw open the library door, not at all sure what he'd find on the other side.

What he did find was…nothing.

No Helena Reeves, and no cloaked wraith drifting through the glass doors, but it was colder in here than it should be, as if the door had just been open, and—

He paused as he caught a subtle shift in the light coming through the glass, the hint of a shadow drifting across the stone terrace and into the garden beyond.

Lady Emma hadn't yet made her escape.

Samuel darted across the library, taking care to stay on the carpets so his footsteps would be muffled. The shadow had vanished by the time he reached the glass doors, but she couldn't have gotten far.

He pushed the door open, closing it behind him as he stepped onto the terrace. He was angry with Lady Emma when he found she'd slipped his grasp this evening, yet for reasons he didn't care to examine, he didn't choose to reveal her secret comings and goings to Madame Marchand.

His labored breaths echoed in his ears as he crossed the garden, hoping he wasn't so far behind her she'd disappear into the darkened streets of London before he could see which way she'd gone, but when he reached the corner, he glimpsed a slight figure hurrying down the street.

No cloak this time, no deep hood to hide her face, but he would have known her anywhere, regardless. So graceful, her movements so fluid— he'd as soon forget the way Lady Emma moved as he would her scent, or the taste of her lips, or the unbearable eroticism of her low, sweet voice.

Samuel went after her, drawing closer, then closer still. He expected her to turn and see him at every moment, alerted by the sound of his footsteps, but she kept on with single-minded purpose, never glancing back.

It wasn't until she was nearly on top of it that Samuel noticed the carriage. It was waiting halfway down a narrow lane, several blocks east of the Pink Pearl, and beside it stood a hulking figure Samuel recognized at once as Lady Crosby's coachman.

The man was strangely menacing for a coachman, and not the sort one wanted to tangle with on a dark London street, but the threat of him didn't deter Samuel. He crept forward, hidden in the shadows of a tall hedge, but just as he drew close enough to hear the low murmur of their voices, he went still.

Lady Emma was standing at the open carriage door, her hand resting on the edge of it as she spoke earnestly to the coachman. A faint glimmer of moonlight fell across the side of her face and over her hands, and—

Samuel stared, his breath catching with a painful hitch in his throat.

A complex web of thin, silvery scars covered her knuckles and crisscrossed in a crazed pattern over her fingers and the back of her hands. They were long since healed now, remnants of wounds that must once have been ugly indeed, to have left such deeply etched scars in that fine, white skin.

Those scars…how could he not have noticed them before, how could he—

She keeps them hidden.

He'd never once seen her bare hands. She kept that secret, marred flesh concealed under layers of silk or fine white kid, as if it were something shameful, a terrible thing *she'd* done, rather than a violence that had been done to her.

Samuel raised his gaze to her face, her profile limned in the muted glow, then lowered it again to her hands, a strange, hollow ache tugging at his heart for his dainty wraith, with her pale, ruined hands.

Chapter Eleven

"Caroline Francis is missing."

Emma was standing in front of the pier glass in the drawing room attempting to smooth a wayward curl before she and Lady Crosby left for the theater, but her fingers stilled at Daniel's words.

Her eyes met his in the glass. "Missing?"

"Aye, lass." Daniel paused in front of Lady Crosby's elegant marble fireplace, his massive shoulders dwarfing the dainty mantel. "She never came back to the Pink Pearl last night."

"Oh, dear." Lady Crosby looked from Emma to Daniel, the color draining from her cheeks. "But what could have become of the poor girl?"

"Nothing good." Daniel's voice was hard.

Emma turned from the glass to face him, her heart crowding into her throat. "Are you certain, Daniel? Is there a chance you might have missed her, or—"

"No, lass. I waited all night for 'er, and spent most of today searching. No one's seen or heard a word from the girl since she left the Pink Pearl the day before yesterday. She's gone."

Gone. Disappeared, just like Amy and Kitty—seemingly dissolved into thin air without a trace, as if they'd never been there at all.

"But…how can she be gone?" Emma asked dumbly. This was London, not a country village in Kent. People didn't vanish without a single person having seen a thing. "Someone must have seen something."

"Of course, they must have, dear." Lady Crosby said, but she looked uncertain. "Someone must have some idea of where she's gone, mustn't they, Daniel?"

"No one who's willing to talk." Daniel's somber eyes met Emma's. "No one could tell me anything other than the lass went off in a black carriage, and never came back to the Pink Pearl."

"Perhaps she went with him willingly?" Lady Crosby asked hopefully. "Perhaps there's nothing so sinister in it, after all."

"Perhaps." But Emma's throat had gone tight with dread.

"I can't speak to that." Daniel's voice was grim. "All we know is 'e sent a carriage to fetch her, she got inside, and no one knows another cursed thing about him."

Emma's hand shook as it crept to her throat. "What of Helena, Daniel? Where is she?"

As soon as Emma saw the expression on Daniel's face, she knew she wasn't going to like the answer. She reached out to grip the back of the settee, bracing herself.

"She's at the Pink Pearl still. I couldn't get a message to her because I couldn't find that little kitchen lad."

"Charles is missing, too?" Emma dropped down onto the settee, stunned.

"We don't know that, lass. All I can tell ye is I couldn't find him."

Emma pressed her fingers to her temples, trying to think, but her head was spinning with something Helena had said last night, like a frenzied flock of birds beating their wings against her skull.

I'm Caroline's only friend here...

If the scoundrel discovered Caroline had stolen his pendant, he'd suspect at once that she'd given it to Helena. Helena was the only one at the Pink Pearl who was in Caroline's confidence, the only person Caroline might have trusted with her secrets.

Dear God. She *had* to get Helena away from the Pink Pearl, and it had to be soon.

But how? Madame Marchand wasn't simply going to hand Helena over to Daniel, nor could Helena simply stroll out the front door. She might be able to sneak out the library doors, but Helena was terrified of Madame Marchand, and would never risk it without Emma there.

Lady Clifford could get Helena out, but if Madame Marchand proved difficult—and she *would*—it could take time, and that was something Helena didn't have.

There had to be another way. There *had* to be someone who could— Emma's head came up.

There was.

But it would mean she'd have to trust Lord Lymington.

Emma trusted very few people, and there wasn't a single marquess among them. She'd learned her lesson about noblemen five years ago, and it wasn't one she'd ever forget.

But what choice did she have? Caroline was missing, and Helena could be next.

It seemed a cruel twist of fate, that after all her tricks and dodges, her cunning and guile honed over five years of practice, that she should end up having to rely on a churlish marquess.

But then Emma recalled the warmth in Lord Lymington's voice yesterday in the rose garden, when he'd spoken about Flora and Lord Lovell, the gentle pressure of his hand on Emma's neck, the tenderness with which he'd kissed her....

She turned to Lady Crosby with her mind made up. "I'm going to leave the theatre early tonight. I'll tell Flora I have a headache, and that I'm going to have Daniel take me home. When I beg you to stay to watch the rest of the play, you must do as I ask, all right?"

Lady Crosby looked troubled, but she nodded. "Yes, I will, dear."

"Thank you." Emma squeezed Lady Crosby's hand. "Shall we go?"

By the time they reached Drury Lane and Emma and Lady Crosby had made their way to their box, they were quite late. Lady Silvester and Lady Flora were already waiting for them, and the opening scene of *Vortigern and Rowena* was well underway, with Vortigern striding from one end of the stage to the other, plotting King Constantius's murder.

"Emma!" Flora let out a joyous little squeal, grabbed Emma's hand, and tugged her down into the seat beside her. "Lord Lovell is here," she whispered, tilting her head to the left. "Do you suppose he'll come speak to us?"

Emma glanced toward the box Flora indicated, and saw Lady Lymington and Lady Lovell seated in the first row. Lady Lovell was surveying the company through a gilt opera glass, and Mr. Humphries was on her right, dozing.

Behind them sat Lord Lovell, breathtakingly handsome in his impeccable evening clothes. He was looking right at them, a warm smile on his lips, but it wasn't Lovell who caught and held Emma's gaze.

It had never been Lovell, because that would have been far too easy, wouldn't it?

Emma tried to avoid meeting Lord Lymington's gaze, but it was a pitiful attempt, especially for a lady who'd never before hesitated to confront her fate.

But then, her fate had never before led her to Lord Lymington. Again and again, she seemed to find herself coming up against him, as if fate, in a fit of mischief, had tied them together and then stood back to see what they would do.

Kiss each other, as it turned out.

That is, he'd kissed her. Yes, that was more accurate. She'd done nothing at all but...

Kiss him back.

Unconsciously, Emma raised a hand to her tingling lips, as if mere moments had passed since his lips had touched hers, and then her head was turning toward him of its own accord, her gaze bypassing every other face, as if she were magnetically drawn to *him*, and no other face, no other gentleman in all of Drury Lane mattered at all.

He was seated next to Lovell, his gloved hands folded on top of the walking stick between his knees, and his gaze was fixed on Emma with such dark intensity she was amazed their box didn't burst into flames.

He wasn't smiling. Watching him now, it occurred to Emma he rarely smiled, as if he were allotted only a finite number of them, and didn't wish to squander any.

She tore her gaze away from him, goosebumps tickling her neck. She didn't want to think of Lord Lymington just yet, of his smiles or his frowns or the gray eyes that seemed to penetrate her every defense, to see her every secret, her every lie.

Instead, she let her restless gaze wander over the crowd in search of a distraction, and it fell to the chaos in the pit below.

The noise from that quarter was deafening, the rabble jeering and heckling the players from one side of their mouths while pouring prodigious quantities of cider into the other. It was a performance that rivaled the one on the stage, and Emma found her gaze moving from the ragged mob below to the private boxes where aristocrats lounged in luxury, their jewels flashing.

London had always been divided thus, but nowhere were the two separate worlds more evident than at the theater, with the unruly mob below, and their betters arrayed in their private boxes above, watching the masses writhe with amused scorn.

Then there were those who were suspended somewhere between them, those like Helena, or Emma herself, dangling over the abyss—

"Emma? Did you hear me?"

Emma forced a smile to her lips. "I beg your pardon, Flora. What did you say?"

"I asked if you thought Lord Lovell would come to our box this evening."

"Oh, yes. I'm certain he will. He can't take his eyes off you, Flora."

"Is he looking now?"

Emma cast a reluctant glance toward their box again, cursing herself. "He is, indeed."

Lovell politely inclined his head, but Lord Lymington remained motionless, still watching her, his eyes still burning into her. This time, it was harder for Emma to drag her gaze from his. His dark eyes held her frozen until at last she tore free with a wrench, a flutter in the deepest pit of her stomach. Her eyes darted this way and that, searching for something else to focus on, someone else....

But it was no use. Her gaze was drawn back to Lord Lymington, as if he'd commanded it with an imperious snap of his fingers. And once she looked—once she gave into his command—she couldn't look away.

A strange feeling swept over Emma as their gazes held, because somehow in that moment she knew, without a word exchanged between them, that he was thinking of their kiss in the garden, just as she was.

He wouldn't let her escape him tonight.

They shifted at the same time—Lord Lymington to murmur in Lady Lymington's ear, and Emma, who leaned over Flora to say to Lady Crosby, "I find myself more fatigued than I expected tonight, grandmother."

"You do look a trifle peaked. You're worn out, you poor child. Come along, then, and we'll go home. We can see the play another time."

Emma shook her head, hiding a smile. Lady Crosby really was a magnificent actress. "No, I don't want you to miss the play. I'll just slip out, and have Daniel take me home."

"All right, dear, if you're sure." Lady Crosby patted her hand.

"Quite sure." Emma turned to Flora with an apologetic smile. "I beg your pardon for abandoning you, Flora, but I don't feel up to the theater this evening."

Flora studied Emma's face, and her brows drew together in concern. "Oh, dear. You don't look well. Are you ill?"

"No, it's just fatigue, but I don't like to aggravate it with all the noise and light. I need a bit of rest, and I'll be back to rights tomorrow."

"Shall I come with you?"

Lady Flora started to rise, but Emma urged her back into her chair with a gentle hand on her shoulder. "No, I'm perfectly well, and you can't leave now. Lord Lovell is sure to come to see you at the break."

That was all it took to coax Flora back into her chair. Emma whispered a quick goodbye to Lady Crosby, then hurried from their box into the hallway beyond.

* * * *

Samuel had nearly convinced himself she wasn't going to come tonight.

He hadn't seen her since their kiss in Lady Tremaine's rose garden. In that time, Samuel had gone walking in Hyde Park, escorted his mother and aunt on a shopping excursion in Bond Street, and spent a tedious two hours with Lovell at Tattersall's, along with every other nobleman in London, all of them crowded shoulder to shoulder in the subscription rooms.

The entire time, he'd thought of nothing but Lady Emma Crosby.

He'd hoped he might see her on Rotten Row, but after an hour squinting at every fair-haired lady in blue, he'd finally given up, and gone home to dress. When he'd arrived at the theater and noticed Lady Silvester and Lady Flora alone in Lady Crosby's box, he'd convinced himself Lady Emma had left London.

He'd even persuaded himself he hoped it was so, until he saw her enter with Lady Crosby and take her seat, as cool as you please, dressed all in blue, the lights catching at the loose strands of her hair.

Before he could stop it, before he could question it, his chest swelled, and he took what felt like his first deep breath since he'd kissed her beneath the rose arbor.

That kiss…it had changed everything.

Samuel jerked his gaze away from Lady Emma's face, but after a day of being deprived of that face, it felt like losing a limb. Even after it was gone one could still feel it, a phantom remnant of something that had once been there, that one could never reconcile oneself to losing.

She'd never looked lovelier than she did tonight, her blue silk gown the exact same shade as her eyes, with her hair caught up in a simple blue silk ribbon, the pale, silky curls trailing over her white shoulders and brushing the bare skin of her neck.

"Stunning, isn't she?" Lovell murmured in Samuel's ear. "Aside from Flora's, I've never seen a prettier face in my life than Lady Emma's."

Samuel grunted. "London is full of lovely faces. There's nothing so special in hers."

Lovell chuckled. "Then why can't you look away from her? You've been staring at her since she sat down. Has the mighty Lord Lymington fallen victim to Cupid's arrow, and been brought low by love at last?"

"*Love?* Don't be absurd, Lovell. I'm not in love with Lady Emma."

It wasn't *love*. It was…well, he didn't have any bloody idea *what* it was.

"Be careful, Lymington. Cupid makes the greatest fools of those who scorn his powers. If a man *were* to fall in love, he could hardly choose better than Lady Emma."

She half-turned toward them then, as if she'd heard them say her name, but she looked quickly away, delicate color washing over her cheeks.

"Ah, just look at that blush. She knows you're watching her, Lymington. Come now, confess the truth. Lady Emma's been driving you mad all season. She's a beauty, and worse, just the sort of beauty you prefer."

"You're mistaken, Lovell. It's you who prefers fair-haired, blue-eyed ladies, not me." He'd never been particularly enamored of fair ladies, and he didn't intend to start mooning over them now, no matter how distracting he found Lady Emma.

No matter that he couldn't forget that kiss. Dreamed about that kiss—

"My fondness for fair-haired ladies was a momentary aberration, nothing more. I've always been partial to dark-haired beauties." Lovell's gaze lingered on Lady Flora, who was seated beside her friend. "But you know very well it's not Lady Emma's face that has you enthralled, Lymington."

"What is it, then? Enlighten me, Lovell. Is it her slippery relationship with the truth? Her sharp tongue?" Her mouth, her lips...Samuel suppressed a shudder at the memory of her kiss, so soft, surprisingly so, tender and giving—

"No. It's that she's not afraid of you. Curious, really, that such a delicate lady should have turned out to have such a rigid spine, but there it is." Lovell waved an airy hand.

As far as Samuel could tell, Lady Emma wasn't afraid of anything at all. "She would have made an excellent naval commander."

Lovell frowned. "No frontal assaults, Lymington. I forbid it."

Samuel didn't answer, his attention caught and held by Lady Emma, as it always was whenever she was near him. Had he kissed the soft skin behind her ear, fingered that errant curl that refused to lay smooth under the blue ribbon? If he hadn't, he should have. He should have spent hours tracing those full red lips with his tongue, stroking that creamy skin and nuzzling his face into the fragrant curve of her neck, caressing those slender curves and inhaling the scent of vanilla and wild roses that clung to her—

Damn the woman. She was driving him mad. "I don't deny she's... attractive, but—"

"Attractive?" Lovell snorted. "That's like saying the Mona Lisa's smile is *pleasing.*"

"What is it about her face?" Samuel muttered, to himself more than to Lovell. "What's so arresting about it? There are dozens of ladies here tonight who's faces rival hers for beauty, and yet..."

Yet he hadn't spared any of them so much as a glance.

It was *her* face that bewitched him, *her* face he couldn't look away from.

"Lady Flora is ravishing, isn't she, Lymington?" Lovell let out a yearning sigh. "Those lovely dark eyes. I've always admired her eyes, but since we've been in London it's as if I'm obsessed with them. I spend hours every day thinking about her eyes."

Samuel seized his chance to turn the subject away from Lady Emma's captivating face. "Lady Flora has turned those fascinating eyes your way more than once tonight. Dare I hope you've charmed you way back into her good graces?"

Lovell's lips quirked in a tender smile as his gaze lingered on Lady Flora. "Charmed? No. Flora's never been susceptible to my charms. Nothing but honesty will do for such a lady."

For the first time that evening, Samuel smiled. "Shall we go over to their box and bid them a good evening?"

"I intend to, I assure you, but not just yet."

"Why not *now*?" Samuel wasn't in a humor to be patient.

Lovell raised an eyebrow. "Because a gentleman doesn't pounce upon a lady who entered her box less than five minutes ago. We'll wait until the end of the first act."

The end of the first act? "For God's sake, Lovell, that's a lifetime away."

"My, you are anxious to speak to Lady Emma, aren't you? I confess I'm relieved at it, Lymington. I was beginning to think your heart was impenetrable."

"It's nothing to do with my heart. It's just...it's the play. It's the dullest thing imaginable."

Lovell chuckled. "Think of it as an ambush, Lymington. Timing is of the essence."

Samuel huffed. "Ambushes are done *quickly*, Lovell."

But Lovell would not be moved. He settled comfortably back in his chair with the air of a man who'd made his plans, and was willing to bide his time until the moment he was waiting for arrived. "All in good time, Lymington. All in good time."

"When did you become such a pillar of patience and good sense, Lovell?" Samuel grumbled.

"Right around the time you lost your head over Lady Emma, cousin." Lovell grinned. "Now be quiet, won't you?"

Samuel shifted in his chair, muttering under his breath, but he knew Lovell was right. Since that night in a dark library in an infamous London brothel, from the moment he'd first heard Lady Emma's voice, he hardly recognized himself.

A few words in that smooth, soft whisper, and his wits had scattered. Then he'd seen her face, and the few wits he'd had left had fled after them—

"That's odd. Is Lady Emma leaving?"

Samuel's head shot up at Lovell's words, and what he saw made his fingers tighten around his walking stick. "Where the devil does she think she's going?"

"Easy, Lymington. I'm sure she'll return as soon as…for God's sake," Lovell hissed, when Samuel rose to his feet. "You're not going to chase her? You promised me no frontal assaults! Just wait until—"

But Samuel was done waiting. He was on his feet and striding from the box before Lovell had even finished his sentence.

Lady Emma had been walking away from him since their first dance together at Almack's.

Not this time. This time, he was going after her.

Chapter Twelve

"If you intend to escape me, Lady Emma, you'll have to run more quickly than that."

Samuel was still half a dozen paces behind her when the growl left his lips. She might have broken into a run then, just as he'd warned her to—she might have fled to her carriage and the protection of her enormous coachman, but instead she froze in the middle of the corridor as if roots had sprouted from the soles of her feet into the thick carpet below them, leaving her at his mercy.

Samuel was behind her in an instant, one arm snaking around her waist. He eased her back against his chest and pressed his lips to her ear. "Shame on you, my lady, leaving without even bidding me a good evening, and in such a hurry, too. Where are you going?"

He shouldn't be touching her, but hadn't years passed since that afternoon at the Royal Academy, when he'd told himself he wouldn't touch her again? Wouldn't stroke her silky skin, inhale the soft scent of vanilla that clung to her, that sweetness so impossible in the midst of the dirt and grime of London?

"Everywhere I've been today, I searched for you." Samuel pressed his nose to the delicious curve between her neck and shoulder, inhaling desperately. "Did you think you could avoid me, after our kiss in the rose garden? You should have known better, Emma."

On some hazy, distant level Samuel was aware he'd lost control of himself—that accosting a lady in a public corridor at Drury Lane Theatre with half the *ton* mere steps away was madness. Wasn't there some rule, some wise aphorism warning gentlemen not to pursue a lady when their blood was rushing in a heated frenzy through their veins, burning them from the inside?

If there was, Samuel didn't know it. He'd never needed such words of wisdom before, because he'd never, in all his thirty-four years, lost control of himself.

Until *her*.

Emma's breath was coming in short, sharp gasps, her slender back rising and falling against his chest. She said nothing, nor did she try to break loose from his hold, but her entire body was trembling, the coldness of her hand gripping his wrist tangible even through the fine kid of her glove.

Shame washed over Samuel, enough shame to make him relax his hold on her, yet not so much he'd let her escape him again. After a day in which he'd gone half-mad with longing for her, she was finally in his arms. He couldn't make himself let her go.

"My carriage," he muttered in her ear, and began striding down the corridor toward the staircase. Emma didn't fight him, or offer any resistance at all. If anyone happened to catch a glimpse of them, they'd see nothing remarkable, nothing untoward.

But Samuel knew Emma. Even in the short time they'd been acquainted he *understood* her, and uneasiness niggled at him as he escorted her down the staircase and through the entrance to the street beyond. Emma was many things, tempting and infuriating in equal parts, but she wasn't docile. If she was coming with him willingly, then something was wrong.

He handed her into his carriage, and took the seat on the bench across from her, determined to put some space between them, and not to say a word until she met his eyes. She shifted uncomfortably against the seat, fussing with her skirts and delaying the inevitable until at last she stilled, and raised her eyes to his.

Samuel sucked in a breath. Her face was as lovely as ever, but now he was close enough to notice the delicate purple smudges beneath her eyes, and all the words he'd meant to say to her froze on his tongue. What he said instead was, "You look fatigued, my lady."

"I am, rather. Yesterday and today have been…difficult."

Samuel struggled briefly with his reply, but he was done with the lies, half-truths, and subterfuge between them. "They might be less so if you spent fewer evenings at the Pink Pearl."

If she was shocked to discover he'd seen her there last night, she didn't show it. She didn't deny it. Her neutral masque never slipped, but now Samuel had seen beneath it, he was no longer fooled by her smooth façade.

"Poor Lady Tremaine was persuaded you were really ill yesterday, but then she didn't kiss you in the rose garden. For a lady suffering from such a dreadful malady, you kiss with great passion, Emma."

Samuel couldn't help a rush of fierce satisfaction as her masque slipped, and color surged into her cheeks. "I beg your pardon, my lord. If you recall, I had a headache earlier that—"

"I recall Lady Flora said so. I also recall thinking she was lying, to give you an excuse to refuse to walk with me." Samuel sat back against his seat, studying her. "I asked you a question yesterday, Lady Emma— about your friend Helena Reeves. Did you think I wouldn't notice that you never answered me?"

"No. I think you notice everything, Lord Lymington."

"Perhaps we're alike in that way," he murmured.

"In more than just that one way, I think."

Samuel thought so too, but he hadn't chased after her tonight to let her distract him a second time. "I spoke with Helena Reeves at the Pink Pearl last night. She told me a half-dozen lies, then sent me on my way."

"Oh? What lies were those, my lord?"

"She claimed she once served as your lady's maid, that she lost her place after some scoundrel seduced her, then fled to London and became a courtesan at the Pink Pearl." Samuel hadn't believed a word of it.

Surprise flickered over Emma's face, but she hid it quickly. "You seem skeptical, my lord, but you must be aware how often young girls are seduced, ruined, and then abandoned to a brutal fate in London."

"I'm aware, yes, but I'm also aware you were at the Pink Pearl last night and that you saw Helena Reeves. I suspect you told her to lie to me."

"I see. Did you overhear a lady asking Helena to lie, and decide her voice was exactly like mine? Not a voice a man forgets—that was your evidence last time, I think."

"No. Not this time."

"What do your base your suspicions on, then?"

Samuel didn't answer. Hardly having once taken his eyes off Emma since they'd met offered him one advantage. The slight uptick of her chin, the near infinitesimal tightening of her lips...he saw them, and knew what they meant.

She was lying.

He didn't know why, but it wouldn't do her any good.

Not with him.

"I know you were there last night, Emma. I arrived just after you left the library, and I followed you down the street. I saw you get into your grandmother's carriage a few blocks away from the Pink Pearl."

"You saw *me*, or you saw a lady in a hood in the street outside the Pink Pearl, and though you didn't see her face, you assumed she must be me?"

"No." His voice was quiet. "You weren't wearing your hood this time. I saw your face, Emma. I also saw your hands."

Silence, so sudden and profound Samuel could feel it against his skin, like a hazy mist enveloping him. "Your coachman leapt down to open the door, but you got to it first. You reached up your hand to open it, and braced your other hand on the side of the door. There wasn't much light, but enough so I saw them, Emma. I saw the scars on your hands."

She turned away to hide her face from him, but it was already too late. Samuel had seen it, a shift, the subtle change in her expression, another tiny crack in her façade.

"I recall thinking it was curious I hadn't once seen you without gloves before that night. But it wasn't curious, was it? It was by design."

He leaned back, away from her, away from the light streaming in through the carriage window, far enough so his face was shrouded in shadow.

And he waited.

She swallowed, her pale throat working, and twisted her hands in her lap, as if she could erase the scars by rubbing the soft silk over them, like marks on a child's slate.

Since that first night at Almack's, Samuel had wanted to shatter her composure, to see an honest reaction from her, but as the movement of her hands grew more urgent, more panicked, he found he couldn't bear it.

"Stop it, Emma." He caught the tips of her gloved fingers, stilling her. "Give me your hands."

"No." She jerked away from him, and folded her hands tightly in her lap. "The scars are...they don't matter. Are you aware, my lord, that Caroline Francis is missing?"

Samuel blinked. "Missing?"

"Yes. Helena says Caroline has been...entertaining a gentleman since the season began—a nobleman who prefers private engagements."

"What nobleman?" Samuel demanded, once Emma's words had sunk in. "Who is he?"

"I don't know that. Helena hasn't seen his face. She knows only that he fetched Caroline from the Pink Pearl yesterday. Caroline was meant to return last night, but she never did, and no one has seen her since."

"It's the same man," Samuel muttered. "It has to be."

"What man, my lord?"

Samuel wasn't certain he wanted Lady Emma knowing his family's secrets, but this business had taken a sudden, ominous turn. If Caroline was missing, the only way he could get her story was from Helena Reeves's lips. He needed to speak to Helena again, and he needed her to tell him the truth this time.

For that, he'd have to go through Lady Emma Crosby.

Samuel didn't believe for a moment that Helena had been Emma's lady's maid, but the truth about the connection between the two women no longer mattered. What did matter was it seemed not a single word would cross Helena's lips without Emma's permission.

"The two housemaids I mentioned, who went missing from my country estate in Kent." Samuel dragged a hand through his hair, his throat tight. "The first, Amy Townshend, disappeared last August, and then Kitty Yardley six weeks later. When Caroline vanished in January, we feared the same fate had befallen her."

"But then she turned up at the Pink Pearl."

"Yes. I brought Lovell to London for the season for Lady Flora, but I also came for Caroline Francis. I hoped she could tell me something about the circumstances under which she left Lymington House, and how she ended up in a London brothel. The scoundrel who seduced her—"

"Is very likely the same man who took Amy and Kitty, and the same man who has Caroline now."

"I don't see how it could be anyone else. But you seem to know a great deal about Caroline's business." And, by default, a great deal about his family's business. "Why is that, Lady Emma?"

She gave him a tight smile. "Helena Reeves is Caroline's only friend at the Pink Pearl, Lord Lymington. Caroline has confided in Helena, and Helena has confided in me."

Damn it. That's what he was afraid of. "Listen to me. If Helena knows Caroline's secrets, then she's in as much danger as Caroline is."

Emma hesitated, then to Samuel's shock she reached out and grasped his hand. "I need your help, my lord. If you agree to assist me, I'll return the favor."

Until she asked, Samuel would have claimed he'd never help Lady Emma, who'd caused him nothing but trouble since he'd first laid eyes on her. But all at once, helping her was the only thing that mattered to him. "What can I do?"

"I need to see Helena at once, but Madame Marchand knows I want to persuade her to leave the Pink Pearl. As you can imagine, Madame doesn't look upon me with a friendly eye. You, however—"

"You want me to go to the Pink Pearl and fetch Helena for you."

"Yes, but I'm afraid it won't be as simple as you imagine. Helena doesn't know or trust you, and she's learned to be wary of noblemen. She won't go with you."

"What, then?"

"Go to the Pink Pearl, and, ah…engage Helena's companionship for the evening. You can be certain Madame Marchand will be delighted to accommodate you. Once you have Helena alone, tell her Lady Emma wants her to come to the library, then return to your carriage at once and wait for us. I can persuade Helena to come with me, but we'll need to leave quickly once she's out. Will you help me?"

"That depends, Lady Emma, on whether or not *you'll* help *me*. Once you free Helena from Madame Marchand's clutches, I want to speak with her. I don't mean her any harm, but I insist she tell me everything Caroline told her. The truth this time, and every word of it."

Emma inclined her head. "She will."

Samuel studied her, looking for any sign of deception. "Don't lie to me, Lady Emma."

"She will. I promise it, my lord." She met his gaze without flinching, with truth in the deep, blue depths of her eyes.

"Well, then. It looks as if we're paying another visit to the Pink Pearl."

* * * *

Don't lie to me, Lady Emma.

The words echoed in Emma's head as she waited in the carriage after Lord Lymington had disappeared inside the Pink Pearl.

Lord Lovell was wrong. Every word out of Lord Lymington's mouth *didn't* sound like a command. He'd said those word to her in a soft, almost pleading voice, one that made Emma wish she could give him the truth he asked for.

But it was only that, a wish, destined to remain unfulfilled, no matter how much her heart urged her to tell him all she knew.

She now believed Lord Lovell was innocent of any crime, despite Caroline's accusations, but she couldn't be certain the real culprit wasn't another member of Samuel's family. What if Lady Lymington had somehow had a hand in it? And what of Felix Humphries? He had unlimited access to Lymington House. At this point she couldn't even rule out Lady Lovell. It seemed unlikely she'd implicate her innocent son in a crime, but Emma had seen wickeder things than even that.

After twenty minutes had passed, Emma left the carriage and made her way through the back garden to the terrace doors. She peered through the glass into the library, her hand on the latch and a prayer on her lips that Helena was there, and had unlocked the door.

She sucked in a breath, then let it out again in a heavy gust when the latch turned in her hand. "Letty?"

A shape detached itself from the deep shadows in one corner of the room. Helena darted forward and threw herself into Emma's arms. "Emma? Oh, thank goodness you're here. Caroline's gone, and Madame Marchand is on a tear, and Lord Lymington—"

"Shh. I know, dearest, I know." Emma stroked a hand down Helena's back. "But it's all right now, Letty. It's going to be all—"

Emma was interrupted by a faint click, and both she and Helena jerked their heads toward the library door. Light spilled through the gap, illuminating a tall, spare figure. "You should know better than to make promises you can't keep, Emma."

Emma froze at the sound of that cold voice, dread overwhelming her at the sight of the narrow chin and sharp, beaky nose that haunted her nightmares.

She was no longer the same helpless, frightened girl she'd been that awful night five years earlier, when she'd left the Pink Pearl behind her, but no matter how old she became, or how many years she put between that night and the present, Madame Marchand's voice still had the power to make her shudder with horror. No sooner would she hear that harsh voice than the memories would come flooding back, as if some hidden lever in her brain had been wrenched, warning her to flee.

"How remarkable, Emma, that you imagine you can just stroll into my establishment and leave with one of my young ladies." Madame Marchand pointed a bony finger at Emma. "I've already lost Caroline. Do you suppose I'll let Helena go, as well?"

Helena's shoulders hunched, and she shrank into herself. "I beg your pardon, Madame. We were just—"

"Such disloyalty, Helena." Madame Marchand tutted. "I didn't believe it when Clarissa told me you'd been sneaking in and out of the library, yet here you are, and after all I've done for you."

"Madame, I—"

Madame Marchand cut her off. "Get out, Helena. I'll deal with you later. As for you, Emma, this will be your last clandestine visit to the Pink Pearl. Charles won't be available to assist you anymore."

A hoarse gasp tore from Helena's throat. "What do you mean? What have you done to Charles?"

Madame Marchand didn't even spare her a glance. "I told you to *get out*."

Emma's stomach lurched as she stepped between Madame Marchand and Helena, but by some miracle, her voice was steady. "Go through the terrace doors behind me, Helena, and out to the front. Lord Lymington's carriage is there, waiting for you."

Light filtered from the open doorway behind her, leaving Madame's face in shadows, but there was no mistaking the steely thread of menace in her voice. "Upstairs this instant, Helena. Don't make me tell you again."

Helena looked between Emma and Madame Marchand, her face a chalky white. Madame's cold gaze remained fixed on Emma, but Emma met Helena's eyes, begging without words for Helena to do as she said, and leave this place now, before she no longer had the choice.

"The seed pearls sewn into that silk gown on your back were very dear, Helena," Madame Marchand said in a matter-of-fact tone, as if she had chests of seed pearls in her bedchamber upstairs, casks of precious jewels, and stacks of golden guineas secreted in every hidden corner of the Pink Pearl, and the loss of these were of little consequence to her.

But they were of grave consequence to Helena.

"Altogether the gown with the trimmings, gloves, and headdress cost me a small fortune," Madame Marchand went on, circling gradually closer to Helena. "Tell me, Helena. Can you pay me what is owed for your ensemble tonight?"

Emma's lips twisted with disgust. Of course, Madame Marchand's first thought was for the money. "Don't listen to her, Helena."

Madame Marchand shrugged, unconcerned. "You may do as you choose, of course, Helena, but if you set foot outside that door, I'll have you taken up for theft before you've taken two steps toward Lord Lymington's carriage."

"Emma?" Helena cast a stricken look at Emma, her chin wobbling.

"It's all right, Helena," Emma said evenly, her gaze on Madame Marchand. "Lady Clifford will bring you your money tomorrow, Madame."

"By tomorrow, Helena will be locked in the debtor's prison at Newgate. Have you ever been inside Newgate, Helena? It's rather unpleasant, I'm afraid."

Madame Marchand's smile chilled Emma's blood. "Helena, listen to me. She's only trying to frighten you—"

"If the idea of Newgate doesn't appeal to you, Helena, you may return to your bedchamber like a good girl, and we'll forget this incident ever happened."

Helena was inching toward the door that led back to the hallway, tears streaming down her cheeks. "I'm sorry, Emma."

"*Helena!*"

Emma darted after her, but Madame Marchand stepped in front of the door, blocking her way. Before Emma could jerk back, Madame grabbed her chin and tilted her face toward the light, studying the angles and curves as if calculating the value of it. "Ah, that face."

The grip of those cold, claw-like fingers made Emma cringe away, but Madame held on, her fingernails leaving deep scratches in Emma's skin. "Such a beauty. I would have made you one of London's greatest courtesans. You might have been a legend, Emma, but you destroyed my plans and your future with a foolish swipe of a blade."

Emma opened her mouth, but no words came.

Madame Marchand released her chin, but she snatched Emma's hand in hers, stripped off her glove and shook her head over the scars. "It's a great pity, but then you never had the temperament of a proper whore. For all your loveliness, you've never been pleasing, Emma."

Pleasing. By that, Madame meant obedient, and Emma had never been that. Not then, and not now. "Yes, if only I'd been quiet when your lord pressed a blade to my throat, instead of making such a fuss. After all, no gentleman wants an uncooperative harlot."

Madame Marchand smiled, but her face was as cold as ice. "You'd be surprised. Tell me, when did you become Lord Lymington's plaything? I can't help but be impressed. A marquess, no less, and a wealthy one at that. I'm *proud* of you, Emma."

Madame's words sank in, rushing like poison through Emma's veins.

Madame Marchand laughed, but it was an ugly sound, edged in cruelty. "Ah, still so haughty, despite your humble beginnings. What you've never understood, Emma, is that once a woman has been a whore, she will always be a whore. No matter how Lady Clifford might dress you up, or how many marquesses you charm with your pretty face, you'll never be anything but a whore."

Emma opened her mouth, but none of the denials inside her head made it to her lips. Something was there, cold and hard, blocking her throat, stealing her voice.

"I'm afraid Helena will be unavailable for the rest of the night, both to you and to Lord Lymington." Madame Marchand nodded at the terrace doors. "Do feel free to go out the way you came in, Emma."

Madame Marchand didn't bother to wait for a reply. She turned, the hems of her magnificent bronze silk gown sweeping across the floor, and left Emma in the dark, cold library, more alone than she'd ever been in her life.

Chapter Thirteen

Emma was right about Madame Marchand. The bawd had been delighted to turn Helena Reeves over to Samuel for the evening. Helena had been less pleased to find herself at his mercy, but when he explained he'd come at Lady Emma's request, she'd allowed him to escort her to the library.

The entire maneuver went as smoothly as Emma predicted. For a sheltered young lady who'd never left Somerset, she had an oddly well-developed talent for intrigue.

When Samuel reemerged from the Pink Pearl after securing Helena, Emma was hovering beside his carriage, her anxious gaze fixed on the entrance. She waited only long enough for his nod, and then she was gone, the hems of her hooded cloak dragging along the ground as she vanished into the darkened garden behind the townhouse.

A strange emotion welled in Samuel's chest as he watched her go, a sort of dull heaviness he didn't understand. He knew only that the Pink Pearl loomed very large, and Emma looked very small as she was swallowed into its depths.

There was nothing for him to do but wait for her return, the darkness pressing in on him as one moment dragged into the next, until it seemed as if they'd spun into an eternity.

When Emma did emerge from the brothel's back garden, she was alone. No Helena Reeves, despite Emma's promises.

Samuel couldn't read her expression, as her face was hidden inside her hood, but she cast more than one glance over her shoulder as she hurried toward him, her skirts clutched in her hands. When she reached the carriage, she climbed inside without a word, and without sparing Samuel a glance.

He climbed in after her, pulling the carriage door closed behind him, but he made no move to signal his driver. Instead, he turned to Emma, who'd tucked herself tightly into the opposite corner of the bench, her head turned away from him. "Where is Helena Reeves?"

No answer. It was as if he hadn't spoken at all.

Samuel tried again. "I left Helena waiting for you in the library, just as you asked. Where is she?"

Still nothing, or at least, not an answer. Emma made a sound—a strangled breath, or a sigh—but she didn't speak.

Slow anger began to burn in Samuel's chest. "We had an agreement, Emma. I trusted you to keep your promise." Foolishly, it seemed. He should have known better than to believe a word she said, given that she'd lied to him before. But somehow, this time her lie tore at him in a way Samuel could never have imagined, had never thought possible.

Had he truly believed a few kisses in a rose garden would change anything between them? He was as ridiculous as every other gentleman who'd fallen victim to her red lips, her dark blue eyes. "I'm waiting for an explanation, Emma."

Emma gazed down at her hands folded tightly in her lap, her deep hood hiding her expression, and remained silent, as if Samuel wasn't even there.

"Nothing to say, my lady?" His harsh voiced seemed far too loud inside the closed carriage. "No wild justifications this time, no lies or excuses?"

Emma turned toward him with her lips parted. "I-I…"

Samuel waited, but when nothing more emerged, his last shred of patience snapped. "Take off that hood, and look at me," he growled, pushing her hood back. She tried to flinch away from him, but he caught her chin in his hand and turned her face to his. "I did as you asked, and you—"

The words froze on Samuel's lips, and his stomach dropped.

All the color was gone from her cheeks, her eyes wide, dark pools in that pale face, fear and shame in their blue depths.

He stared at her, stunned. The vulnerability he'd seen in her face in Lady Tremaine's rose garden, that glimpse of the truth that had made it impossible for him not to kiss her, had been only the barest hint of what she was hiding from the world, a mere shadow of the darkness there.

This was what lurked beneath those devastating eyes, that charming smile.

An overwhelming, inexplicable ocean of pain.

Dear God, what had happened inside the Pink Pearl?

A thousand different questions leapt to Samuel's lips at once, but he didn't ask them. He said nothing, his fingers gentling on her face, and his thumb creeping up to stroke her cheekbone.

The anguish in her eyes, those scars on her hands, the remnants of a painful, violent past—how could they belong to Lady Emma Crosby, the sheltered, indulged daughter of the Earl of Crosby? How could they belong to London's reigning belle?

Samuel's gaze dropped to her hands. They were buried inside the folds of her cloak, covered by the tight silk of her gloves. Hidden, always hidden, but he could see them still, the thin scars etched into her pale flesh. Now he'd seen them once, he could never forget they were there, no matter how she tried to disguise them under layers of linen and silk.

Samuel didn't think about what he did next. He didn't plan it. He simply reached for her, his movements slow so as not to frighten her, and lifted her into his lap.

Emma went rigid in his arms. "I-I can't—"

"Shhh." Samuel cupped her neck in warm, gentle fingers. "It's all right."

It wasn't, not at first, but gradually Emma's hectic breaths slowed, and she began to relax against him, the tension draining from her body bit by bit, until at last she went limp in his arms, and let her cheek rest against his chest.

Samuel closed his eyes then, a long, slow breath leaving his body. He rested his chin on her head, the soft, golden wisps of her hair tickling his skin, and let the truth break over him like a wave unfurling onto the sand, no less inevitable for the slow, gentle drift of it.

I could hold her like this forever.

He traced her jaw, then tipped her face up to his with a finger under her chin. He waited for one breath, two, to give her a chance to pull away, but she only gazed up at him, her blue eyes soft, her lips open, and just like that, he was lost. Time narrowed and contracted until there was just the two of them, her face tipped up to his, their breath mingling.

He pressed his mouth to her forehead and let them linger there, his heart pounding at the sensation of her smooth skin against his lips. He stroked his thumb down her cheek and teased it across her lower lip, the merest brush against that tender skin, once, and then again, and then his lips were on hers, his kiss gentle, coaxing her until she opened her mouth with a soft moan.

He kissed her deeply then, his hands sinking into her hair as he urged her mouth against his, coaxing her lips apart so he could slip inside and tangle his tongue against hers, each slick caress driving him wild until he tore his mouth away at last, his chest heaving. "Emma?"

He met her gaze, and found her looking up at him, her eyes huge with wonder. Then she reached forward with a shy finger and traced the outline of his lips, following the upward curve as he smiled down at her, his heart leaping when she smiled back at him.

"Give me your hand," he murmured, his fingers closing around hers.

She shook her head, but she didn't resist when he drew her hand closer, cradling it in his palm. Samuel traced his thumb over the tiny button of her glove and slowly—so slowly and carefully—slid the button through the silken loop.

She gazed down at his fingers wrapped around hers as if in a daze, as if she'd never seen such a thing before. Her hands were trembling, but her chin rose, and somehow, that little act of bravery made Samuel's heart melt in his chest.

He didn't wait, couldn't wait until he'd bared her skin. He caught her slender hand in his and raised it to his lips, the warm, smooth slide of silk against his mouth sending hot sparks of desire spiraling in his belly.

A tiny sigh left her lips at the caress. "M-madame Marchand was there, and she—"

"Shhh." Samuel didn't want to talk about Madame Marchand, or the Pink Pearl, or Helena Reeves, or Caroline Francis.

He didn't want to talk at all.

* * * *

It made no sense, that his lips could be so gentle.

The firm line of them, the sardonic curl at the corner of them, the grim twist of them...they should be hard, shouldn't they? Demanding. Punishing, even.

How could she have known? How could she ever have imagined how soft they'd be, the sensuous slide of them against the thin silk of her glove?

"Show me your hands, Emma." His voice had dropped to a whisper.

Emma did her best suppress the delicious throb of awareness that uncurled in her belly at that low purr. She didn't move as he took her hand, his touch tender as he began to slowly draw off her glove.

There was a part of Emma that wanted to tug free of him—to snatch her hand from his grasp before he could see what she'd tried for so many years to hide, even from herself, but there was another part of her that was weary, so weary of cowering, that wanted someone to see....

No. Not someone. *Him*. Only him.

She watched, entranced, as he slid the smooth silk down her arm, and she let him, she *let* him, even as she knew what he'd find...

Lower, and lower still, his touch firm, her skin learning the shape of his fingertips. His gaze held hers as he slid each of her fingers free of the silk glove, one by one, his movements languid, unhurried, until her bare hand rested in his gloved one. "There," he whispered, tracing the pattern of lines on the back of her hand.

The scars were faded now, but one had only to look carefully to see them, her brutal past written across her hand, a piece of her history carved into her flesh.

"Your hands are no less beautiful because they bear these scars." He brought her bared hand to his lips and pressed a warm, lingering kiss there. "Have your admirers made you ashamed of them, Emma? Is that why you hide them?"

It was a kiss, only a kiss, a brush of his lips against her hand, but within seconds, Emma's head was swimming. "I...no one..." she whispered, but how could she tell him, how could she explain that no man had ever seen these scars before him? No man but the one who'd inflicted them, and he...he...

But she didn't have to tell him. She didn't have to say a word, because Samuel read the truth in her face. "No man has ever seen them, touched them, kissed them. No man but *me*."

Emma shivered at the possessiveness in his voice, the fierce satisfaction in his face as he bent over her hand and traced the tip of his tongue over the deepest of the scars. "This is part of who you are, Emma. You have no reason to be ashamed of them."

Everything inside Emma ached at his words. She wanted so badly to believe him, but she'd earned the nightmares that came with those scars, had lived those awful moments over and over again, each time she closed her eyes.

Samuel saw the doubt in her face—or perhaps it wasn't doubt, but the fragile hope that rose in her breast at his words—and he turned her hand over and pressed his lips to the center of her palm.

Emma's breath caught. His gaze darted to her face at the soft gasp, his dark eyes holding her captive as, one by one, he pressed kisses to each of her fingertips before trailing his lips up the tender skin of her inner arm.

Emma's own lips parted when the tip of his tongue grazed her skin, but the kiss was over in an instant, leaving only a hint of heat behind. His teasing mouth wandered from her forearm to the curve of her elbow, and he buried his face in the sensitive hollow, a low moan on his lips as he breathed deeply, taking her scent inside him.

She didn't realize how badly she wanted to touch him until, as if in a dream she watched her hand settle gently on the head bent over her arm, and she dragged her fingers through the hair at the back of his neck.

"Oh." Emma let her fingertips drift through the dark strands, her lips parted in wonder at the silky waves tickling her fingers. It seemed impossible such a hard man could have such softness to him, such unexpected tenderness.

Hadn't she thought him a hard man, once? Yes, but it seemed a long time ago now. As she drew her fingers through the impossible softness of his hair, Emma could no longer recall why she should have. "How can it be so soft? It's like dark velvet.."

Samuel had gone still at her touch, but her quiet exclamation of surprise made him raise his head. He gazed at her for a breathless moment, eyes glittering, the gray iris drowning in a sea of black.

"Emma." He gathered her close, holding her against his hard, broad chest as his lips closed over hers in one drugging kiss after another, everywhere he could reach, her skin leaping to attention under the caress of his mouth, as if it had come alive for the first time under his touch. His lips ghosted over the curve of her shoulder to her collarbone, shivers rising in their wake. He lingered at the hollow of her throat, his teasing caresses making her gasp before he dropped a string of sweet kisses over her chin and jaw.

His hands were shaking when he drew back at last and looked into her eyes. "You don't need to hide your scars, Emma. Not from me, and not from anyone."

He didn't give her a chance to answer him before he took her lips again, and Emma didn't allow herself to think of anything but the feel of his hungry mouth on hers, his tongue prodding gently at the seam of her lips. She never even thought to refuse him, but opened for him at once, her hands coming up to rest on his chest as if touching him were the most natural thing in the world.

"You even taste like vanilla." His voice was low and husky, his lips curving against hers in a smile Emma knew was sweet, because she could taste it on his lips.

He wrapped his hands around her waist, squeezing gently as he eased closer, the long, hard length of his thigh brushing against hers. His gaze moved over her face, and then, with one quick flick of his fingers, he plucked at the blue ribbon woven into the locks of her hair.

Dozens of pins were hiding under the simple ribbon, all of them poking into her head and holding the heavy waves in place. Emma raised a hand to her head. "Those absurd curls took hours to pin in place, my lord."

He let out a low chuckle. "I beg your pardon, madam. Does it soothe your injured feelings if I confess removing your ribbon didn't have the result I'd hoped for?"

"Hmmm. Perhaps it would. What did you intend?"

He kissed her temple, then pressed his mouth to her ear. "For your hair to fall in a cascade around your shoulders, of course." He gave one of the offending locks a gentle tug. "If I'd known it would refuse, I wouldn't have bothered with the ribbon at all. Still," he murmured, his voice lowering to a deep drawl as he toyed with the loose wave in his fingers. "It wasn't an entirely wasted effort."

He touched the errant curl to his lips, his eyes darkening as he took in the heightened color in her cheeks, the fluttering pulse at the base of her throat. "The first time I saw you at Almack's, the chandeliers turned your hair to pale gold, like a halo around your head."

Emma gazed at him, mesmerized by his warm eyes, his husky voice.

"Then I heard your voice again, and do you know what my first thought was, Emma?"

Emma swallowed. "That you'd heard my voice before?"

"No. That *should* have been my first thought, but instead, all I could think was that yours was the only face I could ever imagine living up to the promise of that voice."

Emma caught her breath as his words moved through her, into the empty, aching place that lived inside her heart. Men had paid her compliments before, had extolled the beauties of her face, her blue eyes, but their words had never meant anything to Emma. When she'd looked at her reflection in the glass, she'd only ever seen ugliness looking back at her.

But Samuel's words touched her in a way no man's words ever had before, as if through his eyes she could at last see herself as she really was. Not as beautiful, but as...real.

Emma couldn't speak, but she rested her hands on his chest, her palms flat against his waistcoat so she might feel the beat of his heart against her palm, the rise and fall of his chest with his every ragged breath.

The two of them remained like that for long, quiet moments, their breath mingling, until Samuel let out a resigned sigh, and eased her from his lap onto the carriage bench. He didn't kiss her again after that, but he held her hand cradled in his as his coachman drove them through the dark streets of London.

He made no move to release her when the carriage came to a stop in front of Lady Crosby's townhouse, and Emma made no move to pull away. Her

hand felt small wrapped up in his much larger one, and she realized with
a start that he was the only man she'd ever known who made her feel safe.

Or perhaps for the first time ever, she just felt like herself.

Finally, he stirred, and opened the carriage door. He assisted her down,
and escorted her to the entrance of the townhouse. "Good night, my lady,"
he murmured, pressing a soft, final kiss to the inside of her wrist.

He turned to go, but Emma stopped him with a hand on his arm. "As
soon as Helena's free of Madame Marchand, she'll tell you all she knows
about Caroline Francis. I won't go back on my word to you, Samuel."

He looked down at her, his eyes soft. "I know you won't."

The entryway was dark and silent when Emma entered, but she heard
footsteps coming down the hallway as she closed the door behind her,
and a moment later, Daniel appeared. "Helena, lass? Did you fetch her?"

"No." At mention of Helena, the warmth Samuel had kindled inside
Emma cooled to a dull chill. "Madame Marchand put a stop to it before
I could get Helena out."

Daniel grunted. "Lady Clifford, then?"

Emma didn't like to involve Lady Clifford, but there was no way she'd
leave Helena at the Pink Pearl to face Madame Marchand's wrath. She
shuddered as she recalled the way Madame had glared at Helena, the
coldness in her voice when she'd ordered Helena out of the room.

"Yes, I think we must." Madame Marchand wouldn't relinquish Helena
easily, but she *would* relinquish her. Even Madame didn't have the courage
to refuse Lady Clifford. "You'll go?"

"Aye." Daniel gave Emma's shoulder an awkward pat in a rare show
of affection, then he was gone, the heavy thud of his boots on the stone
steps echoing in Emma's ears.

Chapter Fourteen

"Let me have a look at you, my dear." Lady Crosby took both of Emma's hands in hers and stood back to consider her. "It was rather brilliant of you to adopt that shade of blue for the season. It's lovely on you. If I could coax that frown from your pretty face, I think you just might do."

"Am I frowning?" Emma peeked into the pier glass, and found a blue-eyed lady with a creased brow and downturned mouth staring back at her. "I didn't realize."

"You've been frowning since you woke this morning, my dear—in between frequent dreamy smiles, that is. I do believe I've strained my neck, trying to keep pace with your moods." Lady Crosby regarded her with kind brown eyes. "Did, ah...did something happen with Lord Lymington last night?"

Emma opened her mouth to deny that Samuel—that is, Lord Lymington—had a thing to do with it, but she couldn't make the lie leave her lips. *That* had never happened before. Given the dozens of lies she'd be obliged to tell before this business was done, it was worrying, indeed.

It was all Samuel's fault, with his lovely words last night, and his even lovelier kisses. Emma had caught herself with her fingers pressed to her mouth dozens of times today, recalling the delirious brush of his lips against hers, his whispered words in her ear.

Who would have guessed such a gruff gentleman hid such generous passion, such gentle tenderness under his stern appearance? The sweetness of him, the sincerity, the unexpected kindness...

Emma sucked in a trembling breath. Flora had warned her Samuel wasn't at all the haughty lord he appeared to be at first. Emma would have done well to listen to her.

How had Flora put it, again, that first night at Almack's?

He's blunt, but he rather grows on one....

That was all well and good, but it had never occurred to Emma he might grow on *her.*

No gentleman ever had before, yet here they were.

Samuel had been creeping his way under her skin since their dance together the first night of the season. He'd been unforgivably rude to her that night, every inch the high-handed, arrogant marquess, but it seemed she *liked* arrogant marquesses, because she hadn't been able to stop thinking about him since.

She'd tried over and over to convince herself Lord Lymington wasn't any different than any other gentleman, but it was no use. He *was* different. He was *honest,* and somehow, his honesty had compelled hers.

And that...well, that changed everything, because it made it impossible for her to lie to herself any longer. He'd slid under her defenses with all that absurd honesty, and now he was clinging there like a prickly saddle burr. She hadn't any idea how to tear him loose, and worst of all, after last night she wasn't sure she *wanted* to.

Not anymore.

Lady Crosby raised an eyebrow at Emma's silence. "You hardly had a chance to leave our theater box before Lord Lymington leapt to his feet and went after you, Emma. I confess I'd been hoping the two of you had negotiated a truce."

"It was more of an, er...suspension of hostilities than a truce." If making her laugh, and tugging her ribbons loose, and kissing her senseless could be called a suspension of hostilities, that is.

Emma tweaked a curl into place, and made an effort to smooth her brow and will the blush from her cheeks before turning back to Lady Crosby. It wouldn't do to appear at Vauxhall Gardens looking like a cross between a lovestruck schoolgirl and a thundercloud. "There. Is that better?"

Lady Crosby smiled. "Much better, yes. Come along, then. I don't like to keep Lady Flora and Lady Silvester waiting." The four of them were sharing a supper box at Vauxhall Gardens this evening, along with Lord Lovell, Lady Lovell and Mr. Humphries, Lady Lymington, and... Lord Lymington.

Samuel.

Just thinking of him made Emma flush with humiliating heat once again. Dash it, of all the times she could have chosen to become besotted with a gentleman, this was the worst.

But that was the trouble with infatuations. They were rarely convenient.

Caroline Francis was still missing, Helena was trapped inside the Pink Pearl with an infuriated Madame Marchand, and a mysterious nobleman with a missing pendant—a nobleman who might or might not be a murderer—was running loose in London.

And here *she* was, mooning over Lord Lymington.

She sighed as she draped a thin silk shawl over her shoulders, and followed Lady Crosby from the drawing room down to the carriage, which was waiting in front of the townhouse. Daniel Brixton stood beside the open door, ready to hand them in. "Good evening, Daniel."

"Evening, lass."

Daniel's voice was as gruff as ever, but a tiny wrinkle between his brows disturbed his usual dark impassivity, and Emma's stomach gave an uneasy lurch. She'd seen that wrinkle before, and knew what it meant.

Something *else* had gone wrong.

"What is it?" She paused, her hand on his arm. "What's happened?"

Daniel jerked his head toward the carriage. "Ye'll find out soon enough."

Emma's heart gave an anxious thump. She leapt into the carriage without waiting for him to hand her in, but stumbled back before taking her usual seat.

Someone was already there.

A gloved hand grabbed hers to steady her. "Careful, dearest. Here, sit beside me."

"Lady Clifford?" Emma's knees felt suddenly wobbly, and she dropped clumsily onto the carriage bench. They hadn't made any plans to meet today, and Lady Clifford wasn't the impulsive sort. If she was here, then something was very wrong, indeed.

Lady Clifford nodded to Daniel to close the carriage door and smiled a greeting at Lady Crosby before she turned to Emma. "I've got news, and I warn you, dearest. You're not going to like it."

Emma drew her wrap tighter around her shoulders as a chill rushed over her skin. "It's not Sophia, or Cecilia or Georgiana?" She'd been staying with Lady Crosby these past few months, preparing for Lady Emma Crosby's appearance in London society, and had hardly seen her friends at all in that time.

"No, no. They're all very well. It's, ah…it's Helena, Emma."

Emma's stomach dropped, and for one sickening moment the carriage seemed to tilt underneath her. "Tell me."

Lady Clifford sighed. "I went to have a word with Madame Marchand this morning, and she informed me, with a singularly unattractive degree of satisfaction, that Helena had some sort of disagreement with Lord Peabody at the Pink Pearl last night."

Oh, no. *No.*

Emma could well imagine what sort of disagreement Lady Clifford meant. Helena had objected to Lord Peabody's boot heel to her shin, or his hands wrapped around her neck. "What happened? What did he do to her?"

"It's not what he did to her—well, not entirely, anyway. It's what she did to him, deserved as it likely was."

Emma closed her eyes, praying it wasn't as bad as she feared. Helena had a temper, much as Emma herself did. Lady Clifford had taught Emma how to control hers, but Helena was like a wild thing when threatened, striking out at everything in her path.

That animal instinct for survival was how she'd endured for this long.

"Helena clawed Lord Peabody's face, Emma. Her nails left bloody scratches on his cheeks." Lady Clifford shook her head. "Lord Peabody's terribly vain, as you know, and he wasn't inclined to be forgiving. Madame Marchand has sent her away for good this time. Helena won't be returning to the Pink Pearl."

"Lord Peabody provoked her!" Emma cried, but she knew very well it wouldn't make a bit of difference that Lord Peabody had no doubt heartily deserved a clawing. Oh, he'd earned those bloody scratches, but what was the point in saying so?

He had all the power, and Helena none.

Then another thought struck her, and a cold shudder gripped her.

Madame Marchand had done this on purpose.

She'd been furious with both Emma and Helena when she caught them in the library last night. What better way to punish them both than by turning Helena over to a vicious lord with a penchant for violence?

Madame was well aware Helena wouldn't tolerate Lord Peabody's abuse—that she'd fight back, and once she did, it gave Madame the perfect excuse to toss Helena out onto the street. Madame wanted to be rid of her, and handing her over to Lord Peabody was a quick, efficient way to accomplish it.

This was no coincidence, and no accident.

"It doesn't matter what Lord Peabody did, Emma," Lady Clifford said. "You know that as well as I do. The moment he sets foot inside the Pink Pearl, he may do whatever he likes. Helena does not enjoy the same freedom."

Emma fell back against the squabs, a numb haze falling over her. "I tried to tell her, to warn her not to—" She trailed off, realizing too late that Lady Clifford knew nothing of her visits to the Pink Pearl.

Perhaps her ladyship had suspected it all along, though, because instead of scolding Emma, she squeezed her hand.

Emma squeezed back, struggling to quell her rising panic. "I should have made her come with me. I've been to the Pink Pearl over and over again. I never should have let her stay there."

But she'd been too busy kissing Samuel to think about Helena, hadn't she? Now Helena would be made to pay for Emma's foolishness, her cowardice.

Lady Clifford sighed. "I have people looking for her."

"But you haven't found her."

"Not yet, no."

It wouldn't be easy. Helena knew every dark street and filthy alcove in the rookeries. She could choose to make herself elusive if she wished. Emma could only pray Lady Clifford's men would find her before the man who'd taken Caroline began to suspect Helena knew his secrets, and found her himself.

"I debated whether or not to even tell you this, Emma. Even now, I'm not certain I've made the right choice, but I felt you needed to know we no longer have anyone inside the Pink Pearl to assist us."

A sob caught in Emma's throat. "I'll find Helena, my lady. I'll search until I—"

"No, you won't. This business with Lymington House isn't over, Emma. It's taken us weeks to pull it together, and we won't get another chance at it." Lady Clifford's voice was as calm as ever, but there was an unmistakable edge to it that spoke more clearly than her words.

They were moving on as planned, with or without Helena.

They had no choice.

Lady Crosby slid her hand into Emma's empty one, cold inside her glove. "Lady Clifford is right, Emma. Think of those poor girls that have gone missing."

"Missing, at best. At worst, they're dead, and they won't be the last to meet such a disastrous fate if we don't put an end to whatever evil is unfolding at Lymington House. The servants there are in no less danger for Helena's having gone missing, Emma."

The carriage came to an abrupt stop then. Emma peered out the window, and saw they'd arrived at Vauxhall Gardens. A row of fine carriages was lined up in front of the gate at Kennington Lane, ready to disgorge their elegant passengers.

"Look at me, Emma." Lady Clifford lay a hand on Emma's arm to get her attention. "You're to go on just as you have been. Is that understood?"

"Yes, my lady."

"Very good. Go on, then. Lady Silvester and Lady Flora will be looking for you." Lady Clifford retreated into the heavier shadows in the corner of the carriage, and turned her face toward the window.

It was a dismissal, and after all, what was there left to say? Helena was gone, absorbed into the London streets like hundreds of other girls before her, neither her existence nor her disappearance causing a ripple on the surface.

Emma stumbled on the carriage step, only Daniel's firm hand under her arm keeping her from sprawling onto the street. "Steady now, lass," he muttered as he caught her, and he wasn't referring to the steps.

Steady, steady, steady...

Emma repeated the word over and over in her head as she and Lady Crosby made their way from Kennington Lane toward the supper boxes on the far side of the Grand South Walk.

Lady Silvester and Lady Flora were waiting for them there, with Lord Lovell on one side of Lady Flora, and on the other...

Samuel, his dark eyes burning as he watched her approach.

* * * *

Samuel despised Vauxhall Gardens with the unrelenting heat of a thousand suns. Of all the entertainments on offer during the London season, this was the very last one he would have chosen to endure this evening.

He wasn't sure how he'd allowed himself to be coaxed into it, but they'd been here for less than an hour, and he already regretted it. The loud laughter and the endless drone of chatter around him was making his head ache.

Or was that the champagne?

It was flat, and left a sour taste on his tongue, but Samuel lifted the glass to his lips and forced down another swallow. Even dreadful champagne was preferable to sobriety at the moment.

"What ails you tonight, Lymington?" Lovell muttered, leaning closer to Samuel to be heard. "For God's sake, you've got a full glass of champagne in your hand and a supper box of lively company to entertain you. What more could a man ask for?"

"A decent supper? Musicians who know how to tune their instruments, perhaps?" Vauxhall's orchestra was abominable. Every false note clanged through Samuel's aching head like a crash of cymbals. "I'd settle for a single moment of peace."

"This is London during the season, cousin. There's not a moment of peace to be had. Come now, there's no need to look so grim. It's a *pleasure* garden, if you recall. Neither Lady Emma nor Lady Flora have been here before. It will be good fun to show them the Cascade. I'm certain they'll be delighted with it."

Samuel glanced across the supper box where Lady Emma sat. She was flanked by Lady Crosby on one side and Lady Silvester on the other, looking far from delighted.

She'd hardly spoken a word to anyone since she arrived. She was as lovely as ever—so much so it made his chest ache to look at her, but she appeared...distracted tonight. Her gaze darted over the crowd as if she were looking for someone, and both her supper plate and the glass of champagne at her elbow remained untouched.

Something was wrong, but Samuel knew he'd never get a word out of her as long as she was tucked between the two grandmothers. He rose abruptly to his feet, and held out his hand to her. "Shall we walk, Lady Emma? You must be curious to see all the delights the gardens have to offer, having never been to Vauxhall before."

"No, thank you, Lord Lymington. I don't..." She trailed off, her attention caught by a raucous party of gentlemen and a half-dozen or so demireps who'd just risen from a supper box nearby. Lord Peabody was among the party, and Samuel also recognized Clarissa, the redheaded courtesan from the Pink Pearl. With much shouting and laughter, they disappeared down one of the garden pathways.

Lady Emma stared after them, the oddest expression on her face. "Now I think on it, my lord, I believe I would enjoy a walk, after all."

"Oh, yes! Let's walk, shall we?" Lady Flora jumped to her feet. "I'm mad to see the illuminations. They're said to be very clever."

"Then see them you shall, Lady Flora." Lovell rose and offered her his arm with a gallant flourish. "Where shall we go first? The Triumphal Arches?"

"Yes, that sounds lovely." Lady Emma slid her small, gloved hand through Samuel's arm, her slender body vibrating with impatience.

His body leapt to aching attention at her nearness, the scent of her, the press of her fingers on his sleeve, and he was obliged to clear his throat before speaking. "Would anyone else care to accompany us?"

"Not me." Lady Lovell drew herself up with a sniff. "The gardens don't interest me. Unless you'd care for a stroll, Mr. Humphries?"

"No, indeed." Mr. Humphries helped himself to another slice of ham. "I'm comfortable where I am."

"Lady Lymington?" Samuel glanced at his mother, who startled when he said her name. "No, thank you. I daresay you'll enjoy yourselves more without us."

"Indeed. We're perfectly content to stay where we are, aren't we, Henrietta?" Lady Silvester turned to Lady Crosby with a good-natured smile.

"Quite content, yes," Lady Crosby agreed, giving Emma a cheerful wave.

Samuel led them from the deep alcove that sheltered the supper boxes onto the Grand Walk. When she saw the lamps, Lady Flora gasped, her hand over her mouth. "Oh, my goodness. So many colors! Why, how lovely it is! Lady Emma, don't you find it lovely?"

Anyone who'd never before seen the marvel of Vauxhall's colored glass lamps could be expected to pause to marvel at them, but Lady Emma would have marched right past them, without sparing them a glance if Samuel hadn't stopped her with gentle pressure on her arm. "Lady Emma, I believe Lady Flora asked you a question."

Emma seemed to realize she was dragging Samuel and she stopped, her fingers loosening on his coat sleeve. "Oh, er...yes! Quite beautiful, indeed."

Lady Flora sighed with pleasure. "The blue is the prettiest, I think."

Lady Emma was peering down the lane toward the darker walkways at the back, as if searching for something. "Yes, the blue is very...that shade is... did you not say, Lady Flora, that you wished to see the Triumphal Arches?"

Lady Flora's brow furrowed. "Did I, indeed?"

Samuel stood quietly, taking in this odd scene. Lady Emma had risen to her tiptoes, and was peering in the direction of the Center Cross Walk. She was chasing someone through the gardens, and it looked to Samuel as if it was that disreputable pack of drunken rakes who'd turned down the Grand Walk just ahead of them.

Why would Lady Emma be chasing *them*? The look on her face when she'd been watching them from the supper box had been far from admiring. Then again, Emma was good at keeping her secrets, and had been from the start.

Damn it, none of this made sense, and it was driving him mad.

"Shall we wander toward the Triumphal Arches?" Lady Flora peeked up at Lovell from under her lashes, her lips curving in a winning smile.

Lovell gazed back at her, appearing stunned for a moment before clearing his throat. "Whatever you like, my lady. I'm your willing slave."

If Lovell had said it to any other lady, Samuel would have thought it an abominable bit of flirtation, but in Lady Flora's case, it was nothing but the truth.

Lady Flora colored, but she allowed Lovell to lead her toward the Grand South Walk, where the first Triumphal Arch was located. "There are two more besides this one, each of them situated where the pathways cross, and at the end is a transparency."

"Vauxhall's transparencies are meant to be clever. I should like very much to see one." Lady Emma didn't pause to wait for a reply, but slipped her arm free of Samuel's, and turned toward the back of the garden. Lovell and Lady Flora went along willingly enough, leaving Samuel no choice but to follow.

There was no sign of the drunken rakes, but they were likely headed for the darker walks at the back of the garden, where the branches were thicker, and one might take a lady who didn't object to a bit of intrigue. Samuel was now certain Lady Emma was following them, and he was determined to let her have her way, and see what became of their little adventure.

"Ah, that's a handsome one," Lovell exclaimed when they reached the transparency at the end of the walkway. "What say you, Lymington?"

Samuel stepped closer to study the painting on display. It was a military scene, the width of it nearly as wide as the path leading from the Grand South Walk.

"See how the paper has been scraped thin here?" Lovell said to Lady Flora, pointing to one section of the painting where the soldiers' red coats shone with particular brightness. "It allows more of the light to come through, exaggerating the effect of the colors."

"Is it paper, then? I thought it was silk," Lady Flora said, studying the transparency with interest.

"No, it's varnished paper, painted on both sides and illuminated from behind with lamps." Lovell smiled down at her. "It's meant to look like stained glass."

"It's lovely," Lady Flora breathed, but she was looking at Lovell as she said it, as if she found *him* to be the loveliest sight in all of Vauxhall Gardens.

Lovell grinned with such unabashed pleasure Samuel couldn't help but smile himself. Perhaps Lady Emma was right, and it had been presumptuous of him to chase Lady Flora to London for his cousin's sake, but he could hardly regret it, seeing how pleased both Flora and Lovell were now.

Lady Flora was just the lady to make Lovell happy.

That thought led him to recall Lady Emma, who'd gone remarkably quiet while they were studying the illumination. Samuel was still smiling when he turned to her. "Shall we go back? The Cascade is about to—"

His smile vanished instantly.

Lady Emma was gone.

Chapter Fifteen

She'd lost her wits. It was the only explanation.

With every step forward Emma told herself to go back, to return to Lady Crosby and the safety of the supper boxes. The warning repeated itself so many times it became a chant inside her head, the words an echo to each tap of her foot on the pathway.

Yet she didn't go back.

She kept running, her heart in her throat, branches snatching at the silk of her shawl and tearing at her hair as she burst into the thickest part of the garden, the very heart of the Dark Walk.

Young ladies didn't go into the Dark Walk, particularly not alone, and certainly not after a gang of drunken blackguards who behaved as if women were toys to be used and then tossed aside once they'd outlived their usefulness.

What did she intend to do when she caught up to Lord Peabody? Rage at him, or strike him? Demand to know what he'd done to Helena, demand he find her wandering the streets of London, and bring her back? Did she think she could make him admit his perfidy, or apologize for it?

She might do what she liked, but short of a pistol ball buried in the center of Lord Peabody's cold, black heart, it wouldn't change a thing. She couldn't make an earl do anything he didn't wish to do. She had no more power over Lord Peabody than Helena had.

She had no power—

No, it wasn't true. She *did* have power, but it wasn't the same sort of power a weak man like Lord Peabody wielded. Her strength didn't come from her fists or from a title or fortune, but from her mind, her will, her determination and cunning.

And yes, from her heart. Not the part that loved, but the part that *hated*. The deepest, darkest chamber where she hoarded the memories. The part where there was no forgiveness, not even for herself.

There, in the most secret part of her, she wanted to make Lord Peabody pay for his sins.

But when she turned onto the Dark Walk it wasn't Lord Peabody she found tucked into a shallow alcove. It was Clarissa, the redheaded courtesan from the Pink Pearl, who looked as if she were fresh from a liaison with one of Lord Peabody's blackguards.

Clarissa plucked a handkerchief from her plunging bosom and patted at the edges of her painted lips, then her bodice, dabbing at her decolletage with the handkerchief. Emma waited until these repairs were completed before she emerged from the bushes.

Clarissa startled, her hand going to her chest when Emma appeared in front of her. "God in heaven. Where did you come from? If you're looking for Lord Weymouth, he's already gone."

Emma's gown clearly identified her as a lady, not a courtesan, but perhaps Madame Marchand was right. She'd been a whore once, and now would forever be a whore, no matter how fine her gown. Clarissa might not recognize her face, or know her as one of Madame Marchand's former courtesans, but perhaps she could sense the two of them were part of the same world.

"I don't care about Lord Weymouth. I'm looking for Helena Reeves."

"Helena Reeves!" Clarissa's gaze swept over Emma, taking in the fashionable gown and tasteful jewels, and a smirk rose to her lips. "What's a fine lady like you want with a jade like Helena?"

Emma ignored the question. "I understand Helena was made to leave Madame Marchand's employ last night. Do you know where she is now?"

"I don't know, and I don't care. She tore up Lord Peabody's face, didn't she?" Clarissa shrugged. "Helena got what's coming to her, the way I see it."

"That's not what I asked you," Emma gritted out, her jaw tightening at the woman's callousness. "I asked if you knew where she is now. If you know anything, I'll make it worth your while to tell me."

Emma took off her diamond ear bobs. Clarissa watched, her expression calculating as Emma dropped the glittering jewels one by one onto her palm and held them out, so the moonlight would make them sparkle.

Clarissa stared at them with gleaming eyes. "Mayhap I do know something."

Emma had thought as much. Madame Marchand might rule with an iron fist, but every single courtesan under her roof knew everything there was to know about the Pink Pearl, right down to where the tiniest silver teaspoon was hidden. "Tell me, and they're yours."

"I didn't see her myself, mind you, but Lizzie went to the theater earlier, and she said she saw Helena hanging about Drury Lane." Clarissa licked her lips, her eyes on the jewels. "I can't say if she's still there, but it wasn't but two or three hours ago."

Emma took Clarissa's wrist, drew her hand forward and dropped the diamond ear bobs into her palm. "Thank you. Here you are."

Clarissa snatched her hand back, and the jewels disappeared into her bodice with a casual flick of her fingers. "Helena's not worth it, you know," she said, as Emma turned to leave.

Emma didn't bother with an answer, but hurried from the alcove back onto the Dark Walk, her quickened breath rasping in her ears. She could see the faint flow of light from another transparency on the opposite end of the path, but it felt far away, and the tall hedges on each side seemed to close around her, the overgrown branches meeting above her head, blocking out what little moonlight struggled through the clouds above.

Should she go back in the direction from which she'd come? Or stay on this path, dark as it was? If she kept on, she'd soon reach the Grand Walk, and would be back at the supper boxes much more quickly than if she went the long way. She could claim she'd somehow gotten turned around, and lost the others.

Mind made up, Emma hurried off toward the Grand Walk, but before she'd taken a dozen steps an enormous hand closed around her upper arm, and a low, furious voice whispered in her ear. "What the *devil* do you think you're doing?"

Emma jerked back instinctively, tugging at her arm to free herself, but he hurried her toward a shadowy alcove off the Dark Walk.

The sort of shadowy alcove she'd just left. The sort Vauxhall was famous for.

Or infamous.

"Release me this instant!" Emma fought him instinctively, but it was like struggling against a wall of solid stone.

"Emma, it's *me*. I'm not going to hurt—"

But Emma wasn't in any mood to listen. She hissed angrily, even landed a blow or two on him with her flailing fists and kicking feet, but it made no impression on him whatsoever. He held her as if she weighed no more than a child, and deposited her in the alcove with a wrathful grunt.

"Cease that squirming before you hurt yourself, and answer me, Emma! What the *devil* do you think you're doing, wandering off into the darkest part of the gardens by yourself?"

It was pitch black inside the alcove, even darker than the Dark Walk, and his face was cast in shadows, but as his words sank in, she realized it wasn't Lord Peabody who had her in his clutches. Her panic receded enough that she recognized that rough growl.

It was Samuel, and he was *furious*.

She considered darting around him and making a dash for the walkway, but it was as if he'd read her mind. Before she could stir a step, he blocked her with his large body, looming over her, frustration pouring off him in heated waves. "Well, Emma? I've no qualms about keeping you right here until I get an answer out of you, but I hope you won't make poor Lady Flora worry for too long. Offer her that much consideration, even if you won't do the same for yourself."

Emma blinked up at him, taken aback by his words. "What do you mean, consideration for myself?"

"What do I mean? For God's sake, Emma! Don't act as if you don't know how reckless it is for you to enter the Dark Walk by yourself. Unscrupulous men lurk in these shadows, and any one of them would be delighted to find a sweet young lady wandering these pathways alone. Good Lord, you may as well be a fox wandering amongst a pack of slavering, rabid hounds."

Emma shivered. "That's...descriptive."

"It's accurate," he snapped.

"I wasn't on a stroll, my lord. I, er...lost track of you and the others, and—"

"Stop it, Emma," he said, taking her shoulders in his hands. "I told you never to lie to me again."

Emma could feel his big body vibrating with tension, but for all his anger, he touched her so gently, his words more a plea than a command. "I-I'm sorry, Samuel, I—"

"Shh." He stroked his finger down her neck to the hollow of her throat, his eyes following it as if mesmerized. "You skin flushes pink wherever I touch you."

Emma caught her breath, but he didn't give her a chance to say anything more before his lips came down on hers, stealing her reason.

He'd kissed her before, but not like this. Never like this.

His unexpected kiss in Lady Tremaine's rose garden had been hesitant, but there was nothing hesitant about *this* kiss.

If the kiss in the rose garden had been a question, then this kiss was the answer.

A soft, choked sound caught in Emma's throat when his tongue teased at her lower lip, nipping and sucking at it. "Open your mouth for me, sweetheart."

He held her still for him, panting, one hand clamped on the back of her neck and the other wrapped lightly around her throat. When she parted her lips he plunged inside, taking her mouth roughly, his rasping breaths drifting over her damp lips, making her heart pound and her head spin with desire.

"I've dreamed about kissing you here," he whispered as his tongue curled around her earlobe, licking her before his teeth closed down in a gentle nip. He sucked the tiny fold of her skin into his mouth and teased at it with his tongue, his mouth hot and demanding, commanding her response.

"Oh!" Emma gasped, shocked at the sudden heat gathering in her belly. She'd never wanted a man before, nor had she ever imagined she would.

Until now.

That it should be *him*—a gentleman, an aristocrat, a man so far out of her reach he might as well be on the moon—would lead to nothing but heartbreak, but she clung to him, grabbing handfuls of his coat in her fists, her lips opening eagerly under his.

"Is this how an innocent young lady kisses a gentleman?" he growled against her lips.

"Is this how a gentleman kisses an innocent young lady?" She nipped at his full lower lip, the only soft feature in his otherwise stony face, that pouting lip the only hint there was a passionate man his underneath his cool façade.

He groaned and sank his hand into the mass of curls at the back of her neck. "Have you kissed other men like this? Brought them to their knees with that sweet mouth?"

"No. Just you, my lord." It was both the truth and a lie at once. Another man had kissed her, had done whatever he wished to her while she waited, still and cold, for it to be over.

But Samuel was the only man she'd ever kissed because she *wanted* his lips on hers.

A hoarse laugh tore from his chest, and the hand on her throat vanished, giving way to gentle fingertips on her neck, caressing the bare skin with light, teasing strokes. Emma moaned, every inch of her skin quivering in the wake of those caressing fingers, clamoring for more of his touch.

He sank his hands into her hair and urged her head back, baring her neck. "So soft, my lady, like silk," he whispered as he trailed his lips down to the pulse point at her throat. "I've dreamed of tasting you here, too, every night since I first laid eyes on you. Does that gratify you, knowing you haunt my dreams?"

"No." *Yes.* Emma closed her eyes, her lips parting on a silent cry as his teeth grazed her collarbone.

"Why did you chase those men into the garden, Emma?" He slid his hands down her neck and over her ribcage, letting his thumbs brush against the sides of her breasts before they settled on her hips and he jerked her harder against him. "Tell me."

Did he think he could seduce the truth out of her? Weaken her with his drugging kisses until she told him all her secrets? Perhaps the two of them weren't so different, then, but what Samuel didn't know was the truth he demanded wasn't hers to give.

But she'd give him as much as she could—as much as she dared. Emma melted against him, her soft curves molding to his hard angles, the long muscles of his thighs pressing into her belly. "I wasn't following them. I told you, I got lost."

She stroked her fingers back and forth across his neck, then slid them down over his chest. His stomach muscles tightened as her hands drifted lower, over his abdomen and under the edge of his waistcoat before coming to rest on his waist.

Samuel took her wrists and set her away from him, so he could see her face. His lower lip was swollen from her bite, his dark eyes blazing. "I doubt you've been lost a day in your life. Tell me who those men are to you. What do you want with them?"

Emma clung to him, feeling as if she were drowning. "I don't want anything from them. They don't matter."

Warm lips touched her temple, but for all his tenderness, there was a hint of hurt in his voice. "Why do you always lie to me, Emma? What are you hiding from me?"

Emma gripped the thick, dark waves at the back of his neck, still amazed at how soft they were. Another lie rose to her lips, but this time, she couldn't force her tongue to speak it. Not to *him.* "I-I don't want to lie to you."

"Do you want my kisses, my lady? Or do you want me to stop, and return you to your grandmother as pristine as you were when you entered the garden?" He pressed a kiss to the corner of her mouth, the tip of his tongue making her shiver.

She wanted his kisses—wanted *him.* It was the one thing she wouldn't lie about, and the one thing she wouldn't give up. Until she'd kissed him, Emma had never tasted desire such as this, had never believed it was anything more than a fantasy. She'd keep it now, while she could, hold it in desperate hands until it vanished again, like the quiet footsteps passing by them in the garden beyond.

But she didn't tell him this. She didn't say anything at all as she drew him deeper into the alcove, the tall, thick shrubs curving protectively around them, shielding them from prying eyes. It was madness, utter madness, yet she took another step backward, then another until the back of her knees bumped into something hard.

It was a stone bench, tucked into the trees.

They both paused then. It was too dim for Emma to see his face, but she could feel his gaze on her, hot and heavy. She caught her breath as he dragged his fingertips along her jaw, and then he was kissing her—not the hard, demanding kisses of before, but slow, gentle, his lips brushing over hers again and again, soft and coaxing.

She sank her hands into his hair to drag him closer, her entire body leaping to aching awareness when his tongue slipped between her lips. He was warm, so warm, and his mouth so hot and sweet against hers.

It might have been the darkness surrounding them, or the dizzying press of his lips, but everything around Emma faded to nothingness then. She twined her arms around his neck and let it all go, her world suspended as she gave in to the pleasure of his caresses, his lips on hers.

"We need to stop, Emma. I need to take you back to your grandmother," he murmured in a broken whisper, but he didn't release her, nor did his mouth cease its breathtaking progress from her lips to her neck and down her throat, then lower still, until he was pressing open-mouthed kisses on the tops of her breasts.

Emma whimpered as he plucked at her sleeve, dragging it down and baring her shoulder and burying his face in the sensitive arch of her neck. "This is madness. Tell me to stop."

But Emma didn't tell him to stop. She pressed closer still, her body going limp against his as he lifted her and dropped down onto the bench, dragging her over his lap. "Oh." Emma's breath left her lungs in a rush at the hot press of his arousal beneath her.

"Do you feel that?" He moved his hips in a restrained thrust as he settled her more snugly against his erection. "That's what you do to me."

He nuzzled the swells of her breasts, nipping at her skin until her head fell back in invitation, and he sank his hands into her long, silky curls to hold her still while his fingers slipped under the edge of her bodice, dragging the heavy silk down, down...

He opened his mouth to nip at her shoulder, his breathing ragged, and eased his hands higher, giving her a chance to stop him. When she didn't, he cupped her breasts in his hands and brushed the pads of his thumbs over her nipples. "Look how they peak for me, Emma, how they beg for my touch."

Emma's tongue darted out to wet her lips, but a strangled whimper was her only answer.

"God, so pretty," he choked out when he'd bared her to his hungry gaze. "So perfect," he whispered, cupping the generous swell in his palms. "Such creamy skin, tipped with the palest, daintiest pink." He traced a reverent finger around one nipple, his gaze shooting to her face when she shifted in his arms. "You like it when I stroke you here."

"Yes." Emma gripped his shoulders in frantic fingers, afraid one more word, one more touch, another of his heated breaths drifting over her skin would shatter her into a thousand pieces.

She could feel his eyes on her face as he did it again, then again, teasing her, brushing his thumb over her tight nipple until a sharp cry fell from her lips. "I…I…"

But Emma didn't know what to say, what to do, so lost was she in a haze of desire. It wasn't until he touched the peak with his tongue that she understood she needed his mouth.

"My lord." Her eyes dropped closed at the exquisite sensation "Sam—"

"Shhh." He didn't tease her this time before drawing her aching nipple into the dark cavern of his mouth. He suckled at her for long, breathless minutes, the soft, wet sound of his lips against her flesh seeming loud to Emma, obscene, yet nothing would have made her stop his sweet torment.

He didn't release her until he'd reduced her to a moaning, quivering bundle in his lap, her nipples a deep red from his mouth. He rested his cheek against the soft skin between her breasts, a pained groan tearing loose from his chest. "I must be mad, touching you like this."

Emma let out a soft cry of distress. She caught a handful of his thick hair and tried to urge his mouth back to her breasts, but he captured her wrists in his hands.

"No. I want you too much, Emma. You steal my logic, my reason. *This,*" he jerked his hips against her, "is why we can't be alone together in a dark garden. Everything about you—the way you move, your scent, your voice, your wicked, delicious mouth…" He pressed a hard, desperate kiss to her lips. "You make me forget I'm a gentleman."

Emma's breath came in short gasps as she traced his lips with her fingertip, then slid her hands up his chest and wrapped her arms around his neck, so her breasts were flattened against him. "I don't want you to be a gentleman."

* * * *

Samuel was losing his mind. Emma was stealing it from him, one soft moan at a time.

She was enthroned on his lap, her round bottom pressed tightly against him, her tongue in his mouth, and he was mere seconds away from lifting her skirts and sliding into her warm, welcoming heat.

Samuel shuddered against her, easing her closer until he enveloped her, her vanilla scent teasing his senses. He held her there, his body crushed against hers so he could feel the shape of her thighs and her breasts, and dear God, she felt so good, her soft curves such a perfect fit against him, her belly cradling his stiff cock.

Even now, as his mind screamed at him to stop his hand was slipping under the hem of her skirts, his palm sliding up her calf, then higher, higher, over long legs in fine silk stockings until his fingers touched her garters, and then...

The smooth, bare skin of her upper thigh.

He was close, so close to the warm, damp haven between her legs. Once he touched her there, it would be over. He'd take her, right here on this hard stone bench in Vauxhall Gardens, with her grandmother a short walk away in their supper box, drinking champagne with his mother.

Samuel let out a tortured groan, but before he could give in to temptation again, he grasped her hips, moved her off his lap onto the bench beside him, and shot to his feet. He was panting, his cock straining against his falls. He'd never been so hard in his life, had never wanted a woman the way he wanted her, and it took every shred of his control to resist taking her into his arms again, and sinking into her tight heat.

He paced from one end of the tiny alcove to the other, trying to reason with his cock. It was long agonizing minutes before it relented enough for him to be able to turn back to Emma without snatching her up again, and losing himself in her arms.

She was sitting on the bench, her skirts tucked demurely around her ankles. The luscious breasts he'd worshipped had disappeared back into her bodice and the heavy silk was smoothed into place over her shoulders. Her cheeks were flushed, but she sat with her spine straight, and her hands folded neatly in her lap.

To look at her now, he would never guess she'd been writhing on his lap mere moments ago. Samuel stared at her, wondering if he'd imagined the whole thing. Would he wake in his bed alone, sweat pouring off him, his cock jerking against the coverlet, and find he was once again caught in an erotic dream about her?

"I, ah…perhaps you'd better take me to my carriage, my lord. If you could return to the supper box to fetch my grandmother for me afterward, I'd be grateful."

Samuel looked into her dark blue eyes, and shame washed over him. He'd just *pawed* a young lady in a public garden, had nearly taken her, on a stone bench at *Vauxhall*.

"Emma. I shouldn't have…I beg your pardon for—"

"I think it's best if I don't return to fetch her myself." She raised a hand to her tousled hair. "I'm afraid I must look…quite wild."

She laughed a little, then reached up to tuck one of the loose locks behind her ear with a self-conscious gesture that hit Samuel like a blow to the gut. "Emma." He took a step toward her, but froze again when she held her hand up to stop him.

"Please tell my grandmother I was taken with a bout of dizziness, and felt too ill to return to our box."

"I don't like to leave you alone in your carriage while I fetch your grandmother." It was a paltry excuse, but everything inside him rebelled at the thought of coolly delivering her to her carriage, and then abandoning her.

It felt wrong. Dismissive.

"It's all right, my lord. Our coachman is very good, and will take care of me until my grandmother arrives."

Samuel wanted to beg her to return to the supper box with him, but she looked so small and fragile sitting there in the shadows that he couldn't bring himself to argue with her.

So he did the only thing he could do. He held out his arm to her, and led her out of the Dark Walk, avoiding the bright, crowded parts of the garden. The silent walk to the Coach Gate seemed to take far longer than it ever had before, but at last they made it through the archway and onto Kennington Lane.

Lady Crosby's coachman saw them coming. He leapt down from the box and stalked toward them, a hulking figure in the darkness, but it wasn't until the light fell on his face that the hair on Samuel's neck rose in warning.

He'd seen the man before, but never as close as this.

Christ, he looked like a murderer escaped from Newgate.

Samuel caught Emma's hand, stopping her. "Lady Emma, I don't think—"

"It's all right, Lord Lymington. He's harmless to me, despite his, er… menacing appearance." Emma tried to tug her hand free of his, but Samuel held her fast as he sized up the threatening coachman with narrowed eyes.

"Let the lass go, Lymington," the man growled, his enormous arms bulging as he crossed them over his chest. "*Now.*"

Samuel didn't let her go, but stared the man down. "I don't take orders from you."

The man took a threatening step toward him, and things might have gotten ugly, indeed, if Emma hadn't intervened. "Please, Lord Lymington. You promised me you'd fetch my grandmother for me."

Samuel gazed down into those big, dark blue eyes, at those red, trembling lips, and reluctantly released her hand.

"Wise choice, my lord." The coachman held out a hand to Emma. "Come on then, lass."

Samuel watched them go, somewhat mollified by the gentle way the brute took Emma's arm to lead her to the carriage, but his heart gave a curiously miserable thump as she vanished inside, and the coachman closed the door behind her.

Chapter Sixteen

Emma pulled her hood low to hide her face, sweat trickling down the back of her neck even in the cool evening air. If any aristocrats happened to see her wandering around Covent Garden alone at night, searching for a courtesan turned street prostitute, her brief time as Lady Crosby's virtuous granddaughter would come to an abrupt and final end.

She was amazed it hadn't already.

A lady could only tempt the wrath of fate so many times before the consequences caught up to her. This wasn't the first foolish risk Emma had taken in the last few weeks, but it could well be the last.

Yet she kept pushing forward along the edges of Tavistock Row, until she was steps away from the glare of lights emanating from the gaming hells arrayed on King and Henrietta Streets like a row of rotten teeth. She could hear the shouts and drunken laughter from here, the shuffle of feet, the low buzz of fortunes being won, then lost again.

Emma kept her head down as she headed west toward Brydges Street. She was dimly aware she was muttering nervously to herself, prayers and curses both—prayers that Helena was still in the alley behind Drury Lane Theater where Clarissa said she'd last been seen, and curses on Helena's name for putting herself in danger again and ending up *here* on the London streets, the very place Emma had begged her not to go.

Only this time, it was worse. So much worse, because while Helena was accustomed to managing drunken rakes, a kidnapper and murderer was another sort of beast altogether. Whoever had taken Caroline Francis might be searching for Helena even now, and the reckless girl had just made it easier to find her.

Not just find her, but *hurt* her.

Fear flooded Emma's throat, choking her. Dear God, how could Helena not have seen how much danger she'd put herself in? Once a woman found herself down here in the seamiest part of London, it was very difficult to rise to the surface again. Emma could grab Helena by the hair and wrench her from the muck only so many times before Helena sank to the bottom forever.

Then again, Amy and Kitty had met their disastrous fates in the countryside, at Lord Lymington's grand estate, a place where they should have been safe.

For a certain sort of lady, no place was ever safe, even under the best of circumstances, but for Helena to venture onto these streets alone, in the dark, with a conscienceless villain after her?

They were *not* the best of circumstances.

But Emma wouldn't think of that now, nor would she think of the promises she'd made, not only to Lady Crosby and Lady Clifford, but to herself, and to Amy and Kitty, who hadn't done anything to deserve the awful fate that had befallen them.

Drury Lane Theatre was dark, the play having let out already, but tight knots of gentlemen were still hanging about, some of them lounging in front of the theater, others making their way down Russel Street toward the mayhem on offer closer to the center of Covent Garden.

Emma kept to the dark corners of the streets, her gaze darting this way and that. Where there were drunken gentlemen with coins to spare there would always be women, gliding through the darkness like spirits, smiling, whispering, luring. Offering.

There was no telling how long it would take before Helena turned up, but Emma would keep searching for her until she did. All she had to do was stay out of sight, and pray to God no one would see—

"Tempting fate again, I see. Was the Dark Walk not dangerous enough for you, Emma? Whatever ugliness you might encounter there is, admittedly, nothing in comparison to the dangers lurking in Covent Garden at night."

Emma froze at the low hiss in her ear, the voice much closer than it should have been. If she'd been paying proper attention to her surroundings, she would have heard footsteps approach well before he got close enough to be heard in whispers.

Covent Garden at night was not the place to become distracted, but she knew this voice, recognized the touch on her arm, and before she could forbid it, relief flooded through her, so profound her knees shook with it.

"Is that sinister coachman of yours in the habit of letting you wander about the London streets at night, without protection?"

He was not. Emma had been obliged to argue herself hoarse to get Daniel to agree to head north, toward Long Acre, then loop back on Drury Lane. If it had been anything less than Helena's life hanging in the balance, there wasn't a chance he'd have left her side. "Don't blame Daniel."

Samuel dragged a hand down his face, sighing. "Why are you here, Emma?"

"I might ask you the same question, my lord. Did you follow me?"

"Of course I followed you. I've made quite a habit of it of late." He took her arm, as if he were certain she'd attempt to flee, and was determined not to let her slip away from him this time. "Let's try this again, shall we? What are you doing in Covent Garden, alone, at night?"

Emma hesitated. Samuel was already much deeper into this business than she wanted him, but once again, she couldn't quite bring herself to lie to him.

Or perhaps it was just that she didn't want to do this alone, and he...

He hadn't lied to her yet, or pretended to be someone he wasn't. To another person his honesty might have been of little consequence, but to her, it was...everything.

So for the third time in as long as she could remember, Emma told him the truth.

Not all of it, but enough.

"Helena went missing from the Pink Pearl last night after an incident with Lord Peabody. It wasn't her first offense, and Madame Marchand isn't a patient woman." Nor a forgiving one. God knew Madame hadn't forgiven Emma for escaping her clutches five years ago, and now Helena was being made to pay for Emma's sins.

"Madame Marchand has parted ways with Miss Reeves?" Samuel's tone was grim. For all that he was an aristocrat with a grand townhouse in Mayfair and an estate in Kent, he was under no illusions about how an unprotected woman fared on the London streets.

"If by parted ways you mean Madame has tossed Helena onto the street without any means of protecting herself, and doubtless without a shred of remorse, then yes, my lord. They've parted ways."

Emma sucked in a breath of the cool night air to steady herself, but she could hear the fear in her own voice, the bitterness that always lurked under the surface, like a sour aftertaste.

It could have been me, so easily...but for Lady Clifford, it would have been me.

"Is that why you followed Lord Peabody into the gardens tonight? What did you hope to accomplish?" Samuel spoke calmly, but anger vibrated just beneath the surface. "Did you think you could force an apology from him, or make him sorry for what he'd done? Men like Peabody aren't ever sorry for anything, Emma."

"I didn't follow *him*." Not precisely, anyway. "I was following Clarissa, one of the courtesans who was with him."

In truth, Emma hadn't taken any time to reason it out before she'd slipped away from Samuel. When she saw Lord Peabody drinking and laughing without a care in the world while Helena was wandering the streets, prey to every blackguard in London, she hadn't thought at all. She'd simply reacted. "I thought she could tell me if anyone had seen Helena. At the moment, that's all that matters to me."

He gazed down at her with some emotion Emma couldn't read in his dark eyes. She thrust her chin up, expecting him to argue with her, but he only said, "Very well. Where do we start?"

Emma opened her mouth, but any protests she might have made withered on her tongue. It wasn't that she *trusted* him—she didn't trust many people, least of all a haughty nobleman. It was just that the overwhelming bulk of him, his commanding presence were...reassuring.

"On Drury Lane, behind the theatre. Clarissa told me another one of the courtesans from the Pink Pearl saw Helena here earlier this evening."

He nodded, and together they ducked around the corner of the theatre, his hand still wrapped firmly around her upper arm, but aside from a few drunken noblemen wandering about, there was no one there.

Emma wandered from White Horse Yard down as far as Blackmoor Street, peering into every shadowy alcove and around every corner, her hopes dimming with every step. Helena might be anywhere by now, and with each moment that passed, she was in greater danger.

Please, please let us find her...

She made her way back to the corner of Drury Lane and Princes Street where she'd left Samuel, but as she drew closer to him, she noticed he'd gone still, his face tense, his head turned toward Stanhope Street. "Samuel? Are you—"

That was as far as Emma got before he exploded into motion, his heels striking the street, his long legs devouring the distance between Princes Street and Hartford Place.

"Samuel!" Emma ran after him, her heart rushing into her throat.

He didn't slow at her frantic shriek, but charged passed Hartford Place, ducking instead down the dark, narrow alleyway that led to Bennets Court, a tiny courtyard surrounded on all sides by buildings.

"Samuel, wait!" Emma shot after him, stumbling on the hem of her skirts, but within seconds he was already out of sight. "Samuel?" She came to a breathless halt at the mouth of the alleyway and peered inside. It was dark, so dark, but she thought she saw a flash of movement, then the echoing sound of footsteps, a thud of heels on gritty streets, running—

Emma jumped as a terrified scream rent the air, her heart nearly bursting from her chest. It was coming from the direction of the courtyard beyond, so bloodcurdling every hair on Emma's neck rose in reaction.

That voice, she knew it—

"Helena!" Emma didn't hear her own shout, didn't feel her feet slapping against the filthy street as she dashed down the alleyway, only to come to a screeching halt in the middle of the courtyard, her mouth falling open in shock.

Samuel had a howling, thrashing, clawing Helena in his arms. She was incoherent with panic, her face smeared with dirt, the shoulder torn clean off her dress, her lip rapidly swelling, and her neck...

Emma froze in horror.

Bruises, the size and shape of a man's fingers circled her neck.

Bile flooded Emma's throat, but she choked it back and darted forward, her arms outstretched. Helena, who was too overwrought to tell the difference between her attacker and her rescuer, was growing more hysterical by the moment, and Samuel wisely relinquished her into Emma's arms.

"Helena! Helena, it's me!" After a struggle Emma managed to grab Helena's chin and force her to still. "Look at me, Helena! It's Emma."

"Emma?" Helena's eyes stopped their panicked rolling, and she snatched at Emma as if she were drowning, her fingernails sinking into Emma's forearms.

"Yes, dearest. It's all right. You're all right."

Emma patted and crooned and soothed until at last Helena calmed enough to loosen her death grip, whereupon she immediately burst into a storm of hysterical tears.

"I...he grabbed me, Emma, and dragged me—" Helena looked wildly around her. "Dragged me *here*, and it's so dark, and I...I tried to scream, but he put his hand over my mouth, and no one could hear me!"

"I know, dearest, I know, but you're all right now, you see?" Helena *wasn't* all right, but against all odds, she wasn't dead, and for now, for this moment, Emma could only feel gratitude for that small mercy.

The anger, the ugly, all-consuming bitterness and fury would come later. It always did.

Helena grasped Emma's shoulders with desperate fingers. "The pendant, Emma! You remember, I told you about the pendant? He crept up behind me, so I didn't see his face, but it was *him*, the same man who took Caroline!

He demanded the pendant, b-but I don't have it! When I didn't g-give it to him, h-he grabbed me by the neck, and he...he..."

"Shh. Calm down, and let me take you to Daniel."

But Helena was beyond listening, and the words kept tumbling from her bruised lips. "It wasn't Lord Lovell, Emma! We were wrong about him. This man is much bigger, much taller. Lord Lovell didn't take those girls from Lymington House...w-we made a mistake."

Emma squeezed her eyes closed, praying with everything inside her Samuel hadn't heard Helena's words, or by some miracle hadn't understood them, but before she could even turn her head to look at him, she felt him go unnaturally still beside her.

Helena was still clutching at Emma and babbling incoherently, but Emma didn't see her, didn't hear her. For an instant everything went silent as she turned to face Samuel. He was staring at her, his face white but for the blood trickling from his nose, where Helena had struck him with her elbow.

"Lovell? You thought *Lovell* had..."

He trailed off into silence, but Emma could see the wheels turning behind those dark gray eyes, see him fitting the pieces together.

Emma's flirtation with Lovell, her interest in Caroline Francis, the snatches of conversation Samuel had overheard between Emma and Helena that first night at the Pink Pearl, the lie she'd told Lady Tremaine to escape the picnic, and later that night, when Samuel had seen her at the brothel once again...

In the time it took Emma to draw a breath, it went from bad to worse. Samuel's jaw hardened, his hands clenching into fists. Somehow, Emma knew he was recalling their interlude in the rose garden, their yearning kisses in his carriage, their stolen passion at Vauxhall tonight, and drawing his conclusions.

The *wrong* conclusions, but before he'd even said a word, she knew he wouldn't ever believe the kisses they'd shared, the tender moments between them had happened for no other reason than she wanted them.

Wanted *him*.

When he looked at her again, his eyes had gone ice cold.

"Emma?" A shaking hand clutched at Emma's sleeve, and she turned to find Helena staring at her, her dark eyes filled with tears. "I shouldn't have said that about Lord Lovell. I'm sorry."

In all the time Emma had known Helena, she'd never once seen her cry. If Helena's swollen lip and torn gown hadn't been enough to make Emma hold her tongue, Helena's tears should have been, but the look in Samuel's eyes, the accusation there, the pain—everything rose up at once in Emma's breast, every raw, painful, ugly emotion, and the next thing she knew she'd opened her mouth, and it was too late.

"You promised me, Helena."

Helena's face crumpled for an instant, but the anguish was there and then gone as quickly as a flash of lightning, sullen defiance in its place. "It was bound to happen, Emma. Madame Marchand despises me. She's been looking for a reason to turn me out, and—"

"And you gave her one." Emma's voice wasn't quite steady.

The minute the words left her mouth Emma wished them back, but it was as if a dam had burst, and all the misery and confusion and fear that had been pushing against Emma's chest since she'd escaped the Pink Pearl at age fifteen were determined to have their way at last.

After five long years, they refused to be silenced any longer.

Helena made a sound that was perhaps meant to be a laugh, but it was sharp, cutting, like the sound of glass being ground under a boot heel. "What would you have had me do, Emma? Let Lord Peabody beat me bloody? He got what he deserved."

What he deserved? No, he'd gotten far better than that. He deserved to be put down like the rabid animal he was before he got a chance to hurt someone else.

"I warned you to stay away from him, Helena!" Emma cried, knowing how unfair her words were, but unable to make herself stop. "I told you not to—"

"You're right, of course. I should have declined his attentions, shouldn't I? Why, I should have simply told Madame Marchand I preferred to lounge in my bed all evening instead of entertaining the gentlemen. You *know* I didn't have any choice, Emma. Or perhaps you don't know." A bitter smile crossed Helena's lips. "Perhaps you've forgotten."

Helena turned away, but Emma snatched Helena's cold hand in hers, stopping her. "Wait, Helena."

Helena waited, her throat working.

"I…haven't forgotten." How could she? She'd tried to forget those years, to bury the memories so deeply they'd never see the light of consciousness again, but they were like the wraiths floating through Covent Garden. Silent, but haunting. "I'm sorry. I know there was nothing you could do."

Helena face softened then, and incredibly she made a valiant attempt at a smile. "Well, not *nothing*. Lord Peabody came away from it with neat rows of scratches on his cheeks. He was furious when he saw his pretty, ruined face in the glass. Why are the ugliest men always the vainest?"

"And the handsomest gentlemen always the kindest?" Emma murmured, turning her gaze back to Samuel.

He wasn't the handsomest man she'd ever seen, yet to Emma, no gentleman's face could ever compare to Samuel's.

The realization stunned her.

When had she stopped thinking of his face as too harsh, too cold? Was it the first time she'd seen a flash of heat in those cool gray eyes, the first restrained twitch at the corner of those hard lips? His wasn't a kind face at first glance, but the hint of his smile...did it mean more than Lovell's easy grins because it so infrequently graced his lips?

It felt like a gift, that smile, like a reward she'd earned, and then just as quickly squandered, because he wasn't smiling at her now. His expression was dark, his face set into hard, uncompromising lines. He didn't return her gaze, but turned away, as if he couldn't bear to look at her.

Unconsciously, Emma pressed a hand to her chest, right over her heart, as if she could stop it from shattering with a simple touch. An unfamiliar sob rose in her throat, but she choked it back and took Helena's hand. "Come along, dearest. Daniel will be looking for us."

Emma led Helena from Bennets Court back to Drury Lane. Samuel followed without a word, a bedraggled, dejected little band of three.

They met Daniel coming from the other direction down Drury Lane, his eyes wild, and moving at a speed that should have been impossible for a man of his massive size. "That the lass?" he called to Emma, when he caught sight of them.

"Yes, we found her. She's all right." Mostly, and even that had been a near thing.

Some of the tension drained from Daniel's big shoulders, but when he was close enough to see Helena's face, the livid finger marks on her neck, he stiffened again. "Skin of her teeth, by the looks of it. What's his lordship doing here?"

"He, ah...he followed us from Vauxhall Gardens."

Daniel's brows lowered. "Did he, now? What's he want?"

Whatever answer she gave to that question wouldn't sit well with Daniel, so Emma thought it best to ignore it. "You'll see to it Helena is taken care of?" Emma didn't mention Lady Clifford, but she didn't have to, with Daniel. He knew what she wanted.

"Aye. Where are ye going, lass?" Daniel's question was for Emma, but his grim gaze remained fixed on Samuel.

"Lady Emma is coming with me." Samuel wrapped a possessive hand around Emma's wrist. "I'll see she's returned to Lady Crosby."

Daniel's eyebrows shot up, but something in Samuel's face silenced his protest. "Come on then, lass," he said to Helena, his huge hand gentle on her shoulder. "We'll see ye put back to rights again. I'll be waiting for you, Miss Emma," Daniel added, casting a dark look at Samuel over his shoulder as he helped Helena down the street toward Lady Crosby's carriage.

By the time Samuel handed Emma into his carriage, she was trembling with exhaustion. Between her chase through the Dark Walk, Samuel's dizzying kisses in the alcove, the frantic search in Drury Lane, and Helena's attack, she was ready to collapse.

But one glimpse into Samuel's cold, shuttered eyes made her heart shrink inside her chest, and she knew, without him saying a word, that the miseries of this evening were far from over.

* * * *

Since their first meeting at Almack's, Lady Emma had been lying to him. Dozens, tens of dozens of lies, the web pulling tighter around him with every word out of her pretty mouth.

One some level, perhaps Samuel had known it all along. Somewhere, deep inside himself, hadn't he been waiting for the truth to come out? He simply hadn't wanted to believe it could be as bad as this.

But tonight, the truth had slammed into him with brutal clarity.

"Is your name even Emma?"

It wasn't what he'd meant to ask. Given the mountain of lies she'd told him, what did her name matter? It seemed a ludicrous place to start. Her past as a courtesan, her relationship to Lady Crosby, her friendship with Helena Reeves, her flirtation with Lovell, her very identity…

What was a name, when taken against all that?

There was a long pause, then she whispered, "Yes. My name is Emma."

"I don't believe you." Samuel's throat tried to close around the words, but they clawed their way from his throat to his lips. How pathetic was it that he doubted her even in this? That he could no longer trust she wouldn't lie about something as simple as her name?

"Even if it is Emma, it isn't Lady Emma Crosby, is it? Lady Crosby isn't your grandmother, and Helena Reeves was never your lady's maid. You were a courtesan at the Pink Pearl. That's how you know Helena. Caroline too, I suppose."

Strange, that there wasn't any accusation in his voice. There was nothing at all in it—it was flat, inflectionless.

"I don't know Caroline." She looked down at her hands. "She's Helena's friend. I never met her."

It might be the truth, the one small, insignificant truth amid an avalanche of much bigger lies. It hardly mattered. "Your flirtation with Lovell, your interest in him, it was never real, was it?"

"No." Low, nearly inaudible.

For the first time since they'd entered the carriage, he turned and looked at her. She'd crammed herself into the darkest corner, and she looked so small and pale, so lost, nothing at all like the blue-eyed temptress who'd charmed and flirted her way into the dreams of every gentleman in London.

No longer the belle. But then she never had been. Not really.

Samuel's heart gave a miserable thump at how broken she looked, like a discarded doll, but at the same time he was furious that he could still care for her—could feel anything for her—after what she'd done to him, to his family.

"You feigned your regard for Lovell in order to draw him in, because you thought he'd hurt Amy and Kitty and…what? That he seduced Caroline, then abandoned her? How could you think…*why*? Why would you suspect Lovell?" Samuel's voice cracked on the last words.

"I—" she began, but fell silent again, shaking her head.

Some of Samuel's numbness fled in the face of her silence, disintegrated in a hot flash of anger and hurt. He thought of Lovell as he'd been at fifteen, right before Samuel had left England, with his sweet smile, his disheveled mop of dark hair and his eagerness, and it felt as if a knife had been plunged into his chest.

Lovell wasn't a perfect man, no more than any man was, but a kidnapper, a *murderer*?

The unfairness of it stunned him, stopped his breath.

"Why should it have fallen to *you* to determine Lovell's innocence or guilt? Who are *you*, to decide?" Even as the words left his mouth, there was a part of Samuel that hoped she wouldn't answer. Knowing would only draw him deeper into her web.

"I took an interest in Lord Lovell at the request of Lady Clifford." Emma's gaze was on her hands, clenched tightly in her lap.

Samuel stared at her. "Lady *Amanda* Clifford?"

"Two young housemaids went missing from your country estate, Samuel. Vanished, never to be seen again. They—"

"I know that, Emma! I made it my business to discover what became of Amy and Kitty as soon as I returned to England. What I don't understand is why Lady Clifford should think Lovell is involved in it."

Emma's lips parted, but no words emerged.

"Lovell couldn't have committed the crimes you suspect him of. He fought a duel in January, and was nearly killed by a pistol ball to the leg. He's done nothing for weeks but lie in his bed."

"I know that, now."

"If you'd asked me, you might have known it at once, and spared us all of this!" Samuel shouted, gripping his hair in his hands.

Emma flinched at his raised voice. "If I *had* asked, would you have told me?"

No. Samuel couldn't deny it, not even to himself. He'd been suspicious of Emma from the start.

For good reason, as it turned out.

He forced himself to take a deep breath until the ache in his chest loosened enough for him to speak calmly. He wanted this over, but there was one question he had to ask, one thing he had to know before this would ever be over for him.

If Emma had feigned her regard for Lovell, then couldn't she do the same for any man? When she realized she wouldn't get anywhere with Lovell, had she put Samuel in his cousin's place, traded one of them for the other as if they were no more significant than discarded cards tossed carelessly aside after a lost wager?

Samuel swallowed. "Our kiss in Lady Tremaine's garden, my carriage, tonight at Vauxhall. Was that...were you pretending then, too? Was I part of your scheme all along?"

"*No.*" She didn't hesitate, her voice strong and clear.

Her blue eyes were fierce, flashing with conviction, and hope sparked in Samuel's chest. "There's more to this than you've told me. If you truly do care for me, then tell me the truth, Emma. All of it."

Silence stretched between them, thick with anguish. Samuel already knew what her answer would be before she spoke it.

"I-I can't do that, Samuel."

Just like that, the spark was snuffed out, reducing his heart to a drift of hot cinders in his chest. After that, there was nothing more to say.

"I'm leaving London tomorrow, and taking my family back to Kent." Samuel drew in a harsh breath. "Whoever hurt Amy and Kitty will face justice. I'll make sure of it, but I don't...I don't want to see you ever again, Emma."

He didn't look at her after that, nor did he move when the carriage stopped in front of Lady Crosby's townhouse. His coachman jumped down from the box and opened the carriage door, but Emma didn't get out—not right away.

Samuel could feel her gaze on him, but he couldn't bear to look at her.

After a moment he heard a faint rustle of silk, and felt a slight shift in the carriage as she turned away to accept his coachman's hand, and stepped onto the pavement.

His eyes slid shut as the door closed with a quiet click behind her.

Chapter Seventeen

Emma dragged herself through the front door of Lady Crosby's townhouse in a daze, hardly able to believe she'd passed through this same door mere hours earlier.

It should take more time than that, shouldn't it, for a dream to fall apart?

She closed the door and stood there, eyes closed, unsure what to do next. Helena was safe, but Caroline was still missing. Lord Lovell was innocent, but *someone* at Lymington House was guilty, and she was no closer to knowing who it was than she had been when this started.

I'm leaving London tomorrow....I never want to see you again.

Emma bowed her head, her eyes stinging as Samuel's words came back to her on a rush of pain, and with it, the crushing realization that she was unsure what to do next, because there was nothing left *to* do.

It was over. By this time tomorrow Samuel would be on his way to Kent, his family with him. She'd remain in London, left to try and puzzle out the tragedy that had unfolded at Lymington House with the few fragments she held in her hands, and little hope of success.

Amy, Kitty, and Caroline, Lady Clifford, Daniel and Lady Crosby, Flora and Lord Lovell, and even Helena, who'd come so close to dying alone in a filthy alley—Emma could hardly bear to think of it.

She'd failed them all, and she'd failed Samuel.

But most of all, she'd failed herself. She'd had one chance to offer something to all the lost young girls—a chance to do something *good*, to prove to herself she was more than just a whore and a murderess. One chance to carry a torch and stride triumphantly through the flames like Thaïs, and she'd let it slip through her fingers.

And for what? Some childish dream she'd long since given up on.

She'd been a fool to believe even for a moment the fragile tenderness between her and Samuel would flourish, when it was destined from the start to wither on the vine. She should have known it would end the same way it had started—with him wishing he'd never laid eyes on her.

One way or another, it would always end that way.

"Emma?"

Emma looked up to see Lady Crosby hovering by the door to the drawing room, her face drawn with worry. "I'm sorry, my lady. Am I very late?"

"It's all right, dear." Some emotion flickered in Lady Crosby's eyes, but the hallway was too dim, and Emma too exhausted to decipher what it was. "Did you find Helena?"

"I did, and not a moment too soon." Emma swallowed at the memory of Helena's torn gown and bruised neck. "Daniel's taken her to Lady Clifford."

Lady Crosby sagged against the door frame in relief. "Thank goodness. But you look done in, you poor thing. Come to the drawing room, and sit with me for a bit."

Emma took the hand Lady Crosby offered, and allowed herself to be led to the drawing room as if she were a child, and seated on a comfortable settee by the fire. Lady Crosby called for refreshments, then proceeded to fuss over Emma like a mother hen until a footman arrived with a silver tray bearing a bottle of sherry and two glasses.

"Sherry, my lady? At..." Emma glanced at the mantel clock. "Six o'clock in the morning?"

"I'm a great lover of tea, as you know, Emma, but there are occasions when it isn't quite sufficient." Lady Crosby poured a hearty measure of sherry into each glass, and handed one to Emma. "This feels like one of those times."

Emma couldn't argue with that. She raised the glass to her lips and took a grateful sip, but Lady Crosby's next remark had her choking on the sherry.

"You've been with Lord Lymington all night, haven't you, dear?" Lady Crosby took a calm sip from her own glass. "He followed you from Vauxhall, and I imagine he caught up with you. He's not the sort of gentleman one easily escapes, is he?"

It wasn't a question, despite Lady Crosby's enquiring air.

From the start, Emma hadn't kept any secrets from Lady Crosby. Emma's questionable origins, her memorable year at the Pink Pearl, and her history with Lady Clifford—Lady Crosby knew it all, as indeed she must if she and Emma were to work effectively together.

But even so, an unaccountable shyness overtook Emma at mention of Samuel's name, and she found herself stumbling over her reply. "He, ah…we weren't—"

"Now, don't get flustered, dear. Lord Lymington returned to the supper box to deliver your message to me, but he hardly managed to get one sentence out before he shot off again as if his heels were on fire. Of course, I knew he was going after you."

He'd gone after her to help her, and what had he got for his trouble?

Lies, and betrayal.

Emma flushed with shame.

Lady Crosby seized her hand. "There's no need to look so chagrined, my love. I was young once too, you know. We'd hardly embarked on the season before I realized the way that particular wind was blowing."

"*Wind?*" Emma echoed. "I don't—"

"It's a figure of speech, dear. But it's curious, isn't it, how things come to pass? You'd chosen Lord Lovell for this scheme, but then fate chose Lord Lymington for *you*, and so it goes."

Emma let out a bleak laugh. "Fate has her way in the end, doesn't she?" Fate, or divine justice. They could call it whatever they liked, but in the end, the result was the same.

Fate hadn't chosen Samuel to reward Emma. She'd chosen him to punish her.

Samuel wasn't under any illusions about her any longer. What better way to castigate her for her sins than for her to be cursed to tell one lie after another to a man destined from the start to despise her, a man she'd fallen hopelessly in love with—

Love? No, that wasn't…she wasn't *in love* with Samuel. She'd made mistakes these past weeks—a shocking number of them—but surely she couldn't have been such a monumental fool as to fall in love with the Marquess of Lymington?

Emma set her glass aside with shaking fingers when the sherry threatened to come back up again.

It didn't make sense. How could this tremor in her body, this sick feeling in her stomach, this unbearable pain in her heart be *love*? *This* horridness was what Sophia and Cecilia had been going on and on about over these past few months? *This* was why the two of them wore such dreamy smiles, and floated about as if their feet no longer touched the ground?

Lady Crosby, who didn't seem to notice Emma's distress, finished off her sherry and reached for the bottle. "I'm glad of it, for my part. Lord

Lovell is a sweet young man, of course, but he's no match for you, is he, dear? No, you and Lord Lymington are much better suited."

Emma leapt up from the settee. It wasn't a wise choice, given the nausea roiling in her stomach, but she couldn't bear to listen to another word. "Sam—that is, Lord Lymington and I are *not* a match, my lady."

"Well, perhaps not *quite* yet, dear. These things take time, you see, but I'm certain soon enough you'll find—"

"We've no time left." Emma's knees wobbled, and she fell back onto the settee with a clumsy thud. "Lord Lymington told me tonight that he's returning to Kent immediately, and taking his family with him. I'd hoped we'd find our way to Lymington House with them, but there's no question of that now."

Lady Crosby frowned. "What do you mean?"

Emma had no wish to relive those awful moments in the carriage with Samuel, but this discussion was inevitable, and she wanted it over as quickly as possible. "I mean Lord Lymington informed me just now that our, er…friendship is over. I believe he also said something about…" Emma's lower lip began to wobble, and she sucked in a quick, desperate breath to calm herself. "He may have added he hoped never to see my face again. Under the circumstances, I don't think we can expect an invitation to Lymington House anytime soon."

"Oh, dear. That *is* a wrinkle, isn't it?"

Less a wrinkle than an enormous, gaping rent, but then one person's wrinkle was another's heartbreaking catastrophe. "A bit of one, yes."

Lady Crosby's brow furrowed. "Don't lose heart just yet, my dear. Lady Flora may be able to persuade Lord Lovell to invite us to Lymington House."

"It's Lord Lymington's estate, not Lord Lovell's."

"Yes, but Lord Lovell grew up at Lymington House. Surely both he and Lord Lymington consider it his home. I doubt Lord Lymington would begrudge his cousin a visitor or two."

"That depends on the visitors. Lord Lymington may take one look at me and forbid me to cross the threshold."

"Nonsense." Lady Crosby handed Emma's sherry glass back to her. "I'm certain things can't be as bad as that."

They *were* as bad as that, and worse. Emma was tempted to lay her head on Lady Crosby's shoulder and let the story flood from her lips in all its ugliness and hurt, but before she could move, the front door opened, then thudded closed again.

Heavy footsteps echoed in the hallway, then Daniel entered the drawing room. He wasn't given to melodrama, but his face was a mask of murderous fury, tempered with an emotion Emma had never seen there before.

Anguish.

"Daniel!" She shot to her feet, her heart crowding into her throat. "Dear God, what's happened? It's not Helena?"

"Nay, lass. The girl's tucked up safe with Lady Clifford."

Emma let out a long breath, but her relief was short-lived.

"It's t'other one. Caroline Francis."

Lady Crosby rose unsteadily to her feet, her hand going to her throat. "She's been found?"

"Aye, she's been found."

Emma could read the awful truth on Daniel's face, and she reached out to steady herself with a hand on the back of the settee.

Another man might have tried to soften the blow, but Daniel wasn't the sort to skirt the truth, no matter how terrible it was. He and Emma were alike that way. That was how she knew what Daniel was going to say, before he spoke a word.

"She's dead. Found strangled to death in Orange Court."

Lady Crosby gasped, her face going white.

Emma thought of the bruises on Helena's neck tonight, the same size and shape as a man's fingers, and nausea rolled over her again. If she'd lingered at Vauxhall Gardens with Samuel for another moment—if she'd allowed him another kiss, another caress, Helena would be dead.

"Orange Court," Emma repeated faintly, digging her fingertips into the settee. "That's only a few blocks off Drury Lane."

"Aye. Our kidnapper's turned murderer. Like as not he's been a killer all along, but now there's a body to prove it."

Lady Crosby rose unsteadily to her feet. "I think I'd better...I believe I'll retire to my bedchamber for a short time."

"Yes, my lady." Emma's anxious gaze followed Lady Crosby as she made her way to the door of the drawing room. For the first time since Emma had met her, Lady Crosby looked every moment of her age.

If her ladyship fell ill over this, Emma would never forgive herself.

It was yet another thing to worry about.

She sank back down on the settee, every limb trembling with exhaustion. Her eyes felt gritty, and her head was pounding.

"Go on up to yer own rooms for now, lass," Daniel said gruffly. "We can talk on this later. I'll send for ye if there's a need."

But as exhausted as Emma was, she knew she'd never be able to rest. Every time she closed her eyes, she'd be haunted with the waking nightmares of last night. Caroline Francis lying dead in a dark alley. The bruises on Helena's neck, the tears in her eyes. Samuel's face when Helena said Lord Lovell's name, and later, in the carriage, when he'd asked her to tell him the truth.

Was I part of your scheme all along?

He had been, at first, but then...then he hadn't.

Emma wasn't sure when it had changed. That day at Hyde Park, or the next day, in Lady Tremaine's rose garden? That night at Drury Lane, when she'd glanced over at his box and found him staring at her, his gray gaze like a caress.

The way he'd kissed her scars...

It had been all of those moments, and none of them.

There hadn't been a single moment, a single touch, a single kiss. It had crept up on her, and she hadn't even thought to look for it, when nothing—*nothing*—ever crept up on Emma Downing.

Except this had, and before she even knew she held it in her hand, it was already gone.

She slumped back against the settee, and she must have fallen asleep, because it was hours later when she blinked awake to Lady Crosby gently shaking her shoulder. "Emma? Wake up, dearest."

"What time is it?" Emma sat up, rubbing her eyes. Daniel was gone, and late morning sunlight was filtering through the drapes.

"Nearly eleven, and we have a visitor. Tidy your hair a bit, won't you? Oh, dear, your gown is all wrinkles. Well, it's too late to do anything about it now."

Lady Crosby fussed and patted Emma into near-respectability, then sent word for the footman to show their visitor into the drawing room. Emma expected Lady Flora and Lady Silvester to appear, but that wasn't who walked into the room moments later.

It was Lady Lymington.

"Good morning, my lady. How do you do?" Lady Crosby rose to her feet.

It wasn't so shocking that Lady Lymington should call—she and Lady Crosby were friendly, if not intimates—but after what had happened with Samuel, the last person Emma expected to stroll into their drawing room was his mother.

"Lady Crosby, and Lady Emma." Lady Lymington inclined her head, and accepted the seat Lady Crosby indicated. A brief silence fell before Lady Lymington awkwardly cleared her throat. "I beg your pardon for calling so early, but it seems we're to, ah, leave London for Kent later this morning."

Lady Lymington shot a glance at Emma, who struggled to keep her face neutral.

Samuel must have offered his mother *some* explanation for their precipitous departure from London. It was difficult to guess what he'd told her from Lady Lymington's expression, but given Emma had suspected her ladyship's beloved nephew of kidnapping and murder, Emma braced herself for a flood of angry denials and bitter recriminations.

They never came.

What *did* come left both Emma and Lady Crosby momentarily speechless.

Lady Lymington shifted uneasily on the settee. "I didn't like to leave London without seeing you both first."

Emma and Lady Crosby exchanged a glance. Their level of acquaintance with Lady Lymington didn't demand such a courtesy. It was a bit odd, but Lady Crosby, who was all graciousness, leapt into the fray to cover the awkward silence. "That's very kind of you, my lady. We'll miss you very much, won't we, Emma, dear?"

"We will, indeed. The season won't be the same without your family here, Lady Lymington." Those words were truer than any Emma had ever spoken, so true it was as if they'd been wrenched from her soul.

Lady Lymington studied Emma's face, as if gauging her sincerity. "It does seem a great shame we should part now, just as we're all becoming such good friends. That's why I've come, you see."

Emma stared at Lady Lymington. It almost sounded as if she intended to—

"Lady Flora is tremendously fond of Lady Emma, as you know, Lady Crosby, and then you and Lady Silvester are such dear friends. They're both insisting upon accompanying us to Kent, but they've been made rather unhappy over it, I think."

Emma said nothing, but leaned forward, waiting, hoping....

"My nephew doesn't like to see Lady Flora made unhappy in any way, and so I came to see if I might persuade you both to come for a visit at Lymington House."

Lady Crosby covered her gasp of surprise with a dainty cough. "How kind you are, my lady. We'd like that very much, wouldn't we, Emma?"

Emma didn't answer. She'd fallen back against the settee, stunned speechless.

The idea of appearing at Lymington House after that scene with Samuel in his carriage made a cowardly shudder roll down Emma's spine, but even with the mistakes she'd made, the lies and the mess and the heartbreak, she'd never before been a coward.

Lord Lovell was innocent, but someone else at Lymington House was as guilty as the devil himself. Two girls had vanished. Both of them were likely dead, and Caroline Francis had lost her life in a filthy London alley, the breath strangled out of her.

Now, unbelievably, a second chance to bring the murderous villain to justice had just fallen into Emma's lap. How many more girls would meet the same tragic fate if she gave up now? How many more girls just like Helena—just like Emma herself—would find themselves at the mercy of a villain, because Emma was too spineless to face an imperious marquess?

The only way to unravel the rest of this mystery was to uncover the secrets that remained buried in Kent. She *had* to get to Lymington House. It was as simple as that.

"Er, Emma, dear. Lady Lymington has generously invited us to Lymington House." Lady Crosby gave Emma a meaningful look. "Isn't that kind of her?"

"Yes, yes, very kind indeed, my lady." Emma recovered her wits enough to smile gratefully at Lady Lymington. "I've always enjoyed the country, and it's especially delightful in the spring."

"It's settled, then. How wonderful! Lady Flora will be so pleased. I beg your pardon for leaving so abruptly, but Lord Lymington is anxious to be on our way." Lady Lymington rose to her feet, casting another curious glance at Emma.

Emma forced herself to meet Lady Lymington's eyes, then regretted it at once when she saw they were the same lovely dark gray as her son's.

"Of course, I'll see you both again at Lymington House very soon," Lady Lymington added. "Tomorrow, perhaps? The journey is a brief one, and exceedingly pleasant. If you're not too fatigued, may we expect you for a late supper?"

"Certainly, my lady. We're looking forward to it."

Emma smiled at Lady Lymington, but remained where she was while Lady Crosby rose from the settee and accompanied her to the door of the drawing room, chatting amiably about the countryside around Kent, and begging Lady Lymington to send their compliments to Lady Flora and Lady Silvester.

Meanwhile, Emma's head was spinning.

"What an unexpected stroke of good luck!" Lady Crosby joined Emma on the settee once Lady Lymington was gone. "I daresay we were due for some. But you look grave, Emma. What's troubling you?"

Emma hesitated. It *was* a stroke of good luck, but Lady Crosby might not still think so when she knew the plan that was forming in Emma's head. "Perhaps we'd better fetch Daniel, my lady."

Lady Crosby cast her a wary look, but she signaled for a footman to fetch Daniel. They heard the thump of his boots coming down the hallway before he entered the drawing room and took up his place in front of the fire. "All right then, lass?"

Emma gave him a grateful look. "Yes, much better. It looks as if we're leaving for Lymington House tomorrow, Daniel."

One heavy dark eyebrow rose. "That so?"

"Yes. Lady Lymington has cordially invited us for a visit to Kent." Emma glanced at Lady Crosby, and chose her next words carefully. "Which is fortunate, indeed, as I've a notion we'll find our murderer there."

Lady Crosby sucked in a breath, but Daniel only regarded Emma calmly, his massive arms crossed over his chest. "Why is that, lass?"

"Because he's been keeping a close eye on Lord Lymington and Lord Lovell since they arrived in London, and isn't likely to stop now. Given an opportunity, he'll follow them to Kent."

"Aye, that seems likely." Daniel waited, his dark gaze on Emma's face.

"No one will think it odd if he appears, as he's a friend of the family. It's strange, though," Emma said slowly. "As familiar as he is with them, he isn't such an intimate he knows about Lord Lovell's duel. If he did, he'd have known he couldn't implicate Lord Lovell in the crimes."

"Implicate Lord Lovell!" Lady Crosby pressed her fingertips to her lips. "My goodness, how wicked."

"Do ye have any idea who he is, lass?"

"No, not yet, but I will soon enough."

"How's that, then?"

Emma touched the pendant in her pocket, running her fingers over the rough diamonds surrounding the portrait of the young boy. "I have something of his, and he wants it back badly enough he attacked Helena tonight to get it."

"He knows ye have it?"

"I'm not sure he does, no, but he will." Emma pulled the pendant from her pocket, and held her hand out to show Daniel. "I think it will flatter me, don't you? I have just the gown to wear with it."

Lady Crosby looked between Daniel and Emma, her expression baffled and fearful at once, as if she didn't quite understand what Emma meant, but was certain she wouldn't like it.

Daniel glanced at the pendant on Emma's palm, and grunted. "Ye mean to put yerself in his way, then?"

"*What?*" Lady Crosby snatched Emma's hand in a frantic grip. "No. He'll hurt you, Emma!"

Emma had been threatened before, even attacked before, but even she couldn't suppress a shudder at the thought of being the target of a man so cold-blooded. Because of course he'd been the one who'd taken Amy and Kitty from Lymington House, before setting his sights on Caroline Francis.

"I imagine he's desperate to get this pendant back, and desperate criminals are likely to become careless." Emma's gaze met Daniel's. "If he were to find me unexpectedly in his path, the pendant around my neck, who knows what mistakes he might—"

"God in heaven!" Lady Crosby shot to her feet. "That's madness, Emma!"

Lady Crosby had faced every challenge thus far with the aplomb of a lady born for intrigue, but Caroline Francis strangled and left dead in an alley and her dear Emma threatened with a similar fate was too much for her.

"I thought it might come to this, my lady." Emma drew Lady Crosby gently down onto the settee beside her. "I knew how dangerous this could become when I agreed to go ahead with it. Surely, you can understand why I must see it through?"

"But to throw yourself into such a man's path, Emma!" Lady Crosby wailed. "How can you be certain it won't end in tragedy?"

I can't. Emma didn't say it, but Lady Crosby was no fool. "If it's not me, it will be some other lady, one who doesn't know how to defend herself, and doesn't have you and Daniel to help her."

Lady Crosby shook her head, her face crumpling.

"Please, my lady. I can't turn up at Lymington House without my grandmother, can I?" Emma's tone was light, but she needed Lady Crosby as much as she did Daniel. Samuel knew part of the truth about her, but as far as the rest of the *ton* was concerned, she was still Lady Emma Crosby, and Lady Emma Crosby didn't visit the Marquess of Lymington's country estate without a proper chaperone. "Lady Crosby?"

Lady Crosby drew in a shuddering breath. "I don't like it, Emma, but I did agree to this, just as you did, and I won't disappoint you and Daniel and Lady Clifford."

Emma sagged with relief. "Thank you, my lady. Don't forget Daniel will be with us. He's accustomed to dealing with murderous villains."

"That's, ah…very reassuring, Emma."

"We might wish to arrive several hours before supper, so we have time to unpack our things and rest before the evening commences." If they were already ensconced in their rooms, it would be more difficult for Samuel to toss them out.

"Of course, if you wish it, dear," Lady Crosby said dully. "Whatever makes you comfortable, Emma."

"Thank you." Emma pressed Lady Crosby's hand gratefully, but she didn't fool herself into thinking there would be anything comfortable about this visit.

I don't want to see your face ever again, Emma.

No, nothing comfortable, at all.

Chapter Eighteen

Samuel strode into the drawing room, found Lovell and Lady Flora whispering together on the settee in front of the fire, turned without a word, and strode back out again.

"Wait, Lymington," Lovell called, rising to his feet. "A word, if you would?"

Damn. He'd nearly escaped. Maybe he could pretend he hadn't heard—

"I know you heard me, Lymington."

Samuel let out a defeated breath and returned to the drawing room to see Lovell lean close to Flora and whisper something in her ear. Flora's cheeks flushed a becoming pink, and she rose to her feet. She nodded to Samuel, then slipped past him and out the door of the drawing room.

Samuel waited until Flora's footsteps had faded, then crossed the room and threw himself into a chair across from the settee. "Don't let Lady Silvester catch you in here alone with Lady Flora, Lovell."

Lovell chuckled. "Not to worry, Lymington. Lady Silvester left the two of us here alone when she went upstairs to dress for dinner. I think we can assume she trusts me with her granddaughter."

"Both ladies have forgiven you for your wild antics this past year, then. You're a fortunate man, Lovell."

"Indeed," Lovell murmured. "Forgiveness is a divine thing, isn't it?"

"Divine, or unforgivably foolish, depending on the offense." Samuel winced at the resentment that colored his words. Lady Flora was the reason Samuel had insisted they go to London for the season in the first place. Would he sulk now, once he'd gotten precisely what he wanted?

It wasn't that he resented Lovell, or the happiness his cousin had found with Flora.

Not specifically.

No, he resented everything and everyone in equal measure. Lovell, Lady Flora, Lady Silvester, Lady Crosby, Emma—*especially* Emma—but he resented *himself* more, for having been fool enough to be taken in by her wiles, and for continuing in that foolishness now, even after he knew what she was.

He'd returned to Kent determined to banish Emma from his mind forever. She'd lied to him, and used him. He didn't even know her surname, for God's sake. After everything they'd gone through together, she hadn't even given him that much.

This, because she believed his cousin was guilty of a despicable crime.

Lovell had his flaws, but a kidnapper and murderer? Anyone who'd spent any time with Lovell should have known at once he was the furthest thing from a cold-blooded villain.

All the time Emma had been smiling at Samuel, flirting with him and kissing him with those soft, red lips, she'd been plotting to fit Lovell's neck with a noose. It was a betrayal in every way. Every time he thought of it, it was as if a pile of stones had crashed down on his chest, crushing him under the unbearable weight.

Yet somehow, even now, she was all he could think about. He fell asleep every night with her soft, husky voice in his ears, dreamed of her dark blue eyes, and woke every morning, aching for her.

What sort of man pined for a woman who'd told him more lies than truths?

"You've no need to worry about Lady Flora's virtue," Lovell said, recalling Samuel to the present. "I've been the picture of restraint, Lymington—a perfect gentleman."

Samuel gave his cousin a guilty look. He had no business lashing out at Lovell. It wasn't Lovell's fault he was miserable. It was no one's fault but his own, for acting such a damn fool over a pretty face. "You have, indeed. Well done, Lovell."

"If I *have* done well, it's because you didn't abandon me. You've ever been my conscience, Samuel, and I'm grateful to you for fighting for my happiness, even when I didn't deserve it."

Samuel's heart softened at the sincerity in Lovell's blue eyes. At one time he'd feared the good-natured, caring boy Lovell had once been was gone forever, but with every day that passed, he saw more and more of that boy in the man Lovell was becoming. "You're my cousin, Lovell. Your happiness is as important to me as my own."

"Your happiness is just as important to me, so you can imagine how dejected I am to see you wandering about with that woebegone expression."

Samuel grunted. This was the trouble with being around a couple who were madly in love. They expected everyone around them to be as blissful as they were. Samuel was, unfortunately, as far from blissful as a man could get, but he *could* make more of an effort to climb out of the deep pool of self-pity he was wallowing in.

"I beg your pardon if my expression offends you, Lovell," he snapped, then cringed. Damn it. He'd meant to say something gracious.

"You may growl all you like, and welcome. I just wonder what has you so grim. You have no reason to be, from what you've told me."

"No reason to be pleased, either." Samuel kicked at the ornately carved leg of the delicate little table beside his chair. He'd always despised this particular table. Its very daintiness offended him, made him feel big and clumsy.

"Don't assault the table, if you please, Lymington."

Samuel huffed, but he balanced one leg over the other knee in an attempt to save the furnishings.

"It occurs to me something hasn't been resolved to your satisfaction," Lovell went on. "I wonder what it could be?"

"Nothing. I'm perfectly well satisfied."

Lovell snorted. "That must be why you've been stomping about with that dark scowl on your face, terrifying everyone who crosses your path. Yesterday I saw poor Mr. Humphries turn and scurry back up the staircase when he saw you coming."

Samuel gave another irritable grunt. "All the better."

Lovell studied Samuel's expression. "I have a theory about your troubles. Would you like to hear it?"

"Have I any other choice?"

"None whatsoever. It's my considered opinion you've fallen madly in love with a certain lady, but are too stubborn to admit it." Lovell shook his head, as if Samuel were being very tiresome, indeed. "Shall I tell you which lady I think has captured your heart?"

Samuel turned a dark scowl on his cousin. *"No."*

He knew which name was about to fall from his cousin's lips, and he was desperate not to hear it spoken aloud, as if even a whisper would conjure the lady herself—that she'd appear in the drawing room, and break his heart all over again.

Lovell of course, ignored him. "Lady Emma Crosby."

Samuel flinched. Damn it, he'd spent the past day doing whatever he could to forget that name, and the lady attached to it, only to have Lovell blurt it out. "Not *Crosby*, Lovell," he muttered through clenched teeth. "Not *lady* either, as far as we know."

She'd lied about everything else. Why not that as well? And who'd said a single word about love? Not *him*. How could he be madly in love with a lady when he didn't even know her name?

Lovell regarded him calmly. "Her title doesn't make a shred of difference, and you know it. Lady Emma, or just Emma, you love her either way."

Yes, Samuel loved her, but he didn't *want* to love her. That was why he'd told her he didn't wish to ever lay eyes on her again. He could no longer tell whether that had been very wise of him, or very, very foolish, so he confined his answer to a third irritable grunt.

"The question, Lymington, is what you intend to do about it."

"*Do*? Not a damned thing. For God's sake, Lovell, have you forgotten she believed you to be a debaucher, kidnapper, and murderer?"

Meanwhile the real debaucher, kidnapper, and murderer was still running loose, and Samuel *did* intend to do something about that. He wouldn't rest until he discovered who the scoundrel was, and saw him held accountable for his crimes. The trouble was, he had no idea where to start.

"I'm not likely to forget that, Lymington. I confess it's a trifle uncomfortable, Lady Emma's trying to see me hanged, but you'd do well to listen to her explanation, even so. Not for *her* sake, but for yours. This business with her will never be over until you know the truth."

"I *asked* her to explain herself, Lovell! She refused." Samuel dragged his hand down his face. Even if he *could* forgive her for what she'd done, he didn't think he could ever trust her again. "She lied to me."

She'd lied about everything, and her betrayal was lodged in the tissue of his heart like a sliver, leaving a small but painful tear where the point had pierced the tender flesh.

"She did, yes, but it's not her lies you can't forgive."

"No?" Samuel's laugh was grim. "What is it, then?"

Lovell's gaze was steady. "You can't forgive her because you believe she was only pretending to care for you."

"She *was* pretending, Lovell." Emma might expel every breath in her body denying it, but every time Samuel looked into her face, heard the slightest tremor in her voice, wouldn't he always suspect she was lying to him?

All at once, Samuel felt weary to his bones. "None of this makes any dif—"

"Samuel?" Lady Lymington appeared at the drawing room door. "Oh, and Lancelot. Here you both are. Supper is served. Shall we go to the dining room?"

Samuel didn't have any appetite at all, but he managed a half-hearted smile for his mother, and offered her his arm. She didn't take it, but hung back, motioning to Lovell to precede them.

Samuel frowned. "Is something wrong?"

"Nothing at all, only...you will do your best to be gracious to our guests this evening?"

Dear God. Had he really made himself so unbearable his mother felt the need to remind him to behave like a gentleman? "Of course, unless... is there some reason I might be tempted to be ungracious?"

Lady Lymington avoided his gaze. "No, no, I just...well, keep in mind that everything I do, Samuel, I do for your own good."

His own good? Nothing pleasant ever followed *that* sort of observation. God in heaven, now what? "That sounds ominous."

"Nonsense. All is well." Lady Lymington gave a brisk laugh, but she was agitated as she urged Samuel toward the dining room.

Several footmen were moving about, silver serving platters in their hands, and the low murmur of voices was audible from the hallway, but that wasn't what caught Samuel's attention.

It was Lovell. His cousin had come to an abrupt halt in the doorway of the dining room. "What are you doing, Lovell?"

Lovell glanced over his shoulder at Samuel, his eyes wide. "Before you go in, Lymington, let me remind you that the dining room is not a proper place for a frontal assault."

"Frontal assault? What are you on about, Lovell?"

Lovell's gaze slid to Lady Lymington. "Can't say the same for ambushes, I'm afraid."

Samuel blinked. "For God's sake, what has you two in such a lather?"

"Er, well...perhaps it's best if you see for yourself." Lovell stepped aside and gestured Samuel forward.

Samuel didn't make it more than two steps into the dining room before he broke off, his mouth dropping open in shock.

Directly across from the doorway, seated next to her grandmother, dressed in a blue dinner gown that turned her eyes the color of midnight skies, sat Lady Emma Crosby.

* * * *

Emma took one look at Samuel's scowling face, and her heart plunged in her chest.

Dear God. Perhaps this hadn't been such a good idea, after all. It was too late to do anything about it *now*, but it took every bit of determination she possessed not to leap to her feet and flee the dining room.

Lord Lovell was blocking the doorway, his back to the company, murmuring urgently to Samuel, who was a step in front of him, his dark head towering over his cousin's.

Perhaps she could duck under the table—

"You've gone as pale as a ghost, Emma." Lady Crosby seized Emma's hand under the table. "It's all right, you know. He's not going to gobble you up."

Emma wasn't so sure. He looked as if he'd be more than happy to forgo the beef course, and make a meal of *her* instead.

She could never be afraid of him—she knew who Samuel was, under that scowl, knew the caring, tender heart he hid inside that powerful chest, yet still her pulse refused to cease its frantic pounding, because she was afraid of losing him.

Only she *was* losing him, even now, and her heart recognized it, while her head, the organ she relied upon, was still foolishly hoping.

"What are you doing here?"

It took all of Emma's fortitude not to shrink down in her chair as every head at the table turned in her direction.

"My goodness," Lady Crosby muttered in Emma's ear. "He *is* a bit cross, isn't he?"

Samuel was staring at her, his gray eyes as cold as ice. "Why are you in my home? I thought I made myself clear regarding my wishes on that point, *Lady* Emma."

"Samuel!" Lady Lymington exclaimed, shocked. "That is quite enough."

Samuel didn't spare his mother a glance, but took another step into the room, his gaze fixed on Emma. "I beg your pardon, Mother. I didn't anticipate the pleasure of Lady Emma's company at Lymington House."

Emma said nothing, because she couldn't speak. She could only stare at Samuel's face in misery. She'd imagined he'd be angry, but *this*...this was worse than angry.

He was *hurt*. She could see the pain in every line of his face even as he struggled to maintain a neutral expression.

"Now, Lymington," Lord Lovell warned. "There's no need to make a scene."

Emma almost laughed. It was far too late for that. The scene had begun, and it looked as if it were going to unfold in all its awful glory in front of Lord Lymington's dinner guests.

She half-rose from her chair, intending to leave the table, if not the house, but before she could take a step Lady Lymington spoke up, her voice firm. "It's all right, Lady Emma. Do take your seat. I invited Lady Crosby and Lady Emma to Lymington House, Samuel. They are *my* guests, and you will treat them with the same respect you would any guest in this house."

Lady Lymington didn't often assert herself so forcefully, and her words seemed to recall Samuel to his senses. After a long, tense pause, he inclined his head. "Very well, my lady."

"Thank you. Now, go and sit down." Lady Lymington urged him toward the head of the table. To Emma's immense relief he obeyed, but she could tell by his black scowl her reprieve wouldn't extend beyond the last course.

Whatever appetite Emma had fled for its life in the wake of that scowl. Her stomach tied itself in knots, and the few bites she did manage to choke down tasted like sawdust.

It wasn't a comfortable meal for anyone. Lord Lovell and Lady Lymington did their best to smooth over the unpleasantness and act as if nothing untoward had happened, but no one ate much, and Lady Lymington called the ladies from the table as soon as decency allowed.

Lady Flora rushed to Emma's side once they reached the drawing room, a scandalized expression on her pretty face. "If I hadn't seen it with my own eyes, I never would have believed Lord Lymington could behave so dreadfully! He's always been gruff, of course, but...well, perhaps the less said about that scene at supper, the better."

"Yes, I think that's best, Flora." Emma was grateful for her friend's kind words, but her heart was lodged in her throat, and there would be no coaxing it back into her chest until she spoke with Samuel.

"I, for one, am delighted to see you, Emma," Lady Flora added loyally, linking their arms together.

"Thank you, Flora." Emma managed a weak smile, but regret was heavy in her chest. Flora didn't know the truth about her yet, but once she did, their fledgling friendship would come to a swift end.

To Flora's credit, she didn't release her hold on Emma when Lord Lovell and Samuel entered the drawing room, not even when Samuel shot a look in their direction so dark Emma was amazed it didn't leave scorch marks in the carpet.

He didn't waste any time, but stalked across the room toward Emma, pausing to address himself to Lady Crosby. "I'd like to have a word with Lady Emma, alone. With your permission, my lady."

Lady Crosby looked him up and down, her lips tight. "I'm not certain I can permit that after your shocking behavior in the dining room, Lord Lymington."

"Bad form, Lymington," Lord Lovell muttered, shaking his head.

Lady Silvester cast a sympathetic look at Samuel. "I daresay we can trust Lord Lymington to speak with Lady Emma on the far side of the drawing room."

Hardly. If there was ever an altercation that would swell to the size of an entire room, this was it. A hysterical laugh threatened, but Emma bit it back, and with a hasty gulp, rose to her feet. "I'm willing to speak to Lord Lymington in private."

Samuel said nothing, only nodded and gestured her toward the door.

Emma was shaking as he followed her down the hallway, but she kept her head high.

She'd prepared for this moment, and knew just what she had to do.

Tell him the truth. Wasn't it supposed to be easy, to tell the truth? Perhaps it would have been, if she'd been someone else, but Emma felt how a criminal might, when he was destined to swing and caught his first sight of the gibbet.

She couldn't prevent a tremor when Samuel led her to a dimly lit library and closed the door behind them. Oh, why did it have to be a *library*? She didn't have much luck with libraries.

Samuel strode to a sideboard, fetched two crystal glasses, and poured a measure of some dark red liquid into each. Emma stood in the middle of the room, unsure what to do until he gestured her to a chair by the fire, then took the seat across from her, and handed her a tumbler.

Emma took a cautious sip. Port, and it didn't *taste* poisoned.

She sat quietly, sipping her port and waiting for a barrage of accusations to flood from his lips. It was some moments before she realized he was waiting for her to speak.

But she didn't know where to start. It was all so complicated, and confusing, and—

"I really am fond of Reynolds's military portraits," she blurted, then blinked.

Well, that was one way to begin.

"But they aren't the reason you went to the Royal Academy that day." Samuel's face was expressionless, as if he'd never seen her before.

"No," she admitted.

Nothing. Not a word from him, or even a twitch.

"Does everyone at Lymington House know the truth about me?" It wasn't a question likely to endear her to Samuel, but Emma needed to know her situation if she was going to make any progress.

"No. Only my mother, and Lovell. That is, they know what I know. That you're not Lady Emma Crosby, that you work with Lady Amanda Clifford, and that you were attempting to prove Lovell is a murderer." Samuel shot her a dark look. "None of us know the whole truth. We don't even know your real name."

"My real name is Emma Downing. I'm not the Earl of Crosby's daughter, or Lady Crosby's granddaughter. I'm not a lady at all." Emma took a desperate gulp of her port and coughed a little, though she couldn't have said whether it was the wine or her words choking her.

Dear God, how she'd dreaded this moment, even before she'd fallen in love with Samuel. It took every bit of resolve she had to meet his gaze, but Emma forced herself to meet it, and hold it.

"Helena Reeves was never my lady's maid. I know Helena and Madame Marchand because I spent a year at the Pink Pearl, as a courtesan. I was a courtesan." Emma wasn't sure why she felt the need to repeat it a second time, except once you decided to tell the truth, you told *all* of it, without flinching.

She was done pretending to be someone she wasn't.

"I was born in Essex, near Chelmsford. I don't remember either of my parents. I only ever had my grandmother. When she died, I went off to London to find work, as so many other young girls do. I'd been in the city for less than an hour when Madame Marchand plucked me up. She offered me accommodations, and pretty clothes, and made dozens of empty promises. I thought she did it out of kindness." Emma gave a bitter laugh. "I soon found out otherwise. I was fourteen years old."

Emma had dreaded speaking those words, but now they were out she found herself strangely tempted to tell him everything—she, who never talked about that time she'd spent pinned like a broken butterfly under Madame Marchand's thumb. Not even to Helena.

But he didn't care about her story. He wanted to know how Lord Lovell fit into this business, nothing more. "I left the Pink Pearl five years ago, and went to live with Lady Clifford."

Samuel remained silent, but he tensed at mention of Lady Clifford. That was generally how people reacted when they heard her name. Not many people in London knew what Lady Clifford actually *did*, but most of them had heard of her.

"The other day, you asked me why Lady Clifford suspected Lord Lovell was responsible for your missing housemaids. I couldn't tell you why at that time without implicating another person, a person I'd sworn to protect, but that…no longer matters."

Emma thought of Caroline Francis, dying alone in a dark alley, and her stomach lurched. For all the lies Caroline had told, she hadn't deserved such a fate. "We suspected Lord Lovell because Caroline Francis told Helena he seduced her, ruined her, and then abandoned her, and she accused him of nefarious behavior with Amy and Kitty as well."

Samuel stared at her in astonishment. "*What?*"

"Here." Emma reached into the pocket of her skirts, and pulled out the letter she'd asked Caroline to write. "It's all there."

He looked at the paper as if it were a viper about to strike, but he took the folded sheets, and leaned closer to the light of the fire to read them.

Emma waited, watching the expressions play over his face. Confusion, incredulity, and, by the time he'd read the last word, righteous fury. "These are lies. Every last word of it."

"I know that now. I won't pretend I didn't believe Caroline's accusations at first. I did. I had no reason to suspect she was lying, and this past year Lord Lovell has earned himself a reputation as a rake."

"A *rake*, yes." Samuel voice was icy. "Not a murderer."

"Not a murderer, no. From the start your cousin didn't appear to me to be a violent man." Emma didn't say she'd had enough experience with violent men to know one when she saw one. "But it was Flora who made me suspect Caroline was lying about Lord Lovell, though she didn't know it."

"*Flora*? How?"

"She told me Lord Lovell wasn't sent down from Oxford until September of last year. Caroline claimed he returned to Lymington House in August, just before Amy Townshend went missing. Both things couldn't be true, and Flora had no reason to lie."

Samuel scanned the letter again, nodding slowly.

"Lord Lovell couldn't be responsible for Amy's disappearance if he wasn't at Lymington House when she went missing, and I couldn't quite credit the idea that Lymington House was cursed with two murderous scoundrels. Then I found out about Lord Lovell's duel."

"From Lady Flora?"

"Yes, on the day of Lady Tremaine's picnic, when Flora and I were alone together in the parlor. After I learned of the duel, I suspected Lord Lovell was innocent, but I had to be sure. That was why I rushed off to the Pink Pearl that evening, to see Caroline, and ask her—"

"Ask her about the dates."

"Yes. Whoever tried to implicate Lord Lovell for the crimes didn't know about the duel, or else they would have known his prolonged recovery made it impossible for him to seduce Caroline, as she claimed he did. Caroline must not have known of the duel, either."

"What of the second girl, Kitty Yardley?"

"It looks as though Lord Lovell *was* at Lymington House when Kitty disappeared, but there's no reason to suspect he had anything to do with it, aside from Caroline Francis's word, which has proved to be untrustworthy."

"It sounds as if someone went to a great deal of trouble to make Lovell look guilty."

"Yes, they did. My own belief is the villain murdered Amy Townshend in a fit of passion, then panicked, and started looking about for someone to blame."

Samuel frowned. "Why should you think that?"

"Because Amy's disappearance was so sudden. That implies it was an accident, rather than the result of careful planning."

He considered this, and nodded.

"Then there's the issue of the dates. The culprit must have known *someone* would realize Lord Lovell wasn't at Lymington House when Amy disappeared, but he went ahead anyway, because he had to pin the blame on someone. I haven't quite worked out why he thought he could get away pinning it on Lord Lovell, given the discrepancy in the dates, but your cousin had a reputation for wild, unpredictable behavior, so he was the ideal choice for a villain looking for a scapegoat."

"I...hadn't thought of it that way," Samuel admitted reluctantly.

"No, you wouldn't have, because you didn't know your cousin had been implicated in the crimes at all. I believe Kitty Yardley was taken to reinforce the appearance of Lovell's guilt. Caroline Francis as well, though something must have gone wrong there, or Caroline never would have turned up at the Pink Pearl."

Samuel was quiet for some time, his gaze on the fire, then, "You...how did you put it? You took *an interest* in Lovell so you might get close to him, and thus prove his guilt?"

"His guilt, or his innocence, but yes, that was how it started."

Samuel kept his gaze on the fire. "Once you found out his heart belonged to Lady Flora, you transferred your false affections to *me*."

Underneath the anger, Emma heard the uncertainty, the hurt in his voice, and she couldn't bear it. "Do you remember the day we first kissed, in Lady Tremaine's rose garden?"

Samuel let out a harsh laugh. "I remember. How could I forget it? Bravo, Miss Downing. It never even occurred to me you were pretending."

"I wasn't pretending. That kiss happened *after* I suspected Lord Lovell was innocent, Samuel."

It wasn't much, taken against the other lies she'd told. She didn't expect Samuel to ever forgive her for them, but if only she could make him see she hadn't been feigning her regard for him, hadn't used him, perhaps it would help heal his heart.

"Are you trying to persuade me you kissed me because you *wanted* me?"

Emma closed her eyes. How could she make him understand she'd never pretended with him? With every other man, yes, but not with *him*. She'd lied because she hadn't had any other choice, but their kiss in the garden, the moments of tenderness and passion that had followed—that had all been real. "I did want you. I still do."

Samuel thrust the letter back into Emma's hands. "I don't believe you."

Emma had known he wouldn't, but she'd had to say it. She'd sworn to herself she would tell him the truth, no matter how much it hurt when he didn't believe her.

And now she'd said what she needed to say. She'd failed, just as she'd known she would, but she was here, at Lymington House, and that meant there was still a chance she could find justice for Amy, Kitty, and Caroline.

She could do that much.

Emma set her glass down on a table, and rose to her feet. "Caroline Francis was murdered in London last night, my lord. Someone strangled her."

Samuel went unnaturally still.

Emma walked to the door, but paused before leaving, her back to him. "I know you don't want me here, but there's a murderer running loose, and he's somehow connected to Lymington House. I'm here to find out who he is. Once I do, I'll go, and you'll never have to see me again."

"We don't want your help, Miss Downing. I don't see how any of this has anything to do with you anymore."

Emma almost turned to face him again, but it was easier this way—easier not to look. "I have something of his, and he wants it back. Once he realizes that, he'll make himself known. It's only a matter of time."

Silence. Emma waited, but when Samuel didn't speak, she opened the library door and slipped out, closing it quietly behind her.

There was nothing more to say.

Chapter Nineteen

"You look like an angry bear this morning, Lymington."

Samuel stopped in the doorway of the breakfast parlor, his bleary gaze falling on his cousin. "What the devil are you doing downstairs, Lovell? It's not even noon yet."

"And a good morning to you, too, cousin." Lovell looked Samuel up and down, his brow furrowed. "Not a satisfactory hibernation last night, I take it?"

"I haven't the vaguest idea what you're talking about." Samuel strode over to the sideboard, filled a plate, then joined Lovell at the table. He stared gloomily down at his eggs, then shoved them away. He snatched up his coffee instead, but before he could take a sip, he noticed Lovell staring at him from across the table. "*What?*"

"Nothing, just, ah…what's happened there?" Lovell waved a hand at Samuel's head.

Samuel raised a hand to his hair with a frown. "What do you mean? Nothing's happened."

"Oh, something's happened, I assure you. Did Fletcher abandon you this morning?"

Samuel winced at mention of his valet. "No, I sent him away." The last thing he'd wanted after a night spent tossing in his bed was to endure Fletcher's fussing, but he could have dismissed the man with a *bit* more cordiality. It wasn't his poor valet's fault he hadn't slept a wink last night.

Or any night, really, since he'd first laid eyes on Emma Downing.

"Well, that explains it." Lovell took up his teacup, but instead of drinking from it he continued to stare at Samuel over the rim with a perplexed expression.

"For God's sake, Lovell." Samuel slammed his own cup down with more force than he'd intended. "Just say it, whatever it is, and get it over with, so we can move on."

"Very well, then. Your hair is a trifle, er...disheveled."

"Well, what of it?" Samuel grumbled. "What does it matter what my hair looks like?"

"I suppose it doesn't matter, if you don't mind that it looks like a small animal has been burrowing in it. And where's your cravat?"

"My cravat? It's right..." Samuel fumbled at his neck, but his fingertips met only bare skin. "Oh. I thought I'd...I suppose I forgot it."

Lovell's face softened. "Never mind. As you said, it hardly matters. I've an idea, Lymington. Let's have a ride together this morning. A nice, long one. We haven't ridden together in ages."

"What about your leg?" Lovell had only been able to sit a horse for short distances since his injury.

"Better and better every day, and we can always return if it begins to ache. Come, Lymington, no one will wonder about your hair if you've been riding all day."

Samuel returned Lovell's cheeky smile with a half-hearted one of his own. He didn't care for the idea of moping about Lymington House all day, wondering where Emma was, but he didn't fancy a ride, either. He didn't fancy anything. "I don't think I'm up to it today, Lovell."

Lovell's smile vanished. He opened his mouth to reply, but then closed it again, hesitating.

Samuel sighed. "Go on."

"This business with Lady Emma, Samuel. I think perhaps you should—"

"She'd not *Lady* Emma, Lovell. Just Emma, or rather, Miss Emma Downing."

"Emma Downing is her real name?"

"Yes. At least, she says so."

Lovell fiddled with the handle of his cup, a troubled look on his face. "Do you believe her?"

Yes. His answer was instant, surprising Samuel, but doubt followed right on its heels. "I don't know what I believe anymore, Lovell. She's lied to us all, over and over again—"

"Good morning, Lord Lymington, and Lord Lovell."

Samuel's head jerked to the door of the breakfast room. Lady Crosby was standing there, her lips tight with outrage, and beside her stood Emma, her face white.

It was clear they'd overheard every word.

Lovell shot to his feet, his cheeks flushing. "Lady Crosby, and Lady Em—that is, good morning to you both. May I help you each to a plate?"

Lady Crosby gave him an offended sniff. "No, thank you, Lord Lovell. We're perfectly able to help ourselves. Come along, Emma."

Emma trailed after Lady Crosby without a word. Samuel struggled not to follow her with his eyes, but it was no use. No matter how much he might wish it wasn't so, when she was in the room, nothing else existed for him.

But she looked different this morning, unlike herself.

Her hair wasn't disheveled, as his was, nor was a single item of her clothing missing. There was no indication at all she'd spent the night tossing in her bed as Samuel had, but she didn't look anything like the London belle, the lovely, elegant creature who'd set the *ton* atwitter with her triumphant debut at Almack's.

She was lovely still. She could never be anything but lovely to Samuel, despite his resentment toward her, but something had changed, something so subtle no one who hadn't spent hours looking at her face would even notice it.

Samuel *had* spent hours looking at her face, but even he couldn't quite pinpoint what it was. Her eyes were as bewitching a blue as they'd always been, her hair the same silky gold, her lips their usual tempting red, but her practiced charm and coquettish glances, that teasing quirk at the corners of her lips were all gone. It was as if her features had been scrubbed clean, or—

Yes, that was exactly it.

The truth struck Samuel like a blow to the chest. The hard, glittering masque meant to charm, entice, distract had been torn away.

She wasn't Lady Emma Crosby anymore. She was *his* Emma.

That is, not his Emma, but...Emma Downing. Emma Downing was the lady who'd kissed him in Lady Tremaine's rose garden. It had been Emma Downing who'd marched bravely into the Pink Pearl to save Helena Reeves, and Emma Downing who bore the evidence of a past tragedy etched into her hands.

Without realizing he did it, Samuel rose slowly to his feet. Every head turned in his direction, and a hush fell over the room. Samuel gathered his breath and opened his mouth to say...*something*, some words that would sooth this gnawing ache in his chest, that would miraculously put everything to rights again—

"Good morning!" Lady Flora burst into the breakfast room, looking like a sunbeam in her yellow gown, her face wreathed in smiles, but they vanished when she saw them all standing about like statues, glowering at each other.

"Flora, my dear girl, don't stand in front of the...*oh*." Lady Silvester came to an abrupt stop behind her granddaughter, peered around her shoulder and took in the scene with wide eyes. "Oh, dear. What's happened? Have we run out of chocolate?"

Lady Lymington followed after Lady Silvester. "My goodness, is everyone up already, even Lord Lovell? How wonder..." She trailed off when she noticed the expressions on the assembled faces, and turned to her son. "Samuel?"

Another tortuous moment passed with the entire party frozen, but then Lovell managed to gather his wits. He rose to his feet, clearing his throat. "Good morning, Aunt, Lady Silvester, and Lady Flora."

Lady Lymington hurried toward him. "Lancelot. Is everything all right?"

"Yes, yes, perfectly fine." Lovell gave her a pained smile. "Lymington and I were just about to go for a ride—"

"Lady Lymington," Samuel interrupted. "I wish to see you and Emma in my study."

"Or not," Lovell muttered.

"At once." Samuel's voice was calm, but once again every head jerked toward him, as if he'd just fired a pistol in the middle of the breakfast room. He offered them all a stiff bow, then strode to the door and waited, as if it never occurred to him either his mother or Emma would dare to disobey him.

Nor did they. Emma cast a nervous glance at Lady Crosby, but she followed Lady Lymington out of the room, avoiding Samuel's gaze as she passed.

The three of them maintained their tense silence as they made their way from the breakfast room to Samuel's study, but Lady Lymington spoke up as soon as he'd closed the door behind them. "I don't pretend to know what's happened between you and Miss Downing, Samuel, but I refuse to tolerate any more of your scowling and barking orders. You seem to have forgotten you're a gentleman."

"I agree, madam." Samuel offered Emma a stiff bow. "I beg your pardon, Miss Downing."

Deprived of her righteous indignation, Lady Lymington visibly deflated. "Yes, well, that's better. I do hope you'll keep a civil tongue in your head from now on, Samuel, because whatever your personal feelings about Miss Downing may be, we need her help. I can't bear not knowing what's happened to Amy and Kitty a moment longer."

Samuel's first childish impulse was to declare that *he* didn't need Miss Downing for anything at all, but he bit the words back, ashamed of himself. He didn't want Emma here at Lymington House, but there was no arguing with his mother's logic. Whatever his objections to Emma's presence, she'd already proved that she knew a great deal more about his missing housemaids than he did.

"Again, I agree, madam. I've called you both here so we can tell Miss Downing all we know about Amy's and Kitty's disappearances. I thought it might be helpful to her." The sooner they pieced this puzzle together and brought the culprit to justice, the sooner Emma Downing could be gone from Lymington House.

That was what Samuel wanted, for her to be *gone*. He could already feel himself weakening toward her. If she remained under his roof much longer, it would only be a matter of time before he was inviting her to walk in the gardens with him, then the next thing he knew, he'd be feeding her hothouse strawberries at breakfast every morning, or something equally ridiculous.

"That would be helpful, indeed." Emma continued to avoid Samuel's eyes, addressing herself instead to Lady Lymington.

"Please do sit down." Samuel waved them toward a seating area near the fire, and crossed the room to pull the bell to order a tray, since he'd dragged both of them off to his study before they could have a bite of breakfast.

His mother and Emma carried on an excruciatingly polite if stilted conversation while they waited for the tray to arrive and the footman to arrange the dishes on the adjacent table, but once the servant had gone and his mother had poured the tea, Emma didn't waste any time. "It would be helpful, Lady Lymington, if you could tell me what you know about Amy and Kitty first."

Lady Lymington set her teacup aside with a sigh. "I'll tell you what I can, but I don't know how much help it will be."

"Even the smallest detail could prove useful, my lady. You'd be surprised at how often the most insignificant things can shed light on a mystery such as this." Emma gave her an encouraging smile. "Just take your time, and tell me what you can."

"Yes, all right. Amy Townshend was a good girl. Oh, a trifle silly, perhaps, in the way of many young girls, but sweet-natured, with a pretty face and pretty manners. She disappeared in late August, as near as I can tell."

Emma frowned. "As near as you can tell? Is there some confusion over the date she went missing?"

"Yes. You see, I didn't realize Amy had gone missing at all until after Kitty Yardley vanished. Before that, I thought she'd simply run off with her suitor."

"Her suitor?" Emma's blue eyes sharpened. "Amy had a suitor? Who was he?"

"She had a suitor, or a sweetheart, or some such thing, yes. I don't know who he was, or anything much about him, as I try to avoid servant's gossip, but I daresay Hannah could tell you more. She's one of our kitchen maids. She and Amy shared a bedchamber, and were great friends."

"But there was a suitor, or a sweetheart, or some gentleman or other? You're certain about that?"

"Yes, quite certain."

Emma nodded. "You're already proving tremendously helpful, Lady Lymington."

"Am I, indeed?" Lady Lymington's face flushed with pleasure. "I can't tell you how happy that makes me. I do so want to help, Miss Downing."

"You are. Now, you said you thought Amy had run away with her sweetheart, until Kitty also went missing. When was that?"

"About six weeks later, in October, five weeks or so after Lord Lovell was sent down from Oxford and returned to Lymington House."

Emma bit her lip, thinking. "Did Kitty have a sweetheart, as well?"

"Oh, goodness, no. Kitty was a quiet, meek little thing—terribly shy, you know, so much so she didn't have many friends even among the other servants."

"There's no question of Kitty's having run off, then?"

"Well, it did occur to me at first that she might have run off home. She comes from a large, close family, Miss Downing, and I know she was dreadfully homesick for them, but Kitty isn't the sort to leave without giving notice. It wasn't until after Kitty vanished that I began to wonder if Amy hadn't run off, after all. Two missing servants, you know, are a great deal more sinister than one."

"Sinister indeed, my lady."

"I can't tell you how much I regret not realizing it sooner, Miss Downing. It's haunted me for weeks, that I might have been able to prevent Kitty from meeting such a dreadful fate."

"You couldn't have known, Lady Lymington. The sad truth is, young girls like Amy are lured from their homes far more often than they're kidnapped. Given the circumstances, you had no reason to suspect foul play."

"Perhaps that's so, but it's small comfort now." Lady Lymington's eyes filled with tears. "I know it may seem to you as if I don't care about what happened to my housemaids, but I assure you, Miss Downing, that isn't the case. I care very much, indeed."

Samuel reached out to grasp his mother's hand, alarmed at her tears, but before he could say a word, Emma spoke, her voice soft with compassion.

"I can see you do, my lady. Try and remember, won't you, that you're not the villain here? You didn't do anything wrong."

Lady Lymington nodded, sniffling, and Samuel listened, throat tight as Emma murmured soothingly to Lady Lymington while she gathered herself together. Only then did Emma resume her questions. "Can you tell me anything more about either Amy or Kitty, my lady?"

"No, I'm afraid not." Lady Lymington dabbed at her eyes with a handkerchief. "It was a dreadfully confusing time, Miss Downing. Lord Lovell's father had recently passed, and we were all waiting for Samuel to return to England, and then Lovell ran off to London, and got into that dreadful duel. I was torn in a half-dozen different directions, and didn't pay attention as I ought to have done."

"I understand, my lady. When did Lord Lovell leave for London?"

Lady Lymington thought for a moment. "I don't recall the precise date, but it was the middle of January, a week or two after Twelfth Night. It was very bad of him. We were all in mourning for his father at the time, you know."

"In mourning, yes," Emma repeated slowly. "So it might reasonably be expected by anyone who happened to be interested in your movements that you'd all remain at Lymington House for some months. What of Caroline Francis? Did you happen to notice any change in her behavior at this time?"

"I did, yes. She was distracted, and frequently disappeared with no explanation. It occurred to me at the time she'd also found a sweetheart, just as Amy had. You can imagine how displeased I was at *that*, Miss Downing, but before I could question her, poor Lovell was shot, and we all left Lymington House for London."

Samuel was watching Emma, who was now perched on the edge of her chair. "Let me just make certain I have this right, Lady Lymington. The family was here at Lymington House, Lord Lovell included, mourning his father's passing. In that time, Caroline Francis found herself a suitor. Then, against all expectations, Lord Lovell ran off to London, where he was injured in a duel. Is that correct?"

Lady Lymington nodded. "Yes, that's right."

For the first time that morning, Emma's gaze met Samuel's. "Caroline Francis was meant to meet the same fate as Amy and Kitty, and Lord Lovell meant to be blamed for it, but he left for London before the culprit could finish off Caroline. Lovell's sudden departure would have upset all the culprit's plans, as Lovell could hardly be held responsible for Caroline's disappearance if he was no longer at Lymington House."

"That was how she ended up at the Pink Pearl," Samuel said, picking up the thread. "The culprit's plans went badly awry once Lovell left for London, and he was forced to change tactics at the last minute."

"The best-laid plans…" Emma murmured.

"So he brought Caroline to the Pink Pearl, with instructions to spread the lie that Lovell had seduced and abandoned her there, and to implicate him in Amy's and Kitty's disappearances."

"And Caroline did just as he bid her, by telling the lies to Helena, who then told them to me, but neither he nor Caroline knew about Lord Lovell's duel. You must have returned to England very soon after your cousin was shot, Lord Lymington, in order to keep the gossips from discovering it."

"Less than a day afterward, yes."

"You all remained in London for weeks while Lord Lovell recovered, and then decided to stay for the season, so Lord Lovell might woo Lady Flora while Lord Lymington questioned Caroline Francis."

"Yes, but no one would have anticipated we'd come to London for the season at all, given the proper mourning period for Lovell's father. Our presence must have taken the culprit by surprise."

Emma nodded. "I imagine he panicked when you appeared at the Pink Pearl asking for Caroline. So he made certain to keep her away from you by engaging her for private appointments."

Samuel shook his head, stunned. "Dear God, a man such as that, a man of such cold, deliberate calculation must be an utter monster."

Lady Lymington was wringing her hands. "Samuel?"

In all the excitement, Samuel had nearly forgotten his mother. He jerked his attention back to her, shame sweeping over him at the sight of her distress. He shot to his feet, holding his hand out to her. "You're unwell, my lady. I'll take you to your rooms at once."

"Wait, my lord. I beg your pardon, Lady Lymington, but there is one more thing." Emma reached into the pocket of her skirts and withdrew something. "Do either of you recognize this pendant, or the young boy in the portrait?"

She gave it to Lady Lymington, who studied it for a moment, then returned it to Emma, shaking her head. "No. I've never seen it before, and I don't recognize the boy."

"Lord Lymington?" Emma asked, holding the pendant out to him.

The portrait of the dark-haired boy was tiny but exquisite, and the diamonds studding the oval of good quality. "It's very fine." Samuel rubbed the pad of his thumb over the gems, studying the young face. "I'm sorry, but I don't know the piece. Where did you get it?"

Emma took it from him and slipped it back into her pocket. "It's his."

Samuel frowned. "*His*? What, you mean it belongs to the culprit?"

"Yes. Caroline took it from him, the night before she disappeared. She gave it to Helena, and Helena gave it to me." Emma thought for a moment, then turned to Lady Lymington. "I wonder, my lady, if you'd mind doing something for me?"

"Not at all, Miss Downing. What do you need?"

"Would you be so good as to invite your neighbors and friends to Lymington House for a supper, or perhaps a ball? I beg your pardon for putting you to such trouble, but I have good reason to think the culprit wants this pendant back. If he has the chance to turn up at Lymington House without attracting suspicion, I think he'll come after it."

Samuel went still.

Surely, Emma wasn't suggesting she'd use herself to lure the scoundrel into the open? That she'd sacrifice her own safety—even her *life*—to bring the villain to justice? No, she couldn't possibly be so reckless, so foolish.

Except…it had sounded like that was precisely what she meant to do.

"For God's sakes, Emma, have you gone mad?" Samuel rounded on her, grasping her shoulders, fear making his hands shake.

Lady Lymington looked between them with wide eyes. "Er, perhaps I'll just retire to my rooms, then."

"It's a waste of time and effort, Emma! What makes you think he'll risk coming to Lymington House to get that pendant?" In truth, Samuel was terrified the scoundrel *would* come to Lymington House, and he'd find the pendant hanging around Emma's neck.

The very thought made his blood run cold.

"He attacked Helena Reeves in Bennets Court to get the pendant back, Lord Lymington. I hardly think he'll draw the line at coming to Lymington House."

"I'll see you both at tea, then," Lady Lymington said, trying again.

Neither Samuel nor Emma heard her, and neither noticed it when she left the study.

"So you intend to put yourself in his way, so he can attack *you*? No, Emma. I forbid it."

He knew he'd said the wrong thing when her chin shot up. "You *forbid* it? Forgive me, my lord, but it's not your place to forbid me anything."

Dear God, the woman was driving him mad. "The devil it isn't! In case you've forgotten, you're in *my* house, Emma."

"Oh, I'm not likely to forget that, Lord Lymington. In case *you've* forgotten, you nearly threw me out of *your house* last night."

Samuel blinked, taken aback. He hadn't been as bad as that, had he? He was angry with Emma, yes, but he would never dream of doing such a thing.

Emma let out a sigh when he didn't answer. "It's not as if I'm alone in this endeavor, you know. I have help."

"From whom, Lady Crosby? You intend to put a tiny old lady between yourself and a cold-blooded murderer?"

Emma rolled her eyes. "Not Lady Crosby. Don't be absurd."

"Who, then?" For one wild moment, Samuel wanted her to say she had *him*, but she dashed those hopes in an instant.

"Daniel Brixton, my lord."

"What, Lady Crosby's coachman?"

"He's, ah…he's not Lady Crosby's coachman, Lord Lymington. He works for Lady Clifford, just as I do."

Of course, he did.

Samuel gritted his teeth. "Well, that makes sense, at least. It's the one thing you've said in the past few minutes that does, Emma."

Her chin hitched up another notch. "I suppose you have another suggestion, a better way to catch this blackguard? Very well, my lord. I'm listening."

He *did* have another suggestion, that is, he must, but…damn it, he couldn't *think*. "Why are you doing this, Emma? Why would you risk yourself like this?"

"Why?" She gazed up at him, her secrets and nightmares and all the things she hid right there in her eyes. "Because Lady Clifford did it for me, and now it's my turn."

Samuel's hands tightened on her shoulders. He couldn't bear it if something happened to her, if she were hurt in any way. "You can't save them, Emma. Amy, and Kitty and Caroline. It's too late."

"It's too late for them, yes." Emma's smile was sad as she gently disentangled herself from his grasp. "But I can still save myself, Samuel. It's not too late for me."

Chapter Twenty

The ball at Lymington House
Five days later

"I'm amazed Lord Lymington didn't insist upon coming into your bedchamber while you dressed for the ball this evening, Emma."

Emma was sitting at the dressing table, fussing with the blue ribbons Flora's lady's maid had woven into her hair, but after a few half-hearted tugs she gave up, and let the ribbons lie where they might. What did her hair matter, anyway?

She met Lady Crosby's gaze in the mirror. "He *has* been unusually attentive."

"Attentive?" Lady Crosby gave a delicate snort. "The man hasn't let you out of his sight for the past five days. He's like a hound on a scent."

A fierce, growly hound, yes—one that heartily resented the fox it was chasing. "He makes even Daniel look negligent, doesn't he?"

"Positively neglectful, yes. Why, I wouldn't be surprised to find him outside your bedchamber door at this very moment, waiting to pounce on you as soon as you set foot into the hallway."

Emma set her hairbrush aside with a sigh. "Nor would I."

She'd been sure she was imagining it at first, until she caught him trailing behind her one late afternoon as she wandered through the formal gardens. He'd dodged behind a shrub, but it hadn't done much to conceal him, as he was half a head taller than it was.

Since then, every time she turned around, Samuel was there, hovering at the edges, his dark eyes following her every move. He didn't speak to her any more than politeness demanded, or appear inclined to engage her in any way.

Emma couldn't make heads or tails of his behavior, until at last it dawned on her he'd taken it upon himself to defend her from whatever criminals happened to be lurking about Lymington House.

If he'd been another sort of man, his devotion might have raised a fragile hope in her poor, battered heart, but Samuel's fierce protectiveness had little to do with her. He'd do the same for anyone in his house he believed was under threat.

It was simply who he was.

"You look fatigued, my dear." Lady Crosby abandoned her place on the bed and approached Emma, plucking one of the ribbons up from the dressing table and wrapping it expertly around a cluster of curls at the back of Emma's neck. "Pretty as ever, of course, particularly in that gown, but fatigued, nonetheless."

"It's been a long five days, my lady." Who could have imagined facing the man she loved over the breakfast table every morning for days on end while waiting for a murderer to make an attempt on her life could be so exhausting?

Lady Crosby tidied a loose lock of Emma's hair, tucking it neatly under the ribbon. "There we are. The simpler style suits you."

Emma let her head rest against Lady Crosby's arm. "Thank you."

"You will take care this evening, won't you, Emma? No wandering off alone, or taking reckless chances?" Lady Crosby attempted a smile, but her blue eyes were anxious.

Emma reached behind her to squeeze Lady Crosby's hand. "I promise it, my lady."

Lady Crosby had done her best to hold her tongue since she'd made the decision to accompany Emma and Daniel to Lymington House, but she was far from reconciled to Emma's plan to put herself in the way of the villain who'd murdered Caroline Francis.

A villain who might very well be at Lymington House even now, flirting and sipping champagne in the ballroom two floors below. Emma couldn't say whether she was more fearful he'd appear tonight, or that he wouldn't appear at all.

She was out of clever schemes. If this one failed, they'd likely never catch him.

"You look as lovely as an angel, Emma. Shall we go down, then? I'm certain Lord Lymington is waiting for you."

"You go ahead, my lady. I just need to get these ribbons in order, then I'll come down."

"All right, dear. Don't be long."

"I won't." Emma managed a cheerful wave, but she made certain the door had closed behind Lady Crosby before she slid open the top drawer of the dressing table and withdrew the pendant.

She'd wanted to spare Lady Crosby this moment.

There was a tiny loop at the top curve of the oval, where a gold chain could be attached. Emma threaded one of the narrow blue ribbons through the loop, tied the ends under the fall of curls at the back of her head, and adjusted the pendant so it lay flat against her neck.

Her hands shook as she arranged the pendant over the hollow of her throat, where it was impossible to miss, then met her reflection in the glass.

The skin of her neck and throat were smooth and white, not a bruise to be seen, but when Emma looked in the mirror, it wasn't her own neck she saw. It was Helena's, mottled with dark bruises, the imprint of a man's thumbs right over her pulse point, and Caroline, in her mind's eye, with the same bruises around her neck, except darker, and her body limp, like a broken doll.

Emma's breath caught with a painful hitch. For the first time in a long time, she was truly afraid, and even with Lady Crosby waiting for her in the ballroom, and Daniel keeping watch outside, she felt very much alone.

* * * *

Emma wasn't here.

Samuel paused in the entrance of the ballroom, his gaze moving over the crowd, searching for the distinctive shade of blue he'd come to think of as hers alone. Most of his mother's guests had already arrived, many of them twirling about on the dance floor, engaged in a lively country dance.

But Emma wasn't among them. Samuel frowned, scanning the ballroom. Lord Dunn was here, not dancing, but standing on the side of the room, chatting with a group of gentlemen. Lovell and Lady Flora were dancing together, their gazes only for each other, and Lady Silvester was standing a little apart from the rest of the crowd, watching them with a beatific smile on her face.

Samuel strode toward Lady Crosby, who was on the opposite side of the ballroom with his mother, their heads bent together. "Good evening, Lady Lymington, and Lady Crosby." Samuel offered them each a hasty bow before turning his attention to Lady Crosby. "Has Emma come down yet? I don't see her in the ballroom."

"Good evening, Lord Lymington. I imagined you'd turn up, sooner or later." Lady Crosby, who hadn't quite forgiven him for his coldness to Emma, swept a cool gaze over him. "Emma was still primping in front of the glass when I came down, my lord. Young ladies and balls, you know. I daresay she'll be down very soon."

Primping? Samuel frowned. That didn't sound like Emma.

He turned to his mother, but before he could say a word, she quieted him with a hand on his arm. "Won't you go and ask Lady Mary Worthington to dance, Samuel? I do like to see all the young ladies dance the first dance of the evening, and you see, she doesn't have a partner."

Samuel followed his mother's discreet nod, and saw Lady Mary sitting on a gilt chair in a corner of the ballroom, her parents on either side of her, and she looked miserable indeed.

At any other time, he wouldn't have hesitated, but the urge to go upstairs and fetch Emma himself was so overwhelming, it was on the tip of his tongue to refuse.

"Samuel, did you hear me? I asked you to invite Lady Mary to dance."

Samuel huffed out a breath. It was unspeakably rude of him to stand about when a young lady—one of his guests, no less—lacked a partner, and he couldn't simply charge up the stairs and batter down the door of Emma's bedchamber. "Yes, of course."

"Go on then, before the dance is over." Lady Lymington shooed him away with a flick of her fan. "I'm certain Emma will have appeared by the time you return."

The grateful look on Lady Mary's face when Samuel offered her his hand mollified him somewhat, but he kept a sharp eye on the guests wandering in and out of the ballroom as he took Lady Mary through an interminable country dance.

Something was amiss. He could feel it—

"My hand, Lord Lymington."

Lady Mary was gaping up at him, and all at once Samuel realized he was squeezing her hand much too tightly. He dropped it at once. "I beg your pardon, my lady."

The dance dragged on for another ten minutes—ten minutes in which Samuel couldn't have said who was the more miserable of the two of them, himself or Lady Mary. He did his best to smother his impatience, but once he'd returned Lady Mary to her parents, he fled the ballroom as if the devil were chasing him, before his mother cursed him to another dance.

At this point, he could think of nothing but Emma.

Damn it, where was she? He didn't like this.

Perhaps he *could* charge up to Emma's bedchamber, after all.

His mother caught his eye and beckoned to him, but for the first time in as long as Samuel could remember, he ignored her, and strode from the ballroom. He took the stairs two at a time to the guest wing, each of his footfalls a dull thud in his ears, and hurried down the hallway to Emma's bedchamber.

Before he could knock, the door opened and she emerged, wearing a blue silk ballgown, her shoulders bare, her hair a cascade of curls and blue ribbons. Samuel froze, swallowing at the sight of her silhouetted against her bedchamber door. "Emma."

"Lord Lymington." She jumped, startled, then her eyes narrowed. "You haven't been waiting in the hallway for me, have you?"

"No. I've just arrived." Samuel didn't add that he would have been outside her door far sooner if it weren't for his mother. "You've missed the first two dances, and I—"

Samuel broke off as she drew nearer, his gaze dropping to the pendant hanging from a blue ribbon around her neck. He caught the edge of it on his fingertip, his gaze meeting hers. "No. I won't allow this, Emma."

To Emma's credit, she didn't try to pretend she wasn't taking an enormous risk. "This may surprise you, but I do know what I'm doing, my lord, and Daniel will keep me safe—"

"*No*," Samuel repeated through gritted teeth. "A man who'd strangle a woman is vicious, conscienceless—more animal than human. I can't simply stand by while you become his next victim."

"I don't deny he's vicious, Lord Lymington, but he's clearly not a fool. There are dozens of people in your ballroom this evening. He won't dare make a move tonight—"

Samuel tipped her chin up, forcing her to meet his gaze. "This is madness, Emma. You must know that."

Emma jerked her chin from his grasp, her eyes darkening with emotion. "Do you suppose this is the first time I've been in danger, the first time I've been threatened? I was a *courtesan*, my lord. I've faced vicious men before, and survived it."

Unbidden, Samuel's gaze dropped to her hands. White silk gloves stretched from her fingertips to the curve of her elbow, but he'd seen the evidence of her past written on her skin, and he could never unsee it. He reached for her, and stroked his thumb over the back of her hand, over the deepest of her scars. "There must be some other way."

Her eyes softened at the gentle caress, but she shook her head. "There isn't. I'll keep my wits about me, my lord. I always do."

Samuel remained silent as he struggled with himself, but at last he said, "You'll remain in the ballroom at all times. No strolling in the garden, or even venturing onto the terrace."

"Daniel will be in the garden all evening—"

"This isn't a negotiation, Emma. Either you promise to do as I say, or you'll return to your bedchamber, and I'll see to it you don't leave it again for the rest of the..."

Night. Samuel bit off the last word, his face heating.

That had sounded a great deal more suggestive than he'd intended.

Emma's eyes widened, and Samuel hurriedly cleared his throat. "You'll dance either with me, or with Lord Lovell tonight. No one else."

Emma bit her lip. "I've already told Lord Dunn I'll dance with him."

"Dunn!" Samuel's brow lowered.

A small smile curved her lips. "Forgive me, Lord Lymington. I didn't think you'd want to dance with me."

Samuel did want to dance with her, and with no one *but* her, but all he said was, "You'll remain where I can see you for the entire evening. When you're ready to retire, I will escort you to your bedchamber. Is that understood?"

Emma bowed her head, and said meekly, "Yes, my lord."

Samuel's eyes narrowed. "I don't trust your uncharacteristic obedience for a minute, Emma." Still, he offered her his arm, and escorted her downstairs, mainly because he hadn't any other choice.

As soon as they entered the ballroom, a half dozen gentlemen rushed to claim Emma's hand.

She remained true to her promise, dancing only with Dunn and Lovell, and then Samuel himself before claiming a twisted ankle, and retiring to one of the gilt chairs with Lady Crosby for the remainder of the evening.

An interminable evening, and a surprisingly painful one.

Samuel hadn't expected to get any pleasure from this ball, what with a murderer likely running loose in his ballroom, but he also hadn't anticipated the wrench in his chest as he watched Emma holding court from her chair, bestowing one flirtatious smile after another on her crowd of admirers.

He'd hoped never again to be cursed with the sight of Lady Emma Crosby, but as he watched her charm and dazzle the gentlemen who surrounded her, it occurred to him for the first time how difficult it must be for her to wear that masque, how exhausting.

If it caused him this much pain to *watch* Lady Emma Crosby, how much more pain did it cause Emma to *be* her?

The evening dragged on at a miserable crawl until at last the supper hour drew near. Lady Lymington had been glaring at Samuel all evening for leaving his young female guests languishing on the sidelines while he glowered at Emma, so he invited Lady Flora to dance while Emma was safely engaged with Lovell and Lord Dunn on the other side of the ballroom.

"Forgive me, Lord Lymington, but you don't look as if you've enjoyed yourself this evening. Are you not pleased with the ball?" Lady Flora asked as Samuel escorted her to the floor.

Samuel, who'd always been fond of Lady Flora, managed a smile for her. "No. I confess I'm not much in the mood to dance this evening."

"Not since you had your two dances with Lady Emma, at any rate." Lady Flora looked up at him with thoughtful dark eyes. "Oh, but I forgot. It's not Lady Emma, is it? It's Miss Downing."

Samuel blinked, surprised that Lovell had confided such a closely guarded secret to Lady Flora. "I see you're in Lovell's confidence."

"Of course. Lord Lovell and I don't have secrets from each other anymore, Lord Lymington. Honesty between us was one of the conditions of my forgiveness."

"That was...shrewd of you, my lady."

"Not really, my lord. Despite Lord Lovell's struggles this past year, he's never been one to keep secrets. They make him miserable. So you see, this suits us both."

Samuel stared at her, rather amazed at her intuitiveness, but perhaps he shouldn't be. She was no longer the credulous, naïve child she'd been when he left England, any more than Lovell was. "You know, then, about Emma's—that is, Miss Downing's efforts to prove Lovell guilty of a despicable crime?"

Even saying the words aloud tore at Samuel, making the wound in his chest bleed afresh, but Lady Flora looked surprised by his words. "Is that the way you see it, my lord? How odd. I rather think she was trying to prove him *innocent*."

"But—" Samuel began, then broke off as the truth of Lady Flora's words struck him.

Emma had never denied she believed Caroline Francis's accusations against Lovell at first, but that had been at the very start of the season. She'd only known Lovell a few weeks before she began to suspect Caroline was lying, and since then, she'd been working to prove him innocent.

But the lies she'd told Samuel, her betrayal—

"Lord Lymington?" Lady Flora asked, concerned. "Are you unwell?"

"No, I...the lies, Lady Flora." Samuel's voice was hoarse. "How...how did you forgive Lovell for the lies he told you?"

"Ah, the lies. Lies are difficult to forgive, but have you forgotten *you* forgave Lord Lovell's lies, just as I did?"

He had, yes, but that was different than Samuel forgiving Emma. Wasn't it?

"He's my *cousin*, Lady Flora."

"Yes, of course. You care for him, just as I do, and so we both *wanted* to forgive him. We did it for our own sakes as much as for his. We're meant to consider forgiveness divine, but I've always thought there was a trace of selfishness in it."

"What do you mean?"

Lady Flora's brow furrowed, as if she were searching for a way to explain it that Samuel would understand. "Just this, my lord. I didn't *only* consider Lovell's happiness when I chose to forgive him. I also considered my own, just as you must have done. Withholding our forgiveness would have meant giving up Lovell forever. Neither of us ever wanted that."

No, Samuel had never wanted that. Losing his cousin would be unbearable. *Nearly as unbearable as losing Emma.*

Samuel stared down at Lady Flora, stunned. "I, ah...never thought of it that way."

"I don't know that forgiveness *is* divine." Lady Flora cocked her head, considering it. "But the love that compels it, Lord Lymington, does transcend the ordinary. Perhaps that's what Mr. Pope meant, for love without forgiveness isn't much of a love at all, is it?"

Samuel swallowed. "No. It isn't."

The dance ended then, and he delivered Lady Flora to a beaming Lovell, who watched her approach as if he were watching a glorious sunrise, and couldn't tear his gaze away.

Lord Dunn had claimed Emma for supper, so Samuel took his mother's arm instead, but he passed the rest of the evening in a daze.

The guests making the return trip to London that night took their leave soon after the supper ended, but the rest of the company—their neighbors, and those staying at Lymington House—danced into the early hours of the morning.

Throughout the entire evening, Emma never faltered. She flirted and laughed and sipped champagne, but all the while, she was watching, her gaze flitting from one smiling lord to the next, searching for the one who wore the masque.

And all the while, Samuel was watching *her*, his heart in his throat.

When she came to him at last, she looked as if she were ready to collapse with exhaustion. "I'd like to retire to my bedchamber now, Lord Lymington."

Samuel gazed at her pale face, into the blue eyes that had bewitched him from the start, and thought of a love so powerful it transcended the ordinary, and became divine.

Then he took her hand, and led her up the stairs.

Chapter Twenty-one

The corridor outside Emma's bedchamber was dark, the household already on its way to a blissful slumber, but there would be no sleep for Samuel tonight.

Lady Flora's words were running like a fevered dream through his mind. *Love without forgiveness isn't much of a love at all....*

Emma paused outside her door, and turned to face him. "Thank you for your escort, Lord Lymington. Good night."

He could take her into his arms, or he could return to his own rooms alone and chase the dreamless sleep that had eluded him for weeks, a sleep that would never come tonight. He could pretend he didn't want her, and leave her untouched, or he could wait outside her bedchamber door until morning, to ensure no harm came to her.

While he wrestled with himself, Emma slipped quietly away, leaving him alone in the hallway, lost in an agony of indecision. He lingered for a long time after she'd gone, his forehead resting against her door and an ache in his chest, knowing he'd made the wrong choice.

He should have taken her into his arms.

Emma was all that mattered, all that had ever mattered. She'd lied to him, yes—about her name, and her past—but somehow, even amidst the lies she'd had to tell, she'd never told him a single lie about what truly mattered.

She'd never been anyone other than herself. Not with *him*.

Samuel raised his hand to tap on her door, but then lowered it again, sudden doubt overwhelming him. This was madness. She wouldn't open her door to him. Why should she?

Yet as mad as it was, he couldn't make himself leave until he'd seen her again.

He raised his hand a second time, but before his knuckles touched the wood there was a soft click, and the door opened. Emma stood on the other side, clad in a white night rail, her hair in a loose plait draped over one of her shoulders.

They stared at each other, neither of them speaking, until at last Emma drew in a trembling breath and asked, "Is there something wrong, my lord?"

Her words were soft, more breath than sound, and Samuel wondered if he was imagining the tremor in her voice, the uncertain smile gracing the red lips he'd dreamed about every night since he'd first kissed them, weeks ago.

"No, I…may I come in?" Samuel swallowed, his heart pounding with hope and fear as he waited for her to answer him.

She didn't speak. Instead, she drew away from the door, opening it wider, one slender hand beckoning him inside. As he crossed the threshold and closed the door behind him, he realized in some dim corner of his mind that he'd go anywhere if it meant she'd be on the other side, waiting for him.

He'd cross oceans for her.

She gazed up at him, her eyes two mysterious pools of darkness, so close he could inhale her scent with each breath he drew into his lungs, vanilla, delicate and warm.

Samuel devoured the lines of her face, his heart pounding. There was no coy smile this time, no tantalizing glances from beneath her thick eyelashes. There was no teasing, no practiced flirtation. She looked just as she'd done that day in the rose garden, right before he'd kissed her, her blue eyes wide, her body trembling for him.

His mouth went dry as he gazed down at her. Emma hadn't closed her drapes and the moonlight streaming through the window set her bedchamber aglow, gilding her hair to the softest gold, her skin luminescent, a delicate hint of cream beneath her white nightdress. Lace edged the modest neckline, teasing her skin, the hem billowing around her bare feet.

She looked like the wraith he'd once thought her, so delicate and ethereal, yet at the same time she was more alive than anything Samuel had ever known. He ached to draw her into his arms, press her slender, curved body against his, and take her mouth until she was pleading for him, breathless and trembling.

But he only took her hand, and pressed his mouth to her knuckles, his lips touching her scars. Emma let out a soft sigh at the gentle caress. Samuel stilled before slowly raising his eyes to hers, and what he saw in those dark depths made his breath catch.

Uncertainty, hope, desire, and something else that turned her eyes the deepest midnight blue. He reached for her then, cradling her cheek in his palm, and brought his mouth down on hers. Emma let out a soft moan as her hands came up and sank into his hair.

He'd kissed her before, in the rose garden, and again in the darkened alcove at Vauxhall, but this kiss was different, because *he* was different. Samuel held her as if afraid she'd break, overwhelmed with a tenderness that made his throat close, even as she drove his desire to a fever pitch with her soft whimpers.

He caught her hungry exhalations as they left her lips, devouring them as if they were the air he breathed, the blood in his veins. He kissed her for long, slow moments until at last her lips parted, welcoming him into the blissful heat of her mouth.

Samuel darted inside, tasting every corner of her mouth, his head spinning as his body grew more desperate for hers. After a battle that seemed to go on for ages, he drew back with a groan, and rested his forehead against hers.

He couldn't kiss her again. If he did, he wouldn't stop. "Emma—"

"Don't go, Samuel." Emma gripped the front of his shirt before he could draw away, her fingers desperate. "Stay with me tonight."

A sound tore loose from Samuel's chest—a groan, or a sigh—he didn't know which. He knew only that he wanted to sink to his knees for her, and stay there forever. "Yes. I love you, Emma."

Samuel had never thought about what it might feel like to fall in love, but now he knew it should feel just like this, gentle but inevitable, as if he'd been standing on the edge of the sand his whole life, waiting for the wave to reach him.

* * * *

Love. It was, at once, the one word she wanted most to hear Samuel say, and the last word she ever thought he would.

It had only been a week since she stood alone in Lady Crosby's darkened hallway, and thought of love as a spike straight through the tenderest part of her heart.

She'd thought it dreadful—the worst thing she could ever feel, and she'd felt suspended between the real world, where people cared for and loved each other, and the shadows of her past, not a part of either of them.

It had always been thus, for as long as she could remember. She wasn't one thing, and she wasn't the other, but lost somewhere between them. Madame Marchand's ambitions for her had made her an outcast at the

Pink Pearl. A courtesan like the others, yes, but kept apart from them and reserved for the exclusive use of a single gentleman.

Things had been much better after she'd gone to Lady Clifford, but even then, she'd been the last of the four of her friends to arrive—too old to be a schoolgirl, too wounded to be of much use, hiding a cold, damaged heart beneath a pretty face.

A failed courtesan, a pretend schoolgirl, now a mockery of a debutante... they'd all been disguises she'd worn, identities she'd pretended to, until she no longer knew who she was without them.

Until Samuel.

He leaned closer so he could look into her eyes. "Emma? Say something."

Emma's throat worked, but she couldn't speak. Even if she could, she wouldn't know what to say. How could she tell him he'd given her something she'd never thought she'd have, that she'd never dared dream of? How could she put into words that being here, with him, with the moonlight streaming through the window, felt like coming home?

She couldn't say it. She didn't know how to put such emotions into words, so she didn't try. Instead, she took the hand that was stroking her cheek, and led him to her bed.

"Emma?" He searched her face in the moonlight, so hesitant, even as his hands closed around her waist.

"Shhh." Emma moved closer, rising to her tiptoes. She let her mouth hover over his just long enough so she could feel the warm drift of his breath across her lips before she kissed him.

She hadn't told Samuel she loved him, but she put all of her love into her kiss, and surrendered everything to him. He let out a low groan, his fingers tightening around her waist as he took her mouth desperately, coaxing her lips apart, his kiss possessive, as if he would claim every inch of her.

"Samuel." Emma ran her fingers through the thick strands of his hair, hungry for more of his kiss.

More of *him*. *All* of him.

His hands moved restlessly over her sides, stroking her ribs, his long fingers so warm against the thin cotton of her night rail she wanted him to touch her everywhere, until all the frozen parts of her thawed in a rush of heat. "Take me to bed, Samuel."

A low laugh fell from his lips, rich and deep and dark, and full of wicked promises. Emma had never heard such a sound from him before, and it sent a delicious tingle through her.

"Oh, I intend to, but first…" He dragged his thumbs over her collarbones, a wondering smile rising to his lips when his touch left goosebumps on her skin. "I want to see you in the moonlight."

He slid a finger under the capped sleeve of her night rail, easing the flimsy material down until he'd revealed one pale shoulder. He sucked in a breath, his hot gaze drinking in her bared skin like a man dying of thirst. "So beautiful, Emma. I knew you would be."

Emma didn't have a chance to draw a breath before his lips brushed across the skin he'd bared, tasting and teasing until he'd dragged a husky moan from her lips.

"Every inch of you, Emma." Samuel's mouth moved higher to press kisses to her neck. "I want to see and kiss every inch of you."

His cheeks were flushed, his hair tousled from her fingers, his gray eyes wild with desire. This man, so stern and solemn, was falling apart right before her eyes, and Emma couldn't get enough of it. She traced his lips with her fingertip. "Do what you will, my lord."

Samuel nipped at the tip of her finger before pressing his lips to the arch of her neck, then he drifted lower and opened his mouth over the pulse point of her throat. "That little hollow has driven me mad for weeks," he murmured against her skin. "I dream about tasting you there, and here." He dragged his fingers down her throat to the sensitive skin between her breasts.

Emma's sigh became a gasp when his lips followed his stroking finger. "Oh, that's…"

She trailed off, unsure how to put into words what she felt. She'd been touched by a man before, but never by a man she *wanted* to touch her, and never like this, as if she were precious. It was unexpected and breathtaking at once. Her body tingled, clamoring for more of him.

"Such perfect skin, like new cream, and such a rosy red right here." He cupped the curve of her breast, stroking his thumb over her nipple through the thin linen of her night rail.

Emma gasped and dropped her hands to his broad shoulders to steady herself. "*Samuel.*"

"Yes, sweetheart?" Samuel's voice was soothing, but he continued his teasing caresses, stroking her nipple into exquisite stiffness before lowering his head and taking the reddened peak into his mouth.

They both groaned at the sensation, Emma tugging desperately at his hair with each draw of his lips. His mouth was impossibly hot, his tongue a delicious torment, his hands cradling her hips to drag her closer, the hard length of his erection settling against her stomach. "Tell me you want me, Emma. Let me hear you say it."

"I do want you, Samuel, more than anything." His kiss, his touch, his soft whispers in her ear—this was how Emma had always hoped love would feel.

Samuel caught up a fold of her night rail, but he waited, his powerful body shaking with desire, for her to give him permission to remove it. "I want to see all of you, Emma. May I take this off?"

His gentleness, his sweetness, melted Emma's heart. She couldn't speak, but she wrapped her fingers around his wrist and helped him to raise her night rail.

Samuel groaned as he slowly revealed her, the cool air of the room kissing Emma's bare ankles, her calves. She shivered when the hem reached her thighs, not from the chill, but from the heat in his eyes, the curl of desire in her stomach, the insistent pulse between her legs.

"Look at you, with the moonlight gilding your skin," Samuel whispered when she stood bare before him. His warm palm skimmed the curve of her hip and drifted over the gentle swell of her belly. "I've never seen anything as lovely as you, Emma."

He dropped a sweet kiss on her forehead, and then…

Then his hands, his lips were everywhere, gentle but insistent, his palms cupping her hips, one hard thigh pressed between hers. His mouth followed the path of his hands, leaving a trail of damp kisses across skin that reveled in the touch of his lips, shivers rising in their wake.

Emma could only cling to him, her arms around his neck as he dropped kisses behind her ears, nibbled her ear lobe, and sucked the stiff peaks of her nipples until she was crying out for him, a husky plea. He murmured to her as he touched her, his voice dark and rough, his big hands stroking her thighs as he demanded she tell him she needed him, and only him.

Emma gave him everything he asked, her entire body trembling with need and desire and nervousness, because she'd been touched before, but never like this—oh, never like this, and her body was tightening as it readied, straining toward something, but she wasn't sure what she needed, or what she was meant to do—

"Open for me, sweetheart." Samuel's breath was hot on her neck, his fingertips stroking her inner thighs.

Emma did as he bid her, gasping when his fingers slipped between her legs. "God, yes, so warm and wet for me, Emma, so soft, like silk."

"Oh, oh…" Emma's knees went weak as he stroked and teased at her swollen bud, his fingers circling and pinching until she sagged against him. "Please."

Samuel wrapped an arm around her waist to steady her. He never ceased those tormenting strokes, but continued to work her, his breath hot and fast in her ear and she writhed against him, her hips instinctively taking up the rhythm of his fingers.

He drove her higher with each touch, setting her body ablaze, crooning to her as he wound her tighter, his whispers dark and wicked, urging her on, commanding her to take her pleasure, to come for him—

Emma pressed her open mouth to his neck, her moans smothered against his damp skin, the heat between her thighs intensifying, pulling tighter with every nudge of his fingers until it snapped, exploding in a wave of heat, shooting tendrils of pleasure from her core all the way to her fingertips.

Emma stiffened, clinging to Samuel and crying out. He held her against him with one arm, the other hand still stroking gently between her thighs while her pleasure peaked, then melted until it was no more than a delirious echo of itself. When the last tremor faded and she sagged against him, boneless, Samuel scooped her into his arms and lay her down on the bed.

He stood over her, his hot dark eyes sweeping over her as he slowly removed his cravat, coat and waistcoat, then he joined her on the bed, brushing the loose strands of hair from her forehead. His touch was gentle, but his gray eyes fierce as he gazed down into her face. "God, I've never seen anything more erotic in my life than watching you come for me, Emma."

Emma cupped his bristly cheek. "I never have, before."

His heavy-lidded eyes widened. "Never?"

"Never."

Samuel went still for an instant, but then a satisfied smile curved his lips. "Only for *me*."

"Only you." Emma toyed with his damp curls, a lazy smile on her own lips. "I didn't think women could, er...do *that*."

Samuel dragged a finger down her cheek, a hint of sadness in his expression, but then he smiled, and pressed a sweet kiss to her lips. "Shall we do it again, just to be certain?"

Emma couldn't deny it was an appealing idea, but she shook her head. "Not that, but perhaps...something else?"

Samuel was lying half on top of her, but Emma squirmed out from under him, rose to her knees and with one quick, graceful move settled herself over his hips, straddling him.

"Hmmm." Samuel's eyebrows rose, but a smile played about his lips as he settled his big hands on her thighs. His eyes were heavy as he took her in, his gaze lingering on her lips, her nipples, and the curves of her breasts.

Emma gave the hem of his loose linen shirt an impatient tug. "Take this off, please."

That dark eyebrow rose another inch, but he tugged the shirt over his head, tossed it aside, then lay back against the pillows. "Is there anything else I can do to please you, madam?"

"Oh, I'm pleased." Emma ran her hands over the broad expanse of his chest, the dark, springy hair there tickling her palms, and marveled at the width of his shoulders, the muscular curves of his arms, and the taut, flat plane of his belly. "This is very nice."

A low laugh rumbled from Samuel's chest. "What do you intend to do with it?"

"Hmmm. An intriguing question, my lord." Emma leaned down and pressed a soft kiss to his nipple. "I'll start with that, I think."

Samuel's eyes darkened. He didn't speak, but he reached up and caught the ends of her plaited hair. His gaze held hers as he tugged at the bit of thread there and began loosening it, his fingers slow and gentle.

"There," he whispered when he'd finished, and her hair tumbled over her shoulders. "Beautiful."

The glow in his eyes as he gazed up at her made Emma's chest flood with warmth. She leaned over him, and let the long locks of her hair drag over his chest.

Samuel caught his breath.

Emma braced her hands on his shoulders. "Do you like that, my lord?"

The strong column of his throat moved in a swallow. "Yes."

Emma did it again, letting the ends of her hair drag over his nipples. "And this?"

"*Yes.*" He sucked in another breath, his neck arching, the hot, hard length of him twitching beneath her.

Emma gave a restrained wriggle, just the subtlest twitch of her hips, but it made Samuel hiss, and his fingers tightened around her thighs. "*Emma.*"

His voice was hoarse, the sound somewhere between a warning and a plea, but Emma went on stroking his pulsing erection against her core, teasing him, her slow, sinuous movements not enough to satisfy.

Samuel's lips parted, and a flush of color rose to his cheekbones. His hips jerked up hard, seeking more friction, but Emma shook her head. "No, my lord. Not yet."

A low growl tore from his chest, but he did his best to lie still as she undulated on top of him, her own mouth opening as his breath grew hectic, and his cock swelled beneath her.

"Do as I say, and be still." Emma loosened the buttons of his falls and drew the flap down, gasping softly as the head of his cock appeared, swollen and flushed, the tip damp with his arousal.

"Oh." He was magnificent. Emma's tongue dipped into the curve of her bottom lip as she ran her fingertips over the weeping head, gathering the moisture there.

"Ah, God." Samuel arched his back, his pelvis jerking again, and Emma slid her hands from his chest to his hips. She wouldn't be able to hold him once he grew desperate enough to break free, but until then...

She leaned close, pressing her bare breasts to his chest, her hips still moving against his, and traced her tongue over his lower lip.

"Emma," he moaned.

"Yes, my lord?" Emma drew back to gaze at him, lingering over his sweat-sheened chest, his hard nipples, his straining hips, and her core gave a needy throb.

"*Please,*" he gritted, with another desperate surge.

"Shhh." Emma held her finger to his lips. She couldn't deny him for much longer, but dear God, tormenting him until he was maddened with desire was the most arousing thing she'd ever seen. "Soon."

She watched his face as she circled her thumb around the head of his cock. His eyes were closed, his neck corded. "*No,*" he groaned, twisting out of her grip. "I want to be inside you."

Emma's skin was flushed, her entire body trembling as she leaned down to kiss his neck and the sensitive skin behind his ear, a promise on her lips that he could have her, that she would give him anything, everything, but before she could whisper the words, he tensed beneath her, his stomach muscles tightening, and with a powerful surge of his hips, he tumbled her onto her back.

"Samuel!" Emma gasped with surprise, but her cry dissolved into a moan as he fell on top of her, taking care not to crush her. She gazed up at him, her heart pounding. His expression was like nothing she'd ever seen on his face before—wild and fierce and darkly possessive.

He nudged her legs apart and settled his hips between them, his eyelids heavy over glittering gray eyes. "Such a tease, Miss Downing." He nuzzled her neck, then slid lower to kiss the damp skin between her breasts. "I never would have guessed it."

"Nor I. I've never..." She trailed off, cradling his cheek in her palm. She'd never behaved so before, but with him she felt safe enough to seize control where before she'd had none.

Samuel pressed a tender kiss to her lips, as if he understood what she couldn't say. "I want you, Emma." He slid his warm palm over her knee, urging her thigh onto his hip.

"Yes." Emma wrapped her other leg around him, cradling him between her thighs, pressing their hips tightly together and dragging a hoarse groan from his lips.

He stroked the secret skin of her inner thighs before slipping a hand between her legs. Emma writhed under him, arching her back as he stroked and teased until his fingers were slick with her arousal, and she was pleading with him, her fingernails scoring his back.

Samuel's burning eyes slid closed as he pressed the tip of his cock against her, sweat beading his brow as he slid inside, slowly, so slowly, his every move careful. When he was nearly all the way inside her he paused to brush damp strands of hair from her forehead. "Are you all right, love?"

Emma arched into him, taking him those last few inches, until he filled her completely. "Yes. Please, Samuel."

He gazed down at her with parted lips as he began to move, restrained at first, but his strokes quickening as her legs tightened around him. A broken moan tore from his chest as his thrusts deepened, and Emma clung to him as he took them closer to bliss with every snap of his hips.

"Come for me, Emma," he whispered, slipping his fingers between her legs to stroke her swollen core.

"*Oh.*" Emma whimpered at his touch. Heat unfurled in her lower belly, burning hotter with his caresses until she exploded in a sudden burst of pleasure. "*Ah*, Samuel."

"Yes," he growled against her throat, his entire body going rigid as the pulsing of her core around him dragged him over the edge with a deep groan.

He held her, his face buried in her neck until she went limp beneath him, then he drew back to gaze at her face. What he saw there must have pleased him, because his mouth curved, and he pressed a tender kiss to her lips.

"Sleep, sweetheart." He settled on his side and gathered her against his chest, his arm around her waist and his face buried in her hair. "Sleep."

Chapter Twenty-two

Emma was asleep, her head resting on Samuel's shoulder and her hair tickling his chest. He toyed lazily with the long locks, running his fingers through them and admiring the play of moonlight over the silky strands.

He didn't sleep, but spent the rest of the night watching the night give way to the weak glow of dawn, not wishing to lose even a moment of holding her warm, sleeping body in his arms, of feeling the drift of her breath over his bare skin.

She hadn't told him she loved him last night.

Had he imagined that spark of love in her deep blue eyes? Had he persuaded himself there was tenderness in the way she'd clung to him, whispered his name? Or had he simply seen, heard, and felt what he wished to?

Samuel didn't know. He wasn't certain of anything anymore, but for this.

He wasn't letting her go.

"Samuel?" Emma stirred, warm and drowsy against him. "What time is it?"

Samuel didn't answer her, nor did he give her a chance to open her eyes before he was kissing her—her forehead, her cheeks, her chin, and at last, her parted lips. Emma sighed and twined her arms around his neck as his mouth opened over hers, his tongue stealing inside.

He wanted her again. He'd never stop wanting her.

"Mmmm." Emma hummed with pleasure as he trailed hot kisses down her neck. "You make it difficult to banish you from my bed, my lord, but you must return to your own bedchamber before anyone notices we—"

"No." Samuel's mouth drifted lower to taste the soft skin between her breasts. "Not yet."

If he had his way, not ever.

Emma gave his hair a playful tug. "Refusing to leave a lady's bed? You're dreadfully arrogant, Lord Lymington."

"All marquesses are arrogant, Miss Downing." Samuel nibbled at her lower lip, still swollen from his kisses the night before. "Demanding, too, especially in the bedchamber."

"You don't frighten me, my lord." Emma's lips curved in a cheeky smile. "I've never been one to obey commands, and I don't suppose that will change now, even if you are a marquess."

Samuel drew back to gaze down at her, and was instantly bewitched by her mischievous little smile. "Is that a challenge?"

Emma moved one shoulder in a dainty shrug. "Perhaps it is, but not... Samuel! What do you think you're doing?"

In one quick move Samuel had tossed her onto her back and thrown one leg over both of hers, trapping her beneath him. "Never challenge a marquess, Miss Downing, especially in the bedchamber."

"There seem to be quite a lot of rules about marquesses in bedchambers." Emma wriggled underneath him, making a great show of attempting to escape him. "Why, you wicked man."

Samuel had never seen her so playful before, and her breathless laughter was the sweetest sound he'd ever heard. "There's no point in struggling, Miss Downing. I have you now." He dipped his head to nuzzle her neck. "Behave yourself, and perhaps I'll reward you."

"Never!" Emma declared, but her objections didn't carry as much weight as they might have done if she hadn't been stroking her fingers down the back of his thigh, tickling him with her fingernails. "Surrender is for the weak, and I'm not...*oh*." Her laughing protests were swallowed in a gasp. "Oh, my goodness."

Samuel cupped her breasts in his hands, his thumb teasing one nipple as his lips closed around the other one. He circled the swollen peak with his tongue before drawing it into his mouth and sucking, tormenting her with light strokes, easing back only when Emma was gasping.

"Pretty." Samuel flicked the edge of his fingernail over an eager nipple, watching her face as he crooned to her, low and wicked, his words both a tease and an invitation. "Yes, you like that. Do you need more? Beg me sweetly, and I'll give you whatever you want."

He nuzzled her again, dragging his beard-roughened cheek over the tips of her breasts, a dark chuckle falling from his lips when she sank her fingers into his hair to still him and pressed her nipple against his mouth. He obliged her with a lingering lick before pulling away again. "I don't hear a plea, Emma."

Emma arched up to catch his lower lip between her teeth, her gentle nibble distracting him as she dragged her hand down his chest to his stomach and brushed her fingers over his cock, standing at stiff attention against his belly. He was already aching, and when she teased her thumb over the swollen tip his hips jerked forward, thrusting his hard length into her fist.

God, he wanted her so badly, wanted to keep thrusting until he came into that tight, warm hand, but there would be time for that later. Right now, he wanted to make Emma writhe and plead, and then he wanted to give her everything until she fell apart in his arms.

He wrapped his fingers around her wrist and pinned it to the bed, ignoring the insistent throbbing of his cock, and slipped his other hand between her legs.

Emma gasped, her back arching as he dragged one fingertip through her satiny folds, gathering the moisture there.

He stroked her again, then again until she was slick, and he'd coaxed the swollen nub at her core to rise, begging for another stroke of his fingers. "Spread your legs for me, Emma."

This time she did as he commanded at once, all teasing protests melting away as she opened herself to him.

"Yes. God, yes, sweetheart." Samuel shifted his thigh so it rested between hers, gritting his teeth to fight back his climax at the thought of holding her open and pleasuring her relentlessly until she came for him.

He touched her lightly, delicately, his big, rough fingers parting her dainty pink flesh and revealing the pearl at her center, open and blossoming for him. "So eager. You're beautiful like this, Emma." He dragged the pad of his finger over her, lighter than a whisper.

Emma's back bowed at the caress, seeking more of his touch. So Samuel stroked her again, but too lightly to give her what she needed, his lips parting as she squirmed for him.

"Do you need to come, sweetheart?" He was every bit as wicked as she'd accused him of being, because he loved this, loved teasing her, loved making her moan and beg. He could listen to her incoherent pleas forever.

A broken sob left her lips. "Yes! Samuel, I...*please*, make me—"

Samuel stroked her again, groaning when she arched against him, seeking his fingers. He was nearly as frenzied as she was, his cock harder than it had ever been, the tip weeping with his arousal. He allowed himself one desperate stroke down his length, but no more than that, certain another one would send him over the edge.

He leaned over her heaving chest and lowered his mouth to her nipple, suckling her as he continued to brush his fingertips over her, again and again, but slowly, so slowly she began to thrash against the bed, every inch of her creamy skin flushed, his fingers slippery against her quivering flesh.

And still, he kept her on the edge, panting with the effort of holding them both back. "God, look at you, sweetheart." Samuel bit her earlobe as he whispered in her ear. "So needy, so desperate to come. I could watch you forever."

Another frustrated sob left Emma's chest, and her hand slid down, slipping between her own thighs, tearing a groan from Samuel's throat. The thought of her pleasuring herself, of working those pale, delicate fingers between her legs until she climaxed was so erotic, he was forced to clamp down hard on the base of his cock to keep from coming.

But he wouldn't allow it. *He* would be the one to give her pleasure.

"*No.*" Samuel let out a possessive growl, took her hand and pinned it to the bed. "You'll come at my hand only, Emma."

He slid his thigh from between her legs and worked his way down her body, dropping kisses over her sleek stomach as he went, lingering over her inner thighs, the skin there so soft, so impossibly soft, before at last his tongue found her hungry nub. He licked her there, once, then again, soft, quick flicks of his tongue.

"Oh, oh, oh…" Emma cried out, bucking against him.

Samuel held her legs open and pinned to the bed. "Dear God, you're sweet." Her taste was driving him mad. He licked and sucked, nearly snarling as he devoured her like a ravenous animal.

"Please, *please.*" Emma pumped her hips against his mouth, her fingers twisting in his hair, pulling hard when he pointed his tongue and drove it into her. "Ah, yes, please, Samuel."

"That's right, love. Beg for what you need." Samuel was thrusting against the bed, so close to coming he could feel the orgasm tingling in his spine, but he held off, licking her with wild strokes until Emma's entire body went taut.

"*Samuel.*" His name on her lips was part whisper, part moan, her hips surging as a powerful orgasm thundered through her. Samuel closed his eyes and gritted his teeth and held back his own orgasm as he stroked her through hers.

He stayed with her as she trembled against the bed, suckling her through her release until she let out a ragged sigh, and her fingers gentled in his hair. Samuel pressed a kiss to her thighs, one and then the other, but as surely as he'd tormented her, he'd tormented himself, and now he couldn't wait any longer. He was desperate for release, and he needed to be inside her.

He crawled back up her body and settled his hips between her legs. "I need you, sweetheart. Will you have me?"

She might have teased him as mercilessly as he'd teased her, but Emma only smiled, her blue eyes soft. "Yes."

He hissed as she wrapped her long, slender fingers around his cock and drew her hand up his length. "I want you, Emma, more than I've ever wanted anyone."

"Then take me." She tightened her legs around him, pressed his head to her weeping core, and moved her hips against his in invitation.

He paused to press a kiss to her lips, and then he was sinking into her slick, welcoming heat, the pleasure so intense for a moment Samuel had to close his eyes against it. "Ah, God. Emma."

It was all he could do not to drive wildly into her, to seize the pleasure he'd been denying himself, but he forced himself to take slow, shallow thrusts, his jaw tight with the strain of holding back.

If he could last long enough to make her come again...

It took all the restraint he possessed, but Samuel took her with slow, gentle nudges until her breathing quickened, a telltale flush rose in her cheeks, and her mouth opened in a soft moan. "Come with me, Emma."

Another moan escaped, and she caught her lower lip in her teeth.

Samuel's gaze darted to her mouth, and he took her lips in a hot, deep kiss, quickening his pace until their hips were moving together in a timeless rhythm.

Another thrust, then another, but just as Samuel was sure he would explode, Emma let out a soft cry, her neck arching as she came again in a rush of wet heat.

The tight squeeze of her body around his cock tore a guttural moan from Samuel's chest. He threw his head back and fell over the edge in a climax so intense his body shook with it, hot white flashing behind his closed eyes.

They were both still panting when he gathered her against his chest and fell onto his back, taking her with him so she was sprawled on top of him. Once Emma had caught her breath, she struggled onto her elbows, and gazed down at him in wonder. "I—it's never felt like that for me."

He reached up to cup her cheek in his palm. "Nor for me, Emma. Nor for me."

* * * *

Making love was nothing at all like Emma had thought it would be. Making love with Samuel was everything she'd once dreamed it would be, but had long ago ceased hoping for.

She's heard enough from the courtesans at the Pink Pearl to know it wasn't always like this with a man. Indeed, it seemed it was very rarely like this.

Samuel was a consummate lover—Emma knew enough about the act to know that. He was both tender and wicked by turns, with a depth of passion another lady might find unusual in so solemn a gentleman.

But not her. She'd always known it was there, like the spark of an ember just waiting for a chance to burst into flame. From the moment she'd met him she'd instinctively sensed the heat simmering just below his cool surface. Even when she'd despised him, or been furious with him, she'd still been drawn to that heat.

Perhaps she'd known all along he'd be the man who'd melt the ice that imprisoned her heart.

But it was more than that. What had unfolded between them, the passion, his whispered words of desire and adoration, had little to do with his skills as a lover.

He'd said he loved her. He'd whispered those sacred words to her, and she'd longed to say them back to him. They'd hovered just at the edge of her tongue, but somehow, she hadn't been able to speak them into reality.

Yet she did love him. These stolen moments with him were everything to her.

For all that she'd never believed love would be hers, her scarred heart had suddenly learned to beat again, and now it throbbed with a flood of love for him.

Samuel shifted beside her in the bed. Emma's fingers drifted over his chest, and he caught her hand and raised it to his lips, pressing a tender kiss to her fingertips. "Tell me about your scars, Emma."

Emma let out a long, slow breath. She never talked about her scars to anyone. Only Lady Clifford and Daniel knew what had really happened that night. What little Emma could remember she'd vowed to take to her grave.

But now, as she lay safely in Samuel's arms, the words began to fall from her lips. "I've only ever had one other lover."

His hand stilled in her hair. "I don't understand. The Pink Pearl—"

Emma pressed her fingers to his lips to hush him. "I did spend a year at the Pink Pearl, yes, but I never…I wasn't like the other courtesans. I never, er…entertained any gentleman but one. Madame Marchand auctioned off my virginity to him, and I—he—I became his, after that."

Samuel tensed, but he didn't speak. He simply waited, letting her tell him in her own way.

Emma's eyes burned, and she had to close them at the warm pressure of his lips against her temple. "The gentleman who purchased it—*me*—was a violent, brutish man, especially when he was in his cups, which was often. One night when he was particularly bad, I grew frightened and struggled against him. He—" Emma broke off, the familiar panic and horror rising like bile in her throat.

But Samuel was there, his voice gentle, his strong arms tight around her. "What did he do, sweetheart?"

"He, ah…he had a knife, and he held the blade to my throat. I can't remember how…I don't know how I managed it, but before he could hurt me, I wrestled the knife away from him. I don't remember what happened after that, but when I came back to myself, he was lying still on the floor, and my…my hands were covered with blood."

Emma closed her eyes and waited for Samuel to say…what? What could he possibly say, after hearing that? There was nothing.

Samuel didn't say a word. Instead, he did the only thing he could do that would mean anything to her in that moment. He took her hands in his and covered them with tender kisses, his lips moving sweetly over her scars until she was trembling, and tears sheened her eyes.

He held her for long, quiet moments, waiting for her breath to steady, then he raised her face to his. "Emma, look at me. You're the bravest lady I've ever known. Your past has made you who you are, and who you are is everything to me."

A sob caught in Emma's throat, but the tears that fell from her eyes and dampened his chest weren't tears of sorrow, they were tears of gratitude.

For *him*. He was the dearest man she'd ever known.

He held her until her tears dried, and a shaky sigh left her lips.

"I wish we could stay here all day." Dear God, surely she wasn't going to start crying *again*? She tucked her face against his shoulder to hide her expression. "It's nearly dawn. The servants will be up soon."

It wasn't a subtle hint, but Samuel didn't move. "You haven't told me what happened at the ball last night. Did any of the guests react to the pendant?"

"No. At least, not in any noticeable way." Emma stared up at the ceiling as scenes from the ball the night before played through her mind. The villain who'd hurt Caroline, Amy, and Kitty had been there last night, she was certain of it. She couldn't explain how she knew, but she'd sensed him there, watching from the shadows, waiting for a chance to strike.

Emma had hoped he'd make a mistake, that he'd stumble into some word or look that would give him away, but there'd been nothing. Whoever he was, he was cleverer than she'd thought.

"That's the last time you'll wear that pendant, Emma. Either he's seen it already, or he isn't here. There's no purpose in your wearing it again. One time should be sufficiently dangerous even to satisfy *you*."

Emma couldn't have said whether she was frustrated at his arrogance or thrilled at his fierce protectiveness, but he was right about the pendant. It had served its purpose, and now there was nothing to do but wait and see what happened. "I won't wear it again, but I came to Lymington House to finish this, Samuel, and I don't intend to give up until I have."

He gathered her closer, a low growl in his chest. "Tell me what you plan to do, then. I can't bear it otherwise."

In spite of herself, Emma's heart melted. "There's not much I can do but wait. I would like to speak to your kitchen maid, Hannah, again. I'm not certain she told me everything she knows about Amy's sweetheart."

"I'll come with you. I don't like you to wander about the house alone."

"You can't come with me, Samuel, or I won't get a single word out of her. You're the haughty, intimidating marquess, if you recall." Emma took his hand and dropped a kiss onto his palm to take any sting out of her words.

"I'll wait in the hallway outside the kitchen, then."

Dear God, the man was stubborn. "The house is safe enough with so many guests about. One can't stir a step without tumbling over some countess or earl or other."

Emma was hoping for a smile. All she got was a sullen pinch of Samuel's mouth, but somehow even that proved so endearing she couldn't resist pressing a kiss to his pouting lips.

"You'll come to luncheon."

It was a command, not a request, but Emma chose to overlook his imperiousness in favor of getting her way. "Yes, I promise it. Now hurry back to your own bedchamber, before Lady Crosby comes searching for me."

Samuel grumbled as he got out of bed and dragged his breeches over his hips. Emma couldn't prevent a regretful sigh at seeing all that smooth skin and those taut muscles hidden under clothing once again, but she was somewhat mollified by the dozen warm kisses Samuel pressed to her lips before tearing himself away with a reluctant groan.

"Luncheon, Emma," he reminded her, pausing at her bedchamber door.

"Yes. I promise it."

He gave her one last heated look, and then he was gone.

* * * *

In the end, despite their best laid plans, Emma didn't see Samuel after her foray into the kitchens, or at luncheon an hour later. She kept her promise, but when she arrived in the dining room, he wasn't there.

Lord Lovell took her aside and told her Samuel had been waylaid by a gentleman from a neighboring property with pressing estate business, and that he'd see her at tea.

So Emma sat at the luncheon table between Lady Crosby and Lady Lymington, listening to their cheerful chatter, saying very little and eating even less. She was more disappointed by Samuel's absence than a lady who'd sworn to keep her wits should be.

It was the culmination of what had turned out to be a disappointing morning.

Samuel had clearly instructed Lord Lovell to keep a close eye on her in his place, because Lovell followed her about with such determination that afternoon that Emma was finally driven upstairs to Lady Crosby's bedchamber to escape him.

"Well now, Emma, how did you do with the kitchen maid this morning?" Lady Crosby asked, when Emma joined her. "Did Hannah have any secrets to share?"

Emma dropped down onto the edge of the bed with a sigh. "Disappointingly few, though she did confirm what Lady Lymington told me. Amy Townshend did have a sweetheart."

"A sweetheart? I daresay that might lead to something promising. What sort of sweetheart?"

"Hannah didn't know. It seems Amy kept him a closely guarded secret. Hannah claims never to have laid eyes on the man."

"Nonsense. What sort of young girl keeps her sweetheart a secret?"

"A young girl with the sort of sweetheart who wishes to remain anonymous, I imagine."

"Well, if that's the case, that in itself is telling, is it not?"

"Very telling, yes. Amy took up with this man about six weeks before she vanished. She was coy about his name, but Hannah said Amy once let it slip that the man wasn't from Lymington House. It seems Amy used to sneak down to a folly situated near a pond at the edge of the property to meet with him."

Lady Crosby frowned at her reflection in the mirror. "I never saw a pond, or a folly, and we've been all over the gardens since we arrived."

"It's not the sort of place one would stumble upon, my lady. It's behind the kitchens, down a narrow, tree-lined pathway."

"It sounds like a dreadful, muddy place." Lady Crosby shuddered. "Not at all romantic."

"No, but private, and thus ideal for a man who doesn't wish to be seen." Emma twisted a loose thread on the coverlet, thinking. That Amy Townshend should have disappeared six weeks after she found herself a mysterious sweetheart couldn't possibly be a coincidence.

"What of Kitty Yardley?" Lady Crosby asked. "What became of her?"

"I couldn't find out much about Kitty at all. She was shy, and didn't have many friends among the servants. Lady Lymington mentioned she came from a large family, and was dreadfully homesick for them. Hannah said she assumed Kitty had run away back home when she disappeared."

"Thank goodness for you and Lady Clifford, Emma. Poor Lord Lovell might have found himself at the end of a noose, but for you." Lady Crosby slammed her hairbrush down on the dressing table, her cheeks red with anger. "What pure evil, to try and implicate an innocent man in such a wicked crime."

The loose thread Emma had been toying with snapped between her fingers. "That's true enough, but someone's neck *does* deserve to be fitted with a noose, and I've still no idea who's neck it is."

"But you *will*, dearest. I have the utmost faith in you, and so does Lady Clifford."

Emma gave Lady Crosby a grateful smile, but doubt was niggling at her. Perhaps their faith in her was misplaced. "I suppose I'll go and see this folly, then."

Lady Crosby whirled around to face Emma, startled. "Not by yourself, I hope!"

Emma hesitated. She had no wish to tempt fate, and Samuel would be furious if he discovered she'd been wandering the grounds by herself, but their villain must be offered an opportunity to strike, or he'd never show himself. "I'll fetch Daniel to come with me."

"Yes, all right, but do wear a cloak, won't you? It's a cold, drippy sort of afternoon. You'll come and fetch me before tea?"

"Yes, my lady." Emma pressed a quick kiss to Lady Crosby's cheek. "I won't be long."

When Emma reached the first floor, she found Samuel's study door still closed, with muffled masculine voices coming from inside. So she made her way down the servants' staircase to the kitchen door and out to the stables, where she found Daniel fussing over Lady Crosby's carriage horses.

He turned when Emma entered. "Aye, lass?"

"Good afternoon, Daniel. Will you walk down to the pond behind the kitchens with me? There's a folly down there that was apparently the scene of some secret assignations, and I want to have a look at it."

"More secrets, eh? Lymington House is full of 'em." Daniel's face darkened. "Too many aristocrats in one place, if ye ask me."

Emma smothered a smile. "You may be right."

Daniel gave the horse's nose one last rub, then turned toward the door with a grunt. "All right, then, let's go."

The folly was further from the main house than Emma anticipated, a quarter mile or so down a short, steep hill, the pathway hidden from sight by the spreading branches of a stand of English oak. She and Daniel were nearing the end, picking their way over the exposed roots studding the pathway, when a deep voice came out of nowhere.

"Well, good afternoon, Lady Emma!"

Emma nearly jumped out of her skin. "Mr. Humphries! My goodness." she patted the center of her chest to calm her wildly beating heart. "I, er… didn't see you there."

"Beg pardon, my lady. I didn't mean to frighten you."

"That's quite all right, Mr. Humphries." Emma cast a sidelong glance at Daniel, who gestured toward the folly, just visible to the left of the pathway. Emma nodded, and Daniel slipped into the trees, while Emma made her way down the pathway toward Mr. Humphries.

He was perched on the edge of the pond, up to his ankles in mud with an angling rod in his hands. "I didn't expect any young ladies to venture down to the pond. A bit dirty, what?"

Emma looked down at her muddy boots and wrinkled her nose. "Indeed. I didn't realize you were a sportsman, Mr. Humphries."

"Ach, no—not me, my lady. Just a bit of angling now and then, you see. I like the quiet, and it's pretty down here, with the water and the trees." Mr. Humphries chuckled. "I don't catch many fish, I'm afraid."

Emma edged a little closer. The pond was bigger than she'd expected from Hannah's description of it. A towering stand of oaks overhung a good portion of the eastern side of it, and the shadiest parts were still covered with a thin layer of ice from the past winter's freeze. "It is rather pretty, isn't it? Goodness, those trees are enormous. They must be quite old."

"What, Lord Dunn's trees? Oh, yes. It takes hundreds of years, I believe, for them to reach that size."

Emma turned to him, puzzled. "Are those Lord Dunn's trees?"

"Yes, yes, indeed. That's his lordship's property, just there." Mr. Humphries waved a hand toward the other side of the pond. "He's got a tidy little hunting box over there. He's very fond of hunting, is Lord Dunn."

Emma frowned, vaguely recalling that Lady Crosby had said something about Lord Dunn's having purchased a hunting box near Lymington House.

But this was *very* near, much more so than she'd imagined. So close, she couldn't help but wonder why Lord Dunn should need it at all, when he could just as easily hunt from Lymington House. "What, ah…what sort of hunting does Lord Dunn prefer?"

"Oh, birds mostly, I think. He's an avid birdsman, perhaps a bit more so than he should be, if you take my meaning." Mr. Humphries gave her a mischievous wink.

Emma shook her head. "I beg your pardon, Mr. Humphries, but I don't."

"Oh, well, it's just that I saw him out here in February, and he was after the partridge, you know. Partridge season ends on February first," he added, when Emma gave him a blank look.

"*February*? Are you quite sure it was February?" Emma's voice was much more urgent than the conversation warranted, and she clenched her hands inside her pockets to remind herself to give nothing away.

Mr. Humphries gave her a baffled look. "It was February, right enough— the second week of February. I came for Lady Lovell's birthday weekend, but no sooner had I arrived than the family was unexpectedly called away to London."

A chill rushed over Emma's skin, raising the hairs on her neck. She nodded and offered Mr. Humphries a weak smile, but her head was spinning.

Lord Dunn had told her he was in Cornwall with his sister until the end of March. In fact, he'd made quite a point of saying he'd returned just in time for the season.

Lord Dunn had *lied* to her.

Why should he have lied, unless he had something to hide?

Emma hurried back toward firmer ground, anxious to make her way back to Daniel, so she might confer with him about this new development. "Well, I wish you good luck with your angling, Mr. Humphries."

"Oh, well, I was just finishing when you came. It's not as much fun when you're not catching anything," Mr. Humphries said cheerfully. "May I walk you back?"

"No, I thank you. I think I'll go a little further along the bank so I can see the folly."

"All right, then, Lady Emma. Be careful not to slip. That water's cold."

"I will. Thank you, Mr. Humphries."

Anna Bradley

Mr. Humphries gathered his equipment and, with one final tip of his hat, disappeared down the pathway, whistling as he went.

As soon as the sound of his whistle faded, Emma turned and hurried in the direction of the folly.

It was just where Hannah had said it was, tucked into a narrow bend in the pathway, overlooking the pond. It was a pretty little building of white marble, with graceful columns supporting a domed roof with picturesque vines climbing up one side of it.

Emma glanced behind her, but she was at the bottom of the short hill, below Lymington House, and couldn't see it from here, which meant no one who happened to be looking out the window of the kitchen toward the pond could see the folly, either.

It was plainly visible from Lord Dunn's hunting box, however.

Emma hurried toward the folly, the muddy ground sucking at her feet and slowing her progress, but soon enough she reached the archway that led inside. It was open to the outdoors, and she shivered as a gust of cold wind stole under the skirts of her cloak.

She came to an abrupt stop once she was inside, a sense of foreboding crawling up her neck.

It was empty.

"Daniel?" Emma crept forward and peered around the curved wall, hoping he was waiting for her just out of sight on the other side.

But he wasn't there. Emma's gaze darted this way and that, but aside from a few stone benches, the folly was empty. There wasn't a chance she could have missed Daniel, but Emma circled around again anyway, her heart rushing into her throat as the silence around her grew sinister.

"Daniel?" He never would have left her here alone. Not by choice. There was simply no way he would have ever—

"Well, Lady Emma Crosby. Here we are, alone at last."

Emma whirled around, her heart crowding into her throat. A tall, shadowy figure had appeared behind her as if out of nowhere and was looming over her. He was wearing a dark riding coat and a top hat, the brim pulled low, obscuring most of his face, but Emma knew him the moment he spoke.

She sucked in a breath, gathering her energy to scream. "*Dan*—"

Before she could get another syllable out, he slapped a large, gloved hand over her mouth. "I'm afraid your coachman is otherwise engaged, Lady Emma."

Shock made Emma freeze for an instant, rooting her feet to the floor. By the time her wits returned enough for her to struggle, it was too late.

He'd clamped his other arm around her waist, and was dragging her out of the folly, her heels scrabbling uselessly for purchase on the slippery marble underneath her.

"Come along like a good girl, and don't make a fuss." His tone was mocking, his breath hot in her ear, his forearm pressing hard against her throat. "Surrender to your fate, Lady Emma. It's so much easier for us both that way."

Chapter Twenty-three

It had been an afternoon of torture.

Lord Bartleby, an irascible earl from a neighboring estate, had come by after breakfast, demanding an audience over some pressing business regarding a shared wall on the eastern border of their two properties.

At least, Bartleby deemed it pressing. Samuel didn't give a damn one way or another about the wall, but Bartleby could talk on the subject forever, it seemed. By the time he left Samuel's study, Samuel's head was pounding, and he would have sworn there was blood trickling out of his ears.

If it had ever occurred to Samuel the man could drone on and on at such length about height, drainage, and proper English granite, he never would have let the old bounder set foot in his study.

Thanks to Lord Bartleby and his damned border wall it had been an entire afternoon wasted, and now Samuel was late for tea. He flew upstairs and dressed with such haste he left his dressing closet turned upside down and poor, harried Fletcher in despair.

When he entered the drawing room, there was only one thing on his mind—only one thing he wanted.

Emma.

"Good afternoon, Lymington." Lord Dunn was lounging on one of the settees, one booted foot dangling over his knee, a cup of tea in his hand.

Samuel paused in the doorway. Where was Emma? Come to that, where was everyone else? A tea tray rested on the table at Dunn's elbow, but he was alone in the room. "Have I missed tea?"

"Lady Lymington was here, but she's since retired to her rooms with a headache. Lovell's gone for a ride on the eastern edge of the estate, and Lady Flora and Lady Silvester went to the conservatory to see if the apricots had ripened."

Samuel frowned. "What of Lady Crosby and Lady Emma?"

Dunn shrugged. "Still abed, I imagine, after the ball last night."

Lady Crosby, perhaps, but not Emma. She'd promised to meet him for luncheon. He'd been trapped in his study with Bartleby then, but he'd expected he'd see her at tea. "Were they not at luncheon?"

"I've no idea, Lymington. I've only just ventured into tea myself. I drank too much champagne last night, and I've had a devil of a headache all day."

"You haven't been out riding, then?" Dunn's boots were wet, and the hem of his riding coat was splattered with mud. "For a man who's just left his bed, you look a mess."

"Kind of you to say so, Lymington," Dunn drawled, smirking. "An extra lump of sugar in your tea, perhaps, to sweeten your temper?"

Samuel wasn't interested in tea, or in anything else but finding Emma, but he couldn't rush off and abandon Dunn without sharing a cup with him first. Surely, he wasn't quite such a besotted fool he couldn't manage a cup of tea?

"Sugar won't do it, Dunn." The only thing that would restore Samuel to good humor was one fair-haired, blue-eyed lady with the sweetest lips he'd ever kissed, but he strode into the drawing room anyway, joined Dunn by the fire, and served himself a cup of tea.

Before he had a chance to raise the cup to his lips, however, Lady Crosby burst into the drawing room, her hair tumbling from its neat bun, and her face as pale as death. "Oh, Lord Lymington, thank goodness I've found you!"

Samuel shot to his feet, startled by her wild appearance, and his teacup slipped from his hand and tumbled to the carpet. "What is it, Lady Crosby?"

"I can't find Emma! She was supposed to fetch me for tea when she returned, but I fell asleep, and didn't realize she never—"

"Returned from where, Lady Crosby? Where did she go?"

Lady Crosby was wringing her hands. "To the folly! The one behind the kitchens, next to the pond."

"The folly!" Pure panic swept over Samuel. That folly was in a remote part of the grounds, down a wooded pathway, and not visible from the house. "Please tell me she didn't venture so far from the house alone."

"N-no, not alone." Lady Crosby had become so agitated by this point she was struggling to catch her breath. "She fetched Daniel to go with her."

Daniel Brixton should be menacing enough to deter even the most hardened villain, but if his presence had been as discouraging as it ought to have been, then *where was Emma*?

Anna Bradley

"Dunn, go after Lovell, and fetch Felix Humphries. Tell them they're needed at the folly at once, and that I'll meet them there." Samuel didn't wait for an answer, but flew from the drawing room out to the stables at a dead run.

He started calling Brixton's name once the stable was in sight, but there was no answer, and when he burst through the doors, he found the place deserted. Aside from an occasional equine snort and shuffle of hooves, all was still and silent.

Daniel Brixton had been everywhere during the past weeks in London, shadowing Emma's every move, and lurking on the darkened streets outside the Pink Pearl. Whichever way Samuel turned, Brixton was there, shoving his enormous bulk between Samuel and any hope he had of a private moment with Emma.

Now that Samuel actually needed the man, he was nowhere to be found.

Samuel stood in the middle of the stables, his gaze darting helplessly this way and that, as close to panicking as he'd ever been in his life. Emma had been missing for *hours*, now it seemed Brixton was also missing, and Samuel's thoughts were on the verge of scattering into chaos.

But if he let that happen, he'd be no use to Emma at all. He dragged a hand down his face, drew in deep breath, and tried to *think*.

Brixton would never have left Emma by choice. Wherever Emma was, Brixton was with her, so there was no sense waiting here for Brixton to turn up. Samuel would have to go to the folly alone, and hope for the best.

He ran out the stable doors and around the eastern side of the house. The light from the kitchen illuminated the area just outside the window, but beyond that was gloom, the shadows growing longer with every moment as the sun sank below the horizon.

There were no smooth gravel pathways or trimmed hedges *here*, but Samuel plunged ahead, stumbling over tree roots as he tore down the steep hill that led toward the pond, his boots sliding over the loose dirt, threatening to send him crashing to the ground with every step.

But he didn't slow, even as the soil beneath his feet softened, before it disintegrated into muck near the water. By the time he reached the edge of the pond his chest was heaving with his panting breaths. It had been years since he'd been down here, but he remembered the folly was tucked under the stand of oak trees near the end of the pathway.

He paused, straining to see into the distance. "Emma!"

No answer.

He called Emma's name again, but the only sound was the echo of his voice reverberating among the trees, and the squelch of his footsteps as he made his way through the muck toward the folly.

Before he'd even stepped inside, Samuel knew she wasn't here. If she had been, he'd have felt her at once, but he circled around the building nonetheless, searching for...God, he didn't even know what. Some hint of her, some sign she'd been here, but there was nothing, nothing—

He almost missed it. He didn't realize it was there until he stepped on it.

A ribbon, lying on the floor, a familiar, distinctive shade of blue.

Samuel snatched it up, brought it to his face, and inhaled.

Vanilla.

He stood for long, silent moments, the blue silk against his lips, breathing deeply of her scent and forcing himself to calm. She'd been here recently, then, but where was she now?

Young ladies didn't simply vanish without a trace—

Except they did. At Lymington House, they *did.*

Another moment passed, then another, Emma's blue ribbon clutched in Samuel's fist as he tried to decide what to do next. It could be some time before Dunn found Lovell, but shouldn't Humphries be here by now?

Samuel shoved Emma's ribbon in his pocket and ran back up the pathway, leaving the folly behind, intending to retrace his footsteps back to the house.

He'd drag every footman in the house down here if he had—

Snap.

Samuel froze at the sound of a tree branch cracking under someone's foot. He squinted into the blackness. Was that...

It *was.* A flicker of movement, some distance away still, far enough he could hardly make it out, but it looked like...

The shadow of a man, weaving through the trees.

Who would be wandering the estate *now*, in the dark, especially so close to the pond, over grounds made treacherous by slick mud and protruding tree branches?

No one who was up to any good.

Samuel hesitated, wondering if he could risk waiting for Humphries, but the man wasn't likely to be of much use, and the shadow was receding further into the distance as he hesitated. Lovell and Dunn might arrive soon, but by then the man would have disappeared entirely.

Samuel didn't have any time left.

He crept from the pathway into the rough ground closer to the trees, a soft curse leaving his lips when the sharp branches tore at his hair and coat, but he never took his eyes off that threatening shadow.

He picked his way across the slick ground, sucking in a breath as frigid water seeped into his boots and his toes screamed in protest, the icy water stabbing him like knives slashing his skin.

The shock of the cold made him slow, clumsy, but he could see the man clearly now, a dark figure moving slowly through the trees ahead of him, grabbing at branches as he went to steady himself.

Samuel crept after him, his steps careful but his pace quick and steady, one step, two, a dozen, drawing closer with each one…so close he could see the man's broad shoulders and a black-gloved hand resting against a thick tree trunk.

Closer, a little closer and he could leap on the man's back, drag him to the ground—

"Bloody hell!" The man whirled around at the sound of Samuel's footfalls, but it was already too late.

By then, Samuel was on him.

"Oof!" The man landed with a hard thump on his belly on the muddy ground. Samuel was atop him in an instant, shoving the man's face into the muck with a fist to the back of his head. "What have you done with Emma, you blackguard?"

The man wrenched his head free, and a torrent of vile curses fell from his lips. "Hell, and damnation! I might a' known it'd be *you*—"

The man broke off, gagging around a mouthful of mud as Samuel gave his face another shove. "Tell me where she is *now*, or I'll see to it you're buried head first in—"

"Get off me, ye daft devil!"

Samuel had no intention of going anywhere, but by now the man had overcome his shock, and with one mighty heave he managed to crawl to his knees and throw Samuel off him.

Samuel landed on the ground on his back with a thump that knocked the breath out of him, but in an instant he'd rolled into a crouch, a growl on his lips as he readied to leap again.

"It's Brixton, ye damned fool!" Brixton struggled to his feet and bent over, hands on his knees, and sucked one ragged breath after another into his lungs.

"Brixton?" Samuel dragged himself up, swaying as he struggled to stand. "Damn it, man, I've been searching for you! You're doing a bloody poor job of protecting Emma, because she's—"

"Damn it, Lymington, I think ye broke my hand."

Samuel wanted to strangle him. "I don't give a damn about your hand. Christ, Brixton, didn't you hear me? I told you, Emma's missing!"

Daniel spat on the ground. "Dunn took 'er."

"*Dunn?*" Samuel shook his head. "Why should Dunn—"

"Dunn's yer blackguard, Lymington. Did away with those three servant girls."

"Dunn!" Samuel stared at Brixton, stunned speechless. "How do you know?"

"I know 'cause 'e tried to kill me. Coward crept up behind me in the folly. Nearly crushed my skull with a rock, then tossed me in the pond."

"He crushed your skull and tossed you in the pond, and you didn't drown?"

Brixton scowled at him. "Ye ever been in that pond, Lymington? It's half ice still. Woke me right up, it did."

"You're sure it was Dunn?"

"Aye, I'm sure. I crawled onto the bank of the pond and saw the devil drag Miss Emma away. I've been lying there ever since trying to get up, but my head was dizzy, and my legs not right."

None of this made sense. Dunn had been in Samuel's drawing room an hour ago, sipping tea and smiling, just having risen from his bed...except his boots had been wet, and his coat splattered with mud.

Samuel swallowed as those two details took on an ominous significance. "You're telling me Dunn's a villain, and now he has Emma?"

"Aye, that's what I'm telling ye. But don't underestimate Miss Emma. That lass knows what she's about—"

Samuel didn't wait to hear anymore, but whirled in the direction of Dunn's hunting box. "If Dunn has Emma, then why are we still standing here? Let's go!"

"Nay, Lymington. He didn't take her that way." Brixton pointed in front of them. "He took 'er back toward the house."

Toward the *house?* Why would Dunn take her back toward the house, where it was much more likely they'd be seen? It didn't make any sense—

Samuel went still, a chill rolling over him as Brixton's words came back to him.

Ye ever been in that pond, Lymington? It's half ice still.

There was one place Dunn could take Emma where they wouldn't be seen, and where no one was likely to find her...

Samuel met Brixton's eyes. "I know where Emma is."

Chapter Twenty-four

It was a long time before Emma realized Lord Dunn had taken her to the icehouse.

She might have grasped it sooner, but being attacked in a folly and dragged away with a blackguard's hand slapped over her mouth was a harrowing experience.

Shock made her hazy, and nausea swamped her every time she thought about how Lord Dunn might have incapacitated Daniel, who wasn't the sort of man who was easily overcome. Her mind helpfully offered more than one gruesome scenario, until she forced herself to stop dwelling on it, lest her calm deserted her.

Hysterics were out of the question. Things were bad enough, without that.

But the icehouse wasn't a welcoming place, not even in the daylight, and it was far worse now that the sun had slipped below the horizon. It was as dark as Hades, and just as frightening.

Ideal, though, if one were intent on a kidnapping. Certainly, no one would hear her scream from here.

She hadn't thought much about the cold at first—dark places were often cold—but no one could ignore such frigidity for long. It was positively artic, as if the entire building were buried in ice—

Ice. Of course.

It all fell into place, then. The fragments of ice still floating in the pond, the low brick doorway set into the side of the steep hill that wasn't a hill at all, or even a feature of the landscape, as she'd first assumed.

It was a mound, and where there was a mound, there was bound to be a pit. In this case, an ice pit, the excavated earth fashioned into a mound over the top to keep the ice as cold as possible.

It did an admirable job of it. Emma wrapped her arms around herself, shivering. Thank goodness for Lady Crosby, who'd reminded her to wear her cloak.

She didn't bother to try the door—she'd heard a metallic click after Lord Dunn slammed it shut, the scrape of an iron key in a lock—and knew he'd locked her inside.

It could be some time still before Lord Dunn returned to deal with her. He'd want to make certain everyone noticed him at Lymington House, so they'd be less likely to suspect him of any wrongdoing when they discovered she'd gone missing. He might even wait for Lord Lovell to leave the house, so it would be easier to implicate him in her disappearance.

Lord Dunn was clever that way, but in the end, not clever enough. His fate was already sealed, no matter what happened to Emma.

He simply didn't know it yet.

And Emma hadn't been idle, while he'd been gone. It wasn't easy, finding her way about in total darkness, but Lord Dunn had left her plenty of time to orient herself. Foolish of him, really, but he wasn't the first gentleman who'd underestimated her.

She'd taken her time, even sinking to her knees and crawling with her hands out in front of her, searching for the edge of the ice pit. There weren't many ways to make her situation worse than it was now, but falling into the ice pit was one of them.

In the end, all her creeping about paid off, because she'd found what she was looking for. Well, not *precisely* what she was looking for—she would have preferred an ice hook, or better yet an ice pick, as she had a horror of blades—but it was a great stroke of luck she'd found anything at all.

The axe was on the smaller side, and the blade end nearly rusted through. It wasn't in fine condition, which was likely why it had been left behind, but it would do, for her purposes. The edge of the blade was dull, but she could defend herself with it if she swung with enough force. It might be difficult, as her hands had long since gone numb, but she'd simply have to do her best.

Except her knees were a trifle wobbly. Her cloak was damp, and she was already shuddering with cold, her teeth chattering. She might sit on the floor and attempt to regain her equilibrium, but it was stone, and nearly as cold as the ice itself.

If nothing else brought this to a tragic end, the cold would. If she fell asleep out here, she might never wake up. So Emma kept moving, pacing from one end of the icehouse to the other, stamping her feet, rubbing her hands together, and waiting.

It was impossible to keep track of the time down here, so she wasn't sure how long it had been when she heard the muffled thud of a man's boots on the pathway outside the icehouse.

Enough time that she could no longer feel her hands or her feet.

She heard the scrape of the key in the lock, and a moment later, the icehouse door opened. It was much too dark for her to make out Lord Dunn's features—all she saw was the shadowy silhouette of a towering figure looming at the top of the stone steps.

He looked larger than she remembered, larger than he'd ever looked in any ballroom.

"How do you do, Lady Emma? Not too cold, I hope?"

Emma said nothing.

He sauntered down the steps, and offered her a mocking bow. "I regret you were obliged to miss tea, my lady. It did occur to me to take you from the ballroom last night, but it isn't much of a ball without a belle, is it?"

A belle. That was what Lord Dunn saw when he looked at her. For all his cleverness, he'd never seen anything beyond her face. Blue eyes, a charming smile. It was enough, for so many gentlemen.

But not for Samuel. He'd seen past it. He was the only man who'd ever bothered.

The thought made a sob rise in her throat. She choked it back, but Lord Dunn heard it, and let out a heavy sigh "We're not going to have histrionics, I hope. It's nothing personal, Lady Emma. It's just that I fear Caroline Francis has told you some unflattering stories about me, and I can't have the gossip getting out, can I?"

"I've never spoken a word to Caroline Francis in my life."

"No? Helena Reeves, then. Imagine my surprise when Caroline told me you and Helena were such intimate friends. Curious, that a fine lady like yourself would be friends with a whore." Lord Dunn advanced on her, backed her up against the wall behind her, and grabbed her upper arms. It took every bit of courage Emma possessed, but she managed not to jerk out of his grasp.

"Ah, now there's a good girl. No sense in struggling. Now then, let's get to it, shall we? You have something that belongs to me, Lady Emma, and I want it back."

His breath on the side of her face made Emma flinch, but she managed a smile, hoping to put him off his guard. "It's a fine pendant, my lord. Who is the little boy in the portrait?"

Lord Dunn smirked. "Ever charming, aren't you, Lady Emma? He's my eldest nephew, James. I had the pendant made as a Christmas gift for my sister, but unfortunately I was prevented from visiting Cornwall this year."

His nephew. It was as Emma had thought, then. Caroline had realized she was in danger, and had stolen the pendant, hoping it would serve as proof of a connection between herself and Lord Dunn.

And so it had. If Caroline had never been in his company, as Lord Dunn would likely claim, there was no possible way she could have that pendant. "That's a pity, my lord. I daresay that didn't please you."

He gave a curt laugh. "No, it didn't, but I'm afraid that was always the way with Caroline. Nothing about her pleased me, aside from her death."

Emma shuddered at his callousness. He spoke as if strangling a lady and leaving her body in a London alleyway was a trifling matter, of no more significance than a bit of mud on his boots. "Did Amy Townshend displease you, as well?"

That gave him pause. "*Amy*? Well, it seems you know a great deal more than I realized. You are the clever one, Lady Emma. Amy pleased me very well, indeed, right up until she didn't. It was bad of me to lose my temper with her. I didn't mean to hurt her, but so it goes."

"Yes, murder does have a way of defying expectations," Emma said, unable to hide her disgust.

"Ah, I see I've offended you. I beg your pardon, Lady Emma. You're right, of course. Amy put me in rather a bind. It was lucky Lovell happened to be sent down at just that time, but then I've always been a lucky fellow."

"Not quite as lucky as you might have been, if only Lord Lovell had been sent down a few days earlier."

Lord Dunn shrugged. "It's a matter of a few days, and no one at Lymington House knows precisely when Amy went missing."

It was, unfortunately, the truth. Lady Lymington had said the same thing herself. Lord Lovell's alibi wasn't quite as sturdy as Emma might have wished, given the inexact timing of her disappearance. It seemed Lord Dunn had thought of everything.

Nearly everything.

"What of Kitty Yardley, my lord?"

Lord Dunn gave her a blank look. "Kitty? Was that her name? I didn't have anything against her, but *someone* had to vanish after Lovell returned to Lymington House, and the girl happened along at just the right time. Pity, really. Such a quiet, meek little mouse. She hardly made a sound when I strangled her."

Bile crawled up Emma's throat, burning her. "Clever as you are, Lord Dunn, I can't imagine you intended for Caroline to end up at the Pink Pearl."

"No. She was meant to go the way of Amy and Kitty, but then Lovell ran off to London just when I was about finish the business. Disgraceful of him, dashing off like that when he's meant to be in mourning for his father, but you see, it all worked out in the end."

Emma stared up at him, appalled at his disdain when he said Lord Lovell's name. The man dared to judge Lord Lovell's behavior, after the despicable acts he'd committed? "Did it really work out in the end, my lord? I don't deny you did an admirable job covering your tracks, but there's one thing you didn't anticipate."

"Oh?" Lord Dunn chuckled, as if Emma were an amusing child. "What would that be, Lady Emma?"

"Lord Lovell fought a duel in London soon after he left Lymington House in January. He was badly injured by a pistol ball to the leg, and obliged to keep to his bed for weeks. He couldn't have seduced Caroline, or brought her to the Pink Pearl."

Lord Dunn froze, but then he threw his head back in a laugh. "You expect me to believe Lovell fought a duel in London without anyone hearing a word about it? No, Lady Emma. I'm afraid that's impossible, London gossips being what they are."

"Lord Lymington went to great lengths to keep it quiet. He knows all about your crimes, as well, and he'll see you swing for them."

A trace of fear crossed Lord Dunn's face at that, but then his features hardened. "Lymington may do as he likes, but my neck won't find a noose without any proof, and there isn't a shred of that. Even if what you say about the duel is true, it doesn't exonerate Lovell for the two other girls. Caroline's friend Helena, the little dark-haired whore, will be made to testify that Caroline told her Lord Lovell did away with the two servants."

"Yes, I suppose that's true. Of course, she'll also testify that Caroline told her Lord Lovell seduced and ruined *her*. But perhaps the courts can be made to believe Caroline told the truth about Amy and Kitty, but lied about herself. Then there's the matter of the magistrate searching your hunting box, Lord Dunn, for you can be sure Lord Lymington will insist upon it. I wonder what he'll find?"

"Not a blessed thing. Certainly not any bodies. They'll turn up again eventually once the last of the ice melts—a pond can't hide everything—but Lord Lovell could just as easily have disposed of them there as I could. But enough of this. Lymington's on the hunt for you, and I'd prefer to be gone well before he discovers your body. Now, you may hand over the pendant, or I can take it once you're dead. It's your choice, my lady, but it will go much easier for you if you cooperate."

"It's in my pocket." Emma curled her fingers around the handle of the ice axe she was hiding behind a fold of her cloak.

Lord Dunn seized her cloak in his fist. He'd just closed his fingers around the pendant when Emma raised her arm, and holding the axe close to the base of the blade, slammed it down on Lord Dunn's arm with all her strength.

He shrieked in pain as the blade glanced off his wrist. He leapt back, away from her, cradling his injured wrist in his other hand, and slowly raised his eyes to Emma's face, a snarl on his lips. "You bloody little bitch!"

His face was a mask of rage, his eyes narrowed to vicious slits.

This. This was the face the others had seen right before his hands closed around their necks, and squeezed until their breath stopped in their lungs. This was the *real* Lord Dunn, the monster who lurked under that handsome face.

Emma tried to dart around him, but he shoved her back, trapping her against the wall. She raised the axe again, but just as she was about to bring it down a second time, her gaze began to swim in and out of focus.

She blinked, disoriented, and all at once, she wasn't in the icehouse with Lord Dunn anymore. She was in a luxurious bedchamber at the Pink Pearl with a different man, the same man who haunted her nightmares, his face twisted with inhuman rage as he pressed the cold steel of his blade against her neck.

In that dizzying moment, Emma was no longer holding an axe. She was holding a knife, the gleaming blade sharp enough to slice through flesh and bone, and he was so much bigger than she was, so much stronger than she was, and she didn't have a choice, *had never had a choice…*

And there was blood, so much blood, blood everywhere.

It happened in an instant, the vision there and then gone again, and she was back in the icehouse, facing an enraged Lord Dunn. Her fingers tightened around the axe handle, but her hesitation had cost her. In the time it took her to draw a breath, Lord Dunn snatched the axe from her hand and hurled it away.

Then he lunged for her, slamming her against the wall. Her head hit with a thud, the blow knocking the breath out of her. His face, pale and twisted with hate, swam in front of her eyes, advancing and receding again, in and out, and Emma wondered vaguely if she was screaming, or if she'd die like poor Kitty Yardley had, without making a sound.

But there was no time to think about it, no time to do anything at all as Lord Dunn's hands closed around her neck and *squeezed*, his grip punishing, his thumbs digging into her throat. Emma clawed at his hands, but her vision started to darken at the edges, going black, and then...

There was a crash, like a door being ripped off its hinges. Emma thought she'd imagined it, but then someone shouted, and footsteps were pounding across the stone floor, and suddenly, the hands around Emma's neck were gone.

Then, in the next instant *Lord Dunn* was gone, ripped away from her, his body sailing through the air until he hit the opposite wall with a deafening crash, then sank to the floor.

Emma fell to her knees, coughing and gasping and dragging in one desperate breath after another as a battle raged before her eyes, a blur of fists and bared teeth, then Lord Dunn on his hands and knees, crawling up the stone steps.

He didn't get far. Samuel was on him in a flash. Dunn managed to stagger to his feet, but Samuel lunged for him, wrapping his massive arms around Dunn's midsection. Dunn fought him, kicking and clawing and snarling, the blood from his wrist splattering Samuel's shirt.

Just when it looked as if Dunn would escape and flee into the night, there was another shout—Daniel? A third figure leapt into the fray, crashing into the struggling men, and all three of them hurtled back down the stairs, plunging to the bottom in a spray of blood and tangled limbs.

The man who'd landed on top peeled himself off the other two, then reached down and hauled the second one up by the back of his neck. The two of them leaned over the third man, breathing hard, their hands on their knees.

Daniel prodded at Lord Dunn with his foot, then shook his head. "He's out. See to the lass, Lymington."

Emma didn't remember crumpling to the ground, but she must have, because she was sprawled there when Samuel's face, his beautiful face, appeared above her.

"Emma," he whispered, his voice raw with fear, but still so tender it made Emma want to cry.

Maybe she *did* cry, because a pained sound tore from Samuel as he gathered her into his arms and cradled her against his chest. "It's all right, sweetheart. It's over. I've got you. I've got you, Emma."

Emma let out a sob, and buried her face against his warm, solid chest. She thought he was stroking her hair and murmuring to her, but she let her eyes flutter closed.

Because he *did* have her. He'd had her from the start.

And that was all that mattered.

* * * *

"There was no need to knock me down the stairwell, Brixton," Samuel grumbled, glaring at Daniel as he rubbed his sore shoulder.

"I don't know as that's so, Lymington. Looked to me like Dunn had the best of ye."

"The devil he did. He was crawling on his knees up the stairs, for God's sake."

"Eh, well, it didn't look like it from where I was standing." Brixton's lips stretched in a grin that managed to be both menacing and infuriating at once. "Beg pardon, my lord, but it's best to be safe. That's why ye tackled me in the woods, innit? To be *safe*?"

"So that's why you did it? To get me back? Damn it, Brixton, you nearly dislocated my shoulder!"

Brixton shrugged. "Ye broke my hand."

Samuel subsided with a huff, and rested his head against the wall behind him.

They were both silent for a time, then Brixton began making a strange sound—something halfway between a grunt and a wheeze. It took a minute before Samuel realized the disturbing noise was meant to be a laugh. "What's so amusing, Brixton?"

"For a little while there, I thought ye were going to rip Dunn's throat out," Brixton said with unmistakable relish. "I would have liked to see that."

"And I would have liked to rip the villain's throat out."

"I wouldn't have stopped ye, but 'is neck will find a noose soon en—"

A pitiful cry came from the other side of the closed bedchamber door, and Samuel's gaze shot to Brixton's. He saw his own fear reflected in the man's face, and his stomach dropped. If *Brixton* was afraid, then this was bad, indeed. "She, ah...Emma will be all right, won't she?"

"'Course, she will be. She may be a little bit of a thing, but that lass is stronger than she looks."

But Samuel saw Daniel's uneasiness, and fear gripped him, tightening his chest.

He'd carried Emma all the way from the icehouse back to Lymington House, muttering prayers the entire way that his arms around her would warm her, but she'd been so cold, her slender body wracked with deep, uncontrollable shudders.

Lady Crosby had been weeping on the settee when they burst into the drawing room. Lady Silvester and Lady Lymington had been attempting to comfort her, while Lovell and Lady Flora stood silently nearby, their faces pale, and Flora's eyes red from crying.

The moment Lady Crosby saw Emma lying pale and limp in Samuel's arms, however, she'd dried her tears, and leapt into action with all the self-righteous wrath of an aggrieved grandmother.

Samuel had never seen anything more frightening in his life.

She'd ordered Samuel to carry Emma upstairs to her bedchamber at once and put her directly into bed, tucked up as snugly as possible while the fire was built to a roar in the grate. The entire household had converged in Emma's bedchamber by then, but Lady Crosby had banished the lot of them with the fury of a mother hen protecting her baby chick from a pack of hungry foxes, then ordered a hot bath be brought as soon as possible.

Samuel hadn't dared argue with her. Even Brixton had done as he was told.

Now the two of them were standing in the hallway outside Emma's bedchamber as a half dozen servants rushed back and forth between the kitchen and guest wing, the footmen bearing large pails of hot water, and the housemaids with stacks of blankets in their arms.

Once the servants had filed back out, Lady Crosby had closed the bedchamber door with a determined click, without sparing either Samuel or Daniel a glance.

Since then, an eternity had passed.

Another might pass in its wake, and another still, and Samuel wouldn't stir a step from Emma's door. When she woke, she'd find him right by her side, where he belonged.

And if he was obliged to be firm to get past Lady Crosby to Emma, then so be—

"Lord Lymington?"

Samuel whirled around to find Lady Crosby standing at the open bedchamber door. "Lady Crosby! Is Emma—"

"Calm down, my lord. Emma is awake, and asking for you. Now, Daniel." Lady Crosby cast a stern look at Brixton. "You're to come downstairs with me at once, so the doctor can see to your injuries."

"Ye keep your hands to yerself, Lymington," Brixton growled, stopping Samuel before he could close Emma's bedchamber door behind him.

Lady Crosby gave Samuel a sharp look. "Lord Lymington would never be so ungentlemanly as to importune a distressed lady with his attentions, *would you*, my lord?"

"Of course not, my lady," Samuel said, with a provoking smirk for Brixton.

But all his humor vanished as soon as he closed the door and turned to the bed where Emma lay. It looked as if every blanket at Lymington House had been piled atop her. She was so bundled up only the top of her head and the tip of her nose were visible.

Samuel crept forward, wincing as the floorboards squeaked under his weight. He didn't want to wake her—

"Samuel?" The blankets shifted, and a hand appeared, beckoning him forward. "Come here."

Samuel was overcome with an unfamiliar wave of shyness, but he approached the bed and peered down at Emma. Her face was pale, but her eyes were bright, and a soft smile curved her lips. "Closer, please."

Samuel took another hesitant step forward.

"Come, my lord. I've never known you to be bashful before." Emma wriggled her fingers, urging him closer.

Samuel shuffled closer, trying to swallow the lump in his throat. She looked so small lying there, so fragile. If he hadn't burst into the icehouse when he did, if he'd taken even a few seconds longer...

Emma patted the empty space beside her on the bed. "Come lie down next to me."

There was nothing in the world Samuel wanted more than to hold her, but he shook his head. "I'm covered in dirt and blood, Emma—"

"You're warm. I've never known anyone warmer than you." Emma gazed up at him, firelight flickering in her eyes. "Please, Samuel."

Samuel's hesitation melted away at that soft plea. He could refuse her nothing. So he shed his coat and boots and stretched out on the bed next to her. She snuggled close, and he opened his arms to her.

"There, that's better." Emma lay her head on his chest with a happy sigh.

They lay there together listening to the crackling of the fire, Samuel holding her as tightly as he dared, his heart thundering in his chest. Just when he thought she'd fallen asleep, Emma asked quietly, "Lord Dunn?"

"Locked in the icehouse. Lovell and Humphries have gone after the magistrate. They'll see to it he's dealt with."

Samuel said no more, and Emma didn't ask. Neither of them wanted to talk about Dunn. His neck was destined for a noose, just as Brixton had said. As far as Samuel was concerned, there was no reason to ever speak of Dunn again.

All he wanted to think about, all he cared about, was Emma.

Samuel stroked her hair. "You should sleep, love."

"I will, but I need to say something to you first. When I was in the icehouse with Dunn, when he...he attacked me—"

"Emma, please—"

She clutched at his hand, her fingers trembling. "Shh. Let me speak now, Samuel, and we need never mention Lord Dunn again."

Samuel couldn't speak, but he held her as close as he could, so she knew he was there, and she was safe. That she would always be safe in his arms.

"Those moments in the icehouse were...I was frightened, Samuel, but all the terror I felt, all the rage at Lord Dunn for everything he'd done, was nothing at all to the regret I felt for not telling you how much I love you when I had the chance." Emma turned his face down to hers with a hand on his cheek. "I never thought a man could come to mean so much to me, but you hold my whole heart in your hands. You're everything to me. I love you, Samuel."

"Emma, my love." Samuel closed his eyes, buried his face in her hair and let her words sink into him, into the deepest corners of his heart.

They were quiet for a time, content to lie wrapped in each other's arms, until Emma wriggled closer and rested her cheek against his chest. "Your heart is beating so quickly," she murmured sleepily.

"Yes, I'm, ah...a little nervous."

"Nervous? Why should you be nervous?"

Samuel smiled against her hair. "Because I know myself to be a presumptuous, demanding, arrogant marquess, but I'm hoping you'll agree to marry me in spite of it, though I daresay you could find a more agreeable husband."

Emma went so still, for one breathless moment Samuel thought she might refuse him, but then she rose onto her elbow, a smile tugging at her lips as she looked down at him. "I don't *want* an agreeable husband, Lord Lymington. I want *you*."

"Oh, you have me, Miss Downing. You've had me from the start."

"And I know just what to do with you, my lord." Emma dropped a playful kiss on the end of his nose.

Samuel chuckled as he eased her onto her back and pressed his lips to the tempting red ones he loved so well. "Do you, indeed? What's that, then?"

Emma gazed up at him, her blue eyes shining. "Keep you forever, Lord Lymington. Keep you forever."

Epilogue

No. 26 Maddox Street, London
December 1795

"I do believe I've overindulged in Mrs. Beeson's biscuits." Emma licked the corner of her lip where a smidgen of sweet quince preserves lingered, then dropped her hand to her belly.

"It's the preserves that make us do it." Georgiana pushed a crumb-filled plate away from her with a sigh. "We're all helpless against the preserves. For pity's sake, my stomach is nearly as swollen as Cecilia's."

Predictably, Cecilia's cheeks turned as red as a peony. "I beg your pardon, Lady Haslemere, but that's a shocking thing to say."

"Really, Georgiana, you're too ridiculous." Sophia snatched up the tufted pillow on the settee beside her and stuffed it behind her shoulders. "It's plain to see no one's stomach is as swollen as Cecilia's."

Lord Darlington rose from the table in the corner where he was playing chess with Lord Haslemere, and went to his wife's side. "You've never looked more beautiful," he murmured, kissing her cheek.

"You're leaving the game *now*, Darlington?" Lord Haslemere abandoned the chess board and squeezed onto the settee beside his wife. "I was one move away from beating you."

"If I recall, Sophia, your own belly was swollen not so very long ago." Emma shot Sophia a sly look. "And Georgiana's will be too, before long."

"My goodness, Emma, Lord Haslemere and I have only been wed for six months! It's much too soon for children yet." But a dreamy look came into Georgiana's eyes, and she let out a yearning, very un-Georgiana-like sigh. "Though perhaps a little girl would be rather sweet. Lord Haslemere says he wants a half-dozen."

Lord Haslemere chuckled. "At least half a dozen, and all of them girls."

Sophia snorted. "Why, that's a litter! Shame on you, Lord Haslemere. Your wife is a countess, not a hunting dog."

"My wife can do anything she sets her mind to." Lord Haslemere dropped a kiss on Georgiana's forehead, making her flush up to the roots of her hair, and setting all the girls off into gales of laughter. Georgiana had never been one to blush, but her handsome husband's teasing pinkened her cheeks every time.

"Still, I can't help but agree with Lord Haslemere," Sophia went on. "Little girls *are* sweet, especially little girls who have their father's beautiful gray eyes."

"And their mother's beautiful face." Lord Gray looked up from the bundle he held in his arms to give his wife a secret smile.

"Gray eyes are lovely. One might think they'd be cold, but they're not." Emma dropped her voice to a murmur as she turned to smile at Lord Lymington. "Not at all."

Lord Lymington was reclining on a chair across from the settee, a glass of port in his hand and his lips quirked with amusement as he listened to them banter, but the gray eyes in question transformed to a soft silver at Emma's words. "I prefer dark blue eyes, myself."

The drawing room at the Clifford School wasn't a large one, but it had never looked quite so small to Lady Amanda as it did now, with all four of her girls and their growing families crowded around the fire.

It was strange, how things seemed to go on very much as they'd always done, until all at once they didn't, and everything changed, seemingly in the blink of an eye. With one unexpected event coming on the heels of the last as they'd done this year, was it any wonder Lady Amanda had started woolgathering?

Her four dearest girls, two of them now countesses, and the other two marchionesses, of all things. A smile twitched at the corner of Lady Amanda's lips. One might have predicted Sophia would turn out to be a countess, if only through sheer force of will, but sweet, tenderhearted Cecilia, a marchioness? Lady Amanda hadn't predicted *that*, nor had she imagined her practical Georgiana would find love with the Earl of Haslemere, London's most notorious rake.

Or he *had* been a rake, before he'd found Georgiana.

Such was the transformative power of love.

Then there was Emma. Of all her girls, Lady Amanda had feared Emma's ghosts would haunt her forever, but Emma had found her own love in a man who knew her worth, and treasured her heart.

"How does Helena do, Emma?" Lady Amanda asked, rousing herself from her musings. She'd had a notion she might take Helena in at the Clifford School, but Lady Lymington, of all people, had taken a liking to the girl, and invited her to come live at Lymington House.

Emma smiled. "Very well, indeed. Lady Lymington and Lady Flora— that is, she's Lady Lovell, now—both dote on her. Helena gets on so wonderfully in Kent, I begin to think they'll never part with her. Will it trouble you if she doesn't return to London, my lady?"

"Not at all, dearest. I quite like the idea of Helena tucked up quietly in the country rather than in London. It'll do her good, to have some peace."

A companionable silence fell, then Cecilia asked, "Shall we read another chapter of Mrs. Parsons? When we left it, the Countess of Wolfenbach's lady's maid had been murdered, her desecrated corpse left upon the bed."

"Who leaves a corpse on a bed?" Georgiana licked a dollop of the preserves off the end of a spoon. "It hardly seems the proper place for such a messy thing."

"The countess was fleeing her wicked husband, and had no choice but to leave the poor thing where she'd fallen." Cecilia skimmed to the bottom of the page. "Oh, dear. It's lucky she fled, because the castle is about to burn to the ground."

Sophia frowned. "Why don't I recall the lady's maid?"

"You were asleep on Lord Gray's shoulder during that bit, dearest." Emma patted Sophia's hand, grinning.

"Why, how absurd you are, Emma. I never fell asleep!"

Cecilia hid a smile. "Never mind. Let's have another chapter, shall we?"

"By all means, let's have another chapter." Lady Amanda let her eyes drift closed as Cecilia opened the book and began to read, letting the smooth, soft voice lull her into another reverie. She'd never been one for daydreaming, but she'd found herself falling into reveries these past months as her world had changed.

"Then I am an outcast, a forsaken orphan, without friends or protectors!" Cecilia cried, pouring out the heroine's despair before lowering her voice to Mr. Weimar's villainous growl. "Take comfort, my dearest Matilda, permit me to offer you my hand, my heart, and I will be your protector through life."

"Her protector, indeed," Georgiana scoffed. "How can Mathilda be so foolish as to imagine Mr. Weimar is a hero? Why, any lady with any sense can tell he's an utter villain."

"Well, he certainly has a villainous voice!" Emma replied with a laugh. "Really, Cecilia, in another life you might have gone on the stage."

Sophia let out a pensive sigh. "It's a pity there should always be so many villains hanging about, isn't it?"

"There *are* a great many villains, I'm afraid, but there are heroes, too." Emma reached for Lord Lymington, and clasped his big hand between both of hers.

Lady Amanda took in the four masculine faces arrayed around the drawing room, then her gaze wandered to the door, where Daniel stood half hidden in the shadows, listening to Cecilia read, and watching, always watching the four girls he'd guarded since they were in pinafores. For all that he was a hard man, a menacing man, Daniel's heart had been open to *his* girls from the first.

Cecilia finished the chapter, and a companionable silence fell over the room as dusk approached, tinting the shadows on the other side of the window from a pale gray to a darker violet. It was growing late, but there was no place Lady Amanda would rather be than here, tucked into an overstuffed chair, a roaring fire at her feet, with all of her girls surrounding her.

All her girls, but one.

Teresa Anne, Lady Amanda's only child, the daughter she'd cherished, and been unable to save. Teresa had once been a bright, smiling young lady just like the four gathered around the fire tonight, her deep blue eyes so very much like Emma's.

Teresa should be here now, her husband at her side, her belly swollen with a child, but she'd long since succumbed to her fate, the victim of an unscrupulous seducer and a cold, unforgiving father.

Lady Amanda had searched London for her. For years, she'd wandered through every filthy street and down every dark alley, Daniel by her side, praying a fair-haired, blue-eyed girl would appear before her like a phoenix from the ashes, a precious flicker of hope in an ocean of filth.

She'd never found her. In the end, Teresa had gone the way of so many young girls just like her, lost to mothers who'd cherished them, but couldn't save them.

But others had been found, in their places. Others, like Sophia, Cecilia, Georgiana, and Emma who'd been rescued from their sad fates. In their turn they would save others, and so it would go, until there were more girls saved than lost.

And so, one way or another, the phoenix did rise slowly from the ashes.

Cecilia let out a soft laugh, rousing Lady Amanda from her reverie. "Baby Amanda's fallen asleep again. Such a dear, drowsy little thing."

Sophia turned a fond eye on her infant daughter, still held in her father's arms. "She looks so harmless when she's asleep, doesn't she? No one would ever guess how fierce she is, to look at her now."

"I daresay her namesake would," Emma said softly.

All four of them turned to Lady Amanda, who lingered on each rosy face before she held out her arms for the child. "I'll rock her for a while, shall I?"

"Of course." Lord Gray rose, and settled the sleeping child in Lady Amanda's arms. She cooed at the baby girl as she ran a hand over the downy head, cradling the warm body in her arms.

Outside, the shadows had melted into purple, and from purple to a deep black, black enough to hide whatever wicked deeds London's sinners chose to commit tonight.

Where there was darkness, there would always be sinners, but there was no darkness that didn't give way to light. For every villain, there was a hero, and for every broken promise, another one was kept.

For every lost girl, another was found and saved.

The baby girl in Lady Amanda's arms stirred, the tiny, pink rosebud of her lips opened, and a squawk of pure, infantile fury emerged.

"That's it, little one," she whispered into the child's ear. "Make your voice heard, and someday, you and your sisters will change the world."

Author's Notes

Burns, Robert (1786). "Poems, chiefly in the Scottish dialect." Kilmarnock: John Wilson. p. 138. Retrieved 13 February 2014.

Chaucer, Geoffrey. *Troilus and Criseyde.* 1609. Project Gutenberg. https://www.gutenberg.org/files/257/257-h/257-h.htm

This eBook is for the use of anyone anywhere at no cost and with almost no restrictions whatsoever. You may copy it, give it away or re-use it under the terms of the Project Gutenberg License included with this eBook or online at www.gutenberg.org

Ford, David Nash. *Royal Berkshire History.* 2004. The footrace between the Earl of Barrymore that Lord Lovell describes to Lady Flora in Chapter Seven in which Lord Barrymore lost a wager to Mr. Bullock truly happened, though it took place in 1790, not 1795. http://www.berkshirehistory.com/bios/rbarry_eofb.html

Knowles, Rachel. "Finding Your Way Around Vauxhall Gardens in Regency London." March 2019. https://www.regencyhistory.net/2019/03/vauxhall-gardens-finding-your-way-around.html

Murden, Sarah. "William Leftwich and the Ice Well." January 2019. The Guardian Online. https://georgianera.wordpress.com/2019/01/17/william-leftwich-and-the-ice-well/

Parsons, Eliza. *The Castle of Wolfenbach.* London: printed for William Lane, at the Minerva Press, and sold by E. Harlow, 1793. https://digital.library.upenn.edu/women/parsons/castle/castle.html

Pope, Sir Alexander. "An Essay on Criticism." 1711. Project Gutenberg. https://www.gutenberg.org/files/7409/7409-h/7409-h.htm

This eBook is for the use of anyone anywhere at no cost and with almost no restrictions whatsoever. You may copy it, give it away or re-use it under the terms of the Project Gutenberg License included with this eBook or online at www.gutenberg.org

Reynolds, Sir Joshua. *Sir Banestre Tarleton.* 1782. https://ageofrevolution.org/200-object/joshua-reynolds-portrait-sir-banestre-tarleton/

Reynolds, Sir Joshua. *The Ladies Waldergrave.* 1780. Scottish National Gallery. https://www.nationalgalleries.org/art-and-artists/5360/ladies-waldegrave

Romney, George. *Emma Hamilton as a Bacchante*. 1792. https://www.npg.org.uk/whatson/exhibitions/2002/george-romney/emma-hamilton

Stewart, Doug. "To Be...Or Not: The Greatest Shakespeare Forgery." Vortigern and Rowena. https://www.smithsonianmag.com/history/to-beor-not-the-greatest-shakespeare-forgery-136201/

Printed in the United States
by Baker & Taylor Publisher Services